Praise for *New York*

LORI F

"Say YES! to Lori Foster."
—Elizabeth Lowell

"Lori Foster delivers the goods."
—*Publishers Weekly*

"Known for her funny, sexy writing,
Foster doesn't hesitate to turn up the heat."
—*Booklist*

"One of the best writers around of romantic novels
with vibrant sensuality."
—*MyLifetime.com*

"Foster outwrites most of her peers and has
a great sense of the ridiculous."
—*Library Journal*

"Foster proves herself as a bestselling author
time and again."
—*Romantic Times BOOKreviews*

"Filled with Foster's trademark wit, humor,
and sensuality."
—*Booklist* on *Jamie*

"Foster supplies good sex and great humor along
the way in a thoroughly enjoyable romance reminiscent
of Susan Elizabeth Phillips' novels."
—*Booklist* on *Causing Havoc*

"Foster executes with skill...convincing,
heartfelt family drama."
—*Publishers Weekly* on *Causing Havoc*

"Suspenseful, sexy, and humorous."
—*Booklist* on *Just a Hint—Clint*

Also available from

LORI FOSTER

and HQN Books

Scandalous
Caught!
Heartbreakers
Fallen Angels
Enticing

LORI FOSTER
Bodyguard

HQN™

HQN™

Recycling programs
for this product may
not exist in your area.

ISBN-13: 978-0-373-77421-0

BODYGUARD

www.HQNBooks.com

Printed in U.S.A.

CONTENTS

OUTRAGEOUS

chapter 1

SHE HAD THE BIGGEST BROWN EYES JUDD HAD
ever seen.

She also looked innocent as hell, despite the ridiculous
clothes she wore and the huge, frayed canvas tote bag she
carried. Did she actually think she blended in, just because her
coat was tattered and her hat was a little ratty? Did she think
anyone would ever believe her to be homeless? Not likely.

So what was she doing here at this time of night? The lower
east side of Springfield was no place for a lady like her. She
strolled past him again, this time more slowly, and her eyes were
so wide it looked as if they could take in her surroundings in
a single glance. They took in Judd.

He felt a thrill of awareness, sharper than anything he'd ever
felt before. She looked away, but not before he detected the faint
pink blush that washed over her fine features. That blush had
been obvious even in the dim evening light, with only the moon
and corner street lamp for illumination. She had flawless skin.

Dammit. He had enough to worry about without some

damn Miss Priss with manicured nails and salon-styled hair trying to fob herself off as a local. Judd had only stepped outside the bar to get a breath of fresh air. The smell of perfume inside was overwhelming, and enough to turn his stomach.

He could hear the music in the bar grow louder and knew the dancers were coming onstage. In less than ten minutes, he'd have to go back in there, baring himself in the line of duty.

Damn. He hated this cover. What decent, hardworking cop should have to peel off his clothes for a bunch of sex-starved, groping women? For nearly two weeks now he'd been entertaining the female masses with the sight of his body, hoping to uncover enough evidence to make a bust. He was now, at thirty-two, in his prime, more fit than ever and completely alone. Not only did he meet the necessary requirements to pull off such a ludicrous cover, he had a vested, very personal interest this time. He knew for a fact the room above the bar was the site for shady business meetings, yet he hadn't seen hide nor hair of a gun deal. Clayton Donner was lying low.

It was discouraging, but he wasn't giving up.

He was definitely going to get Donner, but that didn't mean he enjoyed displaying himself nightly.

Each of the strippers had a gimmick. He thought his was rather ironic. He played out the tough street cop, complete with black pants held together with strategically placed Velcro. They came off with only the smallest tug. He even had Max's original leather jacket—a prized possession, to be sure—to add to his authenticity. The women loved it.

He wondered if old Max had known how sexy the cop persona was to females. Or if he would have cared.

God, he couldn't think about Max and still do his job, which was to appear unscrupulous enough that Donner would think him available. Clayton always needed new pigeons to run his scams. Judd intended to be the next. It was the only way he could get close enough to make a clean bust.

And the last thing he needed now was a distraction with big brown eyes. Despite his resolve, his gaze wandered back to the woman. She was loitering on the corner beneath the street lamp, holding that large, lumpy bag to her chest and trying to fit in. Judd snorted. That old coat was buttoned so high she was damn near strangling herself. What the hell was she doing here?

He'd just about convinced himself not to care, not to get involved, when three young men seemed to notice her. Judd watched as they approached her. She started to back away, then evidently changed her mind. She nodded a greeting, but it was a wimpy effort. Hell, the men looked determined to get to know her, without any encouragement on her part. She, on the other hand, looked ready to faint.

Walk away, he thought, willing the woman to move. But she stood her ground. He sensed, then he knew for certain, she was getting in over her head. His body was already tensing, his eyes narrowed, waiting for the trouble to start. They seemed to be talking, or, more to the point, she was trying to speak to them. She gestured with her hands, her expression earnest. Then one of the men grabbed her and she let loose a startled screech. In the next instant, those huge brown eyes of hers turned his way, demanding that he help her.

The little twit thought he was a regular street cop. At this rate she'd blow his cover.

Well, hell, he couldn't allow her to be manhandled. He pushed himself away from the doorway and started forward. The men were obviously drunk. One of them was doing his best to pull her close, but she kept sidestepping him. Judd approached them all with a casual air.

"Here now, boys." He kept his tone low and deep, deliberately commanding. "Why don't you leave the lady alone."

Judd could see her trembling, could see the paleness of her face in the yellow light of the street lamp. The man didn't release her; if anything, he tightened his grip. "Go to hell."

The words were slurred, and Judd wondered just how drunk they were. They might believe him to be a cop, but in this neighborhood, being a law enforcement officer carried very little clout and regularly drew vicious disdain. Damn.

He couldn't get into a brawl—he might literally lose his pants. Not that he wouldn't enjoy knocking some heads together, but still…. Where was a real uniformed cop when you needed one?

He turned his gaze on the woman. "Do you want their company?"

She swallowed, her throat working convulsively. "No."

One of the men shook his fist in Judd's face, stumbling drunkenly as he did so. "She's already made a deal with us." The man grinned stupidly at the woman, then added, "You can't expect a little thing like her to run around here without a weapon to protect herself…"

One of the other men slugged the speaker. "Shut up, you fool."

Judd went very still, scrutinizing the woman's face. "Well?"

Again, she swallowed. "Well…what?"

"Why do you need a weapon? You planning to kill someone?" Whisper-soft, his question still demanded an immediate answer.

Shaking her head, then looking around as if desperately seeking a means of escape, she managed to pique his interest. He couldn't walk away now. Whatever she was up to, she didn't want him to know. Because she thought he was a cop?

Disgusted, Judd propped his hands on his hips, his eyebrows

drawn together in a frown. "Do you want the company of these men or not?"

She peered cautiously at the drunken, leering face so close to her own. Her lips tightened in disapproval and disdain. "Ah...no. Not particularly."

A genuine smile tipped his mouth before he caught himself. She had gumption, he'd give her that. She was no bigger than a ten-year-old sickly kid. The coat she wore practically swallowed her up. She was fine-boned, petite, and everything about her seemed fragile. "There you go, fellas. The lady doesn't find you to her liking. Turn her loose and go find something else to do."

"I got somethin' to do already." Her captor's hold seemed to loosen just a bit as he spoke, and taking advantage, she suddenly jerked free. Then she did the dumbest thing Judd had ever seen. She sent her knee into the man's groin.

Unbelievable. Judd shook his head, even as he yanked her behind him, trying to protect her from the ensuing chaos. He couldn't do any real damage to the men without attracting more spectators, which would threaten his cover. And the woman was gasping behind him, scared out of her wits from the sound of it. But damn it all, he definitely *did not* want to lose his pants out here scuffling in the middle of the sidewalk with common drunks. One of the men started to throw a punch.

Judd cursed loudly as the woman ran around him, evidently not as frightened as he'd thought, and leaped onto his attacker's back. She couldn't weigh over a hundred pounds, but she wound her fingers in the man's hair and pulled with all her might.

Enough was enough. A glimpse at his watch told him it was time for his performance. Judd grabbed the man away from her and sent him reeling with a firm kick to the rear end, then stalked the other two, every muscle in his body tensed. Too drunk to persist in their efforts, the men scurried away.

Judd turned to face the woman, and she was... tidying her hair? Good God, was she nuts? He saw her look toward her canvas bag, which now lay in a puddle on the sidewalk, but she made no move to retrieve it.

"You don't want your bag?" he asked with all the sarcasm he could muster.

"Oh." She glanced at him. "Well, of course..." She made a move in its direction, but he shook his head. He could see more raggedy clothing falling out the opening, and if there was one thing this woman didn't need, it was hand-me-downs.

He took her arm in a firm but gentle hold, ignoring her resistance, and started her toward the bar. He automatically moved her to his right side, bringing her between his body and the building, protecting her from passersby. He held his temper for all of about three seconds, then gave up the effort.

"Of all the stupid, *harebrained*...lady, what the hell did you think you were doing back there?" He wondered if she could be a journalist, or a TV newswoman? She damn well wasn't used to living in alleys, or going without. Everything about her screamed money. Even now, with him hustling her down the sidewalk, she had a certain grace, a definite poise, that didn't come from being underprivileged.

She glanced up at him, and he noticed she smelled nice, too. Not heavily perfumed like the women in the bar, just...very feminine. Her wavy shoulder-length hair, a light brown that looked as baby soft as her eyes, bounced as he hurried her along. She was practically running, but he couldn't help that. He was going to be late. He could hear the music for his number starting. Taking off his clothes in public was bad enough. He didn't intend to make a grand entrance by jumping in late.

She cleared her throat. "I appreciate your assistance, Officer."

Without slowing his pace, he glared at her. "Answer my question. Who are you? What the hell are you up to?"

"That's two questions."

He growled, his patience at an end. *"Answer me, dammit!"*

She stumbled, then glared up at him defiantly. "That's really none of your business."

Everything inside his body clenched. "I'm making it my business."

Digging in her heels as he tried to haul her through the front door, she forced him to slow down. She was wide-eyed again and he noticed her mouth was hanging open as he dragged her into the bar. "What are you doing?"

There was a note of shrill panic in her voice as she took in her surroundings. Judd had no time to explain, and no time to consider her delicate sensibilities. Everyone in this part of town thought of him as a money-hungry, oversexed, willing exhibitionist—Clayton Donner included. It was a necessary cover and one he wasn't ready to forfeit. Donner would show up again soon, and once he decided Judd was a familiar face in the area, the gun dealer would make his move. It would happen. He'd make it happen.

Still gripping her arm, Judd trotted her toward the nearest bar stool. *"Stay right here."* He stared down at her, trying to intimidate her with his blackest scowl. The music was picking up tempo, signaling his cue.

She popped right back off the seat, those eyes of hers accurately portraying her shock. "Now see here! I have no intention of waiting—"

He picked her up, dropped her onto the stool again, then called to the bartender. "Keep her here, Freddie. Make certain she doesn't budge."

Freddie, a huge, jovial sort with two front teeth missing, grinned and nodded. "What'd she do?"

"She owes me. Big. Keep your eye on her."

"And if she tries to pike it?"

Judd gave Freddie a conspiratorial wink. "Make her sorry if she so much as flinches."

Freddie looked ferocious, but Judd knew he wouldn't hurt a fly. That was the reason they had not one, but two bouncers on the premises. But the little lady didn't know that, and Judd wanted to find out exactly what she was up to. Gut instinct told him he wouldn't like what he found.

Suddenly the spotlight swirled around the floor. Cursing, then forcing a grin to his mouth, Judd sauntered forward into the light. Women screamed.

In the short time he'd been performing here, he'd discovered a wealth of information about his gun dealer…and become a favorite of the bar. The owner had promised to double his pay, but that was nothing compared to the bills that always ended up stuffed in his skimpy briefs. He refused, absolutely *refused,* to wear a G-string. His naked butt was not something he showed to more than one woman at a time, and even *those* exhibitions were few and far between. But his modesty worked to his advantage. The women customers thought he was a tease, and appreciated his show all the more.

As he moved, he glanced over his shoulder to make certain the lady was still there. She hadn't moved. She didn't look as though she could. Her eyes were even larger now, huge and luminous and filled with shock and disbelief. He held her gaze, and slowly, backing into the center of the floor, slid the zipper down on the leather jacket. He saw her gasp.

Her intent expression, of innocence mixed with curious wonder, annoyed him, making him feel more exposed than he ever had while performing. That he could feel his face heat angered him. He was too old, and too cynical now, to actually blush. *Damn her.*

Purposefully holding her gaze, determined to make her look away, he let his fingers move to the top of his pants. As he slowly unhooked the fly, one snap at a time, teasing his audience, teasing her more, she reeled back and one dainty hand touched her chest. She looked distressed. She looked shocked.

But she didn't look away.

OH, LORD. Oh, Lord. This can't be happening, Emily! It's too outrageous. There can't possibly be a large, gorgeous man peeling his clothes off in front of you.

Even as she told herself she was delirious, that the scene in front of her was a figment of her fantastical imagination, Emily watched him kick off his boots, then with one smooth jerk, toss his pants aside. She wouldn't have missed a single instant of his disrobing. She couldn't. She was spellbound.

Vaguely, in the back of her mind, she heard the crowd yelling, urging him on. He looked away from her finally, releasing her from his dark gaze. But still she watched him.

He was the most beautiful man she'd ever seen. Raw, sexual, but also…gentle. She could feel his gentleness, had felt it outside when she'd first walked past him. It was as if she recognized he didn't belong here, in this seedy neighborhood, any more than she did.

But they *were* both here. Her reason was plain; she needed to find out who had sold her younger brother the gun that backfired, nearly causing him to lose an eye. He would recover, but that wouldn't remove the fact that he'd bought the gun illegally, that he was involved in something he had no business being involved in and that he would probably be scarred for life. Emily had to find the man who'd almost ruined her brother's life. She couldn't imagine what kind of monster would sell a sixteen-year-old a gun—a defective gun, at that.

Her parents refused to take the matter to the police. Luckily, John had only been using the gun for target practice, so no one even knew he had the thing. And more important, no one else had been hurt. When she thought about what could have happened, the consequences...

But that was history. Now all she could do was make certain that the same man didn't continue selling guns to kids. She had no compunction about going to the police once she had solid evidence, enough that she didn't have to involve her brother.

Her parents would never forgive her if she sullied the family name. Again.

Her heart raced, climbing into her throat to choke her when the officer—obviously *not* an officer—started toward her. She couldn't take her eyes off his bare, hair-brushed chest, his long, naked thighs. The way the shiny black briefs cupped him... Oh God, it was getting warm in here...

Well-bred ladies most definitely did not react this way!

There were social standards to uphold, a certain degree of expected poise... The litany she'd been reciting to herself came to a screeching halt as the man stopped in front of her.

His eyes, a fierce green, reflected the spotlight. He stared directly at her, then moved so close she could smell the clean male fragrance of him, could feel his body heat. And God, he was hot.

Panting, Emily realized he was waiting for her to give him money. Of all the insane notions...but there were numerous dollars sticking out of those small briefs, and she knew, with unwavering instinct, he wouldn't budge until she'd done as he silently demanded.

Blindly, unable to pull her gaze away, she fumbled in the

huge pockets of her worn coat until her fist closed on a bill. She stuck out her hand, offering the money to him.

Wicked was the only way to describe his smile. With a small, barely discernible motion, he shook his head. She dropped her gaze for an instant to where his briefs held all the cash. She'd watched the women put the money there, trying to touch him, but he'd eluded their grasping hands. He'd played up to the audience, getting only close enough to collect a few dollars, then dancing away.

She didn't want to touch him.

Oh, what a lie! She wanted to touch him, all right, but she wouldn't, not here in front of an audience, not ever. She was a respectable lady, she was… She squeaked, leaning back on her seat as he put one hand on the light frame over the bar, the other beside her on the bar stool. She was caged in, unable to breathe. She could see the light sheen of sweat caught in his chest hair, see the small, dark tuft of fine hair under his arm. It seemed almost indecent, and somehow very personal, to see his armpit.

Her body throbbed with heat, and she couldn't swallow. He stood there, demanding, insistent, so very carefully, using only her fingertips, she tucked the bill into his shorts. She registered warm, taut skin, and a sprinkling of crisp hair.

Still holding her gaze, he smiled, his eyes narrowing only the slightest bit. He leaned down next to her face, then placed a small, chaste kiss on her cheek. It had been whisper-light, almost not there, but so potent she felt herself close to fainting.

The audience screamed, loving it, loving him. He laughed, his expression filled with satisfaction, then went back to his dancing. Women begged for the same attention he'd given her, but he didn't comply. Emily figured one pawn in the audience was enough.

Though his focus was now directed elsewhere, it still took Emily several minutes to calm her galloping heartbeat. She continued to watch him, and that kept her tense, because despite everything she'd been brought up to believe, the man excited her.

His dark hair, long in the back, was damp with sweat and beginning to curl. With each movement he made, his shoulders flexed, displaying well-defined muscles and sinew. His backside, held tight in the black briefs, was trim and taut. And his thighs, so long and well-sculpted, looked like the legs of an athlete.

His face was beautiful, almost too beautiful. It was the kind of face that should make innocent women wary of losing their virtue. Green eyes, framed by deliciously long dark lashes and thick eyebrows, held cynical humor and were painfully direct and probing when he chose to use them that way. His nose was straight and narrow, his jaw firm.

Emily realized she was being fanciful, and silently gathered her thoughts. She needed to concentrate on what she'd come to do—finding the gun dealer. According to her brother, who at sixteen had no business hanging out in this part of town, he'd bought the gun on this street. It had been a shady trade-off from the start, cash for the illegal weapon. But John was in a rebellious stage, and his companions of late had ranged from minor gang members to very experienced young ladies. Emily prayed she could help him get back on the straight and narrow, that he could find his peace on an easier road than she'd taken. When she thought of the scars he'd have to live with, the regrets, she knew, deep in her heart, the only way to give him that peace was to find enough evidence to put the gun dealer away.

Though Emily planned to change his mind, John thought his life was over. What attractive, popular teenager could handle the idea of going through life with his face scarred? Then she thought of other kids—kids who might buy a duplicate of the same gun; kids who might be blinded rather than scarred. Or worse. The way the gun had exploded, it could easily have killed someone. And despite her parents' wishes, Emily couldn't stand back and allow that to happen. Her conscience wouldn't allow it.

The show finally ended, the music fading with the lighting until the floor was in darkness. The applause was deafening. And seconds later, the officer was back, his leather jacket slung over his shoulder, his pants and boots in his hand. He thanked the bartender, then took Emily's arm without any explanation, and rapidly pulled her toward an inside door. They narrowly missed the mob of advancing women.

Emily wanted to run, but she'd never in her life resorted to such a display. Besides, now that she knew he wasn't really a policeman, a plan was forming in her mind.

He pulled her into a back room, shut the door, then flipped on a light switch. Emily found herself in a storage closet of sorts, lined with shelves where cleaning supplies sat and a smelly mop tainted the air. A leather satchel rested in the corner. He didn't bother dressing. Instead, he tossed his clothes to the side and moved to stand a hairbreadth away from her.

"You gave me a fifty."

Emily blinked. His words were nowhere near what she'd expected to hear. She tucked in her chin. "I beg your pardon?"

He pulled the cash from his briefs, stacking the bills together neatly in his large hands. "You gave me a fifty-dollar bill. I hadn't realized my show was quite that good."

A fifty! Oh, Lord, Emily. She had no intention of telling him it hadn't been deliberate, that she'd been unable to pull her gaze away from him long enough to find the proper bills. What she'd given him was part of the money earmarked for buying information.

Maybe she could still do that.

Shrugging, she forced her eyes away from his body and stared at the dingy mop. "Since you're not a law enforcement officer, I was hoping the money would...entice you to help me."

He snorted, not buying her line for a second. Emily was relieved he was gentleman enough not to say so. He gave her a look that curled her toes, then asked, "What kind of *help* do you need, lady?"

It was unbelievably difficult to talk with him so near, and so nearly naked. He smelled delicious, of warm, damp male flesh, though she tried her best not to notice. But his body was too fine to ignore for long, despite her resolve not to give in to unladylike tendencies—such as overwhelming lust—ever again.

She licked her dry lips, then met his eyes. His gaze lingered on her mouth, then slowly coasted over the rest of her body. She knew she wasn't particularly attractive. She had pondered many disguises for this night, disguises ranging anywhere from that of a frumpy homeless lady, to a streetwalker. Somehow, she couldn't imagine herself making a convincing hooker. She was slight of build and her body had never quite...bloomed, as she'd always hoped for. She did, however, think she made an adequate transient.

She cleared her throat. Stiffening her spine, which already felt close to snapping, she said, "I need information."

"Your little trio of drunks didn't tell you enough?"

Since he appeared to have guessed her mission, she didn't bother denying it. "No. They didn't really know anything. And I had to be careful. They didn't seem all that trustworthy. But it's imperative I find out some facts. You...you seem well acquainted with the area?"

She'd said it as a question, and he answered with a nod.

"Good. I want to know of anyone who's selling guns."

He closed his eyes, his mouth twisting in an ironic smirk. "Guns? Just like that, you want to know who's dealing in guns? God, lady, you look like you could go to the nearest reputable dealer and buy any damn thing you wanted." He took a step closer, reaching out his hand to flip a piece of her hair. "I don't know who you thought you'd fool, but you walk like money, talk like money…hell, you even smell like money. What is it? The thrill of going slumming that has you traipsing around here dressed in that getup?"

Emily sucked in her breath at his vulgar question and felt her temper rise. "You have fifty dollars of my money. The least you can do is behave in a civilized, polite manner."

"Wrong." He stepped even closer, the dark, sweat-damp hair on his chest nearly brushing against the tip of her nose. He had to bend low to look her in the eyes, but he managed. "The least I can do is steer your fancy little tail back where you belong. Go home, little girl. Get your thrills somewhere else, somewhere where it's safe."

Suffused with heat at both his nearness and his derisive attitude, it was all Emily could do to keep from cowering. She clicked her teeth together, then swallowed hard. "You don't want to help me. Fine. I'm certain I'll find someone else who will. After all, I'm willing to pay a thousand dollars." Then, turning to make a grand exit, certain she'd made him sorry over losing out on so much money, she said over her shoulder, "I imagine I'll find someone much more agreeable than you within the hour. Goodbye."

There was a split second of stunned silence, then an explosive curse, and Emily decided good breeding could take second place to caution. She reached for the door and almost had it open, when his large hand landed on the wood with a loud crack, slamming it shut again. His warm, hard chest pressed to her back, pinning her to the door. She could barely move; she could barely breathe.

Then his lips touched her ear, whisper-soft, and he said, "You're not going anywhere, sweetheart."

chapter 2

SHE FELT LIGHT-HEADED, BUT SHE SUMMONED A cool smile. He was deliberately trying to frighten her—she didn't know how she knew that, but she was certain of it. Slowly turning in what little space he allowed her, Emily faced him, her chin held high. "Would you mind giving me a little breathing room, please?"

"I might."

Might mind, or might move? Emily shook her head. "You have a rather nasty habit of looming over me, Mr....?"

For a moment, he remained still and silent, then thankfully, he took two steps back. He looked at her as if she might not be entirely sane. Emily stuck out her hand. "I'm Emily Cooper."

His gaze dropped to her hand, then with a resigned look of disgust, he enfolded her small hand in his much larger one, pumping it twice before abruptly releasing her. He stared at the ceiling. "Judd Sanders."

"It's very nice to meet you, Mr. San—"

"Judd will do." He shook his head, and his gaze came back

to her face. "Look, lady, you can't just come to this part of town and start waving money around. You'll get yourself dragged into a dark alley and mugged, possibly raped. Or worse."

Emily wondered what exactly could be worse than being mugged and raped in a dark alley, but she didn't bother asking him. She felt certain he'd come up with some dire consequence to frighten her.

He was watching her closely, and she tried to decide if it was actual concern she saw on his face. She liked to think so. Things still didn't fit. He didn't seem any more suited to this part of town than she did, regardless of his crude manners and bossy disposition.

But now that he'd backed up and given her some room, she was able to think again. "I made certain to stay in front of the stores and in plain sight at all times. If mischief had started, someone surely would have offered assistance." Her eyebrows lifted and she smiled. "You did."

He muttered under his breath, and pointed an accusing finger at her. "You're a menace."

Glaring at him wouldn't get her anywhere, she decided. She needed help, that much was obvious. And who better to help her than a man who evidently knew his way around this part of town, and was well acquainted with its inhabitants. She cleared her throat. "I realize I don't entirely understand how things should be done. Although I'm familiar with the neighborhood, since I work in the soup kitchen twice a week..." She hesitated, then added, "I bought this coat from one of the ladies who comes in regularly. On her, it looked authentic enough. That was even her bag I carried—"

"Miss Cooper."

He said her name in a long, drawn-out sigh. Emily cleared her throat again, then laced her fingers together. "Anyway, while I know the area, at least during the day, I'm not at all acquainted with the workings of the criminal mind. That's why, as I said, I'd like to hire you."

"Because you think *I* do understand the criminal mind?"

"I meant no insult." She felt a little uncertain with him glaring at her like that. "I did get the impression you could handle yourself in almost any situation. Look at how well you took care of those drunkards? You didn't even get bruised, and there were three of them."

"Yeah. But you'd already laid one of them low."

She could feel the blush starting at her hairline and traveling down to cover her entire face. "Yes, well…"

He seemed to give up. One minute he was rigid, his posture so imposing she had to use all her willpower not to cower. Then suddenly, he was idly rubbing his forehead. "Let's get out of here and you can tell me exactly what you want."

Oh, no. She wouldn't tell him that, because what she wanted from him and what was proper were two very different things. But she forgave herself the mental transgression. No woman could possibly be in the same room with this man without having a few fantasies wing through her mind.

Trying for some vagrant humor to lighten his sour mood, she asked, "Wouldn't you like to change first?"

Staring at her, his jaw worked as if he was grinding his teeth. Then he gave one brisk nod. "Turn your head."

Emily blinked. "Turn my… Now wait just a minute! I'll go out to the bar and—"

"No way. I can't trust you not to disappear. Just turn around and stare at the door. I'll only be a minute."

"But I'll know what you're doing!"

He smirked, that was the only word for it. "What's the

matter, honey? You afraid you won't be able to resist peeking, knowing I'll be buck naked?"

That was a pretty accurate guess. Emily shook her head. "Don't be ridiculous. It just isn't right, that's all."

"Afraid one of your society friends might meander along and catch you doing something naughty?" He snorted. "Trust me. Not too many upper-crust types visit this part of town. You won't catch yourself in the middle of a scandal."

But she had been caught once, and it had been the most humiliating experience of her life. She'd been alienated from her family ever since.

She thought of that horrid man and nearly cringed. She'd thought herself so above her parents, so understanding of the underprivileged. And she still believed that way. A gentleman was a gentleman, no matter his circumstances. Decency wasn't something that could be bought. But the man who had swept her off her feet, shown her passion and excitement, had proven himself to be anything but decent.

She'd nearly married him before she'd realized he only wanted her money. Not her. Never her. He'd used her, used her family, made a newsworthy pest of himself, and her parents had never forgiven her for it.

She could still hear herself trying to explain her actions. But her mother believed a lady didn't involve herself in such situations, under any circumstances.

A lady never lost her head to something as primal as lust.

Lifting her chin, Emily gave Judd the frostiest stare she could devise. "I can most certainly control myself." Then she turned her back on him. "Go right ahead, Mr. Sanders. But please make it quick. It is getting rather late."

Emily heard him chuckling, heard the rustle of clothing, and she held her breath. It was only a matter of a minute and a half before he told her she could turn around.

Very slowly, just in case he was toying with her, Emily peered at him. He was dressed in jeans, and had pulled on a flannel shirt. He was sitting on a crate, tugging on low boots. When he stood to fasten his shirt, Emily noticed he hadn't yet done up his jeans. She tried not to blush, but it was a futile effort.

He ignored her embarrassment. "So, Emily. Where exactly are you from?"

Her gaze was on his hands as he shoved his shirttails into his pants. "The Crystal Lakes area," she said. "And you?"

He gave a low, soft whistle. "The Crystal Lakes? Damn. No kidding?"

Annoyed, she finally forced her attention to his face. "I certainly wouldn't lie about it."

He took her arm and led her out of the storeroom. He had stuffed his dance props into the leather satchel he carried in his other hand. "I'll bet you live in a big old place with plenty of rooms, don't you?"

Emily eyed him with a wary frown. She wasn't certain how much she should tell him about herself. "I have enough space, I suppose."

He asked abruptly, "How did you get here?"

"Actually, I took the bus. I didn't think parking my car here would be such a good idea."

"No doubt. What do you drive, anyway? A Rolls?"

"Of course not."

"So?" He pulled her out the door and into the brisk night. "What do you tool around in?"

"Tool around? I drive a Saab."

"Ah."

"What does that mean? Ah?" He was moving her along

again, treating her like a dog on a leash. And with his long-legged stride, it was all she could do to keep up. He stopped near a back alley, and Emily realized they were at the rear of the bar. "Why didn't we just go out the back door instead of walking all the way around?"

"'Ah' means your choice of transportation shouldn't surprise me. And we came this way so I could spare you from being harassed. Believe me, the men working in the back would have a field day with an innocent like you."

Don't ask. Don't ask. "What makes you believe I'm an innocent?"

Judd opened the door to a rusty, disreputable pickup truck and motioned for her to get inside. She hesitated, suddenly not certain she should trust him.

But he only stood there, watching her with that intense, probing green gaze. Finally, Emily grabbed the door frame to hoist herself inside.

Judd shook his head. "And you ask how I know you're an innocent?"

Before Emily could reply, he slammed the door and walked around to get in behind the wheel. "Buckle up."

She watched his profile as he steered the truck out of the alley and onto the main road. The lights from well-spaced street lamps flashed across his features. Trying to avoid staring at him, she looked around the truck and she saw a strip of delicate black lace draped over the rearview mirror.

Judd noticed her fascination with the sheer lace and grinned. "A memento of my youth."

Trying for disinterest, Emily muttered, "Really."

"I was sixteen, she was eighteen."

Sixteen. The same age as her brother—and obviously into as much mischief as John.

Judd ran his fingers down the lace as if in fond memory. "We were in such a hurry, we ripped her panties getting them off." He flashed her a grin. "Black lace still makes me crazy."

Emily went perfectly quiet, then tightly crossed her legs. *There's no way he can know what your panties look like, Emily,* she told herself. But still, she made an effort to bring the conversation back to her purpose. She had to find a way to help John.

Reminded of the reason she was with Judd in the first place, Emily turned to him. Taking a deep breath, she said, "I need to find out who's selling semiautomatic weapons to kids. I...I know a boy who had one blow up in his face. He was badly injured. Luckily, no one else was around."

The truck swerved, and Judd shot her a look that could have cut ice. *"Blew up?"*

His tone was harsh, and Emily couldn't help huddling closer against her door. "Yes. He very nearly lost an eye."

Judd muttered a curse, but when he glanced at her again, his expression was carefully controlled. "Did you go to the police?"

"I can't." She tightened her lips, feeling frustrated all over again. "The boy's parents won't allow him to be implicated. They refuse to realize just how serious this situation is. They have money, so they took him out of the country to be treated. They won't return until they're certain he's safe."

"Yeah. A lot of parents believe bad things will go away if you ignore them. Unfortunately, that's not true. But Emily, you have to know, there's nothing you can do to stop the crime on these streets. The drugs, the gangs and the selling of illegal arms, it'll go on forever."

"I refuse to believe that!" She turned in her seat, taking her frustration out on him. "I have to do something. Maybe I can figure out a way to stop this guy who sold that gun. If everyone would get involved—"

Judd laughed, cutting her off. "Like the folks who whisked their baby boy out of the country? How old was this kid, anyway? Old enough to know better, I'll bet." He shook his head, giving her a look that blatantly called her a fool. "Don't waste your time. Go back to your rich neighborhood, your fancy car and your fancier friends. Let the cops take care of things."

She was so angry, she nearly cried. It had always been that way. She never shed a tear over pain or hurt feelings, but let her get really mad, and she bawled like an infant. His attitude toward her brother infuriated her.

Judd stopped at a traffic light, and she jerked her door open, trying to step out. His long hard fingers immediately wrapped around her upper arm, preventing her from leaving.

"What the hell do you think you're doing?"

"Let me go." She was proud of her feral tone. "Did you hear me? Get your hands off me." She struggled, pulling against his hold.

"Dammit! Get back in this truck!"

The light had changed and the driver of the car behind them blasted his horn. "I've changed my mind, Mr. Sanders," she told him. "I no longer require your help. I'll find someone else, someone who won't choose to ridicule me every other second."

He peered at her closely, then sighed. "Aw, hell. Don't tell me you're going to cry."

"No, I am not going to cry!" But she could feel the tears stinging her eyes, which angered her all the more. How could she have been so wrong about him—and he so wrong about her? She didn't have fancy friends; she didn't have any friends. Most of the time, she didn't have anybody—except her brother. She loved him dearly, and John trusted her. When the rest of her family had turned their backs on her, her brother had been there for her, making her laugh, giving her the support she needed to get through it all.

She couldn't let him down now, even if he didn't realize he needed her help. He was the only loving family she could claim, the only one who still cared about her, despite her numerous faults. And she knew, regardless of the gun incident, John was a good person.

Several cars were blaring their horns now, and Judd yanked her back inside, retaining his hold as he moved out of the stream of traffic and over to the curb. He didn't release her. "Look, I'm sorry. Don't go and get weepy on me, okay?"

"You, Mr. Sanders, are an obnoxious ass!" Emily jerked against him, but he held firm. "I always cry when I'm angry."

"Well...don't be angry then."

Unbelievable. The man had been derisive, insulting and arrogant from the moment she'd met him, but now his tone had changed to a soft, gentle rebuke. He had a problem with female tears? She almost considered giving in to a real tantrum just to make him suffer, but that had never been her way. The last thing she wanted from Judd was pity.

"Ignore me," she muttered, feeling like a fool. "It's been a trying week. But I am determined to see this thing through. I'll find the man who sold that gun. I have a plan, a very solid plan. I could certainly use your help, but if you're only going to be nasty, I believe I'd rather just find someone else."

JUDD WAS AMAZED by her speech. Then his eyes narrowed. No way in hell was he going to let her run loose. She was a menace. She was a pain.

She was unbelievably innocent and naive.

Judd shook his head, then steered the truck back into the street. "Believe me, lady. I'm about as nice as you're going to find in these parts. Besides, I think I might be interested in your little plan, after all. I mean, what the hell? A thousand bucks is a thousand bucks. That was the agreed amount, right?"

Emily nodded.

Lifting one shoulder, Judd said, "Can't very well turn down money like that."

"No. No, I wouldn't think so." She watched him warily, and Judd thought, what the hell? It would be easier to work with her, than around her. If he turned her down, she'd only manage to get in his way, or get herself hurt. That was such a repugnant thought, he actually groaned.

He'd have to keep his cool, maintain his cover, and while he was at it, he could keep an eye on her. Maybe he could pretend to help her, but actually steer her far enough away from the trouble that she wouldn't be any problem at all.

Yeah, right.

It would probably be better to try to convince her to give up her ridiculous plan first. He glanced at her, saw the rigid way she held herself, and knew exactly how to dissuade her. "There are a few conditions we should discuss."

Emily heaved a deep breath. "Conditions?"

"Yeah. The money's great. But I'll still have to work nights at the bar. Actually, only Tuesdays and Thursdays. *Ladies'* nights."

Emily hastened to reassure him. "I don't have a problem with that. I wouldn't want to interfere with your...career."

His laugh was quick and sharp, then he shook his head. "Right. My career." He glanced at her again, grinning, wondering if she could possibly realize how uncomfortable he was with that particular career. "That's not the only thing, though."

"There's something else?"

"Yeah. You see, we'll need a place to meet. Neutral ground and all that. Someplace away from prying eyes."

Emily stared.

"You stand out like a sore thumb, honey. We can't just have you traipsing around in that neighborhood. People will wonder what you're up to. It could blow the whole thing."

"I see."

"My apartment is close to here. No one would pay any attention to you coming in or out. It wouldn't even matter what time we met. We'll need to work closely together, finesse these plans of yours. What d'ya say?"

Her mouth opened, but all that came out was, "Oh God."

Lifting one dark eyebrow, Judd felt triumphant. She was already realizing the implications of spending so much time alone with him. He hid his relief and said, "Come again?"

Emily shook her head, then at the same time said, "Yes, that is…I suppose…" She heaved a sigh, straightened her back, and then nodded. "Okay."

Judd stared at her, trying not to show his disbelief. "What do you mean, okay?" He'd thought for certain, since everything else had failed, that this would send her running. But no. She seemed to like the damn idea. She was actually smiling now.

"I mean, if you think we could successfully operate from your apartment, I'll agree to meet you there."

Contrary female. "Emily…" He faltered. He liked saying her name, liked how it sounded, all fresh and pure. She looked at him, with those huge, doe eyes steady on his face. She was too trusting. She was a danger to herself. If he didn't keep close tabs on her, she'd end up in trouble. He was sure of it.

"You were going to say something, Mr. Sanders?"

Nothing she would like hearing. He shook his head. "Just be quiet and let me think."

Obediently, she turned away and stared out her window. He wasn't buying her compliance for a minute. He had a gut feeling there wasn't an obedient bone in her slim body. He also suspected she was as stubborn as all hell, once she'd set her mind on something. And she was set to find a gun dealer.

The truck was heating up. It was late spring and even though the nights were still a little chilly, the days were warming up into the seventies. Without any fanfare, and apparently trying not to draw undue attention to herself, Emily began unbuttoning the oversize coat. Judd watched from the corner of his eye.

Just to razz her, because she took the bait so easily, he asked, "Would you like me to give you a drumroll?"

She turned to face him. "I beg your pardon?"

She looked honestly confused. He tried to hide his grin. "Every good striptease needs music."

"I'm not stripping!"

He shrugged, amused by the blush on her cheeks that was visible even in the dark interior of the truck. She was apparently unused to masculine teasing, maybe even to men in general.

He snorted at his own foolishness. It was men like himself, coarse and inelegant, that she wasn't used to. He imagined she had plenty of sophisticated guys clamoring for her attention. And that fact nettled him, even though it shouldn't. Grumbling, he said, "You should try it. Everyone should experience stripping just once. It's a rush."

She held her coat together with clenched fingers, her look incredulous. If she knew him better, she'd know what a lie he'd just told. He hated taking off his clothes in front of so many voracious women. But she didn't know him, and most likely never would. He should keep that fact in mind before he did something stupid. *Like what, you idiot? Like promising you'd take care of her gun dealer for her, so she could take her cute little backside and big brown eyes back home where it's safe?* No, he most definitely couldn't do that, no matter how much he'd like to.

They came to the entrance to Crystal Lakes. "Which way?"

He'd startled her. She'd practically jumped out of her seat, and he was left wondering exactly where her mind had been. "Which way to your place? You didn't think I'd take you to my apartment tonight, did you? In case you haven't noticed, lady, it's after midnight. And I've put in a full day. Tomorrow will be soon enough."

The truck was left to idle while they stared at each other. Finally in a small voice filled with suspicion, Emily said, "You're not just getting rid of me, are you? You'll really help me?"

Those eyes of hers could be lethal. He wanted nothing more than to tug her close and promise her he wouldn't leave her, that he'd take care of everything, that he'd... She looked so damn vulnerable. It didn't make a bit of sense. Usually people with big money went around feeling confident that money would get them anything. They didn't bother with doubts.

Irritated now, he rubbed the bridge of his nose, then said in a low tone, "Since I haven't gotten my thousand bucks yet, you can be sure I'll be sticking around."

After heaving a small sigh, she said, "Of course."

Now, why did she have to sound so disappointed? And why did he feel like such a jerk?

"Left, up the hill, then the first street on the right."

Judd knew he had no business forming fantasies over a woman who blushed every time she spoke. Especially since he'd have to keep her close, more to protect her than anything else. She didn't understand the magnitude of what she was tampering with, the lethal hold gun dealers had on the city.

An idea had been forming in his mind ever since he'd realized he couldn't discourage her from trying to save the world. He'd thought, if he became aggressive enough, she'd run back home to safety.

Instead, she'd only threatened to find someone else to help her. And he couldn't let that happen. She might get herself killed, or maybe she'd actually find out something and inadvertently get in the way. He'd worked too hard for that to happen. He wouldn't allow anything—or anyone—to interfere. He *would* get the bastard who'd shot Max. But damn, he'd never expected Emily to openly accept his plans.

Crystal Lakes, as exclusive and ritzy as it was, sat only about twenty-five minutes from the lower east side. It was one of those areas where you could feel the gradual change as you left hell and entered heaven. The grass started looking greener, the business district slipped away, and eventually everything was clean and untainted.

Emily pointed out her house, a large white Colonial, with a huge front porch. It looked as if it had been standing there for more than a hundred years, and was surprisingly different from the newer, immense homes recently built in the area.

There were golden lights in every window, providing a sense of warmth. A profusion of freshly planted spring flowers surrounded the perimeter, and blooming dogwoods randomly filled the yard. All in all, the place was very impressive, but not quite what he'd expected. Somehow, he'd envisioned her stationed in real money. Any truly successful businessperson could afford this house.

Judd stared around the isolated grounds. "Do you live here by yourself?"

She nodded, not quite looking at him, her hands clasped nervously in her lap.

"No husband or little ones to help fill up the space?"

"No. No husband. No children."

"Why not? I thought all debutantes were married off at an early age."

He didn't think she'd answer at first, but then she licked her lips and her skittish gaze settled on his face. "I was…engaged once. But things didn't work out." She rushed through her words, seemingly unable to stop herself. "I bought this house about a year ago. My parents don't particularly like it—it's one of the smaller homes in the community. But it was an original estate, not one built when the Lakes was developed. It's been renovated, and I think it's charming."

She said the words defensively, as if she expected some scathing comment from him. Judd didn't like being affected this way, but there was something about Emily that touched him. He could *feel* her emotions, had been feeling them since first making eye contact with her. And right now, she seemed almost wounded.

Very gently, he asked, "Did you see to the renovations yourself?"

"Yes."

He looked around the dark, secluded yard and shook his head. "Your parents approve of your living here alone?"

"No, but it doesn't matter what they think. When my grandmother died, she left me a large inheritance. My parents expected me to buy a condo near them and then invest the rest using their suggestions." Her hands tightened in her lap and she swallowed. "But I loved this house on sight. I'd already planned to buy it, and receiving the inheritance let me do so sooner than I'd planned. I don't regret a single penny I spent on the place. Everything is just as I want it."

"What if you hadn't gotten the inheritance?"

"I would have found a job. I'm educated. I'm not helpless." She gave him a narrow-eyed look. "But this way, I don't have to. I'm financially independent."

And alone. "How old are you, Emily?"

She raised her chin, a curious habit he'd noticed she used whenever she felt threatened. "Thirty."

He couldn't hide his surprise. "You don't look more than twenty." Without thinking, he reached out and touched her cheek, his fingertips drifting over her fine, porcelain skin. "Twenty and untouched."

She jerked away. "Are we going to sit in the driveway all night? Go around the back, to the kitchen door."

He shouldn't let her give him orders, but what the hell. He put the truck in gear and did as directed.

The darkness of the hour had hidden quite a few things. There was a small lake behind her property, pretty with the moon reflecting off its surface. Of course, there were some twenty such lakes in the Crystal Lakes community, so he shouldn't have been surprised.

"Is the lake stocked?"

"Yes. But it's seldom used. Occasionally, one or two of the neighborhood children come here to fish. My lake is the most shallow, so it's the safest. And it's the only one on this side of the community. Most of the lakes are farther up."

"You don't mind the kids trampling around your yard?"

"Of course not. They're good kids. They usually feed the ducks and catch a frog or two. I enjoy watching them."

Judd stared back at the house. There was a large window that faced the backyard and the lake. He could picture her sitting there, content to watch the children play. Maybe longing for things she didn't have. Things money couldn't buy.

Hell, he was becoming fanciful.

Disgusted with himself, knowing he'd been away from normal society too long and that was probably the reason she seemed so appealing, he parked the truck and got out. The fresh air cleared his head.

He opened Emily's door to help her out, but she held back, watching him nervously. "I'll make sure you get inside okay, then I'll take off. We can hook up again tomorrow morning."

"Oh. Yes. That will be fine."

She sounded relieved that he didn't intend to come inside tonight, and perversely, he changed his mind. He'd come in, all right, but with his imagination so active, he couldn't trust himself to be alone with her any length of time. Anyway, he told himself, she wasn't his type—not even close. She was much too small and frail. He liked his women big, with bountiful breasts and lush hips.

As far as he could tell, Emily didn't have a figure.

But those eyes... She walked up a small, tidy patio fronted by three shallow steps, then unlocked the back door and flipped a switch. Bright fluorescent light cascaded through a spotless kitchen and spilled outside onto the patio. Judd saw flowerpots everywhere, filled with spring flowers, and a small outdoor seating group arranged to his right. Everything seemed cheery and colorful...like a real home, and not at all what he'd expected.

Damn, he'd have to find some way to dissuade her from her plan before he got in over his head.

She turned and gave him a small, uncertain smile. "About tomorrow..."

He interrupted her, coming up the three steps and catching her gaze. "Let's make sure we understand each other, Emily, so there won't be any mistakes."

She nodded, and he deliberately stepped closer, watching with satisfaction as she tried to pull back, even though there was no place to go. Good, he thought. At least she had some sense of self-preservation.

He braced his hands on the door frame, deliberately looming over her. "From this second on, I call the shots, with no arguments from you. If you really want my help, you'll do as I tell you, whatever I tell you." He waited until she'd backed all the way into the kitchen, then he added, "You understand all that?"

chapter 3

EMILY'S MOUTH OPENED TWICE, BUT NOTHING
came out. She was too stunned to think rationally, too appalled
to react with any real thought. Judd dropped his arms and
stepped completely into the kitchen, watching her, and by reflex
alone, she started sidling toward the hall door. She had made a
terrible mistake. Her instincts had been off by a long shot.

Judd's smile was pure wickedness. "Where ya' goin', Emily?"

"I, ah, I just thought of something…"

Like a loud blast, his laugh erupted, filling the silence of
the kitchen.

She halted, a spark of suspicion beginning to form. "*What*
is so funny?"

"The look on your face. Did you think I had visions of
taking you instead of the money?" He shook his head, and
Emily felt her cheeks flame. He was still chuckling when he
said, "It only makes sense that I'd be in charge—after all, that's
what you'll be paying me for. Like I told you, a rich little lady
like yourself would only draw a lot of unnecessary attention

hanging around that area. You'll have to follow my lead, and do as I tell you if you want to stay safe. And another thing, we need to figure out some reason for you being there at all. I think we'll have to do a little acting. Your part will be easy, since you'll just be the rich lady. That leaves me as the kept man." He spread his arms wide. "As far as everyone will be concerned, I'm yours. There's no other reason why a woman like you would be around a man like me, unless she was slumming. So that's the reason we'll use."

She was so mortified, she wanted to die. Stiff-backed, she turned away from him and walked over to lean against the tiled counter near the sink. She heard Judd close the door, and seconds later, his hands landed on her shoulders, holding her firm.

"Don't get all huffy now. We have things to discuss. Serious things."

"You mean, you don't intend to taunt me anymore? My goodness, how gracious."

"You've got a real smart mouth, don't you? No, don't answer that. I'm sorry I teased you, but I couldn't resist. You're just too damn easy to fluster." He turned her to face him, then tipped up her chin.

"Here, now, don't go blushing again. Not that you don't look cute when you do, but I really think we should talk."

Emily stepped carefully away, not wanting him to know how his nearness, his touch, affected her. Even after all his taunting, she still went breathless and too warm inside when he was close. And ridiculously, it angered her when he belittled himself, claiming she could have no interest in him other than as a sex partner. The physical appeal was there, but it was more than that. Much more. He had helped her. He'd actually taken on three inebriated men to protect her, even though he wasn't a real cop. And he was willing to help her again. She discounted the money; what she was asking could put his life at risk. He must be motivated by more than money to get involved.

But for now, she couldn't sort it all out. Especially not with her senses still rioting at his nearness. She drew a deep breath, then let it out again. "I thought we were going to wait until morning to make any plans. It is getting rather late."

"No, I've decided it can't wait. But I won't keep you long. Pull up a chair and get comfortable."

Emily didn't particularly want to get comfortable, but she also didn't want to risk driving Judd away. For the moment, he was the best hope she had of ever finding the man who'd sold her brother the gun. She knew her limitations, and fitting in around the lower east side of Springfield was probably the biggest of them. She needed him.

As she headed for a chair, Judd caught the back of her coat, drawing her up short. "It's warm in here. Why don't you take this off?"

He was watching her closely again, and she couldn't fathom his thoughts. She shrugged, then started to slip the shabby wool coat from her shoulders. Judd's eyes went immediately to the tiny camera she wore on a strap around her neck.

"What the hell is that?"

She jumped, then lost her temper with his barking tone. "Will you please quit cursing at me!"

He seemed stunned by her outburst, but he did nod. "Answer me."

"It's rather obviously a camera."

Closing his eyes and looking as though he were involved in deep prayer, Judd said, "Please tell me you weren't taking pictures tonight."

"No. I didn't take any." She lifted her chin, knowing what his reaction would be, then added, "Tonight."

"You just had to clarify that, didn't you, before I could really relax." His sigh was long and drawn out, then he led her to the polished pine table sitting in the middle of her quarry-stone kitchen floor. He pulled out a chair for her, silently insisting that she sit. "So when did you take pictures?"

"I've been checking that area for three nights now." She ignored his wide-eyed amazement, and his muttered cursing. "The first night, I took some shots of things that didn't look quite right. You know, groups of men who were huddled together talking. Cars that were parked where they probably shouldn't be. Things like that. Not that I really suspected them of anything. But I didn't want to come home empty-handed.

"I was hoping to find something concrete tonight, so I brought the camera again. Let's face it. If I did find out anything, I doubt the police would simply take my word for it. I mean, if they were at all concerned with that awful man who's selling defective guns, well…they'd be doing something right now." Judd cringed, but Emily rushed on. "If I had something on film, I'd have solid evidence. The police would have to get involved. But there wasn't anything incriminating."

Judd's mouth was tight and his eyes grew more narrow with each word she spoke. "You've been hanging out in the lower east side for three days…rather, nights?"

"Yes."

His palm slapped the table and he leaned forward to loom over her again, caging her in her chair. Emily slid back in her seat, stunned by his fury. And he *was* furious, she had no doubt of that.

"Never again, you got that!" He was so close, his breath hit her face in hot gusts. "From this day on, you don't even think about going anywhere, especially to the lower east side, without me. Ever. You got that?"

Emily bolted upright, forcing him to move away so they wouldn't smack noses. "You don't give me orders, Mr. Sanders!"

"Judd, dammit," he said, now sounding merely disgruntled. "I told you to call me Judd."

"I hired you, *Judd,* not the other way around."

He grabbed her shoulders and pushed her into her seat. His tone was lower, but no less firm. "I'm serious, Emily. You obviously don't have the sense God gave a goose, and if you want my help on this, I insist you stay in one piece. That won't happen if you go wandering around in areas where you shouldn't be. It's too dangerous. Hell, it's a wonder you've survived as long as you have."

Emily tried to calm herself, but he was so close, she couldn't think straight. She recognized his real concern, something money couldn't possibly buy. Satisfied that her instincts hadn't failed her after all, she tried to reassure him. Her voice emerged as a whisper. "I have been careful, Judd. I promise. No one saw me take the pictures. But just in case, I took shots of inconsequential things, too. Like the children who were playing in the street, and the vagrant standing on the corner. If anyone saw me, they'd just think I was doing an exposé. They'd be flattered, not concerned."

"You can't know that."

He, too, was easing back, as if suddenly aware of their positions. Slipping the camera off over her head, he said, "I'll take this, in case there is anything important on the film."

Emily started to object, even though she truly didn't believe she had photographed anything relevant. Then she noticed where his gaze had wandered. Very briefly, his eyes lit on her mouth, then her throat. Emily could feel her pulse racing there.

Still frowning, but also looking a little confused, Judd laid the camera on the table, then caught the lapels of her coat and eased them wide. He just stood there, holding her coat open, looking at her. He didn't move, but his look was so hot, and he was still so near she grew breathless.

She felt choked by the neck of her dress, a high-collared affair that buttoned up the front and was long enough to hang to midcalf. It was sprinkled with small, dainty blue flowers, a little outdated maybe, but she liked it. She'd long ago accepted she had no fashion sense, so she bought what pleased her, not what the designers dictated.

Judd lifted a finger, almost reluctantly, and touched the small blue bow that tied her collar at her throat. She could hear his breathing, could see his intense concentration as he watched the movement of his hand. With a slow, gentle tug, he released the bow, and the pad of his finger touched her warm skin.

Emily parted her lips to breathe. She wasn't thinking about what he was doing or why. She was only feeling, the sensations overwhelming, swamping her senses. She surrendered to them—to Judd—without a whimper, good sense and caution lost in the need to be wanted, to share herself with another person.

Judd lifted his gaze to her face. He searched her expression for a timeless moment, his eyes hard and bright. Then abruptly, he moved away. He stalked to the door, his head down, his hands fisted on his hips.

He inhaled deeply, and Emily watched the play of muscles across his back. "I want your promise, Emily. I don't want you to make a single move without me."

Gruff and low, it took a second for his words to filter into her mind. They were so different from her own thoughts, so distant from the mood he'd created. She cleared her throat and tried to clear her mind. Judd still had his back to her, his arms now crossed over his chest. He sounded almost angry, and she didn't understand him. Could he, who barely knew her, truly be so concerned for her well-being? "You'll help me? You're not just putting me off?"

"I'll help. But we move when I say, and not before."

She wished he'd look at her so she could see his face, but he didn't. "Since I assume you know the best time to find information, I'll wait."

Finally, he turned to her. "This house is secure?"

"Very."

He picked up the camera, then opened the door. "I've got to go. I have a few things to do yet. But I want you to promise me you'll stay inside—no more investigating tonight."

Nervously, Emily fingered the loose ties to her bow. She considered retying it, but decided against drawing any further attention to the silly thing. Judd glanced down at her fingers, and his expression hardened. "Promise me you'll stay in your castle, princess. We can talk more in the morning."

"Yes. I won't go anywhere else tonight." She tried to make her tone firm, but some of her fear came through in her next question. "How will I reach you tomorrow?"

Judd stood silently watching her a minute longer. "You got a pen and paper anywhere around here?"

Emily opened a drawer and pulled out a pad and pencil. Judd quickly scrawled several lines. "This is my number at the apartment, and this is the one at the bar. And just in case, here's my address. Now, I mean it, Emily. Don't make a move without me."

She tried not to look too greedy when she snatched the paper out of his hand. "I promise."

He hesitated another moment, then stepped outside, pulling the door shut behind him. Emily watched through the window as his truck drove away, wondering where he was going, but knowing she didn't have the right to ask. Perhaps he had a lady friend waiting on him.

Of course he does, Emily, she told herself. *A man like him probably has dozens of women.* But they're not ladies. He wouldn't want a lady.

And for some reason, that thought sent a small, forbidden thrill curling through her insides.

ANGER AND FRUSTRATION were not a good combination. Judd didn't understand himself. Or more to the point, he didn't understand his reaction to Emily.

He'd been a hairbreadth away from kissing her. Not a sweet little peck. No, he'd wanted his tongue in her mouth, his lips covering hers, feeling her urgency. He'd wanted, dammit, to devour her completely.

And she would have loved it, he could tell that much from her racing pulse and her soft, inviting eyes. She may play the proper little Miss Priss to perfection, but she had fire. Enough to burn him if he let her.

It wasn't the time and she wasn't the person for him to be getting ideas about. But he'd taunted her without mercy, wanting to conquer her, to show her he was male to her female. To prove...what? That he could and would protect her? That he'd solve her problems so she could smile more? He didn't know.

He'd had women, of course, but none that meant anything beyond physical pleasure. None that he'd wanted to claim, to brand in the most primal, basic way. He didn't know what it was, but Emily was simply different. And she affected him differently.

That dress of hers...so feminine, so deceiving. He'd always heard other men joke about having a lady in the parlor and a wanton in the bedroom. The dress had looked innocent enough, but her eyes...

He knew, even though he wasn't happy knowing, that Emily fit the descriptive mix of lady and wanton to a tee. It was an explosive fantasy, the thought of having a woman who would unleash her passion for just one man, that no one would ever guess unless they were with her, covering her, inside her.

Beneath her dress, he could make out the faint, delicate curve of her breasts, her narrow rib cage. She was so slight of build, but so feminine. She had the finest skin he'd ever seen, warm and smooth and pale. And loyalty. She must be damn loyal to this kid—whoever he was—to take such risks for him.

Judd's thighs clenched and his heart raced. He hadn't been able to resist touching her, and she hadn't protested when he did.

She was too trusting for her own good. And he was too intuitive to be fooled by her prissy demeanor. Emily Cooper had more than her fair share of backbone, and that was almost as sexy as her eyes.

Stopping at a corner drugstore and leaving the truck at the curb, Judd got out to use the lighted pay phone. He never used the phone in his apartment to contact headquarters, in case there were prying ears. To his disgust, his hands shook as he fished a quarter out of his jeans pocket. He made the call, and then waited.

Lieutenant Howell picked up on the first ring. "Yeah?"

"Sanders here."

"It's about time. Where the hell have you been?"

Judd closed his eyes, not relishing the chore ahead of him. This wasn't going to be easy. He took a deep breath, then told his boss, "We have a little problem."

"I'm waiting."

"I met a lady tonight."

"Is that supposed to surprise me, Judd? Hell, you're working as a male stripper. I imagine you meet a lot of broads every damn night."

"Not a broad," Judd said, the edge in his tone evident. "A

lady. And she was actively looking for Donner, though she hasn't put a name to him yet. Seems she knows a kid who had a faulty automatic blow up in his face, and she's pegged Donner as the seller."

There was a low whistle, then, "No kidding?"

"The kid's alive, but from what I understand, he's in pretty bad shape. His parents have taken him out of the country." Then, in a drier tone, Judd added, "They're upper-league."

Judd expected the cursing, then the inevitable demand for details. The telling took all of three minutes, and during that time, Howell didn't make a single sound. Judd tried to downplay his initial meeting with Emily and the fact she'd seen him perform, but there was no way to get around it completely. When Judd finished, he heard a rough rumble from Howell that could have been either a chuckle or a curse. "She could throw a wrench into the works."

Judd chose his words very carefully. "Maybe not. I've been thinking about it, and it might actually strengthen my case. Being a stripper in such a sleazy joint makes me look pretty unethical. And I've made it known I'd do just about anything, including stripping, to make a fast buck."

"But Donner hasn't taken the bait yet."

"He will." Judd was certain of that. Donner always used available locals. That was how he worked. "It will happen. But maybe, with a classy woman hanging around to make me look all the more unscrupulous, Donner will buy in a little quicker."

"You think he'll figure the little lady is keeping you?"

"What else would he think? We're hardly the perfect couple. As long as she's informed and close enough for me to keep an eye on her, she'll be safe. And Donner will definitely get curious. Besides, I don't have much choice. She made it real plain she'd investigate on her own if I didn't see fit to help her. It's a sure bet she'd tip Donner off and send him running."

Howell chuckled. "Sounds like you got everything nicely under control."

No. He didn't have his libido under control, or his protective male instincts that had him wanting to look after her despite his obligations to the job and his loyalty to Max. "I can handle things, I think. It would have been better not to have a civilian involved, but my options are limited now."

"I could have her picked up for some trumped-up violation. That might buy you a little time to settle things without her around."

The thought of Emily being humiliated that way, being harassed—by anyone other than himself, was unthinkable. "No. I'll keep an eye on her. Besides, she's so clean, she squeaks. I doubt you'd find anything. And I already tried scaring her off, but she's sticking to her guns."

"Determined, huh?"

Judd snorted. "I almost think she wants Donner as bad as I do. She was taking pictures. Can you imagine? I took the film. I don't think there's anything important on it, but I don't want to take any chances. Not with this case." *And not with her.* "So I'll let her hang around a while, and use the situation to our advantage. In any case, she'll probably be with me when I perform at the bar on Tuesday."

"Keep me posted as soon as you know about the film. And in the meantime, watch your backside. Don't go getting romantic ideas and blow this whole thing."

"Fat chance." He hoped he sounded convincing. "I just wanted you to know what was going on."

"You need any backup on hand, just in case?"

"No." Everything had gone better than he could have hoped.

His performance was convincing, even superior to the other dancers'. But he didn't intend to share all that over the phone. It was humiliating. "I don't want to take a chance on blowing it now. I'm accepted. No one suspects me of being anything but a stripper."

"Yeah, you fit the bill real good."

Judd ignored that taunting comment. They'd checked the place over in minute detail before setting up the stakeout. Donner definitely used the room above the bar to make his deals and meet contacts. So it was imperative that Judd be on hand. Unfortunately, the bar was such a damn landmark, having been there for generations, the only transient positions available were the dancers'. The bartenders had been there for years and the bar's ownership hadn't changed hands except within the same family. If Judd wanted Donner he was stuck stripping. And he wanted Donner real bad.

"As I said, it's a believable cover, but I hope like hell we can wrap it up soon. I don't want to take any unnecessary chances."

And he didn't want Emily to get caught in the middle of his own personal war.

"Judd? Is there something you're not telling me? Has something happened? Is it time?"

His instincts told him things would come to a head soon, but he kept that thought to himself. "Hell, it's past time, but who knows? Something's bound to break soon. Either a deal or my back. Those ladies can be real demanding when you're peeling off your clothes."

As he'd intended, his cryptic complaints lightened the mood. "You're the perfect guy for the job. Just don't start enjoying yourself and decide to leave us for bigger and better things." Howell laughed, then cleared his throat. "Stay in touch, and for God's sake, stay alert. Get the hell out if things go sour."

"I'll keep my eyes open."

Judd felt a certain finality settle over him as he replaced the receiver. His superior hadn't nixed his plans with Emily, and it was too late to call off the cover, regardless of his personal feelings. He'd be spending a lot of time in Emily's company. And that filled him with both dread and sizzling anticipation.

HE HADN'T SLEPT a wink. The combination of worry and excitement from his vivid dreams of Emily worked to keep him tossing all night. But the knock on the apartment door sounded insistent, so he reluctantly forced himself out from under the sheet, then wrapped it around himself to cover his nudity.

"Just a damn minute!" On his way out of the room, he picked up his watch and saw it was only eight-thirty. Just dandy.

Carrying his pistol, he looked out the peephole, then cursed. He stuck the gun in a drawer, just before jerking the door open. He managed to startle Emily, who nearly dropped a large basket she was holding in both hands. "Are you one of those perverse people who rises with the sun?"

Emily didn't look at his face. She was too busy staring at his body. Judd sighed in disgust. "I'm showing less now than I did last night, and you didn't faint then, so please, pull it together, will ya?"

That moony-eyed look of hers was going to be the death of him. A man could take only so much.

And she was looking especially fetching this morning in some kind of light, spring dress. It was just as concealing as the one she'd worn last night, but there was no tie at her throat, only a pearl brooch that looked as if it cost a small fortune. This dress nipped in at the waist, and showed how tiny she was. He could easily span her waist with his hands. His palms tingled at the thought.

"What the hell are you doing here, Emily? It's still early."

"I…actually, I thought we might have breakfast. You did say we would talk this morning."

"Eager to get started, are you?" Turning away, Judd stared toward the kitchen, then back to Emily. "I wasn't up yet. If you want coffee, you'll have to make it."

Emily seemed to shake herself. "Ah, no. Actually, I thought… you know, to thank you for everything you did for me last night…taking me home and all that, well…I cooked for you."

She ended in a shrug, and Judd realized how embarrassed she was. Or maybe she thought he'd mock her again, ridicule her for her consideration.

He raked a hand through his hair, still holding the sheet with a fist. "What have you got in there?"

He indicated the basket with a toss of his head. Emily's smile was fleeting, and very relieved. She glanced around the room, taking in the apartment's minimal furnishings: a couch, a small table with two chairs, a few lamps, a stereo, but no television. His bedroom sat off to the right, where the open door allowed her to see a small night table and a rumpled bed. The kitchen was merely a room divided by a small, three-foot bar.

He liked the place, even though the neighborhood was rough and the tenants noisy. It wasn't home, but then he'd never really had a home, at least not one of his own. He'd lived with Max Henley a while, and that had seemed as close as he'd ever get to having a family. But that was before Max died. Ever since, his life had been centered on nailing Donner. Where he lived was a trivial matter.

He waited to see Emily's reactions to the apartment, but she didn't so much as blink. After a brief smile, she set the basket on the wobbly table, then opened it with a flourish. "Blueberry muffins, sausage links and fresh fruit." She flashed him a quick, sweet smile. "And coffee."

He was touched, he couldn't help it. "I can't believe you made me breakfast."

"It's not fancy, but you didn't strike me as a man who would want escargots so early in the morning."

He grimaced, then ended with a smile. "And you didn't strike me as the type who would cook for a man."

"I like to cook. My mother thinks it's some faulty gene inherited from my ancestors. But since I'm not married, I don't get to indulge very often."

"What about dates? You could do some real nice entertaining in your house."

She busied herself with setting out the food. "I don't go out much."

He wasn't immune to her vulnerability. He reached out and touched her hand. "No woman has ever cooked for me before."

She stared at him, shocked. "You're kidding."

Feeling a little stupid now for mentioning it, Judd shook his head. "Nope."

"What about your mother?"

"Left when I was real little. My father raised me."

"Oh." Then she tilted her head. "The two of you are close?"

He laughed. "Hardly. Dad stayed drunk most of the time, and I tried to stay out of his hair, 'cause Dad could get real mean when he drank."

"That's awful!" She looked so outraged on his behalf, he grinned.

"It wasn't as bad as all that, Em."

"Of course it was. I think it sounds horrid. Did you have any brothers or sisters?"

"Nope."

"So you were all alone?"

That was the softest, saddest voice he'd ever heard, and for some fool reason, he liked hearing it from her. "Naw. I had Max."

"Max?"

"Yeah. See, I wasn't all that respectable when I was younger, and Max Henley busted me trying to steal the tip he'd left for a waitress. With Max being a cop and all, I thought I'd end up in jail. But instead, he bought me lunch, chewed me out real good, then made me listen to about two hours' worth of lectures on right and wrong and being a good man. I was only fourteen, so I can't say I paid that much attention. When I finally got out of that restaurant, I didn't think I'd ever go back. But I did. See, I knew Max ate his lunch there every day, so the next day, when he saw me hanging around, he invited me to join him. It became a routine, and that summer, he gave me a job keeping up his yard. After a while, Max kind of became like family to me."

Emily was grinning now, too. "He was a father figure?"

"Father, mother, and sometimes as grumpy as an old schoolmarm. But he took good care of me. I guess you could say he was a complete 'family figure.'" *And Donner had robbed Judd of that family.*

"He sounds like a wonderful man."

"Yeah." Judd looked away, wishing he'd never brought up the subject. "Max was the best. He's dead now."

"I'm sorry."

Judd bit his upper lip, barely controlling the urge to hug her close. She had spoken so softly, with so much sincerity, her words felt like a caress. Somehow, she managed to lessen the pain he always felt whenever he thought of Max. God, he still missed him, though it had been nearly six months since Donner had killed him.

Judd nodded, then waited through an awkward silence while Emily looked around for something to do.

She went back to unloading her basket. As she opened the dishes, Judd inhaled the aromas. "Mmm. Smells good. Why don't you get things ready while I put on some pants. Okay?"

"I'll have the table set in a snap." Then she grinned again. "I hope you're hungry. I made plenty."

Judd shook his head. She was wooing him with breakfast, a ploy as old as mankind, and he was succumbing without a struggle. If he was ever going to keep her safe, he'd have to keep his head and maintain the control. The only way to do that was to make certain some distance existed between them. He couldn't be moved by every small gesture she made.

When he emerged from the bedroom two minutes later, Emily had everything on plates. He noticed there were two settings, so obviously she planned to eat with him. He also saw that, other than coffee mugs, she'd found only paper plates and plastic cutlery in his kitchen. But she didn't seem put off by that fact. A tall thermos of coffee sat in the middle of the table. It smelled strong, just the way he liked it.

"This is terrific, Emily. I appreciate it." Normally, he didn't eat breakfast, but his stomach growled as he approached the table, and he couldn't deny how hungry he was.

Emily poured his coffee, still smiling. "I thought we could talk while we eat. Maybe get to know each other a little better. I mean, we will be working together, and we're practically strangers."

He glanced up at her. "I wouldn't say that."

She blinked, then looked away. "How long have you been... ah..."

"Stripping?"

"Yes." There was another bright blush on her cheeks. Judd wondered how she kept from catching fire.

"A while," he said, keeping his answer vague.

"You...you like it?"

Good Lord. He laid down his fork and stared at her. She was the most unpredictable woman he'd ever met. Watching her eyes, he said, "Everyone should experience stripping at least once. It's a fantasy, but most people don't have the guts to try it."

She sucked in her breath. The fork she had in front of her held a piece of sausage, ready to fall off. She looked guilty.

Ah. He smiled, reading her thoughts. "Admit it, Emily. You've thought of it, haven't you? Imagine the men, or even one man, getting hotter with every piece of clothing you remove. Imagine his eyes staring at you, imagine him wanting you so bad he can't stand it. But you make him wait, until you're ready, until you're completely...naked."

She trembled, then put down her fork, folding her hands in her lap. Judd didn't feel like smiling now; he felt like laying her across the table, tossing the skirt of her dress up around her shoulders and viewing all of her, naked. For him. He wanted to drive into her slim body and hear her scream his name. It angered him, the unaccountable way she could provoke his emotions, leaving him raw.

"You want to strip for me, Emily? I'll be a willing audience, I can promise you that."

"Why are you doing this?"

Her tone was breathless, faint. With arousal or humiliation? He slashed his hand in the air, disgusted with himself. "Eat your breakfast."

"Judd..."

"I'm sorry, Emily. I'm not usually such a bastard. Just forget it, all right?"

She didn't look as though she wanted to. Instead, she looked ready to launch into another round of questions and he couldn't take it. He began eating, ignoring her, giving all his attention to his food.

He waited until she'd taken a bite of her muffin, then said, "I've decided if I'm going to help you, I'll need more information."

Emily swallowed quickly and looked at him, her eyes wide. "I told you everything."

"No. I need the whole truth now, Emily. How you're involved, and why. What really happened." He took a sip of coffee, watching her over the rim of his mug. "Who's the kid? But most of all, what does he have to do with you?"

chapter 4

EMILY KNEW HER LUCK HAD JUST RUN OUT. AND though it surprised her he'd figured her out so soon, she had expected it. Judd wasn't an idiot, far from it. And she supposed it was his obvious intelligence and insight that made her feel so sure he would help her.

How much to tell him was her quandary.

Judd evidently grew impatient with her silence. "Stop trying to think up some elaborate lie. You're no good at it, anyway. Hell, if I can tell you're planning to lie, you'll never be able to carry it off. So just the truth, if you please. Now."

Emily frowned at him. He didn't have to sound so surly. And he didn't have to look so...sexy. He'd shocked her but good, answering the door near-naked. Even now, with his pants on, he still looked sleep-rumpled and much too appealing. She cleared her throat and stared down at her plate.

"All I can tell you is that someone I hold dear was injured when that gun misfired. Since I know no one else is going to do anything about it, I have to. And the only thing I can think of is to make sure that the man who sold the gun is brought to justice."

"Is the guy a lover?"

Emily blinked. "Who?"

"The man who is *dear to you*."

His sneering tone had her leaning back in surprise. "Don't be ridiculous. He's just a boy. Only sixteen."

Judd shrugged. "So who is he? A relative?"

Why wouldn't he just let it rest? Why wouldn't he—

"Dammit, Emily, who is he?"

He shocked her so badly with his sudden shout, she blurted out, "My brother!"

"Ah. I suppose that could motivate a person. Never having had a brother myself, I wouldn't know for certain, of course. But I can see where you'd want to protect a little brother." Judd rubbed his whiskered jaw, then added, "Why don't your parents just go to the police?"

Emily stood up and walked away from the table. How had he gotten her to reveal so much, so easily? She knew she had no talent for subterfuge, but she hadn't thought she'd crack so quickly. When she turned to face Judd again, she caught him staring at her ankles. Her silence drew his attention, and when his gaze lifted to her face, he didn't apologize, but merely lifted a dark eyebrow.

Trying to ignore the heat in her face, Emily folded her hands over her waist and said, "My parents hate scandal more than anything. They'd rather move to another country than have their name sullied with damaging speculation."

"Don't they love their son?"

"Well, of course they do." Appalled that she'd given him the wrong impression, Emily took her seat again, leaning forward to get his attention. "It's just that they've got some pretty stringent notions about propriety. Their reputations, and the family name, mean a lot to them."

"More than their son, evidently." Then Judd shook his head. "No, Emily, don't start defending them again. I really don't give a damn what kind of parents you have. But it seems to me, if they're willing to sweep the incident under the carpet, you should be, too. What can you hope to prove, anyway?"

This was the tricky part, trying to make him understand how important it was for John to see now, before it was too late, exactly what road he was choosing. She didn't want to see the same disdain in Judd's eyes when she mentioned her brother as he apparently felt for her parents. Why his opinion mattered to her, she didn't know. But it did.

Keeping her voice low, she said, "John bought the gun, I think, because he wanted my parents' attention. You'd have to understand how hard he tried to find his…niche. I remember last Christmas, John was crushed when my parents sent him a gift from Europe." Her lips tilted in a vague smile. "It was a check, a substantial check, but still, it was only money. John sat in front of the stupid Christmas tree, seven feet high and professionally decorated, and he cried. I didn't let him know I was there because I knew it would embarrass him."

Judd looked down at his feet. "I never had a Christmas tree until Max took me in. It was only a spindly little thing, but I liked it. It beat the hell out of seeing my father passed out drunk in the front room where the Christmas tree should have been but wasn't."

"Oh, Judd."

"Now, don't start, Em. We're talking about John, remember? I only mentioned that memory because I guess I always assumed people with money had a better holiday. I mean, more gifts, better food, a lot of cheer and all that." He shook his head. "Shoots that theory all to hell, doesn't it?"

"People usually think having money is wonderful, but that's not always true. Sometimes…money spoils things. It can make people self-centered, maybe even neglectful. Because it's so easy to do what you want, when you want, it's easy to forget about the others who…might depend on you. It's easy to forget that everyone can't be bought, and money doesn't solve every problem."

Judd didn't say a word, but his hand, so large and warm and rough, curled around her fingers and held on. Emily started, surprised at the gentleness of his touch, at how comforting it felt to make physical contact with him. She glanced up, and his eyes held hers. There was no more derision, and certainly no pity. Only understanding.

It was nearly her undoing.

"My…my brother, he's a good kid, Judd, just a bit misguided. And though he's trying to play it tough right now, he's scared. He doesn't know if he'll ever look the same as he did before the accident. My parents keep assuring him they'll find a good plastic surgeon to take care of everything, but he's hurting. Not physically, but inside. He wanted my parents' attention, but all he's gained is their annoyance. They never once asked him why he bought the gun or how. They only complained about him doing something so stupid. And they made it clear, had he wanted a gun, they could have bought the finest hunting rifle available, and supplied him with lessons on how to handle it."

"They missed the point entirely."

Emily felt his deep voice wash over her, and she smiled. "Yes, they did."

"Okay. So what will nailing the guy who sold him the gun prove to your brother?"

"That I love him. That I know what's right and wrong, and that he knows it, too, if he'll only open his eyes and realize that he is a good person, that he doesn't need affirmation from anyone but himself."

"Is that what you learned, honey? Do you understand your brother so well, because you've gone through the same thing?"

Emily forced a laugh and tried to pull her hand free, but Judd wouldn't let her go. He wouldn't let her look away, either. His gaze held her as securely as his fingers held her hand. "I've never felt the need to purchase a gun, Judd."

"No, but you must have wanted approval from your family as much as your brother does. What did you do, Emily, to get them to notice you?"

She cleared her throat and tried to change the subject. "This is ridiculous. It doesn't have anything to do with our deal."

"To hell with the deal. What did you do, Em?"

Panic began to edge through her. Not for anything would she lay the humiliation she'd suffered out for him to see. Besides, she'd buried the memory deep. It was no longer a part of her. At least, she hoped it wasn't.

"I've made my fair share of mistakes," she told him. "But I've forgiven myself and gotten on with my life. That's all any of us can do." Once she said that, she came to her feet, knowing she had to do something, occupy herself somehow, or she'd become maudlin. A display of emotions wouldn't serve her purpose.

But as she stood, so did Judd, and before she could move away, he had her tugged close. The morning whiskers on his jaw felt slightly abrasive, and arousing, as he brushed against her cheek. The warmth of his palms seeped through her dress to her back where he carefully stroked her in a comforting, soothing manner. She could smell his musky, male scent, and breathed deeply, filling herself with him, uncaring what had brought on this show of concern. It simply felt too good to have him hold her.

"You should always remember, Em, what a good person you are. Don't let anyone convince you otherwise."

His raspy tone sounded close to her ear, sending gooseflesh up her arms. And her emotions must have been closer to the surface than she'd wanted to admit, because she could feel the sting of tears behind her lids.

Not wanting Judd to know how he affected her, she hid her face in his shoulder and tried a laugh. It sounded a little wobbly, but it was the best she could produce. "You hardly know me, Judd. What makes you think I'm such a fine specimen of humanity?"

He rocked her from side to side, and she could hear the smile in his voice when he spoke. "Are you kidding me? You're obviously damn loyal since you're willing to risk your pretty little neck for your brother, just to keep him on the right track. You've opened your property to the neighborhood kids, not caring that they might trample your flowers or muddy up your yard. And you told me you volunteer at the soup kitchen. I'll bet you've got a whole group of charity organizations you donate to, don't you?"

Emily squeezed herself closer, loving the solid feel of his chest against her cheek, the strength of his arms around her. She couldn't recall ever feeling so safe. "I'm the one who benefits from the organizations. I've met so many really good, caring people, who just need a little help to get their lives straightened out. We talk, we laugh. Sometimes…I don't know what I'd do without them."

Judd groaned, and then his hand was beneath her chin, tilting her face up. Emily smiled, thinking he had a few more questions for her, when his mouth closed over hers and she couldn't think at all.

Heat was her first impression. The added warmth seemed to be everything, touching her everywhere. She felt it in her toes as he lifted her to meet him better, to fit her more fully against him. She felt it in her breasts, pressed tight against his chest. And in her stomach, as the heat curled and expanded.

His mouth was firm, his tongue wet as he licked over her lips, insisting she open. When she did, he tasted her deeply, his hands coming up to hold her face still as he slanted his mouth over hers again and again.

Emily had never known such a kiss. She'd thought she'd experienced lust while she was engaged, but it had been nothing like this. She made a small sound of surprise, wanting the contact to go on forever—and suddenly Judd pulled away.

Emily grabbed the back of the chair to keep herself grounded. Judd stared at her, looking appalled and fascinated and…hungry. *Oh, Lord, Emily, now you've really done it.*

She should have felt guilty for behaving so improperly, but all her mind kept repeating was, *Let's do it again.* She shook her head at herself, dismissing that errant notion and trying to remember her purpose. Judd must have misunderstood, because he turned away.

"I'm sorry," he said.

Emily blinked several times. "I beg your pardon?"

Judd whirled to face her, once again furious. "I said, I'm sorry, dammit. I shouldn't have done that. It won't happen again."

Oh, darn. "No, of course not. It was my fault. I shouldn't have been telling you all my problems and—"

"Shut up, Emily."

She did, and stared at him, waiting to see what he would do, what he wanted her to do.

"Damn." He snatched her close again, pressed another hard, entirely too quick kiss to her lips, then set her away. "I take it back. It probably will happen again. Hopefully, not for a while, but…I'm not making any promises. If you don't want me ever to touch you, just say so, all right?"

Emily remained perfectly still, unwilling to take a chance that he might misunderstand her response if she moved. She prided herself on the fact she wasn't a hypocrite. No, she wanted Judd, and she was thrilled beyond reason that he apparently wanted her, too. And since he held rather obvious scorn for her background—that of money and privilege—he wouldn't expect her to play the part of the proper lady. No, Judd had already made it clear where his preferences lay. Any man who could strip for a living was obviously on the earthy side, primal and lusty and…her heart skipped two beats while she waited to see what he'd do next.

He laughed. It wasn't a humorous laugh, but one of wonder and disbelief. "You're something else, Emily, you know that? Here, sit down." He loosened her death grip on the chair back and nudged her toward the seat. "Don't go away. I'm going to shower and finish getting dressed, then we'll make some plans, okay?"

She sat. She nodded. She felt ready to explode with anticipation.

Judd ruffled her hair, still shaking his head, and left the room.

HE MADE CERTAIN it was a cold shower, but the temperature of the water didn't help to cool the heat of his body. Never could he remember being hit so hard. Holding her felt right, talking to her felt right. Hell, kissing her had been as right as it could get—bordering on blissful death.

He could only imagine how it would feel to…no. He'd better not imagine or he'd find himself right back in the shower.

How could one woman be so damn sweet? He'd have thought all that money and her parents' attitudes would have soured her, but it hadn't. Emily loved. She loved her brother, she loved the children in her neighborhood. She even loved the homeless who visited the kitchen where she volunteered. He'd heard it in her tone, seen it in her eyes.

God, she was killing him.

He had to stay objective, and that meant getting back to business. He finished dragging a comb through his damp hair and left the bathroom.

Emily hadn't moved a single inch. And if he hadn't already had a little taste of her, he'd believe her prissy pose, with her knees pressed tightly together, and her slim hands folded in her lap. Ha! What a facade. He dragged his eyes away from her wary gaze and began stuffing her thermos and empty dishes back into the basket. "You ready to go?"

"Ah...go where?"

He flicked an impatient glance her way. "To find your gun dealer. I thought we'd hit some of the local establishments. The pool hall, first. Then maybe the diner. And tonight, the bar."

"Are you...dancing tonight?"

"No. I've got all weekend free. I only dance on Tuesdays and Thursdays, remember?" He noticed her sigh of relief and frowned at her. "But you will be there when I dance, Em. To pull this off, you're going to have to be my biggest fan. Everyone will have to believe I'm yours. You can be as territorial as you like. Besides, I can use you as a smoke screen. If the ladies all believe I'm already spoken for, they might not be so persistent."

Emily pursed her lips, her shoulders going a little straighter. "Are you certain that's what you want? I don't wish to interfere in your social life."

"You know, Em, you don't sound the least bit sincere."

She looked totally flustered now, and it was all he could do not to laugh. "Come on, let's get going."

Holding her arm, a manner that felt as right as everything else he did with her, Judd hustled her down to the street and into his truck. He waited until she'd settled herself, then asked, "Did your brother mention what the guy who sold him the gun looked like?"

Emily shook her head. "He wasn't in much condition to talk when I saw him last. I did get him to tell me where he'd bought it, though. But all he said about the man was that he'd grinned when he sold him the gun."

Judd noticed she'd tucked her hands into fists again, and he reached over to entwine her fingers with his. "When was your brother hurt?"

"Not quite a month ago. I saw him right afterward and then my parents took him away as soon as the hospital allowed it. I didn't even get to say goodbye."

"So you have no idea how he's doing?"

Emily turned away to stare out the side window. Her voice dropped to a low pitch, indicating her worry. "I've talked to him on the phone. He...he's very depressed. Though my parents evidently refuse to believe it, the plastic surgeons have already done all they can. The worst of the scars have been minimized. But the burns from the backfire did some extensive damage to the underlying tissue around his upper cheek and temple. He claims his face still looks horrid, but I don't believe it's as bad as he thinks. He's...he's always been popular in school, especially with the girls. I guess he thinks his life is over. I tried to make him look on the positive side, that his eyesight wasn't permanently damaged, but I don't suppose he can see a bright side right now."

Her voice broke, but Judd pretended he hadn't heard. He instinctively knew she wouldn't appreciate her loss of control. For such a small woman, she had an overabundance of pride and gumption, and he had no intention of denting it.

He squeezed her fingers again and kept his eyes focused on the road. "When will he be home again?"

"I don't know. I haven't spoken with my parents." She sent him a tilted smile. "They're blaming me for this. They say I'm a bad influence on him."

"You?" Judd couldn't hide his surprise.

"I work with the underprivileged. I don't own a single fur coat. And I live in an old house that constantly needs repair."

"Your house? I thought your house was terrific."

She seemed genuinely pleased by his praise. "Thank you. But the plumbing is dreadful. I've had almost everything replaced, but now the hot-water heater is about to go. Either the water is ice-cold, or so hot it could scald you. I thought my father would disown me when he burned his hand on the kitchen faucet. But even more than my house, my parents hate that I refuse to marry a man they approve of. They want me to 'settle into my station in life.'" Emily laughed. "Doesn't that sound ridiculous?"

"Settling down? Not really. I think you'd make a fantastic wife and mother." Dead silence followed his claim, and Judd could have bitten his tongue in two. It was bad enough that he still yearned for a real family. But to say as much to Emily? She was probably worried, especially after that kiss he'd given her, that he might have designs on her.

He slanted a look her way, and noticed a bright blush on her cheeks. Trying to put her at ease, he said, "You look like a domestic little creature, Em. That's all I meant."

Those wide brown eyes of hers blinked, and then she started mumbling to herself. He couldn't quite catch what she was saying. Judging from the tone, though, he probably wouldn't want to hear it, anyway. He had the suspicion she was giving him a proper set-down—in her own, polite way.

Judd was contemplating her reaction, and the reason for it, when they pulled up in front of the pool hall. It was still early, well before noon, so he didn't expect the place to be overly crowded. Only the regulars would be there, the men who made shooting pool an active part of their livelihood.

Clayton Donner was one of those men.

Judd didn't expect to see him here today, but he never knew when he might get lucky. And in the meantime, he'd find out a little more about Donner.

Emily was silent as he led her into the smoky interior. Unlike the lighting at the bar, it was bright here, and country music twanged from a jukebox in the far corner. Some of the men looked as if they'd been there all night and the low-hanging fluorescent lights added a gray cast to their skin. Others looked merely bored, and still others were intent on their game. But they all looked up at Emily. Judd could feel her uneasiness, but for the moment, he played his role and, other than put his arm around her shoulders to mark his claim, he paid her little attention.

Leaning down to whisper in her ear, he said, "Play along with me now. And remember, no matter what happens, don't lose your cool." Then he gave her a kiss on the cheek and a swat on the behind. "Get me a drink, will ya, honey?"

He gave a silent prayer she'd do as she was told, then sauntered over to the nearest table. "Hey, Frog. You been here all night?"

Frog, as his friends called him, had a croak for a voice, due to a chop to the larynx that had damaged his throat during a street fight. Frog didn't croak now, though. He was too busy watching Emily as she made her way cautiously to the bar, careful not to touch anyone or anything.

Judd gave a feral grin. "That's mine, Frog, so put your eyes back in your head."

Frog grunted. "What the hell are you doing with her? She ain't your type."

Judd shrugged. "She's rich. She's my type."

Frog thought that was hilarious, and was still laughing when Emily carried a glass of cola to Judd. He took a sip, then choked. Glaring in mock anger, Judd demanded, "What the hell is that?"

Emily raised her eyebrows, but didn't look particularly intimidated by his tone. "A drink?"

"Damn, I don't want soda. I meant a real drink." Actually, Judd never touched liquor. He knew alcoholism tended to run in families, and after living with his father, he wouldn't ever take the chance of becoming like him. Still, he handed the glass back to Emily, then said with disgust, "You drink it. And stay out of my way. I'm going to shoot some pool here with Frog."

Emily huffed. She started to walk away, but Judd caught her arm and she landed against his chest. Before she could draw a breath, he kissed her. It wasn't a killer kiss like the one he'd given her earlier, but it was enough to show everyone they were definitely an item. He drew away, but couldn't resist giving her a quick, soft peck before adding, "Behave yourself, honey. I won't be long."

Emily nodded, apparently appeased, and went to perch on a stool. Judd looked at her a moment longer, appreciating the pretty picture she made, waiting there for him. She dutifully smiled, and looked as if she'd wait all day if that was what he wanted.

It was the kind of fantasy he could really get into, having a woman like Emily for his own. But he couldn't spare the time or the energy to get involved with her or anyone else. He needed, and wanted, to focus all his attention on taking Donner off the streets. The man had stolen a huge hunk of his life when he'd killed Max. Judd wasn't ever going to forget that.

So instead of indulging in the pleasure he got by simply watching Emily, he turned away. He knew she didn't realize what he'd done, making her look like a woman he could control with just a little physical contact, but every man in the room understood.

And even though that had been his intent, Judd hated every damn one of them for thinking that about Emily. It was bad enough that he'd sold himself to trap Donner, but now he was selling Emily, too. It didn't sit right with him, but at the moment, his choices were limited, and the only alternative was to postpone his plans. Which was really no alternative at all.

EMILY HAD NO IDEA investigating could be so exhausting, though Judd did the actual work. All she did was pretend to be his ornament. It rankled, but until she could get him alone and set him straight about how this little partnership was going to work, she didn't want to take the chance of messing things up.

Judd had been shooting pool for quite some time when the door opened and three men walked in. One was a heavyset man, dirty and dressed all in black, with the name Jonesie written across his T-shirt. Another was a relatively young man, looking somewhat awed by his own presence.

It was the third man, though, that caught and held Emily's attention. There was something about him, a sense of self-confidence, that set him apart. He didn't look like a criminal, but something about him made Emily uncomfortable. He wore only a pair of pleated slacks and a polo shirt. His blond ponytail was interesting, but not actually unusual. In truth, Emily supposed he could be called handsome, but he held no appeal for her. He simply seemed too…pompous.

When his gaze landed on her, she quickly looked away and kept her eyes focused on Judd. And because she was watching

Judd so intently, she saw the almost imperceptible stiffening of his body. He'd only glanced up once to see who had walked in, then he'd continued with his shot, smoothly pocketing the nine ball. But Emily felt she was coming to know him well enough to see the tension in his body.

She was still pondering the meaning of that tension when the men approached where she sat.

"Hey, Clay, you want something to drink?"

The blonde smiled toward Emily and took the stool next to her before answering Jonesie. "No. I'm fine. I think I'll just watch the…scenery, for a while."

Emily wanted to move away, but she didn't. Not even on the threat of death would she turn and meet that smile, though she felt it as the man, Clay, continued to watch her. When he touched her arm, she jumped.

"Well, now, honey. No need to be nervous. I was only going to get acquainted."

Emily shook her head and tried to shrug his hand away. Instead of complying with her obvious wish, his well-manicured fingers curled around her arm. His touch repulsed her. She jumped off the stool and stepped back…right into the younger of the three men. She was caught.

This was nothing like talking to the drunks the other night. She'd felt some sense of control then. But now, as Clay chuckled at her reaction and reached out to stroke her cheek, she felt a scream catch in her throat. His fingers almost touched her skin—and then Judd was there, gripping the man's arm by the wrist and looking as impenetrable as a stone wall.

"The lady is mine. And no one touches her but me."

JUDD NARROWED his eyes, hoping, without the benefit of common sense, that Clayton would take him up on his challenge. He knew he wasn't thinking straight. He could destroy his entire case if he unleashed his temper now, but at the moment, none of that mattered.

He'd kept Donner in his sights from the moment he'd walked in, and he'd thought he'd be able to keep his cool even after Donner noticed Emily. But he hadn't counted on Emily's reaction.

When he'd seen her face and realized she was frightened, all he'd cared about was getting to her, staking his claim and making certain she knew there was nothing to fear. The fact that she was afraid should have angered him, and probably would once he had time to think about it. Didn't she know he wouldn't let anyone hurt her? Hell, he'd take the whole place apart before he'd see her hair get mussed.

But he supposed she couldn't know that, because even now, with him beside her, she still looked horrified. And then she got a hold of herself and smiled, a false smile, to be sure, and stepped to his side. "It's okay, Judd. Really."

Clayton looked down at his wrist where Judd still held him. The gesture was a silent command to be released, but Judd wasn't exactly in an accommodating mood. He tightened his hold for the briefest of seconds, gaining a raised eyebrow from Donner, then he let go. The younger man took a step forward, and Judd bared his teeth in a parody of a grin, encouraging him.

Emily seemed nearly frantic now, saying, "Come on, Judd. Let's go."

But he had no intention of going anywhere. Emily didn't know, couldn't know, the riot of emotions he was suffering right now. His desire to avenge Max mixed with his need to protect Emily, and he felt ready to explode with repressed energy. This was what he'd been waiting for. He could feel Donner's interest, his curiosity, and he knew he'd finally succeeded. If Donner's crony wanted to take him on, he was ready. More than ready.

At this point, Donner would only be impressed with his ruth-lessness. His muscles twitched in anticipation.

Then Donner laughed. "Don't be a fool, Mick. Our friend here is only trying to protect his interests. I can understand that."

The young man, Mick, moved away, but he did so reluc-tantly. Judd flexed his hands and tried to get himself under control. He stared at Clayton, then nodded and turned away, making certain he blocked Emily with his body. He knew Donner wouldn't like being dismissed, but he also didn't want to appear too eager.

Frog was standing at the pool table with his mouth hanging open, and Judd had to remind him it was his shot.

"No more for me," Frog said. "I'm done."

And in the next instant, Clayton was there, slapping Frog on the back and smiling. "So, what do you have for me, Frog?"

Frog pulled money out of his pocket, looking decidedly un-comfortable, and handed the bills to Clayton. As he counted, Clayton continued to smile, and then he asked, "That's it?"

Frog shifted his feet, glancing up at Judd and then away again. "I lost some of it."

"Is that so?"

Judd carefully laid his pool cue on the table then faced Clayton with a smile. He couldn't have asked for a better setup. "It seems I was having a lucky morning." His smile turned de-liberately mocking, and he flicked his own stack of bills.

Again, Mick started forward, clearly unwilling to overlook such an insult to Clayton, and this time Jonesie was with him. But again, Clayton raised a hand. "Let's not be hasty." And to Judd, he said, "I'd like to meet the man who just took two hundred dollars of my money."

Judd heard Emily gasp, but he ignored her surprise. "Your money? Now, how can that be, when Frog told me he'd won that money last night shooting pool? And now that I've won it, I'd say it's my money."

Clayton lost his smile. "Do I know you from somewhere?"

Mick blurted out, "He's one of them strippers. I seen him at the bar the other night."

"Ah, that's right. I remember now. You've been something of a sensation, haven't you?"

Judd shrugged. "Hey, I make a buck wherever I can. A man can't be overly choosy."

"Obviously." Clayton looked down a moment, then his smile reappeared. "Maybe we can do business together sometime. I have several different ventures that might interest you. Especially since you're not choosy."

Again, Judd shrugged, careful not to show his savage satisfaction. Then he took Emily by the arm. "Maybe." He deliberately dismissed Clayton once more, knowing it would infuriate him, but probably intrigue him, as well. As he started out the door, he said, "You can look me up if anything really... interesting comes along."

They were barely out the door, when Emily started to speak. Judd squeezed her arm. "Not a word, Em. Not one single word."

The tension was still rushing through him, and he knew Clayton was watching them through the large front glass of the pool hall. Playing it cool had never been so difficult; no other assignment had been so personal. Playing up to Donner turned his stomach and filled him with rage. He wanted to hit something. He wanted to shout.

He wanted to make love to Emily.

But, he couldn't do any of those things, so he had to content himself with the knowledge he'd set Clayton up good. Not only had he more or less managed to steal two hundred dollars Clayton had earmarked as his own, but he knew damn well

Clayton didn't consider their business finished. Not by a long shot. He'd hear from Donner again, and soon.

He only hoped he could manage to keep Emily out of the way.

chapter 5

EMILY THOUGHT SHE'D SHOWN GREAT RESTRAINT and a good deal of patience. But her patience was now at an end.

Judd had refused to talk to her while he aimlessly drove around the lower east side, burning off his sour mood and occasionally grunting at the questions she asked. Twice they had stopped while he got out of the truck and talked to different people loitering on the sidewalk. Emily had been instructed to wait in the pickup.

When she asked him what he was doing, he'd said only, "Investigating." When she asked what he'd found out, he'd said, "Quiet. Let me think."

It had been nearly two hours since they'd left the pool hall, and her frustration had grown with each passing minute. She tried to maintain her decorum, tried to keep her temper in check and behave in a civilized manner, but he was making that impossible. *You're the boss here, Emily. You hired him. Demand a few answers.* She decided she would do exactly that, when Judd pulled up in front of the diner.

Apparently, he expected her to get out and follow him like a well-trained puppy, because he stepped out and started to walk away without a single word to her. She refused to budge.

Of course, Judd was halfway through the diner door before he realized she was still in the truck. Then he did an about-face, and stomped back to her side, looking very put out. "What's the holdup?"

Emily gave him a serene smile. "I want to talk to you."

"So? Let's get a seat inside and you can talk. God knows, that's all you've done for the past hour, anyway."

She stiffened with the insult, but refused to lower herself to his irritating level. "You're not going to make me angry, Judd. I know you're just trying to get me off the track. But I want to know what that was all about in the pool hall. And don't you dare shake your head at me again!"

He looked undecided for a long moment, then let out a disgusted sigh. "All right, all right. Come in, sit, and we'll...talk."

Emily wasn't certain she believed him, he still looked as stubborn as a mule, but she left the truck and allowed Judd to lead her inside. They sat at a back booth, and a waitress immediately came to take their order. The woman seemed a little hostile to Emily, then she all but melted over Judd.

Judd treated her to a full smile and a wink. "You got anything for me, Suze?"

You got anything for me, Suze, Emily silently repeated, thinking Suze had just received a much warmer greeting from Judd than she herself had managed to garner all day.

The waitress looked over at Emily, one slim eyebrow lifted, and Judd grinned. "She's fine. Just tell me what you've got."

"Well..."

Emily rolled her eyes. Suze obviously had a flair for the dramatic, given the way she glanced around the diner in a

covert manner, as if she were preparing to part with government secrets. She also patted her platinum blond hair and
primped for a good ten seconds before finally exalting them
with her supposed wisdom. *What a waste of time.*

Emily no sooner had that thought than she regretted it.
Suze turned out to be a fount of information.

"He's been in twice since we spoke and something is definitely going down. He met with the same guy both times, that
punk kid who distributes for him. I'd say something will happen
within a week or two. That's usually the routine, you know."

"You couldn't catch an actual date?"

"Hell, no, sugar. If Donner caught me snooping, he'd
have my fanny."

Judd reached out to smack the fanny-in-peril. "We wouldn't
want that to happen. But Suze? If anything more concrete
comes up, you know where to find me."

She knew where to find him? Emily knew she had no right to
be jealous. After all, her relationship with Judd was strictly
business. But still, she didn't like the idea of him...consorting
with this woman. Of course, Suze seemed to know a great deal
about the gun dealer. In fact, she seemed to know almost too
much. Emily narrowed her eyes, wondering exactly when Judd
had contacted this woman, and what their relationship might
be. Judd seemed to be on awfully familiar terms with her.

But Suze did appear to be helping, and Emily certainly had
no claims on Judd. She decided to concentrate on that fact, but
she couldn't keep herself from glaring at the waitress. Suze
didn't seem to notice.

She was back to primping. "Of course I know where you'll
be. I wouldn't miss an act. Do something special for me Tuesday
night, all right?"

Judd laughed and shook his head.

Suddenly, Suze was all business. "You two want anything to drink or something? It don't look right me standing here gabbing without you orderin' anything."

"Two coffees, Suze. That's it."

Emily barely waited for the waitress to go swaying away before she leaned across the table and demanded Judd's attention. "Was she talking about who I think she was talking about?"

"Who did you think she was—"

"That's not funny, Judd!"

"No, I guess it isn't. And yes, she was talking about our friendly, neighborhood gun trafficker."

Emily was aghast. "She *knows* him?" She couldn't believe the waitress had called him by name. Why, if he was that well known...

"Everyone knows who commits the crimes, Em. It's just coming up with proof that's so damn difficult."

Her breath caught in her throat and she choked. "You know who he is, too?"

Judd shrugged, his eyes dropping to the top of the table. Then he quirked a sardonic smile. "You met him yourself, honey."

"I did..." Suddenly it fit, and Emily fell back against the seat. "The guy at the pool hall?"

"Yep. That was him. Clayton Donner."

It took her a minute, and then she felt the steam. It had to be coming out her ears, she was so enraged. Judd had let her get close to the man who'd hurt her brother, and he hadn't even told her.

He was speaking to her now, but she couldn't hear him over the ringing in her ears. Her entire body felt taut, and her stomach felt queasy. No wonder she had reacted so strongly to that man. He'd been that close and...

Emily didn't make a conscious decision on what to do. She just suddenly found herself standing then walking toward the door. She somehow knew Judd was following, though she didn't turn to look. When she stepped outside, and started past his truck, he grabbed her arm and pulled her around to face him.

"Dammit, Emily! What the hell is the matter with you?"

"Let me go." She felt proud of the strength in her voice, though she knew she might fall apart at any moment.

"Are you kidding? I've tried every damn intimidation tactic I could think of—"

"Ha! So you admit to bullying me?"

"—to send you running, but you clung like flypaper. And now, with one little scare, you want me to turn you loose?"

Flypaper! How dare he compare her to… No, Emily, don't get side-tracked by a measly insult. The man deceived you. She lifted her chin and met his gaze. "I wish to leave now. Alone."

"No way, baby. You wanted in, and now you're in."

Her heartbeat shook her, it pounded so hard, and her fingers ached from being held in such tight fists. If she wasn't a lady, she'd smack him one, but good. "When were you going to tell me, Judd? When?"

Judd stiffened, and his jaw went hard. "Get in the truck, Em."

"I will not. I…"

"Get in the damn truck!"

Well. Put that way… Emily became aware of people watching, and also that Judd was every bit as angry as she was. But why? What possible reason did he have for being so mad? She was the one who'd been misled, kept in the dark, lied to…well, not really. But lies of omission definitely counted, and Judd had omitted telling her a great deal.

And after he'd insisted she bare her soul.

When he continued to glare at her, she realized how foolish they both must appear, and she opened the truck door to get in. It wouldn't do to make a public spectacle of herself.

"Put your seat belt on."

Emily stared out her window, determined not to answer him, to ignore him as completely as he'd ignored her all day. But then she muttered, *"Flypaper."*

She heard Judd make a small sound that could have been a chuckle but she didn't look to see. If the man dared to smile, she'd probably forget all about avoiding a scene. But then, thoughts of attacking that gorgeous body left her a little breathless, and she decided ignoring him was better, by far.

Judd reached over and strapped her in. He stayed leaning close for a second or two, then flicked his finger over her bottom lip. "Stop pouting, Em, and act like an adult."

It took a major effort, but she didn't bite that finger. She could just imagine how appalled her parents would have been by that thought.

Judd's sigh was long and drawn-out. "Fine. Have it your way, honey. But if you decide you want to talk, just speak up."

Fifteen minutes later, Emily was wishing she could do just that. Judd pulled into her driveway with the obvious intent of being well rid of her, and she desperately didn't want him to go. She felt confused and still angry and...hurt. If he could explain, then maybe she could forgive him and... *And what, Emily? Maybe he'd let you have one of those killer smiles like the one he gave Suze?* She'd been taken in by one man, and though she honestly believed Judd was different, she wouldn't, couldn't, put all her trust in him. Not on blind faith. Not without some explanations.

When all was said and done, he worked for her, and she deserved to know what was going on. She had to find evidence against Donner, and she needed Judd to do that. But only if he didn't shut her out.

He stopped the truck, and she sat there, trying to think of

some way, without losing every ounce of pride, to talk things out with him.

But Judd saved her the trouble. He got out of the pickup, slamming his door then stomping over to the passenger side. She stared at him, her eyes wide with surprise, when he opened the door and hauled her out.

"What do you think you're doing?" His hold was gentle on her arm as he led her up the steps to her back door. She practically had to run to keep up with his long-legged, impatient stride.

"We're going to talk, Em. I don't like you treating me as if I've just kicked your puppy."

Uh-oh. He sounded even angrier than she'd first assumed. "I don't even have a dog—"

Judd snatched her key from her hand, unlocked the door and ushered her inside. "Do you need to punch in your code for the alarm system?"

It took her a second to comprehend his words since her mind still wrestled with why he was in her house, and what he planned to do there. "Oh, ah, no. I only turn it on when I'm in the house. The rest of the time, I just lock up."

Judd stared. "Why the hell would you get a fancy alarm system, and not use it?"

"Because twice I forgot to turn it off when I came in, and the outside alarms went off, and then several neighbors showed up at my door and the central office called, and it was embarrassing." Judd rolled his eyes in exasperation, and Emily felt her cheeks heat. She hadn't meant to tell him all that. "Judd? I don't want to talk about my alarm system."

Looking restless and still a bit angry, Judd paced across the kitchen. Then he stalked back to her. "Tell me this, Emily. What would you have done if I'd spoken up and introduced you to Donner?"

She watched as he propped his hands on his hips and glared at her. "I don't know what I would have done. But I know I would have done…something."

"Something like accuse him? Or something like demand he give himself up? I thought you needed proof. I thought that was what we were doing, trying to nail him."

His scowl was much more fierce than her own, and her anger diminished to mere exasperation. The man could be so remarkably impossible. "We?" she asked, lacing her tone with sarcasm. "There was certainly no 'we' today. You've refused to tell me anything." When he crossed his arms, looking determined, she added in a gentler tone, "Judd, I can't very well find evidence against this Donner person if I don't know who he is."

Judd came to stand in front of her and gripped her shoulders. "I was working on finding evidence. Or did you think I just enjoyed toying with that bastard? Besides, you were scared out of your wits, Em. And that was without knowing who he was. He had a damn strange effect on you, which now that I think of it again, isn't very complimentary for me. I thought you knew I wouldn't let anyone hurt you."

Emily swallowed, feeling a tinge of guilt. "I'm sorry. Of course I assume you'll protect me, but—"

"Don't assume, Emily. Know. As long as you do as I tell you and follow my lead, you won't get hurt."

"Just like that? You tell me what to do, and I do it, no questions asked? I'm not a child, Judd—"

"So I noticed."

"And… You noticed?" Emily quickly shook her head so she wouldn't get sidetracked. "If you want me to trust you, you have to be totally honest with me, not just expect me to sit around and watch you work, without telling me what you're working on."

"You're making too much of this. I was only shooting pool."

"But you had a goal in mind. And you kept that from me. I despise dishonesty, Judd. I won't tolerate it." He winced, but she didn't give him time to interrupt. "I had no idea today that you were deliberately taking money from one of Donner's men. If I had known, maybe I wouldn't have been so surprised…"

"Exactly. Do you think I want Donner or any other punk to look at you and think you know the score?"

That silenced Emily for a moment. Why would Judd care what other men thought of her? "I quit worrying about others' opinions long ago."

"Why?"

"What do you mean, 'why'?"

"Everyone cares what other people think, even when they know it shouldn't matter."

Busying her fingers by pleating and unpleating her skirt, Emily felt her exasperation grow. "Certain things…happened in my past, that assured me public opinion meant very little, but that honesty meant a great deal."

"Like what?"

When she didn't answer, he said, "Okay, we'll come back to that later."

"No, we won't."

"Dammit, Em. I'd much rather you come off looking like an innocent out for a few kicks, than to have some jerk assume you've been around."

Emily swallowed hard. Judd had evidently made some incorrect assumptions about her character, and it was up to her to explain the truth. "Judd, I don't know why you persist in thinking I'm…I'm innocent. I believe I told you once that I'd been engaged. Well…"

She couldn't look at him, her eyes were locked on her busy

fingers. And then she heard him chuckle. Her gaze shot to his face, and she was treated to the most tender smile she'd ever seen.

"Honey, it wouldn't matter if you'd been engaged twenty times. You're still so damn innocent, you terrify me."

Emily didn't understand that statement, or the way he reached out and touched her cheek, then smoothed her hair behind her ear.

She felt disoriented, and much too warm. She wanted to lean into Judd, but she knew she had to settle things before she forgot what it was that she wanted settled. Once before she'd let her passionate nature guide her. That had been a huge error, and this was too important to be sidetracked by anything—including Judd's heated effect on her.

"The thing is, Em, this whole deal will work out better if your reactions to Donner and his men are real. You can't lie worth a damn, and I don't think, if Donner got close again, you'd be able to hide your feelings from him. You could blow everything."

She cleared her throat and spoke with more conviction than she actually felt. "You don't know that for sure."

His expression hardened, turning grim. "And I'm not willing to take the risk. Things could backfire real easy, and someone could get hurt."

She understood his reasoning, but she couldn't accept it. "This isn't going to work, Judd. Not unless you're willing to tell me everything."

He stared at her, hard, then muttered a curse and looked away. "No, you're right. It won't work. Which is why I've come up with an alternate plan. I decided I'd just find this guy for you, but on my own. You can stay in your little palace and play it safe."

"What?"

"You heard me. From here on, you're out of it."

Emily sputtered, then stiffened her spine. "You said I was 'in,' remember?"

"I've changed my mind."

"Well, you can just unchange it, because I'm not going to be left out."

"I refuse to risk your getting hurt, and your reaction today was proof positive you aren't ready to mingle with the meaner side of life. Let's face it, Em, you're just a baby."

"Oh, no, you don't." She propped her hands on her hips and glared at him. "You're not going to pull me into an argument by slinging horrid insults at me. We had a deal and you're the one who isn't following the rules. Well, you can just stop it right now."

He blinked at her in amazement. "I wasn't insulting you, dammit!"

Emily could tell by his expression he hadn't seen anything insulting in his attitude. But that only made the insult worse. She pursed her lips and tilted her head back so she could look down her nose at him. "I'm not entirely helpless, Judd. I can take care of myself."

There was a minute curving of his lips before he shook his head and spoke in a gentle, but firm, tone. "I'm sorry, Em. My mind's made up."

He acted as if he hadn't just dumped her, as if he hadn't just let her down and destroyed all her plans. But it was even more than her plans now. It was Judd, and she cared about him. She took one step closer and poked him in the chest with her finger. "Okay, fine. You don't want to help me, then I'll find another way."

Startled, he grabbed her finger and held on. "You already have a way. Me. I can do this, you know. I'm more than capable, and I damn sure don't need you looking after me. It'll be easier without you."

That hurt, but she didn't show it. She lifted her chin and met his intent gaze. "No. I won't let you risk yourself for me, not while I sit around and do nothing."

Judd bit his upper lip and his eyes narrowed. He suddenly looked...dangerous, and Emily shivered in expectation of what he might say. She knew it would be something outrageous, but she was prepared for the worst.

"So you'll pay me a five-hundred-dollar bonus. No big deal."

He had a very credible sneer. Emily frowned. She couldn't believe he'd just said that. And she couldn't believe he was really doing this only for the money. She couldn't have been that wrong.

A deep breath didn't help to relieve the sudden pain in her chest, or the tightness in her throat. She still sounded strained as she whispered, "Fine, if money's the issue, I'll pay you to forget you ever met me." She waited for his reaction, and though Judd remained rigid, she noticed his hands were now curled into tight fists.

There's a reaction for you, Emily. He doesn't seem at all pleased by being bought off. She decided to push him, just to see what it would take to force him to drop his charade. "Five thousand dollars, Judd. But I don't want you risking yourself. Take it or leave it." Then she opened the door and waited to see if he would actually leave.

"Damn you, Emily." The door slammed shut and she found herself pinned to the wall by his hard chest, his arms caging her in, his lips pressed to her hair. She could hear him panting, struggling for control of his temper.

Relief washed over her—and hot excitement. "Judd?"

He didn't answer. He kissed her instead, and if the first kiss had been hungry, this one was ravenous. Emily moaned and wrapped her arms around him, holding him tight as his tongue pushed deep into her mouth. How she'd come to care so much about him so quickly, she didn't know. Perhaps it was because she sensed the same emptiness in him that she'd often felt. When he'd told of his past, as different as it was from hers, she still saw a lot of similarities.

Emily knew she was being fanciful, but she couldn't deny the way she felt. It seemed to her sometimes there were no real heroes left in the world, people willing to do what was right— just because it was the right thing to do.

But Judd was a hero, despite his chosen profession, despite his lack of manners and sometimes overbearing arrogance. A hero was a man who could do what needed to be done, when it was needed. And Judd was as capable as they came.

"Oh, Em." His mouth touched her throat, her chin, then her lips again. "I have to stop."

She tried to shake her head, since stopping was the last thing she wanted, but she couldn't. His hands cupped her cheeks and he had her pressed flush against the wall, pinned from chest to knees, his erection hard and throbbing against her belly. It was glorious. She was well and truly trapped, and she loved it. "Judd…"

"No, honey." He was still breathing hard, his mouth touching soft and warm against her flesh, planting small biting kisses that tingled and tickled and stole her breath. "Neither one of us is ready for this. Hell, you've got me so crazy, I don't know what I'm doing. I need time to think. And so do you."

Don't beg, Emily. Don't beg. "Judd…I—"

He touched her lips with his thumb, then his eyes dropped to where she knew her nipples puckered tight against the front of her dress. His voice, when he spoke, was a low, raspy growl. "You're killing me, Em. Please understand."

"I've never felt like this before, Judd."

He groaned, then kissed her again, this time so soft and sweet, she trembled. He pressed his hips hard against her once, then forcibly pulled away. When he touched her cheek, his hand shook. "I'll call you later tonight, okay?"

She swallowed hard, not wanting him to leave, but knowing he was right. It *was* too soon to make a commitment.

It was difficult, but she managed to pull herself together. He was leaving; she knew that was for the best. But she had to recall what had started this whole argument and make certain he understood her position. "I was serious about what I said, Judd. I don't want you doing anything on your own. I don't want the...responsibility of your safety."

He pressed his forehead to hers and gave a loud sigh. "I know. I promise not to do anything until we've figured it all out." Then he chuckled, and it sounded so nice to her ears, she laughed, too. "I must be crazy." He gave her one more quick, hard kiss, then moved her away from the door. "I have to go before I forget my good intentions and ravish you right here. Any red-blooded male can only take so much provocation, you know. And honey, you're damn provoking."

She smiled again, and as he stepped out, Judd said, "Emily? Thanks again for breakfast."

Emily contained herself until she saw Judd drive away. Then she whirled and laughed. Her emotions had been on a roller coaster all day. Whether it had been good or bad, it had definitely been exciting. In fact, her time spent with Judd was easily the most exciting time she'd ever known.

He thought her provocative, and because of that, she felt provocative. That, too, was new, but decidedly delicious. She should feel guilty, since she hadn't done anything to help her brother yet. But she couldn't manage a single dollop of guilt. She simply felt too exhilarated.

HOURS LATER, Emily stood looking out her kitchen window, impatiently waiting for Judd's call. The house was dark and dim, just like her yard. She hadn't bothered to turn on the lights as she'd watched the sunset. The kitchen was her favorite room in the house. The pine cabinets had a warm golden hue, and the antique Tiffany lamp that hung over her table provided a touch of bright color. She thought of Judd sitting at that table with her, of the kiss he'd given her against the wall, and she wondered what he was up to, if he was safe…if he was with Suze.

That vagrant thought had her scowling, and she decided a soothing cup of chamomile tea was just what she needed. Without turning on the lights, she retrieved a cup from the cabinet and turned on the hot water. She knew her kitchen well and didn't need the light intruding on her warm, intimate mood.

It wasn't until she heard a sound and looked up that she realized she'd never reset the alarm. Her heart lodged in her throat as she saw a large body looming outside her kitchen door. Frozen in fear, she stood there as the hot water grew hotter and steam wafted upward around her face. A soft click sounded, and then another. When the door swung silently open and a man entered, his body a shadowed silhouette, she finally reacted. Emily let out the loudest ear-piercing scream she could manage. And after a stunned second and a low curse, the man pounced on her.

Emily didn't have time to run.

chapter 6

JUDD WHISTLED AS HE KICKED OFF HIS SHOES AND dropped back onto the lumpy couch. God, it felt good to get off his feet. And to finally get home. He wanted to talk to Emily. He needed to make certain she'd understood his motives this afternoon. He'd seen the shock on her face, then the determination when she'd thought he was dumping her.

It had felt as if she'd snatched his heart right out of his chest. But what the hell else was he supposed to do? Watch her get involved? He hadn't counted on every guy around, including Donner, wanting to cozy up to her. He supposed that elusive sensuality he'd noticed in her right away was as visible to every other guy around as it was to him.

But he didn't like it. He didn't like other men looking at her and seeing tangled sheets and mussed hair and warm silky skin. He didn't like other guys thinking the thoughts he had.

He also couldn't hurt her. He'd just have to find a way to keep her close, and himself detached. That was going to be the real trick, especially when she did crazy things like offering him money just to keep him safe. He sure wasn't used to anyone trying to protect him, not since Max had been killed.

But he could get used to it, if he let himself.

His eyes narrowed at the thought. He couldn't get distracted from his purpose now, not when he was so close. Emily was a danger, and she didn't even realize it. She had the power to help him forget, and he didn't want that. Donner had hurt her brother, but he'd taken the only family Judd had ever known. Whenever he remembered Max's face, usually smiling, sometimes solemn, occasionally stern, his stomach tightened into a knot. Max was the finest, most honest person Judd had ever known, the only one who'd really cared about him.

Except for Emily.

Judd squeezed his eyes shut to block the thought. What Emily felt or didn't feel for him couldn't matter. Not now. Probably not ever. Judd wouldn't give up until Donner was put away. And after that, he'd have no more reason to be with her.

He was just reaching for the phone to call Emily, when the damn thing rang, causing him to jump. He snatched the receiver. "Yeah?"

"Judd, I'm glad I could reach you. Are you sitting down?"

Startled, it took Judd a second to answer. The lieutenant knew better than to call him at his apartment. It was a real breach of security. Something big must have happened. Trying to sound casual, he said, "As a matter of fact, I'd just propped my feet up. I've had a hell of a long—"

Howell interrupted. "Well, your day's about to get a whole lot longer." He hesitated, then added, "You remember that little lady you mentioned to me the other day? The rich one. She still hanging around with you?"

"Emily?" Judd didn't say that he couldn't forget her even if he tried. He cleared his throat. Even though he was as sure as he could be that no bugs existed in the apartment, he wouldn't take any chances. "Sure. In fact, I was just thinking about her. I guess we've got a regular thing going, at least for a while."

"I see." Judd could hear the restrained frustration in Howell's tone. "That being the case and all, I thought you ought to know, I just heard the little lady had her house broken into."

Judd felt his stomach lurch. "What?"

There was an expectant silence, then, "I recognize that tone, Judd. Just calm down and let me tell you what I know."

"Is Emily all right?"

"She's fine, just a little shaken up, I gather. It only happened a few minutes ago, but I thought... Judd?"

Judd cursed and pushed his feet back into his shoes, "I'm on my way."

He vaguely heard Howell protesting, and knew he'd catch hell later for hanging up on the lieutenant, but the only thought that mattered was seeing Emily. He raced out the front door, only stopping long enough to grab his jacket and his Beretta.

Ten minutes and three red lights later—which he ran—Judd decided he was too old to take this kind of stress. His palms were sweating and his head was pounding. He hadn't felt this kind of nauseating fear since the call telling him Max had been shot in the line of duty. But Judd hadn't made it then. He'd gotten to the hospital too late. Max had died only minutes before he arrived.

He stepped more firmly on the accelerator, pushing the old truck and thanking the powers that be for the near-empty roads that lessened the danger of his recklessness. His hands tightened on the wheel as his urgency increased. He could literally taste his fear.

When he sped into the curving driveway and saw the two black and whites parked there, he didn't stop to think about an excuse for his timely arrival. He simply busted through the door, his eyes searching until he found Emily.

She sat at the kitchen table holding an ice pack to her cheek. That alone was enough to make his blood freeze. She looked up, and the moment she saw him, her eyes widened, and then she smiled. "Judd."

He stalked toward her, sank to the floor beside her seat and took her hand in his. With his other hand, he lifted the ice pack so he could survey the damage. "Are you all right?"

She blinked away tears then glanced nervously at the hovering officers. "I'm fine, Judd. But how—"

Already her cheek was bruising and her eye was a bit puffy. Still holding her hand, Judd came to his feet and glared at the officers. "Who did this?"

"We don't know, Detective. We're still trying to find out all the details."

"Did you check the house? Has anyone searched the yard?" He didn't wait for an answer, but bent back to Emily. "Tell me what happened, honey."

She gave a nervous laugh, then quickly sobered. "Really, Judd, there's no reason to yell at the nice officers. They came almost as soon as I called."

"Why didn't you call me?"

He realized what a ridiculous question that was almost as soon as he made the demand. Emily thought he was a male stripper. Why would she call him? That fact had his temper rising again.

She leaned toward him and patted his shoulder. "Shh. It's all right, Judd. Just calm down."

She was trying to soothe him? Judd gave her a blank stare, then shook his head. "Emily…"

"I was waiting for your call. I guess after you left…I forgot to reset the alarm, because I was making tea when suddenly someone started opening the door."

"Oh, honey." Judd wrapped her in his arms, lifting her from the seat at the same time. "You must have been scared half to death."

Emily had to speak against his chest, since he was still holding her tight. He couldn't let her go just yet. He was still suffering from all the terrible thoughts that had raced through his head after Lieutenant Howell's call.

"I suppose I was scared at first," she said. "I know I screamed loud enough to startle the ducks on the lake. Then the man sort of just jumped toward me. And without really thinking about it, I turned the faucet sprayer on him." She leaned back to see Judd's face. "Do you remember me telling you the water heater was in need of repair? Well, I had the water running hot for my tea, and when he came at me, I just grabbed the hose and aimed at his face. At least, I think I hit his face. It was dark in here and everything happened so fast. I do know he yelled really loud, so I think the hot water must have hurt him."

Judd touched his fingers to her bruised cheek. "How did this happen?"

Emily looked very sheepish now, and her cheeks turned a bright pink. "It's really rather silly. You see, after the man yelled, I jerked away and ran for the library so I could use the phone. But, uh…" It was obvious to Judd she was embarrassed as her eyes again went to the two cops. "I tripped just inside the door. I hit my cheek on the leg of a chair."

Bemused, Judd asked, "The guy who broke in didn't do this to you?"

"No. I did it to myself. I think he left right after I shot him with the water. I locked the library door and called the police. When they got here, he was gone."

One of the cops cleared his throat. "We checked the water in her faucet. It's scalding hot. It's a wonder she hasn't burned herself before." Then he grinned. "You might want to get that checked."

Judd stared.

Emily pulled on his sleeve, regaining his attention. "Do you remember me telling you about my father burning his hand on the faucet? It really does get hot, hot enough to make tea without boiling the water. I wouldn't be at all surprised if the fellow has a serious burn on his face."

Feeling as though he'd walked into bedlam, Judd shook his head then turned his attention to the two officers. "Call Howell and tell him I'm spending the night here. And go check the area. With any luck, the bastard might still be out there if he's burned all that bad."

Both men nodded and started away. Judd turned to Emily, ready to lecture her on the importance of keeping her alarm set, when he felt her stiffen. She looked paper-white and her bottom lip trembled. He grabbed her arm and gently forced her back into her chair.

"Emily, I thought you said you were all right."

Her lips moved, but she didn't make a sound.

"Are you going to faint? Are you hurt somewhere?" He very carefully shook her. "Tell me what's wrong."

His urgency must have gotten through to her, for she suddenly cleared her throat, and her expression slowly changed to a suspicious frown. "One of the officers called you detective. And you're ordering them around as if you have the right. And even more ridiculous than that, they're letting you."

"Oh, hell." Judd wondered if there was any way for him to get out of this one. How could he have been so careless? Howell would surely have his head. His mind whirled with possible lies, but he couldn't see Emily believing any of them. She wasn't stupid, after all, just a bit naive.

He watched her face as he tried to come up with a logical, believable explanation, and he saw the confusion in her eyes, then the growing anger. One of the uniforms came around the corner and said, "Detective, I have Lieutenant Howell on the phone. He said he needed to talk to you, sir, uh…now." And Judd knew Emily had finally guessed the truth.

Before she could move, he cupped her cheeks, being especially gentle with her injury. "I can explain, honey. I swear. Just sit tight a second, okay? Right now, I have to pacify an enraged superior."

"Oh, I'll wait right here, Detective. You can count on it."

Judd didn't like the sound of that one little bit. But it was her look, one of mean anticipation, that had him frowning. This whole damn day had been screwy, starting with Emily cooking him breakfast. He should have known right then he wouldn't end it with his safe little world intact.

No, Emily had turned him upside down.

The hell of it was, he liked it.

EMILY LISTENED as Judd went through a long series of explanations over the phone. Yes, he could handle everything… No, his cover wasn't blown as long as Howell set things right with the two officers. Ha! His cover was most definitely *blown*. Emily wanted to interject at that point, but Judd watched her as he spoke, and so she kept herself still, her expression masked, she hoped.

Her cheek was still stinging, but not as much as her pride. *Lord, Emily, you've been a fool*. Hadn't she known from the start that Judd didn't belong in the east side of Springfield? He talked the talk, and dressed the code, but something about him had been completely out of sync. He could be every bit as hard and cynical as the other roughnecks, but his behavior was forced. It wasn't something that came to him naturally.

She closed her eyes as she remembered offering him money to drop the case. If he reminded her of that, she just might...no. She would not lower herself to his level of deceit.

That decision did her little good when Judd hung up the phone and came back to kneel by her chair. He lifted the ice pack again and surveyed her bruised cheek with a worried frown. "I wonder if you should go to the hospital and have this checked."

"No."

Her curt response didn't put him off. "Does it hurt?"

"No."

His fingertips touched her, coasting over her abraded skin and causing goose bumps to rise on her arms. He ended by cupping her cheek and slowly rubbing his thumb over her lips. Then he sighed. "Just sit tight and I'll make you that tea. After everyone's cleared out, we'll talk."

Emily watched him bustle around the kitchen, thinking he looked curiously *right* there. It was almost as if the room had been built for his masculine presence.

The quarry-stone floor seemed every bit as sturdy and hard as Judd, the thick, polished pine cabinets just as comforting. There were no frilly curtains, no pastel colors to clash with his no-nonsense demeanor.

Emily made a disgusted face at herself. Comparing Judd to a kitchen? Maybe she had hit her head harder than she thought.

When he sat the tea in front of her, she accepted it with a mumbled thanks. Moments later, the officer who'd been outside came in and shook his head. "Not a sign of anything. It doesn't even look as if the door was tampered with."

Judd turned to Emily with a stern expression. "It was locked, wasn't it?"

Since she was already mortified over the evening's events, she didn't bother to try to hide her blush. "I really have no idea. I can't recall locking it, but sometimes I just do it by rote."

"Emily…"

She knew that tone. "Don't lecture me now, *Detective*. I'm really not in the mood."

She was saved from his annoyance by the remaining officer coming downstairs. "I checked out the other rooms. They're clean. I don't believe he ever left the kitchen. Probably took off right after she splashed him, going out the way he came in."

Judd worked his jaw. "I suppose you're right. You guys can take off now. I'll stay with Miss Cooper."

Since Emily had a lot of questions she wanted answered, she didn't refute him. It took the officers another five minutes to actually go, and then finally, she and Judd were alone. Sitting opposite him at the table, Emily prepared to launch into her diatribe on the importance of honesty and to vent her feelings of abuse, when Judd spoke in a low, nearly inaudible tone.

"Clayton Donner shot Max about six months ago. I was out on assignment, and by the time I got to the hospital, Max was dead. I've made it my personal business to get Donner, and I'll damn well do whatever I have to until he's locked up."

Emily didn't move. She heard the unspoken words, telling her he wouldn't let her—or her feelings for him—get in his way. She'd thought she had a good personal reason to want Donner, but her motivation was nothing compared to Judd's. Without thinking, she reached out and took his hand. She didn't say a word, and after a few seconds, Judd continued.

"I told you Max had taken me in. He was everything to me, the only family I'd ever had. He was a regular street cop, and his run-in with Donner was pure coincidence. Max had only been doing a routine check on a disturbance, but he inadvertently got too close to the place where Donner was making a deal." Suddenly Judd's fist slammed down on the table and he squeezed his eyes shut.

"Judd?"

"Max got shot in the back." Judd drew a deep breath and squeezed Emily's hand. She squeezed back. He wouldn't look at her, but she could see his jaw was rigid, his eyes red. Her heart felt as though it were crumbling.

"We all knew it was Donner, but we couldn't get anything concrete on him. And to try him without enough evidence, and take the chance of letting him go free...I don't think I could stand it. I have to see him put away. Regardless of anything, or anyone, I'll get him."

Wishing he'd told her all this because he wanted to, not because he'd been forced, wouldn't get Emily anywhere. And she couldn't, in good conscience, interfere. Not when she could see how much getting Donner meant to him. "I understand."

"Do you?" For the first time, Judd looked up at her, and that look held so many different emotions, Emily couldn't begin to name them all. But the determination, the obsession, was clear, and it scared her. "I left everything behind when I followed Donner here," he said. "Springfield is just like my own home ground. Every city has an area with run-down housing and poverty, a place where kids are forgotten or ignored, where crime is commonplace and accepted. I fit in there, Em. I'm right at home. Sooner or later, I will get Donner. But not if you blow my cover. What happened tonight can't happen again."

Emily knew he wasn't talking about the break-in. "What— exactly—did happen, Judd?"

"I lost my head, and that's bad. I can't be sidetracked from this assignment."

"You know I want Donner, too."

"Not like I do."

She would have liked to probe that a little more, but she held her tongue. She was afraid he was trying to find a way to say goodbye, to explain why he couldn't see her anymore. "What do you want me to do?"

Judd shot from his chair with an excess of energy. He shoved his hands into his back pockets and stalked the perimeter of the room as if seeking an escape. Finally, he stopped in front of the window, keeping his back to Emily. "I want you to understand that I can't let you get in my way. I can't...can't care about you. But when I think about what might have happened tonight..."

"You need me to stay out of your way?" Emily heard the trembling in her tone, but hoped Judd hadn't.

He whirled to face her. "No. Just the opposite, in fact."

She blinked twice and tried to still the frantic pounding of her pulse.

Again, Judd took his seat. "I work as a stripper in the bar because Donner does a lot of his business in the office upstairs. I've set myself up to get hired by him."

"That's what you were doing in the pool hall," Emily said with sudden insight. "You were impressing him, by being like him."

Judd nodded. "Everyone around there believes I'm out for a fast buck, a little fun, and not much else. That makes me Donner's ideal man. Making contact with him today was important. He'll be coming to me soon, I'm sure of it. He's intrigued, because he doesn't like people to refuse him, the way I refused him at the pool hall. I'd like to steer clear of you, to keep you uninvolved." He cast her a frustrated glance. "But it's too late for that."

Her stomach curled. "It is?"

One brisk nod was her answer. "I need you, Em. My superior thinks it's risky to make any changes now. He's already furious that you know my cover, but that can't be helped, short of calling everything off. And I don't want that. He'll pull the officers who were here tonight, because by rights, they screwed up, too. They shouldn't have acknowledged me as a detective, but they're rookies and…" He trailed off, then frowned at her. "If you suddenly stopped hanging around, after the scene we played out today at the pool hall, Donner might get suspicious. The whole deal could be blown. And it's too late for that."

Emily tried to look understanding, but she was still reacting to Judd's casual words. *He needs you, Emily.* She knew she would do whatever she could for him. "Has…has something come up? Something definite?"

"I think so. I visited Frog again after I left here. Next Wednesday night, Donner will be making a pickup."

"What kind of pickup?"

"He gets the guns dirt cheap since they're usually stolen. Then he sells them on the street for a much higher price. The man he buys from has a shipment ready. That would be the best time to bust him. In fact, it's probably the only way to make sure we nail him."

Seeing the determination in his eyes, Emily knew Judd would find a way to get Clayton Donner, with or without her help. But she wanted to be near him any way she could. "Since I still have my own reasons for wanting him caught, I'll be glad to help however I can." She hesitated, then asked, "You're certain Donner is the one who sold my brother the gun?"

"As certain as I can be. We traced him to Springfield by the weapons he sold. One whole shipment was faulty guns. I don't know yet how Donner got hold of them, but from what you told me, it's safe to say your brother got one of them."

A resurgence of anger flooded through her. So Donner had known the guns were faulty before he sold them? He had deliberately risked her brother's life, and that fact made her determination almost equal to Judd's. "I look forward to doing whatever I can to help."

Judd let out a long breath. Then he leaned across the table and took both her hands. "I don't want to have to worry about you. I want your word that you won't try anything on your own. I don't even want you in that part of town without me. Promise me."

"I work there at the soup kitchen…"

"Not until this is over, Em. I mean it. It's just too risky. Promise me."

"Judd—"

"I lost Max, dammit! Isn't that enough?"

His sudden loss of control shook her. She stared at his eyes, hard now with determination and an emotion that closely resembled fear. Reluctantly, she nodded. The last thing she wanted to do was distract him. Already, it seemed to her, he was too emotionally involved, and that weakened his objectivity, putting him in danger. It was obvious that Max Henley had been, and still was, the most important person in the world to Judd. Emily decided she might very well be able to keep an eye on Judd as long as he let her stay close. And evidently, the only way to do that, was to agree to his rules.

"All right. I promise. But I want a promise from you, too, Judd."

It took him a moment to regain his calm demeanor. Then he lifted an eyebrow in question.

"From now on, you have to be honest with me," she said. "There are few things I really abhor, but lying is one of them. You've lied to me from the start."

Judd turned his head. "I was on assignment, Em. And you just came tripping into my case, nearly messing everything up. I did what I thought was best."

"And of course telling me the truth never entered your mind?" When he gave her a severe frown, she quickly added, "Okay, not at first. But since then? Surely you had to realize I wasn't a threat?"

His stare was hard. "You're a bigger threat than you know."

Emily had no idea what that was supposed to mean. And while she did understand Judd's position, she couldn't help feeling like a fool. First she thought he was a cop, then she believed he was a stripper. Now she finds out he actually is a cop. A small, humorless laugh escaped her. "I suppose it really is funny. Did you laugh at the irony of it, Judd?"

"Not once."

"Oh, come on. I must have looked like an idiot. And here you were, trying to keep the poor naive little fool out of trouble."

"It wasn't like that, Em."

She stood, suddenly wanting to be alone. "I should have learned my lesson long ago." She knew Judd had no idea what she was talking about, that she was remembering her sad lack of judgment so many years ago. She shook her head, not at all certain she'd ever tell him. Lord, she probably wouldn't have the chance to tell him. Once this ordeal with Donner was over—and, according to Judd, it would be over soon—Judd would go on about his business, and she would have to forget about him.

"I wonder if my parents were right."

Judd hadn't moved. He sat in the chair watching her. "About what?"

"About me being such a bad judge of character. They always claim I have a very unrealistic perception of mankind, they say that I should accept the world, and my place in it, and stop trying to change things. I suppose I ought to give up and let them have their way."

Judd stiffened, and his expression looked dangerous. "You don't mean that."

With a shake of her head and another small smile, Emily turned to leave. Just before she reached the hallway entrance, she stopped. "One more thing, Judd."

She turned to face him and her gaze locked with his. "The man who came in here? He mumbled something, just before I ran, about only wanting the film."

Judd shot to his feet. *"What?"*

Her smile turned a bit crooked. "I didn't want to tell the police, because I thought it might be important. I was going to wait and tell you so we could figure out what the man meant. But now, since you are the police…" She shrugged.

Judd was busy cursing.

"What are you going to do?" she asked him.

"First, I'm going to get someone over here to check your door for fingerprints."

"It won't do any good. He wore gloves. I felt them when he grabbed me."

"Another tidbit you were saving only for me?"

"Uh-huh. I honestly don't know anything else, though." She stifled a forced yawn. "I think I'll get ready for bed now."

Judd moved to stand directly in front of her. "I'm staying the night, Em."

"That's not necessary." *But, oh, it would be so nice.* She sincerely hoped he would insist. For some reason, the thought of being all alone was very unsettling. And even more unsettling was the thought of letting Judd out of her sight.

"I think it is. I won't bother you, if that's what you're worried about."

"I wasn't worried."

He accepted that statement with a smile of his own. "Good. Why don't you show me where you want me to sleep? Then I've got a few more calls to make."

Since Emily wouldn't show him where she really wanted him to sleep, which was with her, she led him to the room down the hall from her bedroom. Decorated in muted shades of blue, it had only a twin bed and was considered her guest room. There were two other bedrooms, one was John's room, since he dropped in often whenever there were problems with her parents, and the other room served as a small upstairs sitting room.

Judd nodded his approval, then took Emily's shoulders. "Try to sleep. But honey, if you need anything, don't hesitate to let me know."

He doesn't mean what you're thinking, Em. Didn't he just tell you earlier tonight it was too soon? "Thank you, Judd. Good night." Emily forced her feet to move down the hall, then she forced herself inside her room and closed the door. Her forehead made a soft *thwack* when she dropped it against the wood, and her cheek started throbbing again.

But none of it was as apparent as the drumming of her heart. It was all just beginning to sink in, from the slapstick beginning to the frightening end. Judd was an officer, who chose to take his clothes off in an undercover case, using a police uniform as a costume. It was too ironic. And Lord help her, so was her situation.

She was falling in love with a thoroughly outrageous man.

JUDD LAY in the narrow bed, stripped down to his underwear, with only the sheet covering him. His arms were propped behind his head and he listened to the strange sounds of the house as it settled. He'd left the door open in case Emily needed him.

God, what a mess.

Howell had raised holy hell with him, and for good reason. He'd behaved like a rookie with no experience at all. He knew better, hell, he was damn good at his job. But he just kept thinking of what could have happened. The thought of Emily being hurt was untenable. He had to find some way to wrap this operation up, and quickly. He didn't want to be involved with her, didn't want to care about her. But he knew it was too late.

Did two people ever come from more different backgrounds? Emily was cultured, refined, elegant. She had a poise that never seemed to leave her, and a way of talking that implied gentleness and kindness and…all the things he wasn't. That refined speech of hers turned him on. Everything about her turned him on.

He had to quell those thoughts. Emily wasn't for him. From what he knew of her parents, they would balk at the mere mention of her getting involved with someone like him. And he didn't want to add to her problems there. She evidently had some very real differences with her parents, but at least she had parents. And probably aunts and uncles and grandparents, all of them educated and smelling of old money.

The only smells Judd had been familiar with around his house were stale beer and unwashed dishes. Max had tried to teach him a better way, but Max had been a simple man with simple manners. He hadn't owned a speck of real silver, yet that was exactly what Emily stirred her tea with. And he couldn't be certain, but he thought the teacup she'd used earlier was authentic china. It had seemed delicate and fragile—just like Emily.

He squeezed his eyes shut, trying to close out the image of her lying soft and warm in her own bed, her dark hair fanned out on the pillow, those big brown eyes sleepy, her skin flushed. He wanted her, more than he'd ever wanted anything in his life. He hadn't known a man could want this much and live through it. She was right down the hall, and he suspected if he went to her, she wouldn't send him away.

But as bad as he wanted her, he also knew he had no right to her. So he continued to stare at the ceiling.

Somewhere downstairs he heard a clock chime eleven. Then he heard a different noise, one he hadn't heard yet, and he turned his head on the pillow to look toward the door.

Emily stood there, a slight form silhouetted by the vague light of the moon coming through the window. He couldn't quite draw a breath deep enough to chase away the tightness in his chest. When she didn't move, he leaned up on one elbow. His voice sounded low and rough when he spoke. "Are you all right, babe?"

She made another small, helpless sound, then took a tiny step into the room. Every muscle in his body tensed.

He couldn't make out her face, but he could tell her gown was long and pale and he could feel her nervousness. He didn't know why she was here, but his body had a few ideas and was reacting accordingly. He was instantly and painfully aroused. "Em?"

She took another step, then whispered in a trembling tone, "I know you said it was too soon. And you're right, of course. I told myself this wasn't proper, that I should behave with some decorum." Her hands twisted together and she drew a deep, shaky breath. "But you see, the thing is…"

Judd knew his heart was going to slam right through his ribs. He couldn't wait another second for her to finish her sketchy explanation. She was here, she wanted him, and despite all the reasons he'd just given himself for why he shouldn't, he knew he wanted her too badly to send her away.

He stared at her in the darkness, and then lifted the sheet. "Come here, Emily."

chapter 7

SHE MOVED SO FAST, JUDD BARELY HAD TIME TO brace himself for her weight. Not that she weighed anything at all. She was soft and sweet and she smelled so incredibly inviting—like a woman aroused. Like feminine heat and excitement. Her brushed-cotton gown tangled around his legs when he turned and pinned her beneath him. He felt her body sigh into his, her slim legs parting, her pelvis arching up. In the next instant, her hands cupped his face and she kissed him. It wasn't a gentle kiss. She ate at his mouth, hungry and anxious and needy.

So many feelings swamped him. Lust, of course, since Emily always inspired that base craving, even when she wasn't intent on seducing him. And need, a need he didn't like acknowledging, but one that was so powerful, so all-consuming, he couldn't minimize it as anything less than what it was.

But first and foremost was tenderness, laced with a touch of relief that he wouldn't have to pull back this time; she would finally be his. She had come to him, and she was kissing him as if she wanted him every bit as badly as he wanted her. That wasn't possible, but if her need was anywhere close to his, they both might damn well explode.

"Emily…"

Her kisses, hot and urgent, landed against his jaw, his chin, the side of his mouth. Her nipples were taut against his chest, her breath hot and fast. He wanted to touch her everywhere, all at once, and he wanted to simply hold her, to let her know how precious she was. He slid one hand down her side, felt her shiver, heard her moan, and he nearly lost his mind. He gripped her small backside with both hands and urged her higher against his throbbing erection, rubbing sinuously, slow and deep, again and again. He wanted to drown in the hot friction, the sensual feel of her warm body giving way to him. Her legs parted wide and she bent her knees, cradling him, offering herself.

Judd groaned low in his throat and went still, aware of the soft heat between her thighs now touching him. He knew she was excited, and the fact was making him crazy. "Too fast, honey. Way too fast."

Emily wasn't listening. Her hands frantically stroked his naked back and her legs shifted restlessly, rubbing against his, holding him. She continued to lift her hips into him, exciting herself, exciting him more. Judd dropped his full weight on her to keep her still, then carefully caged her face. She whimpered, trying to move.

"Shh. It's all right, Em. We've got all night." Then he kissed her. She tasted hot and sweet, and when he slipped his tongue between her lips, she sucked on him with greedy excitement.

Judd had never known kissing to be such a deeply sensual experience. To him, it had always been pleasant, sometimes a prelude to sex, sometimes not. But he'd never felt such a keen desire just from kissing. Emily was driving him over the edge, and he hadn't even touched her yet.

He caught her slim wrists in one hand and trapped them over her head. He had to take control or he'd never last. She muttered a low protest and her hips moved, rubbing and seeking beneath his, finding his erection and grinding against it. Her nightgown was in his way and he knotted one fist in the material and lifted, urgently. He needed to touch all of her, to explore her body, to brand her as his own. Emily squirmed to accommodate him, allowing the material to be jerked above her waist. When Judd felt her bare, slender thighs against his own, he growled and pushed against her.

It almost struck him as funny, the effect she had on him. Prim, polite, proper little Emily. He dipped his head and nuzzled her breasts at the same time he slid his hand over her silky mound, letting his fingers tangle in her damp curls. Emily stopped moving; she even stopped breathing. Judd felt her suspended anticipation.

He released her wrists long enough to jerk the buttons open on the bodice of her nightgown so he could taste her nipples, feel the heat of her flesh, and then he wedged his hand back between her thighs. He pressed his face to her breast and kissed her soft skin, his mouth open and wet. Emily shifted so her puckered nipple brushed against his cheek and Judd smiled, then began to suckle, drawing her in deep, stroking with his tongue, nipping with his teeth.

Her ragged moan was low and so damn sexy he moaned with her. His fingers slid over the tight curls, felt her slick and wet, hot and swollen with wanting him, and then he slid a finger deep inside her. She was incredibly tight and he added another finger, hearing her groan, feeling her body clasp his fingers as he forced them a bit deeper, stretching her.

He began a smooth rhythm, and with a breathless moan, her body moved with him. His thumb lifted to glide over the apex of her mound, finding her most sensitive flesh and stroking it, while his mouth still drew greedily on her nipple, and Emily suddenly stiffened, then screamed out her climax. Judd went still with shock.

Her slim body shuddered and lifted beneath his, her face pulled tight in her pleasure. He watched her every movement, her intense delight expressed in her narrowed eyes, her parted lips, the sweet sounds she made. Judd knew he had never seen anything so beautiful, so right. It seemed to go on and on, and as her cries turned to low breathless moans, he kissed her, taking her pleasure into himself.

When she stilled, he continued to cuddle her close, his own need now put on hold. A tenderness he'd never experienced before swirled through him, and he couldn't help smiling. Miss Cooper was a red-hot firecracker, and he must be the luckiest man alive. "You okay, Em?"

She didn't answer. Her breasts were still heaving and her heartbeat thundered against his chest. Judd placed one last gentle kiss on her open mouth, then lifted himself away to reach for his pants. He fumbled in the pockets until he found his wallet and located a condom. When he turned back to Emily, he saw her watching him, her dark eyes so wide they filled her face. Her bottom lip trembled as she slowly drew in uneven breaths. Damp curls framed her face and her expression was wary.

She was probably a bit embarrassed by her unrestrained display. He didn't have time to soothe her, though. He needed to be inside her, right now, feeling her body clasped tight around his erection just as it had clasped his fingers. With the help of the moonlight, he could see her pale belly and still-open thighs. He bent and pressed his mouth to her moist female flesh, breathing in her scent and his need for her overwhelmed him. His tongue flicked out, stroking her, rasping over her delicate tissues and he gained one small taste of her excitement before Emily gasped and began struggling away.

He caught the hem of her gown and wrestled it over her head, chuckling at the way she tried to stop him. She slapped at his hands, and when she realized he had won the tug-of-war, she covered her face with her hands. Once the gown was free, Judd tossed it aside and then immediately pulled her hands away from her face. The feel of her naked body, so warm and soft and ready, made him shudder. He covered her completely and said in the same breath, "You are so beautiful, Em. I've never known a woman like you."

She peeked one eye open and studied him. "Really?"

"Oh, yes," he answered in his most fervent tone.

She said a small, "Oh," and then he lifted her knees with his hands, spread her legs wide and pushed inside her. She was tight and hot and so wet… Slowly, her body accepted his length, taking him in by inches, her softness giving way to his hardness. Judd had to clench his teeth and strain for control. She made small sounds of distress, and he knew he was stretching her, but she didn't fight him, didn't push him away. Her small hands clenched on his shoulders and held him close.

It didn't take her long to forget her embarrassment once he was fully inside her. He ground against her, his gaze holding her own, seeing her eyes go hot and dark and intent. She pulled her bottom lip between her teeth and arched her neck.

"That's it, sweetheart." He drew a deep breath and began moving. Emily rocked against him, meeting his rhythm, holding him tight. He pressed his lips to her neck, breathing in her scent. He slid his hands down her back and cupped her soft bottom, lifting her higher. He felt her nipples rasp against his chest. Every touch, every breath, seemed to heighten his arousal.

When she tightened her thighs and sobbed, her internal muscles milking his erection until he wanted to die, he gave up any effort at control and climaxed with a low, rough endless growl.

It took him a few minutes to realize he was probably squashing Emily. She didn't complain, but then, she wouldn't.

He lifted up and stared at her face. His eyes had adjusted to the darkness, and he could see her fine, dark hair lying in disheveled curls on the pillow. Her eyes were closed, her lashes weaving long thick shadows across her cheeks. The whiteness of her breasts reflected the moonlight, and Judd couldn't resist leaning down to softly lathe a smooth, pink nipple. It immediately puckered.

He smiled and blew against her skin.

Emily squirmed. "You're still inside me."

"Mmm. I'm still hard, too."

"I noticed."

Her shy, quiet voice touched him and he smoothed her hair away from her forehead. "I've wanted you a long time, Emily."

"We haven't known each other a long time."

She still hadn't opened her eyes. He kissed the tip of her nose. "I've wanted you for as long as I can remember. It doesn't matter that we hadn't met yet." She shivered and Judd touched his tongue to her shoulder. "Your skin is so damn soft and smooth. I love touching you. And tasting you."

He licked a path up her throat, then over to her earlobe. "I could stay like this forever."

Emily drew in a shuddering breath. "No, you couldn't."

He laughed, knowing she'd felt the involuntary flex of his erection deep inside her. He wanted her again. "If I get another condom, do you promise to stay exactly like this?"

"Will you let me touch you a little this time, too?"

His stomach tightened at the thought. And he hurriedly

searched through the wallet he'd tossed on the floor only minutes earlier.

But once he was ready, he still couldn't let Emily have her way. Watching her react, touching her and seeing his effect on her, was stimulant enough. He'd thought to go slowly this time, to savor his time with her. But every little sound she made drove him closer to the edge. And when he entered her, the friction felt so unbearably good, he knew he wouldn't be able to slow down.

He'd told her the truth. He'd been waiting for her forever. But now he had her, and he didn't want to let her go.

EMILY WOKE the next day feeling fuzzy and warm and remarkably content. Then she realized Judd was beside her, one arm thrown over her hips, his face pressed into her breasts. His chest hair tickled her belly and their legs were entwined. They were both buck naked.

She should have been appalled, but seeing Judd looking so vulnerable, his hair mussed, his face relaxed, made her heart swell with emotion. Very carefully, so she wouldn't awaken him, she sifted her fingers through his hair. It felt cool and silky soft. Emily wouldn't have guessed there was anything soft about Judd. She placed a very careful kiss on his crown.

He shifted slightly, nuzzling closer to her breasts and she held her breath. But he continued sleeping. She was used to seeing the shadow of a beard on his face, but feeling it against her tender skin added something to the experience. She looked down the length of their bodies, and the vivid contrast excited her. He was so dark, so hard and muscled, while she was smooth and pale and seemed nearly fragile beside him.

She almost wished he would wake up, but he appeared

totally exhausted. His breathing was deep and even, and when she slipped away from him, he merely grumbled a complaint and rolled over onto his back.

Lord help him. The man did have a fine body. It was certainly shameful of her to stand there leering at him, but she couldn't quite pull her eyes away. Dark hair covered his body in very strategic places, sometimes concealing, sometimes enhancing his masculinity. And Judd Sanders was most definitely masculine. He took her breath away.

Emily might have stood there gawking until he did wake up, if she hadn't heard a knock on her front door. She gave a guilty start, her hand going to her throat, before she realized Judd had slept through the sound, and the person at the door had no notion she was presently entertaining herself with the sight of a naked man.

She snatched her gown, then ran to her own bedroom to retrieve the matching robe. By the time she got downstairs, the knocking had become much louder. "Just a minute," she mumbled.

When she peeked out the small window in the door, she couldn't have been more surprised. For the longest moment, she simply stood there, crying and laughing. When her brother shook his head and laughed back, she remembered to open the door and let him in.

She grabbed him into her arms, even though he stood much taller than herself, and squeezed him as tight as she could. She couldn't stem the tide of tears, and didn't bother trying. "Oh, John, it's so good to see you."

"You, too, Emmie. What took you so long to let me in?"

Emily froze. Uh-oh.

"Emmie? Hey, what's up?"

She shook her head. "What are you doing here, John? I

thought you were still out of the country. Did Mother and Father come with you?"

He set two suitcases just inside the door then walked past her, heading for the kitchen. Ever since she'd bought the house, the kitchen had become a kind of informal meeting place. Whenever John visited, they sat at the kitchen table and talked until late into the night.

"John?"

"Could I have something to drink first, Em? It's been a long trip."

Emily stared at John, trying to be objective. He looked better, so much better. The scars on his right temple and upper cheek had diminished, and now only a thin, jagged line cut through his eyebrow. He'd healed nicely, but his eyes still worried her. They seemed tired and sad and...hopeless.

"You look wonderful, John. The plastic surgeons did a great job."

He scoffed. "You call this a great job? This is as good as it gets, Em, though Mom keeps insisting she'll find a better surgeon who'll make me look as 'good as new.' She refuses to believe nothing more can be done."

Emily closed her eyes, wondering why her mother couldn't see the hurt she caused with such careless comments. "John, I never thought the scars were that bad. I was more concerned about your eyesight, and once we realized there wouldn't be any permanent damage there, I was grateful. You should be, too."

"Oh, yeah. I'm real grateful to look like a freak."

For one of the few times in her life, Emily lost her temper with her baby brother. It was so rare for her to be angry with John, she almost didn't recognize the feeling. And then she slammed her hand onto the counter and whirled to face him.

"Don't you ever say something so horrible again! You're my brother, dammit, and I love you. You are not a freak."

John seemed stunned by her display. He sat there, silently watching her, his dark eyes round, his body still. Emily covered her mouth with her hand and tried to collect her emotions. Then she cleared her throat. "Are you hungry?"

A small, relieved smile quirked on his lips. "Yeah, a little."

"I'll start breakfast. The coffee should be ready in just a minute. There's also juice in the refrigerator."

John tilted his head. "Since when do you drink coffee? The last time I asked, you said it was bad for me and gave me tea instead."

"Uh…" She'd bought the coffee for Judd, but it didn't seem prudent to tell John that. "You're older now. I see no reason why you can't drink coffee if you like."

"Okay." John still seemed a little bemused, but then he squared his shoulders. "I ran away, Emmie. Mom and Dad refused to bring me home, and I couldn't take another minute of sitting around waiting to see which doctor they'd produce next."

Suddenly, Emily felt so tired she wanted to collapse. "They'll be worried sick, John."

"Ha! I left them a note. You watch. When they can't reach me at home, they'll call here, probably blame you somehow, then carry on as if they're on vacation. We both know they'll be glad to be rid of me. Lately, I've been an *embarrassment*."

Since Emily had suffered similarly at the hands of her parents, she knew she couldn't truthfully deny what he said. She decided to stick to the facts, and to try to figure out what to do. "You came straight here from the airport?"

"Yeah. Mom and Dad probably don't even realize I'm gone yet. They had a couple of parties to attend."

The disdain, and the hurt, were obvious in his tone. She

wished she could make it all better for John, but she didn't have any answers. "You know you're welcome here as long as you like."

John stared at his feet. "Thanks."

"You also know you'll have to face them again sooner or later."

"I don't see why," he said. "They're disgusted with me now, but they won't say so. They never really say anything. You know how they are. I won't hang around and let them treat me the way they treat you. Do you remember how they acted when that fiancé of yours tried to scam them for money? Did they offer you support or comfort? No, they wouldn't even come right out and yell at you. They just made you feel like dirt. And they never forget. I don't think you've been to the house since, that Mom didn't manage to bring it up, always in some polite way, that she'd been right all along about him, that you'd been used by that jerk, just so he could get his hands on your money." John shook his head. "No thanks, I don't want to put up with that. I can just imagine…how…I'd…"

Emily looked up from pouring the coffee when John's voice trailed off. She'd heard it all before, his anger on her behalf, his indignation that she let her parents indulge in their little barbs.

She didn't understand what had silenced him now until she followed his gaze and saw Judd leaning against the doorjamb. He had his jeans on—just barely. The top button was undone and they rode low on his hips. His feet were bare, he wore no shirt and his hair fell over his forehead in disarray. He looked incredibly sexy, and the way he watched her, with so much heat, instantly had her blushing.

Then John stood. "Who the hell are you, and what are you doing in my sister's house?"

JUDD WISHED Emily's little brother had waited just a bit longer before noticing him. The conversation had taken a rather interesting turn, and he wouldn't have minded gaining a little more insight into Emily. But he supposed he could question her later on this fiancé of hers and find out exactly what had happened.

He was careful not to look overlong at the boy's scars, not that they were really all that noticeable, anyway. But just from the little he'd heard, he knew John was very sensitive about them. He was actually a good-looking kid, with the all-American look of wealth. Now, however, he appeared mightily provoked and ready to attack.

Judd ignored him.

His gaze locked on Emily, and suddenly he was cursing. "Damn, Em, are you okay?"

Emily faltered. "What?"

He strode forward until he could gently touch the side of her face. "You've got a black eye."

"I do?" Her hand went instantly to her cheek.

"It's not bad, babe. But it looks like it might hurt like hell."

She cleared her throat and cast a nervous glance at her brother. "No, it feels fine."

Judd smiled, then deliberately leaned down to press a gentle kiss to the bruise. Before Emily could step away, he caught her hands and lifted them out to her sides. In a low, husky tone, he said, "Look at you." His eyes skimmed over the white cotton eyelet robe. The hem of her gown was visible beneath and showed a row of lace and ice-blue satin trim. It was feminine and romantic and had him hard in a heartbeat.

Leaning down by her ear, Judd whispered in a low tone so her brother wouldn't hear, "I woke up and missed you. You shouldn't have left me."

He could feel the heat of her blush and smiled to himself, then turned to greet her brother. The kid looked about to self-destruct. Judd stuck out his hand. "Hi. Judd Sanders."

John glared. "What are you doing in my sister's house?" he repeated.

"That's none of your damn business." Then in the next breath, Judd asked, "Didn't you notice Emily's black eye?"

John stiffened, a guilty flush staining his lean cheeks. "It's not that noticeable. And besides, Emily was asking about me, so I didn't have time—"

"Yeah, right." Judd turned to Emily. "Why don't you sit down and rest? I'll fix breakfast. What do you feel like eating?"

"Hey, wait a minute!" John's neck had turned red now, too. He apparently didn't like being ignored.

Judd sighed. "What?"

For a moment, John seemed to forget what he wanted. He opened his mouth twice, and his hand went self-consciously to his scar. Then he asked, with a good dose of suspicion, "How did Emmie get a black eye?"

Judd smiled to himself. He folded his arms over his chest and braced his bare feet apart. "Some guy broke in here—"

"It was nothing, John." Emily frowned at Judd and then rushed toward her brother. "Would you like to go freshen up, John, before breakfast?"

"Women freshen up, Em. Not men."

She glared at Judd for that observation.

Judd lifted his eyebrow. "He has every right to know what happened to you. He's your brother and you care about him, so it only stands to reason that he cares for you, too." Judd looked toward John. "Am I right?"

"Yeah." John stepped forward. "What did happen?"

Emily looked so harassed, Judd took pity on her. "Why don't you go upstairs and...freshen up, Em, or change or whatever. I'll entertain your brother for you and start breakfast." Then he leaned down close to her ear. "Not that I don't like what you're wearing. You look damn sexy. But little brother looks ready to attack."

Her eyes widened and she cast a quick glance at John. "Yes, well, I suppose I ought to get dressed…" She rushed from the room. Judd watched her go, admiring the way her delectable rear swayed in the soft gown.

"What did you say to her?"

Little brothers were apparently a pain in the butt, and Judd wasn't known for his patience. But he supposed, for Emily, he ought to make the effort. "I told her how attractive she is. I get the feeling she isn't used to hearing compliments very often." The way he said it placed part of the blame for that condition directly on John. Judd didn't think it would hurt him to know Emily needed comforting every bit as much as anyone else. "Emily's a woman. They like to know when they look nice."

As he spoke, Judd opened the cabinets and rummaged around for pancake mix and syrup. It was one of the few breakfast things he knew how to make. He wanted to pamper Emily, to make her realize how special she was.

Last night had been unexpected, something he hadn't dared dream about, something he supposed shouldn't have happened. But it had happened, and even though he didn't know what he was going to do about it yet, how to balance his feelings for Emily with his need to get Donner, he knew he didn't want her to be uncomfortable around him.

He thought breakfast might be a good start. Besides, he owed her one from yesterday.

John interrupted his thoughts with a lot of grousing and grumbling. "I'm good to Emily."

"Are you?" He pulled out a couple of eggs to put in the mix, his mind whirling on possible ways to proceed against Donner, while keeping Emily uninvolved. Perhaps having her brother here would distract her from capturing the gun dealer.

"She's been worried about me."

Judd glanced at John as he pulled down a large glass mixing bowl. "I don't see why. You seem healthy and strong. Hell, you're twice her size." He took the milk from the refrigerator and added it to the mix.

"I nearly lost my eyesight not too long ago. And now I've got these damn scars."

Judd gave up for a moment on the pancakes. He turned to give John his full attention. "That little scar on the side of your face?"

John nearly choked. "Little?"

"It's not that big a deal. So you've got a scar? You're a man. Men are expected to get banged up a little. Happens all the time. It's not like you're disabled or anything. You'll still be able to work and support yourself, won't you?"

"I'm only sixteen."

Judd shrugged. "I was thinking long term."

"My face is ruined."

"Naw. You're still a good-lookin' kid. And in a few more years, that scar will most likely fade until you can barely see it. Besides, you'll probably get all kinds of sympathy from the females once you hit college. So what's the problem?"

John collapsed back in his chair. "You really don't think the scars are all that bad?"

Judd went back to mixing the batter. "I didn't even notice them at first. Of course, with Emily around that's not saying much. I wouldn't notice an elephant at the table when she looks at me with those big brown eyes. Your sister is a real charmer."

There was a stretch of silence. "You and Emily got something going?"

"Yeah. Something. I'm not sure what. Hey, how many pancakes can you eat? About ten?"

"I suppose. I didn't know Emily was dating anyone."

"We aren't actually dating."

"Oh." Another silence. "Should I be worried about this?"

That brought Judd around. "Well, hallelujah. I didn't think anyone ever worried about Em."

John frowned. "She's my sister. Of course I worry about her."

"Good. But no, you don't have to worry right now. I'll take care of her."

"And I'm just supposed to believe you because you say so?"

He almost smiled again. John sounded just like his sister. "Why not? Emily does."

That brought a laugh. "My parents would have a field day with that analogy. They don't think Emily has very good judgment."

"And what do you think?"

"I think she's too naive, too trusting and a very good person."

Judd grinned. "Me, too."

"So tell me how she got the black eye."

Suddenly, John looked much older, and very serious. Judd gave one sharp nod. "You can set the table while I talk."

Fifteen minutes later, Judd had three plates full of pancakes, and he'd finished a rather convoluted explanation of Emily's exploits. It was an abridged version, because even though Judd admitted to helping Emily, he didn't say anything about going undercover as a male stripper, or his overwhelming attraction to Emily, or their newly discovered sexual chemistry. In fact, he wasn't certain yet just what that chemistry was, so he sure as hell wasn't about to discuss it with anyone, let alone Emily's little brother.

John was appalled to learn what steps Emily had taken to try to help him.

And he hadn't even noticed her black eye.

Judd knew he was feeling guilty, which hopefully would help bring him out of his self-pity. "So you can see how serious Emily is about this."

"Damn." John rubbed one hand over his scar, then across his neck. "What can I do to help?"

Ah. Just the reaction he'd hoped for. From what Emily had told him about John, Judd hadn't known for sure what to expect. By all accounts, John could have been a very spoiled, selfish punk. But then, he had Emily for a sister, so that scenario didn't seem entirely feasible. "You want to help? Stay out of the east end. And stay out of trouble."

"But there must be something—"

"No." When John started to object, Judd cursed. "I'm having enough trouble keeping an eye on Emily. And she has enough to do without worrying about you more than she already does. Give her a rest, John. Get your act together and keep it together."

"That's easy for you to say. You don't know my parents."

"No. But I do know your sister. If she turned out so great, I suppose you can, too."

John laughed. "That's one way of looking at it."

Emily walked into the room just then, and Judd immediately went to her. He tried to keep his eyes on her face as he talked to her, but she was wearing another one of those soft, ladylike dresses. But what really drove him insane was the white lace tie that circled her throat and ended in a bow. Without meaning to, his fingers began toying with it. "I told your brother what happened."

The frown she gave him showed both irritation and concern. "Judd."

"Hey, it's okay," John said as he took a plate of pancakes and smothered them in warm syrup. "I'm glad he told me. And I'm glad he's looking after you."

"Judd is not looking after me. He's a...well, a partner of sorts."

Judd lowered his eyebrows as if in deep thought, then gave a slow, very serious nod. "Of sorts."

The look she sent him insisted he behave himself. He wasn't going to, though. A slight tug on the bow brought her an inch or two closer. His eyes drifted from her neatly brushed hair, her slender stockinged legs and her flat, black shoes. Her attire was casual, but also very elegant. "You look real pretty in that dress, Em. Do you always wear such...feminine stuff?"

Trying to act as though she wasn't flushed a bright pink, Emily stepped out of his reach and picked up her own plate. She stared at the huge stack of pancakes. "Most of my wardrobe is similar, yes. This is one of my older dresses because I have some work to do today."

"I like it."

John suddenly laughed. "I think you've caught a live one, Emmie. I don't remember what's-his-name ever acting this outrageous. He always tried to suck up to Mom and Dad by being as stuffy and proper as they are."

After frowning at her brother and giving a quick shake of her head, she said, "I can't truly imagine Judd ever 'sucking up' to anyone. Can you?"

"It'll be interesting to see what the folks think of him."

An expression of horror passed over her face. "For heaven's sake, John. I doubt Judd has any interest in meeting our parents."

Judd narrowed his eyes at the way she'd said that. So she didn't want him to meet them? It was no skin off his nose. He wasn't into doing the family thing, anyway. He couldn't remember one single woman he'd ever dated who wanted to rush him home to meet her mama.

But somehow, coming from Emily, the implicit rejection smarted. "There wouldn't be any reason for me to meet them. Especially since they're out of the country, right?"

Emily stared at her fork. "Yes. And we should have everything resolved before they return if we're as close to finishing this business as you say."

And once everything was resolved, there would be no reason to keep him around? Judd wanted to ask, but he couldn't. It was annoying to admit, but he felt vulnerable. He couldn't quite credit Emily with using him; she simply wasn't that mercenary. But that didn't mean she wouldn't gladly take advantage of a situation when it presented itself. He'd known from the start that she wanted him. They'd met, and sparks had shot off all around them. And if she wanted to have a fling on what she considered "the wild side of life," Judd was more than willing to oblige. For a time.

He would get a great deal of satisfaction when Donner was taken care of, and he'd be able to return to his normal routine: life without a driving purpose. He'd be alone again, without Max and without the overwhelming need to avenge him. Actually, he'd have no commitments, no obligations at all, unless Emily...

Judd shook his head. With any luck, he'd be wrong in what he was feeling, and he wouldn't miss her. The time he had with Emily right now would be enough.

Hell, he'd make it enough.

With that thought in mind, he urged Emily to eat, and he dug into his own pancakes. When she was almost finished, curiosity got the better of him and he asked, "So who was this bozo who tried to schmooze your parents?"

Emily choked. He took the time to whack her on the back a few times, then caught her chin and turned her face his way. "Emily?"

When she didn't answer right away, John spoke up. "Emmie was engaged to a guy for a while. She loved him, but he only wanted to use her to get in good with my parents. Luckily, everyone found out in time, before the wedding."

"Thank you very much, John."

"Oh, come on, sis. It wasn't your fault. The guy was a con artist."

"Yes, he was. And that is all in the past. I'd appreciate it if we found something else to talk about."

Judd transferred his gaze to John. "Your folks are pretty hard on her about it still?"

"God, yes. And she lets them. I don't think I've ever heard her really defend herself, though I'd like to see her tell them where to go. They even try to bully her into giving up her work with the homeless. They keep reminding her how she got burned once. It was a real embarrassing event. The papers got wind of it and all of society knew." John made a face, then added, "My parents really hate being publicly embarrassed."

With a disgusted sound of protest, Emily stood and took her plate to the sink. Judd glanced toward her, then back to John. "She's still a little touchy about it."

"Yeah. It was pretty hard on her. But Emmie is tough, and she doesn't let anything really get her down. Including Mom and Dad. That's why she moved here, away from my folks. She won't argue with them, but she will walk away. Of course, they hate this house, too. I don't know why she puts up with them."

Swiveling in his chair, Judd saw the stiff set to Emily's shoulders, the way she clenched her hands on the sink counter. He wanted to hold her, to comfort her, but the time wasn't right. Later, though… "Did you love him, Em?"

It took her so long to answer, Judd thought she'd decided to ignore him. It wasn't any of his business, but he wanted to know. The thought of her still pining over some guy didn't sit right with him.

Then she finally shook her head. "I suppose I thought I did...maybe I did. But now, it doesn't seem like I could have. I was so wrong about him. He was out of work and needed me, and I thought he cared about me, too. But he turned out to be a really horrible man."

Judd was out of his seat and standing behind her in a heartbeat. "That was one incident."

She turned and smiled at him. "Are you thinking I might decide I was wrong about you, too, Detective?"

"Since I don't know what you think about me, how am I supposed to answer that?"

When it came, her smile was sweet enough and warm enough to make his muscles clench. He caged her waist between his hands and waited.

"I think you're probably a real-life hero, Judd, and unlike any man I've ever known."

The words hit him like a blow. He stared into her dark eyes, dumbfounded. He saw her acceptance, her giving. He was a man with no family, no ties, a cop out to do a job, and willing to use her to do it. He was certainly no hero. But if that was what Emily wanted...

John cleared his throat. "Maybe I should make myself scarce."

Remembering where they were and who was with them, Judd forced himself to release Emily and take two steps back— away from temptation. "No. You can help me do the dishes while Emily calls to see if she can get someone here to repair the hot-water heater."

"Do the dishes? But I don't know how..."

Judd smirked. "It's easy. I'll show you what to do."

"But—"

"Do you want to be able to take care of yourself or not?"

Emily laughed. "Well put. I'll leave you two to tend to your chores." But she stopped at the doorway. "By the way, Judd. What if there was something on that film?"

"I'm picking it up today. Then we'll know."

"I'll go with you."

"No, you won't."

"But…"

His sigh was exaggerated. "You're as bad as your brother, Em. I thought we had an agreement."

When she turned around and practically stomped away without a word, Judd decided she was mad. "Well, hell."

John only laughed. "Gee, I'm really tired. Too much traveling, I guess. I think I might need to spend a lot of time in my room, resting up."

"What's that supposed to mean?"

With a buddy-type punch in the shoulder, John said, "I think you're going to have your hands full with Emmie. She can be as stubborn as a mule, and it's no telling who will win. I don't want to get caught in the crossfire."

And I don't want Emily caught in the crossfire, he thought. *Which is why I'm leaving her here.* There was really no other choice. He would get Donner, one way or another. The past, and Max, couldn't be forgotten. And he couldn't pretend it had never happened, not without finding some justice.

It would be only too easy to get wrapped up in Emily's problems. *It would be much too easy to get wrapped up in Emily.* But he wouldn't. Judd was afraid Emily could easily make him reevaluate himself and his purpose. Arresting Donner and seeing him prosecuted had to remain a priority. But he was beginning to feel like a juggler in a circus, wanting his time with Emily, and still needing to seek vengeance on Donner.

He'd have all weekend to spend with Emily before anything more could be done on the case. His body tightened in anticipation with just the thought. Somehow he'd have to manage—without letting her get hurt.

He only hoped Emily understood his motivations.

chapter 8

"I WANT YOU, EM."

Emily jumped, her heart lodging in her throat. "Good heavens, Judd. You startled me."

His hands slid from her waist to her hips, then pulled her back against him. She could feel the heat of his body on her back, her bottom… "Judd, stop that before John sees."

His growl reverberated along her spine, his mouth nipping on her nape. "John's taking a nap. He's still suffering jet lag."

With shaking hands, Emily carefully laid aside the picture she'd been looking at. She already knew Judd wanted her. He'd made that clear with every look he sent her way. But her brother was here now, and she wasn't comfortable being intimate with John in the house. She cleared her throat and tried to come up with a distraction.

"I don't see anything in these pictures that would prompt anyone to steal them."

Judd pressed closer and his hands came around her waist to rest on her belly. She sucked in a quick breath. His deep voice, so close to her ear, added to her growing excitement. "You have innocent eyes, honey."

"What do you mean?"

"Innocent, sexy eyes." He leaned over to see her face, his gaze dark and searching. "You really don't know what sexy eyes you have, do you?"

It took her a second to remember what she'd been talking about. "No, I… The pictures, Judd?"

His gaze dropped to her mouth and he gave her a soft, warm kiss, then picked up one of the photos. His expression changed as he looked at it, turning dark and threatening. "The guy in the doorway of the deli is an associate of Donner's. My guess is, he only visits this part of town when making a deal. Since the deal surely concerns guns, I'd say he's the one who instigated your break-in."

Emily gave the photo another look. "Really?"

Judd cursed, then tossed the picture back on the kitchen counter. "Unfortunately, I can't do anything about it yet without taking the risk of tipping off Donner and blowing my cover. If we grab this guy, we put a halt to the deal, and lose our advantage." He tightened his mouth. "That's not something I'm willing to do."

"I see." But she didn't, not really. Why was Judd so upset?

"Do you? Do you have any idea how I'd love to get my hands on that guy—*now*—for scaring you like he did?"

His possessive tone made her heart flutter, and she had to force herself to think about the case. "Then you think he was the one who broke in here?"

"Probably not. Like Donner, he has flunkies to do that kind of thing for him. But your taking this picture has obviously annoyed him. Hopefully, it'll help strengthen our case against

Donner, too, and we'll be able to make another connection there once we prosecute."

Emily licked her lips and tried for a casual tone. "Do you think the picture alone will be enough to incriminate Donner?"

Judd shrugged. "Possibly. But I don't want to incriminate him. I want to nail the bastard red-handed."

Emily had known that would be his answer, but still… "Judd, maybe it's time to rethink all this. I mean, is it really worth risking your life—"

He laid his finger across her lips before she could finish. "I'm not giving up, Em. I've already gone too far, and I have no intention of letting Donner win. But in the meantime, until he's put away and everything's settled, I don't want you staying here alone."

So. There it was. Emily knew he was up to something the minute he came back in with the developed pictures. She'd been surveying the pictures, not seeing anything out of the ordinary, when Judd started acting amorous.

Acting, Emily? Can't you feel the man's body behind you? He's not acting. No, and as much as that tempted her, she had to remember he only wanted to stay at her house to protect her. It had nothing to do with actually wanting her. Well, maybe it had a little to do with that, but wanting her wasn't his primary motive. She had to remember that.

Smiling slightly, she said over her shoulder, "My brother will be here with me."

He opened his thighs and pulled her bottom closer to him, his hand still firm on her belly, now caressing. "Not good enough. I want to be certain you're safe."

"I…I'll remember to turn on the alarm system." *Lord, Emily. You sound as if you've run five miles.*

Apparently done with talking, Judd dipped his hand lower and his fingers stroked between her thighs, urging her legs apart and moving in a slow, deep rhythm. The material of her dress slid over her as his fingers probed. Heat rushed through her, flushing her face, making her legs tremble, her nipples tighten. She slumped back against him and her head fell to his shoulder. How could she let this happen again when she still felt embarrassed over her wild display the night before? It was as if she had no control of her reactions.

Judd lifted his other hand to her breast, his fingertips finding a taut nipple then gently plucking.

"Judd—"

"Let me." He nuzzled her throat, his warm breath wafting over her skin. "I love how you feel, Em. I love how you come apart for me."

But you don't love me. She almost cried out at the realization that she wanted his love. She wanted it so bad. All the old insecurities returned, the memories of how she'd tried, just as her brother was trying, to gain a modicum of real emotion, real affection from someone. They all swamped her and suddenly she couldn't breathe. She jerked away, hitting her hip on the counter and hanging her head so Judd couldn't see her face. She felt breathless and frightened and so damn foolish.

His hand touched her shoulder, then tightened when she flinched. "Shh. I'm sorry, babe. I didn't mean to push you."

He turned her to hold her in his arms, no longer seducing, but comforting. And that seemed even worse. The tears started and she couldn't stop them.

His palm cradled the back of her head, his fingers kneading her scalp, tangling in her hair. "Tell me what's wrong, Em. I'll fix it if I can."

Through her tears, she managed a laugh. He was the most wondrous man. She pulled away to retrieve a tissue, then cleaned up her tear-stained face before turning back to him.

He looked so concerned, so caring, she almost blurted out, *I love you*. But she managed to keep the words inside. She had no idea how Judd would feel about such a declaration, but she couldn't imagine him welcoming it, not now, not while he had to concentrate on getting Donner.

"I guess I'm just a little overwrought," she said lamely. She quickly added, "I mean, with my brother being here, and worrying over him and the break-in."

Judd still looked concerned, but he nodded. "I understand. Would you like to take a nap, too?"

She'd never be able to sleep. "No. I have housework to do, and the yard needs some work. And I thought I'd put on a roast to cook for dinner."

Looking sheepish, and somewhat anxious, Judd asked, "You mind if I hang around and help?"

He could be so adorable... *Lord, Emily, are you crazy? The man is devastating, not adorable.* "Of course you're welcome to stay. But you don't have to help out. And I'm still not certain that it's a good idea for you to stay overnight."

"I think it's a hell of an idea. And I insist." When she frowned, he added, "It'll only be for a few days. I have to be back at the bar Tuesday. I have the feeling Donner will approach me then. He's getting restless, and he's made it clear he thinks we'll work well together. Since he doesn't like losing, he'll probably make me an offer that no normal stripper could refuse."

It was a small grab for humor, so Emily dutifully smiled. But inside, she felt like crying. The thought of Judd getting more involved with Donner made her skin crawl. They both knew how dangerous he could be.

"Stop frowning, Em. I should be able to set something up with him, find out when and where his next shipment will be, and then I'll bust him. It'll be over with before you know it."

And he'd go out of her life as quickly as he'd entered it. Emily bit her lip. "I'm worried, Judd."

"Don't be. I can take care of myself."

She supposed that was true, since he'd been doing just that since he'd been a child. But for once, she'd like to see him taken care of.

Just that quick, she had a change of heart. Judd might never love her, but he deserved to be loved. And she could easily smother him with affection. She'd enjoy taking care of him, and maybe, just maybe, he'd enjoy it, too.

They spent the day together, and though she tried, Judd didn't let her do any actual work around the house. She couldn't convince him that she enjoyed getting her hands dirty once in a while, and since he seemed so determined to have his way, she allowed it. Judd followed her direction, and she simply enjoyed her time with him.

He was a pleasure to watch, to talk to. He moved with easy grace, his muscles flexing and bunching. It was almost a shame he wasn't a real stripper, for he was certainly suited for the job.

When Judd suddenly stripped off his shirt, Emily thought he might have read her mind. He didn't look at her, though, merely went back to work. She heard herself say, "Are you performing for me, Judd?"

She'd meant only to tease him, but he slowly turned to face her, and his eyes were intent, almost hot as he caught and held her gaze. "I could be convinced to...in a private performance."

Not a single answer came to mind. She sat there, staring stupidly. Judd walked to her, pulled her close then kissed her. It was such a devouring kiss, Emily had to hold on to him. His tongue pushed into her mouth, hot and wet and insistent. Judd slanted his head and continued to kiss her until they were both breathless.

When he pulled away, she stared up at him, dazed. He drew a deep breath and tipped up her chin. "Anytime, Emily. You just let me know."

After that, she refrained from provoking comments. Judd might handle them very well, but she didn't think she'd live through another one. Instead, she asked about Max, Judd's past, and about his work. She wanted to know everything about him.

Emily went out of her way to show Judd, again and again, how important he was to her. At times he looked bemused, and at times wary. But more often than not, he looked frustrated.

She understood that frustration since she felt a measure of her own. But having her brother there did inhibit her a bit. Of course, so did her unaccountable response to Judd. It was scandalous, the way he could make her feel. But she suspected he didn't mind, even if it did embarrass her, so she decided she'd try to see to his frustration—and her own—once John had gone to bed for the evening.

That thought kept her flushed and filled with forbidden anticipation the entire time they worked.

Midafternoon, John joined them, and Emily was amazed to see how John reacted to Judd. It had startled her that morning when John had spoken so openly to Judd. Usually, her brother was stubbornly quiet, refusing to give up his thoughts, brooding in his silence. But with Judd, he seemed almost anxious to talk. And Judd listened.

Emily was so proud of Judd, she could have cried again. No one had ever reached her brother so easily. In a way, she was jealous, because she'd tried so hard to help John. But she supposed it took a male to understand, and Judd not only listened, he gave glimpses into his own past, allowing John to make a connection of sorts. They found a lot of things in common, though their upbringings had been worlds apart.

Emily decided she was seeing male bonding at its best, and went inside to give them more privacy.

She was starting dinner when they both walked in, looking windblown and handsome. Judd winked at Emily when he caught her eye, and John laughed.

"A man's coming tomorrow to replace my water heater." She more or less blurted that out from sheer nervousness when Judd started her way. He had that glint in his eyes again, and she truly felt embarrassed carrying on in front of her brother.

But Judd only placed a kiss on her cheek, and flicked a finger over the tip of her nose. "Good." Then he turned to John. "Make sure you're here when he comes. I don't think Emily should be alone in this big house with a strange man."

"I'll be here."

Emily might have objected to their protective attitudes, except that she heard a new strength in John's tone, that of confidence and maturity. She gave both men a tender smile. They stared back in obvious confusion.

Backing out of the room, John said, "I think I'll go watch some TV." But he glanced at Judd, then back to Emily. "Uh…that is, unless you need me to do anything else?"

"No. You can go do whatever you like."

Once he'd left the room, Emily turned a wondering look on Judd. "How did you do that?"

His grin was smug. "Do what?"

"Turn my little brother into a helpful stranger."

He laughed outright. "First of all, you could stop calling him your little brother. He's a head taller than you, Em. Respect his maturity."

"I hadn't realized he possessed any maturity."

"No, I guess you haven't seen that side of him. But I know Max had to work hard at getting me turned around. And the first thing he did was explain that I was old enough to know better. Put that way, I felt too embarrassed to act like a kid. And little by little, Max pointed out ways to distinguish what it takes to be an adult. Your brother's no different. He just needed some new choices."

Emily stood there feeling dumbfounded by his logic. She had enough sense to know it wasn't that simple, to realize what John needed was someone to identify with, someone who cared. That Judd was that man only made her love him more. "Thank you."

Judd stared at her, his gaze traveling from her eyes to her mouth, then slowly moving down her body. He muttered a quiet curse, and started toward her. Emily felt her heart trip. But the phone gave a sudden loud peal, and Judd halted.

Hoping she looked apologetic rather than relieved, Emily asked, "Could you get that, please?"

It rang two more times before Judd turned and picked up the receiver.

She knew right away that asking him to answer the phone had been a mistake. The look on Judd's face as he tried to explain who he was would have been comical if Emily hadn't already suspected who her caller was.

When Judd held a palm over the mouthpiece and turned to her, she braced herself.

"It's your father, and he wants to talk to John. By the way, he also wants to know who I am and what I'm doing here an- swering your phone." Judd tilted his head. "What do you want me to tell him, babe?"

Lord, Emily. You're in for it now.

"IT'S OVER and done with, Em. You might as well forget it."

Ha! That was easy for Judd to say. Emily had no doubt her parents were headed home right this minute. Of course, it would take them time to get here, but still, she was already dreading that confrontation.

"Come on, Emily. You know John didn't mean to upset you."

"Of course he didn't. It's just that my parents could rattle anyone." But why did John have to tell them Judd was her boyfriend. Lord, if they showed up before everything was settled, she'd either have to admit Judd was a detective, and accept their unending annoyance for involving herself in something they'd expressly forbidden, or she'd have to tell them he was a...a stripper. She could just imagine their reactions to that.

"I wish I'd talked to them, instead of John."

Judd turned his face away from her. "I offered you the phone, honey. But you just gave me a blank look. I didn't think you wanted to talk to them. And even if you had, what could you have told them? That I was a traveling salesman who just picks up other people's phones?"

She shook her head. "No. But I might have thought of something. And John's been so solemn since he talked with Father. I have no idea what they talked about—other than their conversation about me—but I know it couldn't have been pleasant. John's been sullen and sulky ever since, barely eating his dinner and running off to bed early. I wish he'd talk to me about it."

"He's all right, Em. He just needs a little time to himself."

Emily barely heard him. She stood up and started to pace the room, her mind whirling. Then she threw up her hands in frustration. "Oh, this is just awful. What am I going to do?" She didn't really expect Judd to answer, since he'd only been watching her with a strange look on his face. "You can't possibly realize what a trial my father can be. He's so judgmental, so rigid. Once he takes a stand, he never backs down."

Judd put his hand at the small of her back and nudged her toward the stairs. "Come on. It won't do you any good sitting down here and worrying about it. I'd say you probably have a couple of days before your folks get here, and by then, I'll be gone. So you're probably worrying about nothing."

They were halfway up the stairs, when Emily realized what he'd said. She turned to him and gripped his arm. "What are you talking about?"

He wouldn't look at her, but continued up the steps. "I don't want to cause you any problems. So I'll make certain I'm out of the way before they get here. Maybe John can say he misunderstood the situation, or something."

Judd started to go to the room Emily had given him the night before. She rushed up the remaining steps to catch him. "Wait a minute."

Judd lifted one dark eyebrow in question. "What?"

What are you going to do now, Emily? Just blurt out that you want him? He doesn't really seem all that interested anymore. She swallowed and tried to find a way to phrase her request without sounding too outrageous. "I...um."

Judd frowned and walked closer to her. "What is it?"

She glanced toward her brother's room, then took Judd's hand and urged him away from the door. When they were outside her bedroom, she stopped. Judd made a quick glance at the door, and this time both his eyebrows lifted.

Emily drew a calming breath. "I don't want to disturb John. And I don't want you to misunderstand."

Judd waited.

"It's about what I said before. I didn't mean that I wanted you to leave. I was worrying about John, not myself. My parents might not approve of my having you here, but then, they approve of very little when it comes to me. I'm almost immune to their criticism. But John isn't."

"So you're worried about him, not yourself?"

She didn't want to lie to him, that wouldn't be fair. "I can't say I'm looking forward to explaining you. After all, if I tell them the truth, they might interfere, and then your case could be jeopardized."

"What will you tell them?"

Judd had slowly moved closer to her until he stood only a few inches away. Already she was responding to him, and he hadn't even touched her yet. "I don't know. But I don't want you to—"

He laid one finger against her lips. "You've told me all kinds of things you don't want, Emily. Now tell me what you *do* want."

"You."

The way his eyes blazed after she said it reassured her. Her fingers trembled when she reached up to touch his chest. "I want you, Judd. It's a little overwhelming, what you make me feel. I've never felt anything like it before. But last night, you gave a part of yourself to me. Now, I want to do the same for you."

His eyes closed and he drew a deep breath.

Emily took his hand and placed it against her heart. "Do you see what you do to me? It's probably wrong of me to like it so much—" She had to stop to clear her throat as Judd's fingers curled around her breast. The heat in her face told her she was blushing, both with excitement and with her audacity, but she was determined to tell him all of it. "When I was engaged, I thought I knew what excitement was, and it was wonderful because it was forbidden. I felt wild, and just a little bit sinful. But that was nothing compared to how I feel with you."

"How do you feel?"

"Alive. Carnal." She felt the heat in her cheeks intensify with her outrageous admission, but she continued, "Not the least bit refined."

"God, Emily, you're the most refined, the most graceful

woman I've ever seen." His tone dropped and his thumb rubbed over her nipple. "You're also remarkably feminine and sexy. Just thinking about how wild you get makes me so hard I hurt."

She licked her lips, then stepped closer still so she could hide her face against his chest. "There are…things, I've wanted to do to you, Judd."

His body seemed to clench, and his voice, when he spoke, was hoarse, "What…things?"

Smiling, Emily whispered, "Don't you think we ought to get out of the hall before we…ah, discuss it?"

She'd barely finished speaking before Judd had opened her bedroom door and ushered her inside. The light was out, but Judd quickly flipped the wall switch. Now that they were out of the dim hall and she had his undivided attention, Emily felt very uncertain about what she had to say. But Judd was staring intently, and waiting, so she forged ahead.

"The last time…well, I know I took you by surprise."

He traced her mouth with a finger. "You can surprise me anytime you like."

"That's not what I mean. You see, even though I try very hard to be proper…" She glanced at his face, saw his fascination, then carefully pulled his teasing fingertip between her lips. Her tongue curled around him as she gently sucked and she heard him gasp. She licked at his flesh, lightly biting him.

"Oh, Emily."

She forgot he watched her with intense scrutiny. She forgot that such displays could be embarrassing. She could only think of the many things she wanted…

She released his finger and he dropped his hand to her buttocks, cuddling her. With a deep breath and a nervous smile, she blurted out, "I'm afraid I'm a fraud. I'm not at all proper. At least, you see, not when I'm…"

"Turned on?" His words were a breathless rasp.

She gave a painful nod of agreement.

There was no smile now, but his eyes showed wicked anticipation, and a touch of something more, something she couldn't recognize. "Are you turned on now, Em?"

The rapid beating of her heart shook her. Heat pulsed beneath her skin, making her warm all over, making her nipples taut, her belly tingle. It was so debilitating, wanting him like this. "Very."

"And you want to do…things? To me?"

Again, she nodded, feeling the husky timbre of his voice deep inside herself. "If you wouldn't mind."

His long fingers curved over her bottom and began a rhythmic caressing. "Tell me what things, Em."

Pressed so close to his body, it was impossible to ignore the length of his erection against her belly, or the warmth of his breath fanning her cheek. She went on tiptoe and nuzzled her mouth against his throat. "I want to taste you…everywhere."

His hands stilled, then clenched tight on her flesh. Against her ear, he whispered, "Oh, yeah."

She pulled his shirt open, and rubbed her cheek over the soft, curling hair there. "I'd like to have you…beneath me, so I could watch your face. You are such an incredibly handsome man, Judd. When you stripped for me…at least, it felt like it was just for me…"

"It was. It made me crazy, the way you ate me up with your eyes. I had to fight damn hard to keep from embarrassing myself that day."

Not quite understanding what he meant, she tilted her head back and stared up at him. "How so?"

His lips twitched into a smile. "You make me hard, Em, without even trying. But watching you watch me… It was the first time I thought stripping was a turn-on. Before that, it was only damn embarrassing."

"I'm looking forward to watching you again."

He groaned, then kissed her, sucking her tongue into his mouth. Emily almost forgot that she wanted to control things this time, but with a soft moan, she pushed Judd away.

"Emily…"

"No, wait." She had to pant for breath, but she was determined. "Will you take your clothes off for me, Judd?"

He blinked. "Will I… How about we take them off together?"

Reaching for his shirt, she said, "Of course," but Judd stopped her hands.

"I meant, we should take *our* clothes off, Em. I want you naked, too. All those things you want to do to me, well, I want to do them to you."

Her mouth went dry. Just the thought of Judd kissing her… She shook her head. "No. Not a good idea. This is my turn…"

"Let's not argue about it, okay?"

She could see the humor in his gaze, and his crooked smile. He was so endearing, so charming, so… "I've never undressed for anyone before."

There. She'd made that admission. She knew her face was scarlet, but she simply hadn't considered that he might want her to display herself. He was the stripper, not her.

Even as his fingers went to the waistband of his jeans, Judd murmured, "Fair's fair, Em." His eyes challenged her, and while her fascinated gaze stayed glued to his busily working fingers, Emily nodded.

She started to untie the bow to her dress, but Judd caught her hands. "No. This one is mine. I thought about doing this— so many times—since we first met." He took the very tip of the lace tie between his finger and thumb, then gently tugged.

It pulled open and the ends landed, curling around her breasts. Judd carefully separated the looped strips, while the backs of his fingers brushed over her nipples again and again. Then he slid the tie—so very slowly—out of her collar. Through it all, Emily didn't move.

It was the most erotic thing she'd ever had done to her.

She barely noticed when Judd tucked the lace tie into the back pocket of his jeans. And then he began stripping again, prompting her with a look to do the same. She felt horribly awkward, and very self-conscious. Her body wasn't perfect like his, but rather too slim, too slight. Where Judd looked like every woman's vision of masculine perfection, she was a far sight from the women's bodies displayed in men's magazines.

After unbuttoning her dress, she stepped out of her shoes, trying to concentrate on what Judd was doing, rather than on her own actions. Next, she took off her nylons, tossing them onto the chair by her bed. She saw Judd go still for a moment, then saw his nostrils flare. It hit her that her disrobing excited him. He'd already removed his shirt, and now his jeans, along with his underwear, were shoved down his legs. He stepped out of them, then fully naked, he turned his attention to watching her. There was no disguising his state of arousal. His stomach muscles were pulled tight, and his erection was long and thick and throbbing.

She drew a shuddering breath. "Judd?"

"Go on, honey." When she still hesitated, he said, "You're doing fine, Em. Now, take off the dress."

His words hit her with the impact of a loud drumroll, and she couldn't swallow, her throat was so tight. She saw a slight smile hover on his mouth, and he said, "I've had some fantasies, too, babe. And seeing you strip is one of them."

"I can't."

"I'm not talking about doing it in front of an audience. It'll just be you and me." Then he lowered his gaze to where her hands knotted in the dress. "Take it off, Em."

She wanted to, she really did. But it wasn't in her to flaunt her body, not when she felt she had nothing to flaunt. She looked away, feeling like a failure, afraid she'd disappointed him. Tears of frustration gathered in her eyes, and just when she would have begun a stammering explanation, Judd touched her.

"Shh. It doesn't matter, honey." He pulled her close again. Emily kept her face averted.

Judd pushed the dress down her shoulders, then worked it lower. The soft material slid over her arms and caught, for just a heartbeat, on her narrow hips, then went smoothly to the floor.

Judd's breath left him in a whoosh as his gaze dropped to her black lace panties and stayed there. Emily suddenly didn't feel quite so awkward, not with the intense, heated way he watched her, as if she were the most fascinating woman he'd ever seen. She skimmed off her bra, then offered him a small, nervous smile.

"Incredible." His gaze finally lifted from her panties to her face. "If I'd known what you were wearing under that dress, I never would have lasted this long." He lowered his head for another long, heated kiss, and at the same time, slid his hands into her underwear, his large warm palms cradling her bottom. His fingers explored, probing and stroking, and Emily clung to him. Before the kiss was over, her panties had joined the rest of their clothes and then she urged Judd to sit on the side of the bed. She dropped gracefully to her knees before him, then reached out and encircled his erection with both hands. He was breathing hard, his thighs tensed, his hands fisted on the bed at his sides. Emily leaned forward, feeling her heart pound, and took a small, tentative lick. He jerked, and a rough broken groan escaped him.

Emily felt encouraged and anxious and excited. She leaned forward again, rubbing her breasts against his thighs, her nipples tingling against his hairy legs. Then she closed her mouth around him, gently suckling and sliding her tongue around him, feeling him shudder and stiffen. Judd gave a long, low, ragged groan and twined his fingers in her hair, leaning over her and holding her head between his large palms, urging her to the rhythm he liked. His hands trembled. So did his thighs.

For the first time in her life, Emily was able to indulge in her sensual nature. Judd encouraged her, praised her, pleaded with her. She loved the scent of his masculinity, the texture of his rigid flesh, so silky smooth and velvety. She gave him everything she could, and he gave her the most remarkable night of her life. She knew, if Judd left her now, she wouldn't regret a single minute she'd spent with him.

And she also knew she'd never love another man the way she loved Judd Sanders.

chapter 9

THE BAR WAS CROWDED AS WOMEN WAITED FOR the show to begin. Emily felt a twinge of jealousy, thinking of all those women seeing Judd in his skimpy briefs, but she kept reminding herself it was necessary for him to perform.

She'd left John, still acting contrary and withdrawn, at her house. It seemed it only took one phone call from her father to destroy all the headway Judd had made with her brother. Judd told her not to worry, that he was certain John would work everything out. But John was her little brother, and she couldn't help worrying about him any more than she could stop worrying over Judd.

He was obsessed with catching Donner. Anytime Emily tried to discuss it with him, he went every bit as silent and sullen as John. She supposed he had to get into a certain mind-set to be able to work his cover. After all, not many men could pull off being a stripper. But she hated seeing him act so distant. Even now, as he lounged beside her sucking on an ice cube he'd fished from her cola, she wanted to touch him, to somehow reach him. But he ignored her.

"There aren't any men here tonight. It doesn't seem likely that Donner will come."

She knew Judd had heard her, despite her lowered voice. But he didn't look at her when he replied, "He'll come. I feel it. And there aren't any men because it isn't allowed. It's ladies' night. But Donner has free run of the place. He'll be here."

The look in his eyes, the way he held himself, was so different from the Judd she knew. She felt alone and almost sick to her stomach. She had wanted Donner so badly, but now, she only wanted to protect Judd. From himself. From his feelings. And most especially from his self-designed obligations to a dead man.

Before Emily could comment further, Judd glanced at the watch on his wrist, then said, "I have to go get ready."

He straightened, and Emily tried to think of something to say, anything, that would break his strange mood. Then Judd leaned down and lifted her chin with the edge of his fist. "Do me a favor, babe. Don't watch. If you do, I'll start thinking about last night, and I might not make it."

Emily blinked. "I thought you wanted everyone to believe we had an…intimate association."

"Oh, they'll believe." Then he kissed her. Emily heard the bartender hoot, and she heard a few of the women close by whistle. One particularly brazen woman offered to be next.

Judd practically lifted her from the bar stool, one hand anchored in her hair, the other wrapped around her waist. The kiss was long and thorough, and couldn't have left any doubts about their supposed relationship.

Pulling back by slow degrees, Judd said, "Damn, but I want to be home with you. Alone. Naked."

Emily hastily covered his mouth. "Hush. You'll have me so rattled, I won't remember what I'm doing here."

He kissed her fingers, then straightened again. "Stay out of trouble. And stay where I can see you."

"But don't watch?"

"You've got it." Then he flicked a finger over her cheek and walked away to his "dressing room." Emily couldn't hold back a smile. *He wasn't as indifferent as you thought, was he, Emily? Who knows, this may all work out yet. Maybe, if enough time passes without Donner showing, Judd will finally give up and let someone more objective handle the case.*

Emily was daydreaming about having a future with Judd, when Clayton Donner strolled in the front door, along with his bully boys. Emily sank back on her stool to avoid being noticed. Not that she was all that noticeable, with so many women in the room.

Donner stopped inside the door and spoke with one of his men. He checked his watch, smoothed a hand over his hair, then opened a door leading to a set of stairs. Mick, one of the men from the pool hall, stayed at the bottom. Minutes later, another man entered and spoke quietly with Mick. Emily sucked in a sharp breath as she realized he was the man from the photograph. Fear hit her first, knowing this man had deliberately sent someone to break into her home. But anger quickly followed.

Whoever he was, he could be no better than Donner. And Emily wanted to see them both put away—preferably without involving Judd.

Their heads were bent together in a conspiratorial way, and Emily wished she could hear what they were saying. When Mick led the other man upstairs, she decided she would follow. She felt a certain foreboding, not for herself, but for Judd. She had to protect him.

Her heart pounded with her decision.

Judd was probably the most capable man she'd ever met, but his love for Max would make him vulnerable in ways that could endanger his life. If there was some way, any way, to help predict Donner's actions, she could use the information to help Judd.

With that thought in mind, she waited until Judd had been cued by his music and walked onto the dance floor, then she slipped away. Judd didn't notice since he seemed to be making every effort not to look her way. Women screamed in the background and the music blared. But above it all, Emily heard the rush of blood in her ears and her thundering heart. She tried to look inconspicuous as she made her way to the door.

It opened easily when she turned the knob, and she held her breath, waiting to see if anyone would be standing on the other side. She could always claim to be looking for the ladies' room. But once the door was open, she was faced with a narrow flight of stairs, with another door at the top.

Oh, Lord, Emily, don't lose your nerve now. And stop breathing so hard or they'll hear you. Each step seemed to echo as her weight caused the stairs to squeak. As she neared the top, she could make out faint voices and she strained to listen. Donner's tone was the most prominent, and not easy to miss. He had a distinctive sound of authority that grated on her ears.

Trying to draw a deep, calming breath, Emily leaned against the wall and concentrated on picking up the discussion, hoping she'd hear if anyone moved to open the door. Gradually, she calmed enough to hear complete sentences, and minutes later, she started back down the stairs.

Her hands shook horribly and she thought she might throw up. When she opened the door and stepped back into the loud atmosphere of the bar, her vision clouded over and she had to shake her head to clear it.

Nothing had ever scared her like eavesdropping on Clayton Donner. But she now had what she needed to protect Judd. She knew when, and where, the next shipment would be bought. A plan was forming, and she'd have a little more than a week to perfect it. She'd make it work, and best of all, it wouldn't include Judd.

JUDD FINISHED UP his act just as Emily slid back onto her stool. She was stark white and her face seemed pinched in fear. He felt an immediate surge of anger. Something had upset her, and he wanted to know what.

Ignoring grasping hands as he left the floor, he strode to Emily and stopped in front of her. She met his gaze with wide brown eyes and a forced smile. A crush of women began to close in behind him and he took Emily's arm without a word, then started toward the room where he changed. As he walked, he glanced around, hoping to catch sight of Donner or one of his men. He saw only grinning women.

When he closed the door behind them, she began to chatter. "The crowd seemed especially enthusiastic tonight. It's a shame you're not really a performer. You're obviously very good at it."

Judd didn't offer a comment on that inane remark. He studied her face, saw her fear and wondered what had happened. "Where did you go, Em?"

"Where did I go?"

"That's what I asked." He tossed his props aside and picked up a towel to rub over his body. Emily watched his hands, as she always did, with feminine fascination. "You were gone the entire time I danced."

"Oh." She pulled her gaze up to peer into his face, then shrugged. "I went to the ladies' room."

"Uh-uh. Try again."

She tried to look appalled. "You don't believe me?"

"Not a bit." Maybe she had seen Donner. Maybe the bastard had even spoken to her. Judd felt his shoulders tense. "Where did you go, Em?"

She gave a long sigh, then looked down at her feet. "All right, if you must know, I was jealous."

That set him back. "Come again?"

She waved her hand airily. "All those women were ogling you as if they had the right. I couldn't bear to watch. I suppose I'm just a…a possessive woman."

Judd narrowed his eyes, mulling over what she'd said. She sounded convincing enough, but somehow, her explanation didn't ring true.

Emily gave him a defiant glare when he continued to study her. "How would you feel if the situation were reversed? What if that was me dancing, and other men…were ogling me?"

She blushed fire-red as she made that outrageous suggestion, and Judd felt a smile tug at his mouth, despite his belief she was keeping something from him. He pulled on his jeans and then said to her, "I suppose I'd have to take you home and tie you to the bed. I sure as hell wouldn't sit around while other men enjoyed the sight of you. I'm a little possessive, too."

"There! You see what I… You are?"

Shrugging into his shirt, Judd said, "Yes, I am. And because I'm so possessive, I'd like to know what you're up to."

She immediately tucked in her chin and frowned. Judd was just about ready to shake her, when a knock sounded on the door. He went still, his adrenaline beginning to flow, then he moved Emily out of the way and opened the door.

Mick stood there, an insolent look on his face.

"Yeah?" Judd forced himself not to show any interest.

Mick frowned. "Clay wants to talk to you."

"Tell Clay I'm busy." As he said it, he reached back and wrapped an arm around Emily. She seemed startled that he'd done so.

Mick's gaze slid over Emily, then came back to Judd. "He said to tell you he'd like to discuss a little venture with you."

"Ah. I suppose I can spare a few minutes, then. Where is he?"

"Upstairs. I'll take you there."

"I can take myself. Tell him I'll be there when I finish dressing." He shut the door in Mick's face.

Emily immediately started wringing her hands. "Don't go."

"What? Of course I'm going." He leaned down and jerked on his socks and shoes. His hands shook, the anticipation making simple tasks more difficult. He looked up at Emily. "This is what we've been waiting for. Don't go panicking on me now."

As he was trying to button his shirt, Emily threw herself against him. "It's too dangerous. You could get hurt."

"Em, honey." He didn't want to waste any time, but he couldn't walk out with her so upset. He drew a deep breath to try to collect himself. "Em, listen to me." When he lifted her chin, she reluctantly met his gaze with her own. "It'll be all right. Nothing's going to happen here in the bar. I'm only going to talk to him. I promise."

Her bottom lip quivered and she sank her teeth into it to stop the nervous reaction. Judd bent to kiss her, helping her to forget her worry. "I want you to wait at the bar for me. Stay by Freddie until I come back out. Promise me."

"I'll stay by Freddie."

"Good." He opened the door and urged her out. "Now, go. I won't be long."

Judd leaned out the doorway and watched until Emily had taken a stool in the center of the long Formica bar. He signaled Freddie, waited for his wave, then went back into the room, stuffed his props into his leather bag and hoisted it over his shoulder. He took the steps upstairs two at a time. He rapped sharply on the door. His jaw felt tight and there was a pounding in his temples.

Mick opened it, peeked out, then pulled it wide for him to enter.

Donner stood and came to greet him. "Well, if it isn't our friend, the stripper. Tell me, do the ladies ever follow you home?"

Judd forced his muscles to relax. "They try sometimes. But my calendar is full."

"Ah, yes. I almost forgot. The little bird from the pool hall."

Judd didn't reply. He wanted to smash his fist against Donner's smug, grinning face. Instead, he forced a negligent smile.

"Do you enjoy dancing...Sanders, isn't it?"

"That's right. And no, not particularly." Then he pulled a wad of money from his pocket, all of it bills that had been stuffed into his briefs. "But it pays well."

"I can see that it does. There are easier ways to make money, though."

Judd settled back against the wall and folded his arms across his chest. He was so anxious, his mouth was dry. But he kept his pose, and his tone, almost bored. He gave a slow, relaxed smile, then said, "Why don't you tell me about it."

JUDD WAS still trying to figure out how he was going to keep Emily out of the picture. He couldn't risk her by taking her along, but if she was told the truth, she'd insist on coming with him. They'd argue, and she'd end up with hurt feelings.

He couldn't bear the thought of that. Her feelings were fragile, and she was such a gentle woman, the thought of upsetting her made him feel like an ogre. But dammit all, he had to keep her safe. *Max was dead, but Emily was very much alive.* He had to make certain she would be okay.

Eight days. Not long enough, but then, no amount of time would be enough with Emily. The way he felt about her scared him silly, and it had been a long time since he'd felt fear. Growing up in the wrong part of town, with his father so drunk and angry and unpredictable, he'd gotten used to thinking fast and moving faster. Which was maybe why he'd never settled down with any one woman.

He wouldn't settle down now, either.

He couldn't. Not with Emily. She deserved so much more than he could ever give her, more than he'd ever imagined possessing. Not material things—she had those already, and he wasn't exactly a pauper. He could provide for her. But emotional things? Family and background and happy memories? He couldn't give her that. But he wanted to. So damn much.

She reached over and touched his shoulder as he drove through the dark, quiet streets of Springfield. "What happened, Judd? You've been so quiet since talking with Donner."

He couldn't tell her the truth, so he lied. And hated himself for it. "Nothing happened. He questioned me a little. Tried to feel me out. But he didn't give me a single concrete thing to go on."

"So..." She swallowed, looking wary and relieved. "So you don't know yet what his plans are?"

"No." He flicked her a look. The streetlights flashing by sent a steady rhythm of golden color over her features. She was so beautiful. "I guess we'll have to keep up the cover a little longer. I, ah, suppose I can let you out of it if you think it'll pose a problem. I mean, with John being home now and all."

"No!" She gripped his arm, then suddenly relaxed. "No. I don't mind continuing...as we have been."

A little of his tension eased. He desperately needed a few more days with her. Once it was over, he'd have no further hold on her, and he wouldn't be able to put off doing the right thing. But for now… He tugged on her hand. "Come here, babe."

Emily slid over on the seat until their thighs touched and her seat belt pinched her side. She laid her head on his shoulder. Judd felt a lump of emotion that nearly choked him, and he swallowed hard. For so long, he'd been driven to get Donner and to avenge Max's death. He'd thought doing so would give him peace and allow him to get on with his life. But he realized now, after claiming Emily as his own for such a short time, there would be no peace. His life would be just as empty after Donner was convicted as it had been before. Maybe even more so, because now, he knew what he was missing.

EMILY FELT like a thief. She was getting rather good at sneaking around. It still made her uneasy, but with Judd always watching her so closely, the subterfuge was necessary.

In order to "protect" her, he'd sort of moved in. It was a temporary situation, prompted by Judd's concern over the break-in. He'd never once made mention of any emotional involvement, but his concern for her was obvious. And though it made her plans that much more difficult to follow, she was glad to have him in her home.

During the day he teased her and talked with her; he made her feel special. And at night…the nights were endless and hot and carnal. Judd touched her in ways she'd never imagined, but now craved. The shocking suggestions he whispered in her ear, the things he did to her, and the greedy, anxious way she accepted it all, could only be described as wicked—deliciously wicked. She loved his touch, his scent, the taste of him. She loved him, more with every day.

They had to be discreet, with John in the house, slipping into bed together after he was asleep, and making certain to be up before him. But John seemed to take great pleasure in having Judd around, even trying to emulate him in several ways. The two men had become very close.

Emily had thought long and hard about her situation with Judd, and her main priority was to take every moment she could with him. She suspected John might be aware of their intimate relationship, but since she would never ask either man to leave, there was no help for it. And she simply couldn't feel any shame in loving Judd.

Now, as she slipped from the bedroom an hour before the sun was up, Emily thought of her plan. She knew Donner would be making his deal tomorrow at the abandoned produce warehouse on Fourth Street. She had her camera loaded and ready. If she could get a really good, incriminating picture, there would be no reason for Judd to continue his investigation. He would be safe.

Giving Judd the evidence he needed would be her gift to him, to help him put the past to rest. Then maybe he'd want her to be a part of his future.

She was at the kitchen table studying a map when she heard Judd start down the steps. Seconds later, when he entered the kitchen, she tried not to look guilty. The map, now a wadded, smashed ball of paper, was stuffed safely in a cabinet drawer.

"What are you doing up so early, babe?"

Emily drank in the sight of him, standing there with his hair on end and his eyes blurry. There was so little time left. After tomorrow, his case would be over, the threat would be gone and Judd would leave her. She rushed across the floor in her bare feet and hugged him.

Judd seemed startled for a moment, and then his arms came around her, squeezing tight. "What's wrong, Em?"

"Nothing. I just couldn't sleep."

He set her away from him. "Take a seat and I'll start some coffee."

She sat, and fiddled with the edge of a napkin. "Judd?"

"Hmm?"

"I have some stuff I have to do tomorrow. Around two."

His hand, searching for a coffee mug, stopped in midreach. When he turned around, he wore a cautious expression and his posture seemed too stiff. "Oh? What kind of stuff?"

"Nothing really important. I have a load of clothes to drop off at the shelter, and some packages to send to an aunt for her birthday." She held his gaze, striving for a look of innocence. "And I think I'll do a little grocery shopping, too."

All at once he seemed to relax and his breath escaped in a sigh, as if he'd been holding it. He gifted her with a small smile. "Well, don't worry about me. I'm sure I can find something to occupy my time. In fact, I should go check on my mail and maybe pay a few bills."

Emily congratulated herself on her performance. She'd been brilliant and he'd believed every word. Now, if she could only get him to leave before her so she wouldn't have to try to sneak out. He'd surely notice her clothes, dark slacks and a sweater, since he'd never seen her wear anything like them before. She liked the outfit. It made her feel like 007.

An hour later, all three of them were finishing breakfast. It was a relaxing atmosphere, casual and close, like that of a real family. Emily smiled, thinking how perfect it seemed.

That's when her parents arrived.

THE INTRODUCTIONS were strained and painful. Judd remembered now why he'd never done this. Meeting a mother, especially when you were barefoot and hadn't shaven yet could make the occasion doubly awkward. He thought about bowing out, letting Emily and John have time alone with their parents, but one look at their faces and he knew he wasn't going to budge.

"What is he doing here, Emily?"

"I told you, Mother, he's a friend."

"What kind of friend?"

"What kind do you think, Father?"

Judd winced. He'd never seen Emily act so cool, or so defensive. And her smart reply had Jonathan Sr. turning his way. "I think you should remove yourself."

Judd raised an eyebrow. Well, that was blunt. Before he could come up with a suitable reply, Emily fairly burst beside him.

"You overstep yourself. This is my house, and Judd is my guest."

That startled Judd, but evidently not as much as it did Emily's family. They all stared, and Emily glared back. "Uh, Em..."

"No." She raised one slim, imperious hand. "I want you to stay, Judd."

Evelyn Cooper stepped forth. She was an attractive woman, with hair as dark as Emily's and eyes just as big. For the briefest moment, Judd wondered if this was what Emily would look like when she got older—and he felt bereft that he'd never know.

"We have family business to discuss, Emily. It isn't proper for a stranger to be here."

John snorted. "He isn't a stranger, he's a very good friend. And he already knows all about me. I trust him."

Evelyn narrowed her eyes at her son. "I wasn't talking about your irresponsible behavior. You will, of course, return with us. We've found the perfect surgeon." Then her gaze traveled again to Judd. "I was speaking of Emily's...unseemly conduct."

Judd was still reeling over the way John had just defended him. He was a friend? A very good, trusted friend? He felt like smiling, even though he knew now wasn't the time. Then Evelyn's words sank in. *Unseemly?*

John had told him that Emily never stood up to her parents, that she took their insults and their politely veiled slurs without retaliating. Probably because she still felt guilty for misjudging her fiancé and causing her parents an embarrassment. But to put up with this? He didn't like it, but he also didn't think he should interfere between Emily and her parents. He drew a deep breath, and tried to remain silent.

Emily lifted her chin. "I'm not entirely certain John wants to see another surgeon, or that it's at all necessary."

"John will do as he's told."

"Despite what he wants?"

Jonathan Sr. harrumphed. "He's too young to know what he wants, and certainly too irrational at this point to make a sound decision. It's possible the scars can be completely removed. Appearances being what they are, I think we should explore every avenue."

Judd stood silently while a debate ensued. John made it clear he didn't want any further surgery. The last doctor had been very precise. The scars would diminish with time, and beyond that, nothing more could be done. Judd thought it was a sensible decision on the boy's part, but John's father disagreed. And though he'd told himself he wouldn't interfere, Judd couldn't stop himself from interrupting.

"Will you love your son any less with the scars?"

Both parents went rigid. Then Jonathan shook his head. "This has nothing to do with love!"

"Well, maybe that's the problem."

That brought a long moment of silence. Evelyn looked at her husband, and then at her son. "We only want what's best for you."

"*Then leave me alone.* I'm sick of being picked over by a

bunch of doctors. I did a dumb thing, and now I have some scars. It's not great, but it's not the end of the world, either. They're just scars. I'd like to forget about what happened and get on with my life."

Jonathan frowned. "What life? Skulking around in the slums and getting into more trouble? We won't tolerate any more nonsense."

"Is that why you wanted to keep me out of the country? Dad, I could find trouble anywhere if that's what I really wanted. But I don't." He looked at Judd, then sighed. "I'm sorry for the way I've acted. Really. But I want to stay here now. With Emmie."

Jonathan shared another look with his wife, then narrowed his eyes at Emily. "I'm not certain that's a good idea. Emily's always been a bad influence on you."

Judd waited, but still, Emily offered no defense. It frustrated him, the way she allowed her parents to verbally abuse her. Again, he spoke up, but he kept his tone gentle. "It seems to me Emily's been a great influence. Didn't you just hear your son apologize and promise to stay out of trouble? What more could you ask for?"

Evelyn squeezed her eyes shut as if in pain. "Good Lord, Emily. He's just like the other one, isn't he? How much will it cost us this time to get you out of this mess?"

Judd froze. They couldn't possibly mean what he thought they meant. He looked at Emily, saw her broken expression and lost any claim to calm. But Emily forestalled his show of outrage.

"How dare you?"

She'd said it so softly, he almost hadn't heard her. The way her parents stared, they must have doubted their ears, too.

"How dare you even think to compare them?" Her voice rose, gaining strength. She trembled in her anger. "You don't know him, you have no idea what kind of man he is."

Judd was appalled when he saw the tears in her eyes. He touched her arm. "Emily, honey, don't." She hadn't defended herself, but she was defending him? He couldn't bear to be the cause of dissension between her and her family. It seemed to him they had enough to get straight without his intrusion.

Emily acted as though he weren't there. She drew herself up into a militant stance and said, "I would like you both to leave."

Jonathan glared. "You're throwing us out?"

"Absolutely. I've listened long enough to your accusations and disapproval. I won't ever be the daughter you want, so I'm done trying."

Evelyn laid a hand to her chest. "But we just got here. We came all the way from Europe."

Emily blinked, then gave a short nod. "You may have ten minutes to refresh yourselves. Then I want you gone." And she turned and walked out of the room.

Judd started to go after her when he heard Jonathan say, "You're not good enough for her, you know."

He never slowed his pace. "Yeah, I know."

But before he'd completely left the room, he heard John whisper, his tone filled with disgust, "You're both wrong. They're perfect...for each other."

WHAT DID KIDS KNOW? Judd asked himself that question again and again. So John liked him. That didn't mean he could step in and do something outrageous like ask Emily to marry him. No, he couldn't do that.

But he could let her know how special she was, how perfect...to him.

When he found her in the bedroom, she was no longer crying. She sat still and silent in a chair, her back to the door, staring out a window.

"You okay?"

"I'm fine."

She wasn't and he knew that. He made a quick decision, then knelt beside her chair. After smoothing back her hair, he brushed his thumb over her soft temple. "Maybe you should go talk to them, babe. No yelling, no silent acceptance. Talk. Tell them how you feel, how they *make* you feel. They love you, you know. They don't mean to hurt you."

She didn't look at him. "How do you know they love me?"

Because I love you, and I can't imagine anyone not loving you. "You're a beautiful, giving, caring person. What's not to love?"

Her face tilted toward him, and he saw a fresh rush of tears. He kissed one away from her cheek. "Talk to them, Em. Don't let them leave like this." He stroked her cold fingers, then enfolded them in his own. "Anything can happen, I learned that with Max. Time is too short to waste, and there are too many needy people in the world to turn away those that love you."

She squeezed her eyes shut and tightened her lips, as if trying to silence herself. Judd stood, then pulled her to her feet. "Go. Talk to them. I'll get showered and dressed."

"In other words, you intend to stay out of the way?"

He grinned at her grumbling tone. "I think that might be best. But I'll be here if you need me."

She stared up at him, her eyes huge, her lashes wet with tears, and Judd couldn't stop himself from kissing her. He'd wanted to spend this last day with her, to fill himself with her because after tomorrow, he'd have no reason to be in her house, no reason to keep her close. No reason to love her. He pulled back slowly, but placed another kiss on the corner of her mouth, her chin, the tip of her nose.

"You'd better get a move on before they leave. The ten minutes you gave them is almost up."

She laughed. "If you knew my parents, you'd know how little that mattered. They think I'm on the road to ruin. I doubt they're about to budge one inch." Then she hugged him. "Thank you, Judd. You're the very best."

As she left the bedroom, he grinned, hoping she'd work things out, and wondering at the same time...the best of what?

chapter 10

UNFORTUNATELY, IT RAINED. EMILY FELT THE dampness seep through her thick sweater and slacks. But she supposed the rain was good for one thing—it made her less conspicuous lurking around the back of abandoned warehouses.

Leaving today hadn't been too difficult. Judd had gone on his errands before her, and her parents, though they had stayed in town, hadn't remained at her house. They had talked a long time yesterday, and her mother had said they hoped to "work things out." They'd been apologetic, and they'd listened. Emily wondered at their change of heart, and if they'd still feel the same after she went against their wishes and brought charges against Clayton Donner.

This particular produce warehouse had several gates where a semi could have backed up to unload its goods. Three feet high and disgustingly dirty, the bottom of the gate proved to be a bit of a challenge as Emily tried to hoist herself up. The metal door was raised just enough for her to slip through, and although she still had time before Donner was due to arrive, she wanted to be inside, safely ensconced in her hiding place so there'd be no chance of her being detected.

The flesh of her palms stung as they scraped across the rough concrete ledge. Her feet pedaled air before finding something solid, and then she slid forward, wedging herself under the heavy, rusting door. She blinked several times to adjust her vision, then wrinkled her nose at the stale, fetid air. Donner had certainly picked an excellent place to do his business. It didn't appear as though anyone had been inside in ages.

Emily got to her feet, then hastily looked around for a place where she could hide, and still be able to take her pictures. The warehouse was wide open, so she should be able to capture the deal on film. The entire perimeter was framed with stacks of broken crates and rusted metal shelving, garbage and old machine parts. Not a glimpse of the vague light penetrating the dirty windows reached the corners, so that's where Emily headed. She shuddered with both fear and distaste. But she reminded herself that it could easily have been Judd here, risking his life. That thought proved to be all the incentive she needed.

Just as she neared the corner, she heard the screeching whine of unused pulleys and one of the gates started to move. With her heart in her throat, she ducked behind the crates and crouched as low as she could. She wondered, a little hysterically, if they would hear her heart thundering. She listened as footfalls sounded on the concrete floor, and voices raised and lowered in casual conversation. Then she forced herself to relax; no one was aware of her presence.

When Donner and the man from the picture came to stand directly in front of her, not twenty feet away, Emily silently fumbled for her camera. A van backed up to the gate, and the driver got out—Emily recognized him as Mick—and began unloading wooden cases. She almost smiled in anticipation, despite her nervousness.

Just a few more minutes and… A soft squeaking sounded near her. Emily didn't dare move, her heart once again starting on its wild dance. Then she heard it again. She very carefully tilted her head to the side and peered around her. Then she saw the red eyes. *Oh my Lord, Emily!* A dark, long-bodied rat stared at her.

She drew a slow deep breath and tried to ignore the creature. But it seemed persistent, inching closer behind her where she couldn't see it. She felt the touch of something, and tried not to jerk. The camera was in her hands, she had a clear shot between the crates where she hid, and Donner was winding up his business. All she needed was a single picture.

The rat tried to climb the crate beside her, using her leg as a ladder. Emily bit her lip to keep from breathing too hard. And she was good, very good. She didn't make a single sound.

But the damn rat did.

A broken crate collapsed when the rodent tried to jump toward her, and in a domino effect, other containers followed and Emily found herself exposed. She fell back, trying to hide, but not in time. Within a single heartbeat, she heard the click of a gun, then Donner's voice as he murmured in a silky tone, "Well, well. If it isn't the little bird. This should prove to be interesting."

JUDD CURSED, not quite believing what he'd just seen. How had she known? He'd been so damn careful, even going as far as faking frustration to make her believe that the deal had been called off. But somehow she had found out. And now she was inside, with Donner holding a gun on her. He lowered himself away from the window, then swiped at the mixture of rain and nervous sweat on his forehead. His stomach cramped.

Cold terror swelled through him, worse than anything he'd ever known, but he pushed it aside. He couldn't panic now, not if he hoped to get her out of there alive. His men were stationed around the warehouse, but at a necessary distance so they wouldn't be detected. Judd had planned to make the deal, recording it all through the wire he wore, then walk out just as his men arrived, making a clean bust. Now he'd have to improvise.

Speaking in a whisper so that Donner and the others wouldn't hear, he said into the wire, "Plans have changed. We'll have to move now, but cautiously. There's a woman inside, and I'll personally deal with anyone who endangers her." He allowed himself one calming breath, then said, "I'm going in."

With icy trickles of rain snaking down his neck, he took one final peek through the grimy window, then lowered himself and inched forward until it appeared he'd just arrived directly at the back entrance of the warehouse. His stance changed to one of nonchalance, and he walked through the door beside the gate.

Emily looked up at him in horror. Mick, his grin feral, held her tightly, with her arms pulled behind her back. Donner and the other man stood beside him. Judd feigned surprise, then annoyance. "What the hell is she doing here?"

Donner smiled, then inclined his head. "I'd thought to ask you that when you arrived. You're late."

With a casual flip of his wrist, Judd checked his watch. "Four o'clock exactly. I'm never late. Now, what's she doing here? I didn't want her involved."

"As you can see, she's very much involved." Donner held up a camera. "I believe she had some photography in mind."

"Damn." Then he stomped over to Emily. "I thought I told you to knock that crap off?"

He gave an apologetic grimace to Donner. "She's been thinking of doing a damn exposé on the east end. She's taken pictures of every ragtag kid, every gutter drunk or gang punk she can find. Annoys the hell out of me with that garbage."

Donner gave a lazy blink. "I think she's stepped a little over the line this time."

Judd lifted an eyebrow. "Got some interesting pictures, did she?" He turned to Emily, chiding her. "You just don't know when to quit, do you?"

"Actually," Donner persisted, "I don't think she took a single photo. But that's not the point, now, is it?"

Judd crossed his arms over his chest. "If you mean what I think you mean, forget it. I'm not done with her."

"Oh?"

"She promised to buy me a Porsche. I've been wanting one of those a long time."

Donner moved his gaze to Emily. With a nod from him, Mick pulled her arms a little tighter. The dark sweater stretched over her breasts and her back arched. Judd had to lock his jaw.

"After today, you won't need her. We can make plenty of money together." He dropped the small camera and ground it beneath his heel, then paced away from Emily. "Get it over with. We've been here too long already and there's plenty more to do." As he spoke, he watched Judd.

Knowing Donner was waiting for a reaction, Judd did his very best to maintain an air of disgust. But his mind raced and he tried to gauge his chances of taking on all three of them. He planned his move, his body tense, his mind clear.

The man from the picture grinned. He hefted an automatic weapon in his hand, the very same make that had been sold to Emily's brother. He held the gun high in his outstretched hand and aimed at Emily. Judd roared, lurching toward him, just as the gun exploded.

EMILY SQUEEZED her eyes shut, so many regrets going through her mind, all in a single second. She'd been a fool, a naive fool, thinking she could help, thinking she might make a difference. She'd ruined everything, and now Judd would die, because of her.

She heard the blast of the gun and jerked. But she felt no pain. A loud scream tore through the warehouse, echoing off the stark walls. She opened her eyes and realized the man who'd intended to shoot her was now crouching on the cold floor, his blackened face held in his hands. Blood oozed from between his fingers. The gun had backfired?

Judd reacted with enraged energy. His fist landed against Donner, who seemed shocked by what had just happened. She felt Mick loosen his hold and she threw herself forward, landing hard on her knees and palms, her shoulders jarring from the impact.

And then the room was flooded with men.

There was so much activity, it took Emily a moment to realize it was all over, that Donner and his men were being arrested. Judd appeared at her side, helping her to sit up.

"Are you all right?"

His voice sounded strange, very distant and cold. She brushed off her palms, trying to convince her heart that everything was now as it should be. Her throat ached and speaking proved difficult. "I'm fine. Just a little shaken."

Lifting her hands, Judd stared at her skinned palms, and his eyes narrowed. "I think you should go to the hospital to get checked over."

After flexing her shoulders, still sore from the way Mick had held her and the impact on the hard floor, Emily rubbed her knees. "No. That's not necessary—"

"Dammit! For once, will you just do as I tell you?"

Her heart finally slowed, in fact it almost stopped. He sounded so angry. She supposed he had the right. After all, she'd really messed things up and nearly gotten them both killed. *You might as well begin apologizing now, Emily. From the looks of him, it's going to take a lot to gain his forgiveness.* She reached out to take his hand. "Judd, I—"

He came to his feet in a rush and his eyes went over her, lingering on the dark slacks. He ground his jaw and looked away. An ambulance sounded in the distance, and when Emily looked around, she realized the man who'd been about to shoot her was very seriously wounded. Donner looked as though he wasn't feeling too well, either. He'd been close enough to receive some of the blast from the gun, and he bore a few bruises and bloody gashes from his struggle with Judd.

A passing officer caught Judd's eye, and he was suddenly hauled over to stand before Emily. Judd seemed filled with annoyance. "See that she gets to the hospital. I want her checked over."

"Yes, sir."

Remarkably, Judd started to walk away. Emily grabbed for him. Her hands shook and her heart ached. "Judd? Will I see you later at the house?"

He didn't look at her. "I already got my stuff out. Your house is your own again. Go home and rest, Em. We can question you later."

She watched him walk away, not quite believing her eyes, not wanting to believe it could end so easily. And then it didn't matter anymore. She wasn't giving up. She may have been a fool, but she refused to remain one. She wanted Judd, and she'd do whatever it took to get him.

HE CUT HER COLD. Emily tried numerous times to reach Judd. Three weeks had passed, and the police no longer needed her as a witness. Evidently, Judd no longer needed her…for anything.

She had no reason to seek him out, but she still tried. He'd remained at the small apartment. She'd been there several times, but he either didn't answer the door, or he was so distantly polite, asking her about her brother, wishing her well, that she couldn't bear it. They might have been mere acquaintances, except that Emily felt so much more. She loved him, and even though her parents tried to convince her not to make a fool of herself, she couldn't give up.

She had tried apologizing to him for mucking things up. That had made him angry all over again, so she'd refrained from mentioning it further. John had gone to him once, to see how he was doing. Judd received her brother much better than he'd received her, and Emily felt a touch of jealousy. It bothered her even more when John claimed Judd was "absolutely miserable."

"He wants you, Emmie. I know he does. He just doesn't realize you want him, too."

Much as she wanted to believe that, she couldn't allow herself false hope. "I've made it more than clear, John. I can't very well force the man to love me."

But John had shrugged, a wicked grin on his face. "Why not? At least then you'd settle things, one way or another."

She thought about that. How could she "force" a man who was nearly a foot taller and outweighed her by ninety pounds? She decided to try talking to him one more time, and went directly to his apartment. His old battered truck sat out front, and as Emily passed, something different caught her eye. At first, she had no idea what it was, and then it struck her.

She bent next to the driver's window and peered inside. The black lace that used to hang so garishly from his rearview mirror had been replaced by the tie from her dress. Emily vaguely remembered that night when Judd had shoved the pale strip of material into his back pocket moments before they'd made love.

And now it had a place of prominence in his truck.

It was ridiculous how flattered she felt by such a silly thing, but she suddenly knew, deep in her heart, that he did care. At least a little.

She remembered the day he'd allowed her to indulge her fantasies. He'd said he had fantasies of his own, and he'd whispered erotic suggestions to her while they made love, wicked things about her really stripping—performing for him. She had been mortified and excited at the same time. Some of the things he'd suggested had been sinfully arousing, and she'd promised herself, once she could gain the courage, she'd fulfill every single one of his fantasies.

But she hadn't. She'd let inhibitions get in her way, even though she knew how wild it would make him. But maybe it wasn't too late. Maybe she could still set things right between them, and show him how much she loved him by giving him everything she possibly could.

She started away from the truck, her confidence restored. But she stopped dead when a little old lady blocked her path.

"What were you doing there, girl?"

"I..." What should she say? That she was admiring an article of her clothing, strung from a rearview mirror like a masculine trophy? That she intended to seduce a man? *Get a grip, Emily.* "I was just about to call on my...brother. I see his truck is here, so I know he must be—"

"He ain't home. He's taken to walkin' in the park every evening. Usually picks up a few necessaries for me while he's out."

"I see." Emily's disappointment was obvious.

"I'm the landlady here. You want me to give him a message?"

"No. I had hoped to...surprise him." Her mind whirled. "It's his birthday today. And since he doesn't have any other family, I thought maybe I could make this day...special."

"His birthday, you say? Well, now we can't let it go by without a little fun, can we? I could let you into the apartment, if that's what you're wantin'."

Already Emily's pulse began racing. "Yes, that would be wonderful. And I promise, he'll be so surprised."

JUDD DRAGGED himself up the steps to his apartment. The weather had been considerably mild lately, and he wore only a T-shirt with his jeans. The early-evening air should have refreshed him, but he still felt hollow. He'd felt that way ever since Emily had been endangered—by his own design.

His drive, his need to see Clayton Donner sent to jail, had clouded his reason and cost him his heart. He'd thought losing Max had been the ultimate hurt, but knowing he'd endangered Emily, knowing he'd risked her life, used her, loved her, was slowly killing him. He couldn't bear to face himself in the mirror.

He also knew he'd love her forever, and it scared the hell out of him. Time and distance hadn't helped to diminish what he felt. But what could he do? Ask her to forgive him, to spend her life with him? How could he? She deserved better than him. Her grace was always with her, whether she was working at the soup kitchen, or sneaking into a warehouse full of danger. She was elegance personified, and he was a man who went to any extreme to get what he wanted, to see a job done, including stripping off his clothes for a pack of hungry women.

Self-disgust washed over him. He rubbed his face, wishing he could undo the past and be what Emily deserved.

Mrs. Cleary met him in the hallway, a huge smile spread over her timeworn features. Struck dumb for a moment, Judd stared.

"Did you fetch my bread and eggs?"

"Here you go, Mrs. Cleary. Are you sure you don't need anything else?" Judd had taken to the older woman with her gruff complaints and constant gossip. He figured she was probably every bit as lonely as he was.

"No, I got all I need. Now you run on home. And happy birthday."

Judd blinked. "But..." She winked at him, and he decided against correcting her assumption. Age could be the very devil, and if she wanted to believe it was his birthday, for whatever reason, he'd let her. "Thanks."

When he reached his apartment and stepped inside, he knew right away that something was different. He could feel it. All his instincts kicked in, and he looked around with a slow, encompassing gaze. His bedroom door was shut.

That seemed odd. Then odder still, music began to play. He recognized the slow, brassy rhythm as one of his favorite CDs, and his instincts took over. Without real thought, he inched his way to the cabinet where he kept his Beretta, slowly slid it into his palm, and crept forward.

The beat of the music swelled and moaned, and Judd flattened himself beside the door. Then, with his left hand, he slowly turned the knob and threw it open.

He waited, but no bodies came hurdling out, and he cautiously, quickly, dipped his head inside then jerked back to flatten himself against the wall.

No. It took his mind a second to assimilate what he'd just seen, and still, he didn't believe it. He blinked several times, then peeked into the room again.

Yes. That was Emily.

Standing in the center of his rumpled bed.

He moved to block the doorway, his gun now held limply at his side. The black leather jacket he'd used as part of his stripping costume hung around her shoulders, the sleeves dropping past her fingertips. It wasn't zipped, and he could see a narrow strip of bare, pale flesh, from her black lace bra to her skimpy lace panties. Her navel was a slight shadow framed by the zipper and black leather.

Max's hat sat at a rakish angle on her head. She grinned.

Sweat on his palms made it necessary for him to set the gun aside. He stumbled to the dresser, then took two steps toward her before he stopped, unsure of himself, unsure of her.

With her eyes closed, her hips swayed to the music. As he watched, her face blossomed with color—and the jacket fell away.

He licked his lips, trying to find some moisture in his suddenly dry mouth. It had been three long weeks, three *endless* weeks, since he'd made love to Emily. She lifted her arms over her head, her nipples almost escaping the sheer lace, and he felt his body harden. His erection grew long and full, pressing against his suddenly tight jeans.

She turned on the bed, not saying a single thing. Judd breathed through his mouth as his body pulsed, his eyes glued to the sight of her small bottom encased in black lace. Her hips swayed and his erection leaped, along with his heart.

Emily reached behind her back to unhook her bra. He took another step closer. He wanted to ask her what this meant, but he was afraid to speak, afraid she'd stop—afraid she wouldn't. When she turned around, she tossed the bra to him.

It hit him in the chest and fell to the floor. He couldn't move. He couldn't blink. He could barely force air past his restricted lungs.

The hat fell off when she bent slightly at the waist, hooking her thumbs in the waistband of her panties. The blush had spread to encompass her throat, her breasts. Her pointed nipples flushed a dark rose. The music picked up, hitting a crescendo and crashing into a final, raging beat.

Emily released the panties and they slid down her slender thighs, landing against his disheveled covers and pooling around her feet.

Judd stared at the triangle of dark glossy curls and his nostrils flared. He started toward her.

She raised one hand and he stopped. "We need to talk, Judd."

"Talk?" His mind felt like mush, his body, like fire.

"I realized desperate measures were necessary to get your attention."

"Believe me, Em. You have my attention." It was an effort, but he managed to force his gaze to her earnest face.

She lifted her chin. Her lips trembled for a moment. "I hope you'll understand. Sometimes we have to do outrageous things to meet our ends. Just as you had to strip to trap Donner, well, I had to strip to…trap you." She clenched her hands together, and then she blurted out, "I love you."

"You…" He'd been engrossed with her odd comparison, and the fact she'd evidently understood his motives all along. And she hadn't blamed him for doing whatever needed to be done. He'd been wrong about that.

But now his thoughts crashed down. She couldn't have said what he thought she'd said. "You…love me?"

"Yes. I love you. I want you. Forever. I realize I'm not quite what you had in mind for a…a woman."

"A wife?"

"Well, yes. That would probably be the most logical thing, considering how I feel."

"You love me?"

She made an exasperated sound and propped her fists on her naked hips. His body throbbed.

"Didn't I just say so? Twice?"

"I believe you did."

"Well? Do you think you can come to love me? I realize this is probably not very…fair of me. To try to seduce you—"

"You passed 'try' when the music began."

"Oh. I see. Well, then, you should know, I expect everything. Our…reactions to each other are…very satisfying, but I want more."

"You want me to marry you?"

She tromped over to the edge of the bed, bringing her breasts a mere foot from his face. He swallowed, then gave up trying to keep his gaze focused.

He put first one knee, then the other on the bed and wrapped his arms around her, pressing his mouth to her soft naked belly. "I love you, too, Em. God, I love you."

Her fingers clenched in his hair. "Really?"

"I was afraid to love you, but it happened, anyway."

"You were afraid?"

He nodded, then nuzzled one pointed nipple. "You deserve so much better."

Her fingers tightened and pulled. Wincing, he looked up at her. "Don't you ever say that again! You're the finest, the most caring man I've ever known."

He saw her intent expression, her anger, and felt himself begin to believe. "Our backgrounds—"

"Damn our backgrounds!"

Judd blinked. Cursing from Emily? He felt shocked, and ridiculously happy.

"You rose above your upbringing, Judd. Despite all your disadvantages, you're a hero." Her fingers tightened again and she brought his head against her. "You're my hero."

"No."

"Yes! I'm not giving you pity, because you don't need it. I'm only giving you the truth. I love everything about you." She swallowed hard, then gentled her hold on his hair, smoothing her hand over his crown. "And you make me feel loved. Nothing else matters. We can work out the rest."

"The rest?"

"I love my house, Judd. I'd like us to live there."

"I'd…I'd like that too. But Emily, I'm not a pauper. I've never had anything to spend my money on, so I have a hefty savings—"

Her fingers touched his mouth. "I never thought you were helpless, Judd. And we'll support each other, okay? That is, if you can tolerate my parents. They do seem to be trying."

He pulled her down until she knelt in front of him. "Marry me, Emily."

Her eyes, those huge, eat-a-man-alive eyes, fairly glowed with happiness. She kissed him, all over his face, his ear, his shoulder. "Yes," she shouted, "Oh, Judd, I love you."

As they both began trying to wrestle his clothes from his body, Judd said, "Promise me you'll strip for me again later. You took me so much by surprise, I think I might have missed something."

Her blush warmed him, and she smiled. "Whatever you say, Detective." And then he made love to her.

★ ★ ★ ★ ★

RILEY

chapter 1

"RAISE YOUR KNEES."

Wide-eyed, breathless and straining, she said, *"No,"* in such a scandalized voice that Riley Moore grinned. That was the thing about Red—she made him laugh, made him feel light-hearted when he hadn't thought such a thing would be possible ever again. Not a bad start.

But he had other things to accomplish here besides smiling.

"I'm not letting you up till you do." Hell, he'd be happy to stay put for hours. Not only did she amuse him, she also aroused him more than any woman he'd ever known. Her body was slight but very soft, a nice cushion under his larger, harder frame. And the warmth he felt in the cradle of her thighs could drive him over the edge.

Her big green eyes darted left and right. "Riley, people are *watching.*"

"I know." He decided to taunt her. After all, this was important. She needed to learn how to handle him. No sense in wasting all his instruction. "They're waiting to see if you've learned anything through all these lessons. Most of them think not. Others are pretty damn doubtful."

New determination drew her slim auburn brows down into a frown and turned her green eyes stormy. Suddenly her knees were along his sides, catching him off guard with the carnality of it. While his mind wandered down a salacious path, she bucked, rolled—and onto his back he went.

Proud as a peahen, she bounced on his abdomen and cheered herself. Wrong move, sweetheart, he thought, and deftly flipped her straight back and into the same position that she'd just escaped, except that this time her legs were trapped around his waist. With the wind temporarily knocked out of her, she gasped.

Half frustrated, half amused, Riley straightened. Because he knew his own ability, even if most others didn't, he always utilized strict control and caution. Especially with women, and most especially with Red. He'd sooner break his own leg than ever bruise her.

He pulled her upright, forced her arms straight up high to help her breathe, and shook his head. "When you get the upper hand on an attacker, honey, you do not stop to congratulate yourself."

Seeing that the display was over, the crowd dispersed, going back to their own training. Riley stood and gently pulled Regina Foxworth to her feet. She wasn't necessarily a short woman, but next to his height, she seemed almost puny. The top of her head reached his shoulder. Her wrists were like chicken bones. Narrow shoulders, a delicate frame…and yet, she wanted him to teach her self-defense.

Riley snorted. Hell, whenever he got this close to her he had things other than fighting on his mind. And the fact that, regardless of what he'd tried to teach her, she still ended up on her back with him in the mounted position put all kinds of considerations in his mind.

Like what it'd be like to have her situated that way, with no clothes between them and without her attempting to escape.

Soon, he promised himself. Very soon.

In a huff, Regina promptly jerked away and began straightening her glorious red hair. If the woman thought half as much about applying herself as she did about her appearance, they'd make more progress.

For her lessons today she'd restrained her hair in a braid as thick as his wrist that hung to the middle of her back. Already silky tendrils had worked loose, giving her a softened, just-laid look. Riley shook his head in awe. He worked with other women and they just got sweaty and rumpled. Not Regina. Somehow, no matter what, the woman always managed to look more appealing.

Watching her tidy her braid sent tension rippling through his muscles. A man could conjure quite a few fantasies over that hair, not to mention the delicate, ultrafeminine body that came with it. Hell, he even found the sprinkling of freckles over her nose adorable.

Riley snatched up a towel. "Quit pouting, Red."

"I'm not." But her bottom lip stuck out in a most becoming way. Normally a princess like her wouldn't have appealed to him. But Red had guts beneath the fussy exterior. And in the time he'd known her, he'd also realized she was gentle, compassionate, understanding, and damn it, he wanted her, had from the very start.

If that had been his only problem, he'd have coaxed her into bed by now. But it was more than that. He hadn't thought to ever want involvement with another woman, but he wanted it with Red.

Riley slung his arm around her shoulders and headed her toward the shower. Not that she needed to shower. The natural fragrance of her skin and hair was warm and womanly. His body tensed a bit more in masculine awareness, on the verge of cramping. "We're wasting our time with these lessons."

"I need to be able to defend myself."

True enough. Three weeks ago, Regina had been caught in a burning building while on assignment for the *Chester Daily Press.* As a reporter, she liked to stick her cute little freckled nose into places where it didn't belong, and that particular building had been in a disreputable part of town. That should have been her first clue not to be there. The fact that the fireworks dealer had already had trouble in the past should have been her second.

She'd forged on anyway and had come damn close to dying for her efforts. Most were inclined to call the fire an accident due to the shoddy management of the owner, who left opened pyrotechnics scattered around. But there was more to it. Long before Red got caught up in that fire, she'd been afraid. Riley first met her while she attempted to interview his friend, Ethan, for commendable work as a firefighter. Even then, she'd been as jumpy as a turkey on Thanksgiving morning. She'd seemed so strained, Riley had expected her to scream at any minute.

The day after the interview, she'd come into his gym and asked for lessons to protect herself. Unlike most of the women who approached him with the same request, Red had seemed more desperate, as if she needed the lessons for an imminent threat, not for general assurances.

Before the fire, he'd discarded her claims of endangerment, as had the county police where he worked as an evidence tech. *They* still didn't believe her, but at thirty-two, through life and some hard lessons, Riley had learned to read people, to sift real from feigned. Red was afraid, and he'd bet she had reason.

Someone was after her. She didn't know why. He didn't care why.

The day she'd almost died in that fire, he'd staked a claim. Little Red just hadn't figured that out yet. But no way in hell would he let anyone hurt her.

"Why don't you shower up and we'll talk about it?"

"Again?" She gave her long-suffering look. "There's nothing more to say. The police don't believe me, nothing else major has happened—"

Riley jumped on her choice of words. "What do you mean, nothing major? Has something minor happened?"

She shrugged, which did interesting things to her petite breasts. Dressed in snug biker shorts and a matching sports tank, there wasn't much of her body left to his imagination. But then, he'd wrestled with her enough and studied her in such detail that Riley already knew she had a discreet rack. Her breasts were small, firm and a definite draw to his eyes.

He could span her waist easily in his big hands, but from there she flared out. Her bottom was fuller, nicely rounded, as he liked. Not that it mattered. He already knew you couldn't judge the woman by the package. A facade of innocence, of kindness, or honor, meant nothing, less than nothing.

Regina could have looked a dozen different ways and he'd still want her because her draw on him went deeper than appearances. He felt an affinity to her, a vague basis he could trust in and that, more than anything, appealed to him. It seemed the moment he'd met her something had sparked.

So far, she'd shut him out.

"My apartment door was vandalized the other day."

Riley stopped dead in his tracks, right in front of the entrance to the women's shower. In a voice low with annoyance and disbelief, he growled, "Why the hell didn't you tell me?"

"I'm telling you now."

"Now is too damn late." He felt like shaking her, but she was so dainty a good shake would rattle her teeth.

"There were three other doors that got egged, so I figured it was random, not personal. And really, there's no threat in an egging, just an aggravation."

"Unless someone is trying to bug you enough to make you move." The fact that she lived in a nice apartment building with good security and lots of neighbors around reassured Riley many a night. It was the only thing that had kept him from forcing his pursuit of her. Because he felt she was safe at night, he intended to let her get used to him at her own pace. Little by little, he'd make his intentions known.

Still, he felt compelled to point out the facts. "I don't care what *you* figured, Red. From now on, tell me everything. I'm the expert here."

Her gaze dipped over his chest, now damp with sweat so that his T-shirt stuck to him. Wrestling with her hadn't caused any exertion, but he'd been in the private studio all morning giving lessons. Besides, just being near Red fired his blood. Having her open and vulnerable beneath him brought out a possessive sweat. He'd conquer her—in his own time.

"Yes, you're an expert, Riley." Staring up at him, her big eyes full of serious regard, she added, "At a lot of things."

"At a…" His voice trailed off. Was she coming on to him? 'Bout damn time. He crowded closer to her, letting her feel the heat of his body, instinctively overpowering her with his size and masculinity and interest. "Just what does that mean, Regina?" He sounded gruff, half-aroused, but then she had that effect on him.

Head tipped way back to meet his gaze, she sighed. "You're an amazing guy, Riley Moore. That's all I meant. I don't know any other man who used to be part of a SWAT team, now serves as a crime scene evidence technician, *and* owns his own gym."

Deflated, mouth flat, Riley said, "No."

With a ludicrous show of innocence, she blinked. "No, what?"

"No, I won't do the damn interview." He should have seen right through her. He was good at deciphering motives, but his perspective was blown around her, clouded by lust. She'd been after an interview for over a week now, but his past was just that: the past. He wouldn't dredge it up for anyone, not even Little Red.

"But—"

At that moment, Rosie Winters shoved her way out of the showers, forcing them both to back up. Now Rosie, bless her, knew how to work out. She got sweaty, red-faced and hot. *Not* more appealing. She cursed, grunted, struggled, and she gave it her all, showing constant improvement without a single thought to her hair or audience.

Like Riley, Rosie fought to win and she was now good enough that she just might stand a chance against a man without Riley's special training. But as ex-SWAT, Riley could be lethal when necessary. His job had taught him how to come out the victor in any scenario. But long before that, when he'd still been a kid, nature had taught him that he didn't like to lose.

At anything.

As one of his best friends, Rosie had been coming to his gym a lot, much to Ethan's dismay. She and Ethan had married last week, but that hadn't slowed down Rosie. Nothing slowed her down. The newlyweds supplied endless hours of entertainment with the way they clashed wills, and the way they loved.

"Hey, Riley." Rosie gave him a resounding smooch on the cheek before turning to Regina. Her brown hair, still wet, hung down her back. "I lingered in the shower so I could talk to you."

Regina lifted her brows. "Really? What about?"

"Prepare yourself," Rosie warned with a lot of suspenseful anticipation. "Your loan went through. You're all set to close on the house!"

That announcement seemed to set off both women. Regina squealed as females are wont to do, and Rosie, who never squealed, laughed heartily. But around Regina, Rosie often got pulled into the more feminine mannerisms. Like now, with Regina holding her hands and dancing in circles and bouncing around.

Watching them, Riley crossed his arms and leaned back against the wall. He just adored women, the way they reacted, their expressions, their unique mind-set that was so different from men's. Rosie and Regina couldn't be more dissimilar in most ways, yet they had similarities, too, just by virtue of being female.

It gave him pleasure to listen in—until it dawned on him what Rosie had said. He shoved away from the wall. "A house? You bought a house?"

They quieted, but both still grinned hugely. "It's adorable," Regina confided. "Just the right size for me."

"And such a great bargain," Rosie added. "Because it's empty, she can have immediate occupancy."

"Immediate occupancy?" The words emerged a dark whisper. "As in alone in a house, unprotected, immediately?"

Rosie paused. "Oh. I hadn't thought of that. I mean, it's in a nice quiet neighborhood with half-acre yards—"

"Great. Just great."

Regina gave him a level look. "Really, Riley. You act like I'll be camping in the open with wild bears all around me. I can lock my doors and windows." When he only narrowed his eyes, she added, "I'll even buy an alarm system, okay?"

"It's a lousy idea. Have you two forgotten that someone recently tried to burn you alive?"

Rosie shuddered. "I'll never forget." She'd gone with Regina that day, and damn near died because of it. "But the police seem to think that it was either vandalism that got out of hand, negligence on the part of the owner, or at the very worst, vengeance aimed at the owner, not at us."

Regina watched Riley closely. "They think we were innocent bystanders."

"Right. And that's why your camera was taken and the owner has disappeared?"

Looking guilty, Rosie turned to Regina. "Maybe he's right."

"No, he is not right. I have to live somewhere, so it might as well be my own house." She patted Riley on the chest. Though she did it negligently, without a single sign of awareness on her part, he felt the damn pat clear through to his masculine being. "I'll get an alarm system *and* a dog. How's that?"

Seeing that he wouldn't win, Riley gave up that particular argument. At least she wanted to take steps in the right direction. A big, well-trained German shepherd or Doberman would certainly be a deterrent to anyone thinking to harm her. In the meantime, he'd just have to see about advancing his courtship. Once she gave in, he'd have the right to keep her close, to watch over her.

And all her spare time would be spent in bed, giving her less time to get into trouble.

With Ethan and Rosie's rushed wedding plans, they'd been forced together more frequently than otherwise. Adding to that her lessons at the gym, he'd seen her almost daily for the past three weeks. Their time together had been platonic because he couldn't possibly wrestle with her and have romantic thoughts without embarrassing them both, and possibly breaking a few sexual harassment laws. He felt certain a boner would have been out of line.

But he knew how he felt. Maybe it was time she knew, too.

It wouldn't be a bad idea to live with her until he felt secure that she'd be safe alone. The benefits to that scenario were more than obvious. To both of them.

"When's the closing on the house?"

Rosie winced.

Resigned, Riley asked again, "How soon, Rosie?"

"Weeeelll…" Rosie cast a quick look at Regina, but she was too busy smiling over her good news to share Rosie's uncertainty. "Because the house was empty and her credit impeccable, I sort of rushed it through. We have a date set for the middle of next week."

Regina squealed again, but with Riley so subdued, she quickly quieted. "You're being such a stick in the mud, Riley. Can't you be just a little happy for me?"

If it weren't such bad timing, he would be. But he worried about her enough already without her being off on her own, away from the safety of the apartment complex. In his mind, she was already his. He wanted to protect her, not leave her safety dependent on a dog and alarm.

He studied her for a long moment, deciding how best to proceed without making her more skittish. Then he realized his stare alone had her squirming uncomfortably. He tried a smile, but it felt more predatory than anything else. "I'll take you to dinner to celebrate." He made it a statement rather than an invitation, on the off chance she thought to refuse.

Her hesitation fell heavy between them. "I don't know…"

Riley took a step closer. "Say yes, Regina."

Rosie's gaze bounced back and forth, watching them with great interest.

A blush tinged Regina's cheeks. "The thing is, I wanted to get my dog today. I figure I might as well potty train him at my apartment so he won't mess up my house."

Riley didn't let her off the hook. He waited, still watching her intently until her unease was palpable.

Finally, she sighed. "If you can come over around six, I can cook dinner at my place."

Now that sounded promising. Much better suited to his purpose than being in a crowded restaurant. "I'm on vacation for the next two weeks, so I'm at your disposal." He realized suddenly that Rosie had a vacuous grin on her face. She knew him better than Regina did, so she'd probably already realized how territorial he felt.

Glancing over his shoulder at the workout area of the gym, he said, "I have to get back on the floor. I have three more hours of personal instruction before I'm free." He touched Regina's cheek. "Promise me you'll be careful, Red."

She blinked, then stepped out of reach. Her laugh sounded forced. "It's the middle of the day. I swear, Riley, you're more fretful than I am."

That's because he knew firsthand the danger that could befall a woman alone. He shook off that dark thought and raised her chin. "Promise?"

"Cross my heart." With a last platonic pat on his chest, she said, "Don't be late."

Riley watched her disappear into the shower room, spellbound until Rosie started snickering. When he gave her his attention, she clutched her heart and pretended to swoon.

"Brat." Riley put her in a chokehold and knuckled the top of her head. Though she was gorgeous and sexy, Rosie was like a pal, permanently safe from any lecherous intentions, especially since she'd married Ethan.

"Hey," she gasped out, "no fair. I don't want to get messy again. I have a showing this afternoon."

Riley released her and got a sharp elbow to his middle. He grunted while Rosie quickly backed away. "Sucker," she said with a grin, then she turned and jogged toward the door.

Riley laughed. He did love Rosie, but he didn't want her. He didn't burn for her.

Not the way he did for Ms. Regina Foxworth.

REGINA KNEW it wasn't the wisest decision she'd ever made. And for a woman who prided herself on only making wise decisions, she should have been appalled at herself. She only had so much money for decorating her new house and putting in the alarm system that she'd promised Riley.

She tried to talk herself out of it, she really did. But as she stared at those big brown eyes, she fell madly in love. He was so cute with the way he laid his enormous ears back on his little round head, how he stared at her with bulging eyes, shivering with uncertainty. He probably wasn't the type of dog Riley had in mind, but the man said they were loyal pets, dedicated to their owners.

"I'll take him." Sometimes things just felt right. Like being a journalist. Like buying the house.

Like being near Riley.

This felt right, too. Now that she'd met this dog, no other would do, so she shelled out the six hundred dollars that she really couldn't spare. Love was love and it should never be denied. Not that she knew a lot about love. But she did know that she wanted it more than anything. And to get it, you had to give it, she reasoned. She could really love this dog.

While she carried him outside, he continued to shake and stare at her with those big, watchful eyes. She'd never seen such a pathetic look in her life. She wanted to crush him close, but he was so puny, she didn't dare. Gently, she stroked his skinny back and rubbed his soft neck.

She'd never felt a dog so soft. He had bunny fur, so cuddly and silky. And he didn't smell like a dog either. She rubbed her nose against his neck and got a tiny lick on the ear in return.

Once in the car, secured in the carrier, his teeny tiny mouth formed an O and he began to howl.

It was both hilarious, the way he looked, and heart-wrenching the way he sounded. The mournful baying continued until Regina was in a near panic. "Shh. What's wrong?" Did he want her to hold him? "I have to drive, sweetie," she explained. "It wouldn't be safe. Soon as we get home, I'll cuddle you again, I promise."

At the sound of her voice, the dog quieted and inched to the edge of the small cage to sniff the air near her. His spindly little hind legs quivered and he continued to look sad, but trusting.

"Awww…" He was just so adorable. Big tears filled her eyes. She *had* made the right decision. Sticking one finger through the carrier, Regina rubbed behind his ear. "You're as soft as a baby bunny, did you know that?"

He cocked his head, listening to her, his ears still down in a woebegone display but he made no sounds of dismay.

"What should I name you?"

The ears came up. Regina marveled at his many expressions.

"How about…Elvis?" His ears pricked, then flattened again and he gave her a sideways look. "No? Then maybe Doe? You do look like a little deer, you know. Hmm. That doesn't appeal to you either? Something more manly then. I know. Butch. Or Butchie when you're being so adorable."

Soothed by her banter, he gave an excited yap of agreement and Regina nodded. "Butch it is."

For the rest of the ride home, Regina alternated her attention between her driving and the dog. She constantly scanned the road and surrounding area, still spooked from the time someone tried to run her off the berm. To calm herself and the dog, she spoke to him, being sure to use his name as the breeder suggested, so he could get used to it.

By the time they pulled into her apartment complex, he was looking around with interest, animated anytime she spoke to him. He continued to shake though.

People were coming and going, keeping the parking lot alive with a safe, surrounding crowd. Feeling secure again, she carried Butch, along with his paraphernalia, into her apartment. She'd bought bowls, food, chew sticks, a toothbrush, leash, collar and a cozy fleece-lined bed. She set Butch down first, watched him cower there on the floor, and decided he needed some encouragement.

Her apartment was small, only one bedroom, a bath, kitchenette and living area. "I'll be right back, Butch." She went to the kitchen to unload all the items, then came back for him. She found him sprinkling her couch.

"Oh, now that's just not right, Butch."

He slunk toward her, his head down in apology.

Regina's heart melted. "Honey, it's okay." She cuddled him close, got a tentative lick on her cheek. He was the most precious perfect dog, she decided, and carried him into the kitchen since that was where he'd spend most of his time. With a kiss to the top of his round head, she put him in his bed, then went back to clean her couch. When she returned to the kitchen, she found three more wet spots. Butch looked so very contrite, she couldn't hold it against him. She understood that he was nervous and needed reassurance. Instead of chastising him, she hugged and petted him some more, trying to let him know he was safe and secure and well loved.

By the time she had dinner going and Riley was due to arrive, Butch had relaxed enough to play a little. He followed Regina everywhere she went, sometimes bounding here or there, sometimes turning excited circles. Charmed, Regina had to keep stopping to pick him up, kiss him and hug him.

Because she was on the second floor, she put a litter box on her small balcony for him to use and in no time he got the hang of going to the glass patio door to scratch. She used a short leash that kept him from reaching the edge of the balcony so he couldn't accidentally fall off and get hurt. He did his business like a trooper and came back in.

Of course, he marked his territory everywhere inside the apartment, too. Regina wasn't yet sure if he was uncertain of his boundaries, stubborn or just not very bright. She hoped the first, because the second and third didn't bode well for her peace of mind.

The chicken was done, the potatoes already mashed, when the knock sounded on her door. She recognized Riley's knock right off. Decisive, firm, just like the man himself.

Though she hated to admit it, she felt that familiar leap of her heart whenever he was near. They'd known each other three weeks now, and so far Riley had been attentive, courteous and understanding.

More important than that, he believed her somewhat wild stories about stalkers and threats when no one else would. Of course, Regina thought his belief just might be attributed to boredom. Riley used to be SWAT, for heaven's sake. He was used to excitement and danger.

In Chester, the most excitement he got was photographing old man Tilburn's house because the neighborhood rascals had toilet-papered it once again. For a man like Riley, a man of his skills and background, that had to add up to a lot of frustration. Even chasing Regina's ghosts had to be better than that.

But she wouldn't complain. Regardless of what motivated him, she needed his help, so she'd take what she could get.

She expected the thrill that skated through her when she started to open the door.

What she didn't anticipate was Butch going into a complete hostile frenzy. He transformed from tiny shivering dog into Tasmanian devil right before her eyes.

Riley called out, "Regina? It's me. Open up."

"Just a second." She picked up Butch, but holding the snarling, rigid, four-pound mass of meanness was nearly impossible. Outrage stiffened every muscle in his lean little body and he fought her to be free—so he could attack her visitor.

What a courageous dog!

Using one hand, Regina turned the locks on the door and then struggled to maintain her hold on Butch while Riley stepped inside. The dog broke free. Regina almost dropped him but managed to get him to the floor, head first.

He rolled, landed on his feet and like a shot, went after Riley.

Riley stood there, brows high, expression arrested, while Butch tried to tear his pant leg off. "What the hell? Is that a rabid squirrel?"

Indignant, Regina closed the door and crossed her arms. "Of course not. It's my dog, Butch."

"*That's* a dog?" Incredulity rang in his voice. "Are you sure?" His head tilted down at the wriggling fury hanging from his leg. "How can you tell?"

Offended on Butch's behalf, Regina huffed. She pulled the dog free and went about soothing him. "Shh. Butchie, it's okay. He's allowed in. Such a good dog. So brave."

Riley looked like he might puke. "That *is* a dog. What the hell is wrong with it?"

Regina sat on the couch. "Nothing. He's perfect."

"He can't weigh more than four pounds."

"He's four exactly." She rubbed Butch's belly and he rolled to his back, his skinny legs falling open, his eyes half-closed.

Riley pulled back. "Good God."

Regina didn't take him to task for that comment. After all, Butch was showing his equipment with no evidence of modesty whatsoever. She cleared her throat. "The breeder said I should have him neutered."

"He'll only weigh three pounds if you do." Grinning at his own joke, Riley took the seat beside her and reached out to pet the dog. Butch went berserk again, his doggy lips pulled back tight, rippling with menace, the whites of his eyes showing. One second he looked so innocent and sweet and the next he appeared like a vicious gnat.

"He needs time to get used to you," Regina explained in a rush, and hoped that was true. If Butch continued to act so contrary, what would she do?

In his usual calm manner, Riley surveyed Butch. "What kind of dog is it?"

"He's a pure bred Chihuahua. His beautiful coloring is very unique." She certainly thought him beautiful. "Red with black brindling."

Riley only nodded. "How much bigger will he get?"

"Oh, he's full-grown." She rubbed Butch's ears and watched his bulgy eyes narrow in bliss. "Isn't he just precious?"

"No." Riley frowned at her. "Please tell me this isn't your idea of a guard dog."

"But he's perfect," she said by way of answer. "You saw how he attacked you."

"And you saw how I held real still so I wouldn't accidentally hurt him."

She had noticed that. Riley was always so cautious with people, so careful. She knew a lot of that had to do with his training and his ability. It would be so easy for him to hurt someone, that he naturally tempered himself in almost all situations. Others might not be aware of his restraint, but Regina had seen it in his intense blue eyes, and she'd felt it during her lessons.

She'd also noticed that he hadn't been startled by Butch's attack. Most people would have jumped, maybe even screeched.

Not Riley. She couldn't imagine anything unsettling Riley enough to wring a screech out of him. With unparalleled calm, he'd taken in the situation and then reacted, without haste, careful not to hurt Butch.

Such an incredible guy.

Nodding, she said, "I did notice. Thank you."

Lounging back in his seat, Riley put one arm along the couch back, almost touching her shoulder. Without leaving Regina's lap, Butch slanted a mean gaze his way, his rumbling growls a warning. Riley continued to watch the dog while speaking to Regina. "When do we eat? It smells good."

Flustered by the compliment, she came to her feet, holding Butch like an infant—which he seemed to enjoy. "It's ready now. We have to eat in the kitchen. I don't have a dining room. Once I get moved in I'll have a dining room, and we can use it then. I mean, if you're ever over for dinner at my new house…." Turning her back on Riley and rolling her eyes at her own rambling nonsense, she rushed into the kitchen. Hostesses should not ramble. They should feed their guests.

Riley followed. "Regina?"

"Hmm?" She turned after setting Butch in his bed. He came right back out of it, still watching Riley, inching closer for a sniff. Now that Regina no longer held him, he was jumpy enough to lurch back a step each time Riley moved.

"We'll be having plenty of dinners together."

The sneaky way the dog advanced distracted her. "We will?"

Butch was at Riley's foot now, his sniffing more purposeful. Knowing what Butch probably intended, Regina scrambled to find a chew stick. In no way did she want Butch to mark Riley. He was not part of the permanent territory and unlikely to become so.

Riley crouched down and held out a hand to Butch. The dog gave his fingers a thorough inspection, donned an angelic expression complete with big innocent eyes and a small doggy smile, and even allowed Riley to rub under his chin. Teasing, Riley said, "You sure he wasn't bred with a rat?"

Regina, too, bent down to hand Butch the rawhide chew. The second she got near, Butch did an about-face. He snapped at Riley in warning, squirmed up close to Regina and accepted the chew.

"Contrary dog," Riley commented while standing up straight again.

Butch retreated to his bed to work over the chew. "He's getting used to you already."

Riley caught her hand and pulled her upright in front of him. Her heart pounded when his strong, warm fingers laced with hers, palm to palm.

"What about you, Red? You getting used to me, too?"

Oh boy, there was a load of innuendo in the way Riley said that. And truthfully, she was so used to him that when he wasn't around, she missed him. Dumb. Regina Foxworth did not allow herself fanciful infatuations. She thought to tell him that yes, she was used to him and why shouldn't she be? He was no different from any other man. But with his callused fingers holding hers, words stuck in her throat. She barely managed a shrug.

With his gaze holding her captive, his hand opened, slid slowly up her arm, over her shoulder and the side of her neck, along her jaw until his fingers curled around the back of her neck. Where he'd touched, gooseflesh sprang up and she trembled.

Softly, Riley whispered, "Wrong answer."

Her startled gasp emerged just as he urged her to her tiptoes. "Riley?"

"You need to accept a few things, Red."

She felt spellbound, uncertain. Anxious. But if she hesitated much longer, her chicken would burn and then she'd make a bad impression. She forced herself to say "Like?"

"Like this." He bent and kissed her.

chapter 2

THE TOUCH OF HIS MOUTH WAS BRIEF, WARM, firm. Regina barely had time to appreciate his taste before he lifted away the tiniest bit.

"Oh." Tentatively, thoughts of chicken obliterated, Regina laid her hands on his chest. He'd dressed in casual chinos and a polo shirt, but the domestic clothes couldn't hide the true nature of the man. The soft cotton fabric served an enticing contrast to the hard muscle, long bones and crisp hair underneath.

His eyes were more gray than blue now, glittering with heat. There was nothing even remotely domestic in the way he watched her. "More than anything," he rumbled low, "I'd like to carry you into your bedroom right now, strip you naked and make love all night." He closed his eyes a moment, drew a breath. When he looked at her again, some of that intense heat had been tempered. "But we've got a lot to get cleared up first."

Regina faltered. Make love all night? *Strip her naked?* They hadn't known each other *that* long. Regardless of her strong attraction to Riley, she wasn't the type of woman to leap into an affair. Responsible people utilized caution and thought before making that type of commitment.

Stepping back from him, she gestured to her tiny two-seater table. Her hand shook and she had to clear her throat twice before she could speak. "Sounds like we have a long talk ahead." Thankfully, her voice was only a little shaky. "Sit down while I serve dinner."

Riley watched her with indecision before silently agreeing. Regina could feel his gaze on her rump when she bent to pull the perfectly browned chicken out of the oven. Martha Stewart would be proud. Ms. Manners would applaud her.

As the delicious scents of stuffing and chicken wafted through the air, Butch perked up, his little nose raised and quivering with interest. Regina looked at him, but Riley said, "I wouldn't. Once you feed him table food, you'll never be able to stop. And it's not good for him anyway."

"Right." She knew that, and since she always tried to do the right thing, she hoped her dog would do the right thing as well. Giving Butch an apologetic shake of her head, she filled his bowl with dog food. Appeased, he began to eat while Regina carried the food to the table. The chicken was placed perfectly on a platter, the potatoes looked fluffy in a decorative bowl, and steam rose from the broccoli with melting butter atop it. She lit a scented candle in the middle of the table and everything was complete. Beautiful.

"What can I do to help?"

Regina stared at Riley, and he stared back, studying her. She'd expected him to sit and admire her dinner preparation skills, not watch her every move. But if he wanted to help...wasn't it a man's job to carve? She'd never had a man around long enough to know, and her father certainly hadn't been the type to worry about how food was cut. He was more a grab-and-stuff-it-in-your-mouth kind of guy.

Regina handed Riley the butcher knife and fork with a flourish. "Iced tea, milk?"

"Tea is fine." He stood to begin slicing apart the chicken. Regina noticed that he did an admirable job. He glanced up at her. "Why are you so nervous, Red?"

"I'm not."

"You are."

She sighed, unable to deny the obvious. "No more so than usual. That is, I'm always nervous." It was a complaint she often got from men. But now, with the man being Riley, she felt doubly unsettled. Add to that some unknown assailant who had tried to hurt her several times and might just try again, and to her way of thinking she had plenty of reason to be nervous.

"Because you're worried?"

"Yes." She poured the iced tea, sat, remembered she wanted music and popped back up. "I'll be right back." Seconds later, the stereo in her bedroom played low, adding soft sounds to the clink of china and silver.

Riley waited for her to return. He held her chair, but when she sat, he didn't retreat. Instead he bent down and kissed the side of her neck. Oh Lord, she'd never get used to this spontaneous kissing of his. At Mach speed, he'd taken them from acquaintances, maybe friends, to something much more intimate.

Fighting the urge to gasp again, she stiffened. Where he'd pressed his mouth, her neck tingled and felt damp. A strange but pleasant warmth rippled through her.

Riley spoke softly into her ear, adding to her awareness. "You need to be comfortable being alone with me, Red."

The way he said that, all seductive and low, made her

stomach flip-flop. "I do?" At this rate, she'd never be able to eat. It'd look like she didn't appreciate her own culinary skills.

"Yeah." He brushed her nape with the back of one finger, then circled the table and sat in his chair, facing her, casual as you please, as if he hadn't just been teasing her, turning her on.

"Um…why?"

He picked up his fork. "Starting today, we're going to be alone together." His gaze caught and held hers. "A lot."

THE FOOD WAS DELICIOUS. He'd had no idea that Regina was such a fine cook. For long moments, they ate in silence. He waited to see what Regina would say to his statement, but she just sat there, watching him cautiously, occasionally nibbling on her food.

He didn't want to spoil her dinner, so he sat back and studied her. "I guess you want me to explain?"

She cleared her throat. "That'd be nice, yes."

A starched linen napkin had been placed beside his plate. Since it was there, Riley used it to pat his mouth. "All right. You're not showing much improvement at the gym."

Her shoulders sank the tiniest bit. Riley wasn't sure if it was disappointment or relief. "I know. I'm not a very physical person."

He intended to hold all judgments on that until he had her in bed. Then he'd see just how physical he could coax her into being. "You don't need physical strength, Regina. But you do have to stop worrying about other people watching you."

She winced. "I know. It's just that I hate looking like a fool."

"Once you know what you're doing, you'll look like a pro."

"Yes, of course," she quickly agreed. "I'll try harder, I promise."

He didn't believe that for a minute. "Regina?"

She glanced up at him, her brows raised quizzically.

"I'm going to give you very private lessons from now on. Just the two of us." He looked at her mouth. "All alone. No spectators."

She stared at him for three seconds. "You are?"

Riley nodded, a little put out that she questioned every damn thing he said, like she couldn't believe it or doubted it to be true. He wasn't a liar, damn it.

Stunned by that mental statement, he shook his head and made a quick amendment: he wouldn't lie to *her,* and not about this. Other lies, lies from his past, were well buried.

Holding on to his patience, Riley continued his explanation. "There's not much room here at your place, so we can't really get going tonight."

Her mouth opened. In anticipation, shock or horror? Riley couldn't quite tell. "You can either come to my place, or the gym after hours."

She held perfectly still. Tonight she had her thick hair twisted at the back of her head and held in place with a fancy gold clip. It had been somewhat loosened by the kiss he'd given her earlier. The fluorescent overhead lights brought out the deeper reds and lighter golds, mixed in with the auburn. It also reflected the wariness in her green eyes.

She wore a freshly pressed sleeveless green V-neck shirt and low-riding cotton slacks. Her sandals showed off her meticulous pedicure.

From the top of her head to the tips of her toes, she was polished to a shine. She'd even managed to do dinner with no additional mess, putting things away as she used them so that no empty pans sat on the stove and no seasonings were out.

Riley wanted to see her mussed.

He wanted to see her sweat.

He wanted to hear Ms. Suzy Homemaker crying out in raw

sexual excitement without a single thought as to how she looked, concerned only with the deep, driving pleasure.

Damn, he had to stop that train of thought or he'd be seducing her right now.

Finally, she nodded. "Thank you." Her voice sounded a little raspy. "It does embarrass me. I think it'll be easier without others watching. But, Riley, mostly it's you that I worry about."

"Me?" Sipping his iced tea, he watched her, thinking it wasn't such a bad thing if he unsettled her. It meant she held at least a small amount of awareness for him as a man.

She pleated her napkin. She straightened her fork. Suddenly she blurted, "Are you attracted to me?"

"Yes."

She seemed surprised by his immediate answer. Then she chewed on her lips. "I'm attracted to you, too."

She made that admission with the same regret she might have given a murder confession.

"I know." He hadn't known. He'd hoped. He was pretty sure. But he'd wanted confirmation.

Now he had it.

"It...bothers me, the idea of you seeing me all messy and sweaty."

Hearing her say it sharpened his desire. "Eventually, I'll see you every way there is." He toyed with his iced tea glass, his gaze never wavering from hers. "When we have sex, you'll definitely be sweaty. Messy, too. That's the way it is with good sex. But I'm willing to bet you'll look hot as hell."

Her breathing deepened and her brows puckered in thought. After a long hesitation, she said, "You, um, you treat Rosie like a pal."

"Rosie is a pal."

"But she's also a very attractive woman."

Leaning back in his seat, Riley nodded. "Agreed."

"And yet you never have romantic thoughts about her because she's become your pal."

Riley had no idea where she was going with this. Women could be so confusing, even to a man who prided himself on getting past the surface stuff. Oh, he could detect some of her thoughts. She was uncertain, interested, wary. But he wanted to know *why* she felt so uncertain.

He eyed her, then decided a little truth couldn't hurt the situation. "Who says?"

Confusion left her face blank. "Who says... Well, Rosie said. She assured me that she loved Ethan and—"

"She does." It had recently become very clear that Rosie had always loved Ethan—she'd just been waiting around for him to come to his senses and realize that he loved her, too.

"—and that Ethan was a good friend of yours."

"He is." With Harris and Buck, they made a regular foursome, but he and Ethan had more in common. They were all friends, but if Riley ever had his back to the wall, he'd trust Ethan more than any other man.

"Then—"

"You think because we're friends, I shouldn't have sexual thoughts about her?" He stretched out his long legs beneath the table and bumped into her small feet. "You and I are friends, and I have plenty of sexual thoughts about you."

Her eyes widened comically. "Plenty?"

It was his turn to smile. "All day, every day, as a matter of fact."

She stewed on that for a bit before speaking again. "But see, that's just it. I thought you felt about me the way you feel about Rosie, except you're closer with her."

"Not a chance."

"You're not close to her?"

"Very close. But the way I feel about you is on the other end of the scale. I don't intend to ever sleep with Rosie." He let his gaze drop to her breasts. "You, however, I intend to get naked with just as soon as it can be arranged."

Her eyes dilated in shock, but he also saw reciprocal interest in the way her breathing deepened and how her skin warmed. Despite all that, she shook her head. "You should probably know, Riley, I don't sleep around."

"You're a virgin?"

More color stained her cheeks and she frowned. "No, I didn't say that." Then she added in a mumble, "For heaven's sake, I'm twenty-eight years old."

"So you're saying you don't want to sleep with me?" He knew damn good and well that wasn't true. But would she be honest?

"Of course I do."

He grinned.

"I mean, I do, but I'm not going to. Not anytime soon, that is. We barely know each other."

He'd known her long enough to understand exactly how he felt. "We've known each other better than three weeks now. That's not exactly a sneeze. And because of the lessons, we've been physically close."

"You're keeping count?"

She was clearly astonished by that. Hell, it still stunned Riley a little, the depth of what he felt. But he didn't want her panicking on him, so he backed off. "Let's finish eating, then we'll talk about it more. By the way, you're a hell of a cook. I'm impressed."

Relieved by the change of topic, she nodded. "I wanted you to be. Impressed, I mean." She caught herself and her gaze jerked up to his. "That is, I try to impress everyone."

"Yeah? Why is that, Red? You don't think just being yourself is good enough?" There was so much he still had to learn about her. Funny how appearances meant nothing to him because they weren't something you could trust. Yet, they meant the world to her.

The contrast in their views might have discouraged him, but he figured he was at least making headway now.

"Maybe." She propped her head on her hand, realized that wasn't the proper way to sit and jerked upright again. "Actually I've thought about this a lot, about why I'm the way I am. Every so often, I wish I could be different because sometimes it has the opposite effect and just drives people nuts."

"What people?"

"Co-workers, friends. Men."

He didn't give a damn what other men thought of her. If they steered clear, hell, he was glad. "Rosie and Ethan and Buck and Harris like you fine." He smiled. "I like you more than fine. But I am curious why you're so worried about what other people think. That is, if you care to talk about it."

She pleated and fussed with her napkin. "It's silly really. Maybe something of a habit left over from when I was young."

"You were a fussy child?"

His teasing put a self-conscious half smile on her face. "Yes. Very fussy, I guess. See, I came from a...a dirty farmhouse." She wrinkled her nose with that confession. "And when I say dirty, I'm not exaggerating. It's awful to admit, but we lived like pigs."

Not sure that he understood, Riley asked, "You were poor?"

"Poor and slovenly are not the same thing, but yes, we were poor, too. I've never been certain if it was necessary, if they just couldn't make enough money or if they simply misman-aged what they made." She shrugged. "My parents sustained us from paycheck to paycheck. If we ran out in the middle of the week, or something came up—as things always do—they'd borrow or beg."

The expression on her face twisted his heart. Softly, he said, "That had to be rough."

"I hated it and it embarrassed me."

The emotional plethora took Riley off guard. Being a private man, he couldn't imagine discussing so much of his personal background. "So you've worked to change your life. There's nothing wrong with that."

"It was never my life." She sipped her tea, scooted her broccoli around on her plate with the edge of her fork. "It was my mother's, my father's and my younger brother's. But not mine."

No, Riley couldn't quite imagine her ever being comfortable in those circumstances. She was so prim, proper and precise now, that it must have been almost painful for her.

"You didn't accept the circumstances of your youth."

"For as far back as I can remember, even as a young kid, I tried to make it different. Everything I owned was old and stained, but I did my best to always keep it clean and pressed." She glanced up at him and gave a low laugh. "My brother used to make fun of me for being so meticulous. The other kids we knew…. They liked to call us names and poke fun at us."

Riley hated that anyone had hurt her feelings, even though it had happened long ago. And her brother… It was ridiculous to be angry at him when he'd been no more than a boy, too. But that didn't change how Riley felt. "Kids can be pretty cruel when no one is teaching them better."

"Maybe. But if you'd ever seen our farm or car or how my parents behaved in public, you'd understand why the kids treated us the way they did. I understood it. And I knew my family would never change. After I graduated high school, I moved away, got a job as an errand girl with a small paper and worked my way up to reporter."

Riley smiled. Reporter was a bit of a stretch considering the small pieces she wrote. Then again, her human-interest stories for the local paper were always entertaining. She'd done a stellar article on Ethan that had made the fire department, as well as the whole town, proud.

Riley thought about it and decided selective sharing was good. It forged a bond that would bring them closer together, and that was his ultimate goal. There were parts of himself he could discuss, parts that weren't buried deep and that wouldn't reveal anything beyond the surface.

He mentally skimmed a variety of topics and settled on his safest bet—family. "My mother isn't immaculate or anything."

Her interest obvious, she glanced up at him with a smile. "No?"

"She keeps the place tidy, but it's always well lived in. I have two younger brothers, one older."

"Four boys? My goodness."

"Yeah, Mom felt the same way." He laughed. "The others still live near to home and they drop in a lot with their broods. Between the three of them, I have ten nieces and nephews."

"Wow. A big family."

He acknowledged that with a shrug. "Mom is old-fashioned, the type who wants to feed you the minute you show up and fusses around you the whole time you're there. I haven't been home to see her in a while." That was something he should remedy, Riley decided. Funny that he hadn't much considered how long it had been until Regina started discussing her family.

Wondering how Regina would react to the casual mess around his mother's house, he pushed his plate away. "Maybe next time I go, you could come along with me."

Her eyes shot wide. "You want me to meet your mother?"

She sounded as if he'd asked her to swim with sharks. "And Dad, too. You'd like them."

She had nothing to say to that so Riley pressed her. "What about your folks? Do you visit with them at all?" He wouldn't really be surprised if she'd broken all ties, but it'd be a shame. When all was said and done, family should be there for you, and vice versa.

"They're gone now." There was a wistful, sad note to her voice. "Mom died years ago from cancer and Dad passed away from a stroke two years after. The farm was sold and my brother and I split the profits. That's how I bought my house. I've been sitting on that money for a while."

Riley had wondered about that. He didn't imagine a small-town reporter earned much income. "I'm sorry."

"It was a long time ago. I loved them, but I was never very close with them. We had a…strained relationship." She hesitated, and Riley wondered if she'd pull back now, if she'd return to being evasive. Instead, she shrugged. "They thought I was snooty."

With almost no prodding at all, she continued to open up to him. In his experience, reporters pried into anyone and everyone's life, but clammed up when it came to their own personal issues. He couldn't help wondering if her openness was a compliment reserved for special people. Did she feel safer with him? Did she trust him?

"Snooty, huh?" He pretended to study her head to toe, then nodded. "Circumspect, yes. Meticulous, maybe. But not snooty."

"Thank you." She tucked in her chin to hide her smile. "My brother still accuses me of thinking I'm better than them."

"Do you?"

"Think I'm better? No. But I'm certainly wiser about how I handle my life." Her long look seemed like a warning, one he fully intended to ignore. He would have her, and soon. "My parents had a great farm that they let go to ruin because they refused to do any real work. It should have been worth five

times as much, but they'd never taken care of it. The house was
so run-down it had to be demolished. There wasn't a piece of
furniture or a dish to be salvaged."

"No mementos at all?"

"A few photographs that my brother and I split. My folks
didn't believe in cherishing the past or planning for the future.
They had the barest medical coverage and of course, it wasn't
enough. Now my brother seems just like them. He flits from
one job to the next, one woman to another."

Sounded like a lot of guys Riley knew, men who wouldn't
grow up and so, at least in his opinion, weren't really men.

"He's already spent his inheritance and doesn't have a thing
to show for it. I asked what he intended to do when he retired,
but he just laughs and says he has a lifetime to worry about it.
He hasn't learned at all."

"But you have?"

"Absolutely." She met his gaze squarely. "The house is an
investment in my future, but I have others as well. If I get sick,
I'll be able to take care of myself, not rely on others or end up
in the care of the state. I'm careful about everything I do and
I don't give in to impulses."

Impulses like sexual desire? Did she hope to deny the chemistry between them? Riley didn't correct her but he knew different. He could be persuasive and he never gave up easily.

At his long silence, her chin lifted. "What about you?"

"What about me?"

She looked self-conscious but forged on. "Do you have a
retirement plan? And you mentioned your place. Do you have
your own house or are you renting?"

The inquisition so surprised him, Riley laughed. "Tell me,
Red, are you curious for personal reasons, sizing me up as husband
material, or are you mentally working on that damn article?"

She stiffened, but she didn't lie. "A little of each maybe, though it's certainly too early to be thinking about anything serious between us."

"You really think so?"

Her face went blank, then pink with confusion. She forged on. "And I wouldn't write the article without your permission. It's just that the whole community hero angle worked so well with Ethan, I know people would eat up a life story on you."

He ignored that because his life wasn't anybody's business. "But you're personally interested, right?"

She chewed on her lips again. "We're not involved, Riley, so it's more curiosity than anything."

"I want to be involved."

She pressed back in her chair. She blinked, studied his face, then looked down at her hands. "You know, Riley, it occurs to me that this could get pretty muddled."

"How so?" Riley felt strangely sated. He'd had a delicious meal, cozy conversation and the sight of Regina seated across from him. It was the kind of setting he could get used to—the kind of setting he hadn't wanted again until he'd met her.

He knew exactly how he'd like to end the day, but after everything she'd confessed, he had his doubts about her cooperation. He could be patient, especially since all indications led him to believe he'd eventually win.

"You say you believe me about the attacks."

"I do."

"Then don't you think we should keep the personal and the professional separate? Won't it be hard for you to be objective if we're...well, sleeping with each other?"

Objectivity had flown out the window within hours of meeting her. He drank the last of his iced tea and nodded at her plate. "What I think is that you should eat some of this great dinner you fixed."

"I am eating." She took two more bites, then went on in a rush. "Why would you believe me when no one else does?"

"It's easy enough to understand. You finish eating and I'll tell you a story, okay?"

"All right."

She still only picked at her food, but he felt better knowing he hadn't completely ruined her meal. "Back when I was a new evidence tech, before I became SWAT, I got called to the scene where a guy had broken into his seventeen-year-old girlfriend's house. The mother had forbidden the girl to see him anymore, but when she left to go shopping, he snuck over. When the girl tried to send him away, he got unreasonably furious, choking her and banging her head on the wall a few times."

Regina's head came up, a broccoli floret dangling from her fork. "Dear God."

"The mom got home in time to pull him off her," Riley assured her, but as usual, the bitter memories filled him with anger. Too many times, he hadn't been able to make a difference. "The detectives got there just before me, but the boyfriend had already fled. They were speaking with the mom and daughter, and the dad who had just arrived home. Patrol tells me that the mom wants to prosecute the guy, but the daughter doesn't. When I explain that her boyfriend committed a Felony One—aggravated burglary—which carries the same sentence as murder, the mom starts backing up, too."

"But her daughter…"

"Has purpling choke marks on her neck and bruises on her cheek and temple. Still, she just kept saying, 'But I love him. He didn't mean to hurt me.'"

Regina threw down her fork. "Well, what in the world did he think would happen when he manhandled her that way?"

"Men like that don't concern themselves with the victim. And with the daughter spouting all the classic I-have-no-self-esteem phrases that you get from abused women, there wasn't much we could do. The dad was noticeably silent, only occasionally saying, 'I think I just need to have a talk with the boy.'"

"Unbelievable."

"No, honey, unfortunately it's all too believable and cops run into that crap every day. We had to leave with no charges filed because the victims wouldn't prosecute. I was pissed, the other detective was scratching his head and then the female officer says, 'I can tell you what's going on in there. Dad's beaten Mom up a few times and the daughter knows it. Mom doesn't want to say anything because she might get another beating and the poor girl thinks this is normal behavior because she's lived with it for years.'"

Riley's hands fisted on the tabletop. He wouldn't tell Regina that eventually the girl had run off with the jerk—and died because of it.

Subdued, Regina left her seat and came around to Riley's side. Immediately, Butch did the same. He ran from his bed, stretched up with his paws on her thigh and begged to be held. Regina scooped him up close, rubbing her nose against his soft fur but speaking to Riley. "I'm sorry."

Riley gave her a one-arm hug, pulling her into his side. Because he was still sitting, his face was level with the subtle swell of her breasts. Well, her breasts and a fuzzed-up, irritable Butch who didn't want Riley to touch her.

The dog was too territorial, but Riley understood how he felt. "Yeah, me, too." He forced his gaze to her face. "But you know what, Red? It taught me something. There are all kinds of perspectives and things we never see. And women, God bless them, are pretty damned intuitive. If you say someone is after you, I'd be an idiot not to take you seriously. And, believe me, I'm not an idiot."

She gave a small, tremulous smile. "Thank you. It... Well, it feels better, safer, just knowing someone isn't writing me off as a nut."

Riley pushed back his chair and came to his feet. Oh yeah, he knew exactly how Butch felt because the urge to hold her was nearly overwhelming. "Tell you what, Red. Let's put the dishes away, then go to the living room and you can tell me everything that's been going on."

"Everything?"

"From the beginning. Maybe we'll be able to sort things out." He put his hand at the small of her back and urged her away from the table. "Do you think Killer can entertain himself a few minutes?"

The dog managed a sideways glare and a roll of his lip, but when Regina put him in his bed, this time he circled, dug at the bedding for a few seconds, then plopped down to sleep with his nose noticeably close to his rump.

Her kitchen was so immaculate, it didn't take any time at all to put things away. The leftovers went into matching containers in the fridge. The dishes were rinsed and put in uniform order in the dishwasher. Regina was so orderly, so clean, it unnerved Riley a bit.

Would she expect everyone to be that tidy? Curious as to how judgmental she might be, Riley said, "You've been to Rosie's place before, right?"

"Yes, why?"

"How'd you like it?" Rosie was tidy, but nowhere near as big a neat freak as Regina.

She thought about it for a moment, then smiled. "From the first time I stepped into Rosie's house, it felt cozy, like a home." She gave a soft laugh that sank into him. "But Rosie's that way. Very warm and open and friendly. I like her a lot."

Satisfied by her answer, Riley smiled. "Yeah, me, too."

Together they washed the pans, Regina cleaning and Riley drying. Damn, but he had a good time doing it. Just being with her calmed something turbulent inside him, making him feel more at peace with himself and his life. But slowly the serenity of the moment expanded into heightened awareness. He wanted her, and not having her was torture.

When her hands were completely submersed in soapy water, Riley moved behind her. Holding her waist so she couldn't slip away, he deliberately pressed in, relishing the feel of her full bottom against his groin. A short groan rumbled in his chest.

One day soon, after she'd accepted him, he'd take her this way, from behind, sinking deep, feeling her buttocks on his abdomen and thighs. He'd be able to cover her breasts with his hands, toy with her stiffened nipples, slip his fingers down her belly to her...

"Riley?"

He ignored the hardening of his body, the surge of lust, to nibble carefully on her ear. Without intentional thought, he further aroused her, letting his breath tickle her ear, using the edge of his tongue to tantalize the sensitive nerve endings along the tendons in her neck. "You don't want to sleep with me yet, Red, but you will soon. In the meantime, a little kissing won't hurt anything, right?" Before she could answer, he dipped his tongue into her ear, then gently sucked her earlobe. His accelerated breaths fanned the delicate, baby-fine hairs at her temple.

"No." Her hands went still, just dangling over the edge of

the sink, not quite in the water, not quite out. She tipped her head back to his shoulder and closed her eyes.

Riley leaned around her to see her face. "No what, honey?" He pressed one hand from her waist to her belly, spreading his fingers wide in masculine possession. His thumb dipped into her navel through her clothes, pressing gently, symbolic of so much more. Few people understood the erogenous zones of a woman's body, how small touches, when combined just right, could elicit carnal reactions.

In his training, he'd learned a lot about pressure points that could cripple, but the reverse was also true. He knew the places where exquisite, almost unbearable pleasure existed.

He could make her come, right here, right now, without undue effort, and that knowledge had his entire body straining in need. But he didn't want to push her. The constraint cost him, making him tremble and turning his voice hoarse. "No, you don't want me to do this, or no, there's nothing wrong with it?"

"There's nothing wrong with it."

A shudder rippled through him; she'd seemed so wary of sexual involvement with him that any capitulation now felt like a major triumph.

Suddenly she turned and plastered herself up against him, breasts to abdomen, belly to groin. "I want to kiss you, Riley. I just don't want you to expect it to lead to bed."

"All right."

Her green eyes narrowed with mingled surprise and uncertainty. "All right, what?"

He settled his hands on her hips, urging her closer still, so he could feel the rounded, feminine contours of her body. "All right, you can kiss me. Go ahead."

"Oh." She looked at his mouth, licked her own, and Riley nearly lost it.

"Hurry up, Red."

"Okay then." With her soapy hands sliding around his neck, she went on tiptoe and her mouth touched his.

Riley waited, his heart thundering, his erection straining, his testicles tight. With ruthless determination, he gathered his control around him and kept his stance relaxed, his expression calm, when in reality his emotions bordered on savage. He'd never wanted any woman the way he wanted Regina.

Her warm velvet tongue licked out again, this time over his lips. "Riley?"

"Yeah?"

"Open your mouth for me."

That did it. As carefully as he could manage considering the tumultuous raging of his libido, Riley gathered her fully against him. With her heartbeat echoing his, he opened his mouth but didn't let her take the lead. His tongue slid in, deep and slow, mating with hers, teasing, showing her with his mouth how he wanted to take her with his body. Their hot breaths mingled, their hands clutched. Her body relaxed and sighed into his, so soft and fluid and feminine; his grew more taut with pounding lust.

He'd promised himself only a few kisses when he started this, but then he hadn't counted on the effect of her full and enthusiastic involvement. Before he'd even had time to think it through, he had a small breast in one hand, a firm, lush cheek in the other.

Their groans sounded at the same time.

Her nipple stiffened against his palm, a plea that he couldn't ignore. Using only his open palm, Riley brushed his hand over her again and again, abrading her nipples, giving her only so much. Her fingers tightened in his hair. She pulled her mouth away to gulp for air. "Riley?"

She said his name as an invitation, an appeal for more. "Regina…"

The sudden furious yapping of the dog startled them both. As if he'd only just then realized their physical closeness, Butch ran wild circles around them, snapping at Riley's leg without actually touching, making his discontent with the situation well known.

It hit Riley that his control had definitely slipped. For that brief moment, he'd lost all sense of himself, acting solely on need. It was an awesome, almost frightening admission. No one, not even his wife, and not even the worst imaginable scene, had so much as caused a flicker of loss in his innate control. He'd considered it an unchangeable part of him, like his height and bone structure.

One glance at Regina's hot face and he wanted to curse. "I'm sorry."

She shook her head. "No. No reason to apologize." She smoothed her hands down the front of her blouse, realized they were wet and tucked them behind her. Her smile was entirely false and self-conscious. "Would you like coffee?"

Strangely insulted, Riley stared at her. They'd shared a killer kiss, he'd had his hands all over her, and she wanted to continue playing proper hostess. "What I'd like," he muttered under his breath, "is to finish what we started."

"Excuse me?"

"Nothing." He needed a distraction and fast. The obvious distraction was now chewing on his heel while growling like a banshee. Riley reached down for Butch, but with his expression so dark the dog tucked in his tail and scurried away with due haste. Issuing a grievous sigh, Riley caught Butch with one hand and held him up close. Regina stood next to him like a fretful mother while the dog tried to brazen it out, grumbling, snarling and looking to Regina for rescue.

"Shh," Riley soothed while stroking the narrow back with

one finger. The dog was smaller than his foot, his legs no thicker than Riley's baby finger and he fit fully into one hand. Butch quieted just a bit, giving Riley a suspicious look reminiscent of Regina's. "Good boy. See, I'm not so evil, huh? I saw that you weren't actually biting me, just trying to scare me off. You don't trust me with Regina. But you're going to have to get used to me touching her, buddy, because I intend to touch her a lot."

Regina said, "You do?"

Riley slanted her a look. "Since we're done here, let's go into the living room. The sooner I can figure out what the hell's going on with your attacker, the sooner we can get beyond it."

Regina dried her hands, neatly folded the dish towel to hang over the bar and hurried after him. "And then what?"

"And then I can concentrate on just you." He smiled at her over his shoulder, a deliberate smile, hot and suggestive. She stopped dead in her tracks, blinked twice, then followed him into the room.

And damned if she didn't wear a coy little smile of her own.

chapter 3

"IT STARTED AFTER MY ASSIGNMENT IN THE PARK."

The second Regina sat beside him, Butch snapped at Riley again and jumped over into her lap. Traitorous dog. "What park? Around here?"

"No, where I used to work before moving to Chester." While she spoke, she absently petted the dog and within minutes Butch was sound asleep again. "It was a new park opening. There'd been a lot of problems with it because some of the bigger businesses wanted to use the area for a parking lot. The arguments were pretty good on both sides: beautify the land with a park to draw visitors to the area, or use it to provide adequate parking so people would come to the stores to shop, thereby actually spending money."

"So I guess the park won?"

She nodded. "It was in the news every day. City hall got more action than it'd seen in months. The mayor had started to look pretty harried before everything got settled. The paper I worked for ran regular articles about it, then they sent me there to get photos and to do a write-up a week before the park officially opened. It was my biggest feature, a two-page spread."

Riley smiled at her enthusiasm. Sitting so close to her, seeing her so animated, made it impossible not to touch her. He reached toward her, and Butch came off her lap like a whirlwind. Riley didn't duck away. He held his hand out while Butch pretended to bite. He came close, but never actually closed his teeth on Riley.

"Just like I thought. All bluster." He kept his tone soft so he wouldn't upset the dog more. "You're ferociously defensive, aren't you, squirt? I like that." And then, despite Butch's complaints, he rubbed his ears. Butch gave up and enjoyed the attention. "So what happened at the park?"

"Everything was going well at first. I took some pictures of the elaborate fountain, the new swing sets, the pond with ducks and geese. It really is a beautiful spot." She glanced down at Butch and blushed. "I even got to meet my favorite politician."

"Yeah? And who's that?"

"Senator Welling. He was there with an intern, doing the same thing I was doing, checking out the park. He'd supported it, you see. He always supports the conservation of land whenever possible. I've admired him so long, I even took a few pictures of him. He waved to the camera for me."

Riley sighed. For a reporter, she sure had a hard time getting around to the point. "So what happened, Red? Did someone attack you in the park? Did the good senator try to come on to you—"

"No! Senator Welling isn't like that." She looked genuinely annoyed by his teasing remarks. "The reason I admire him so much is because he's such a dedicated family man. He's a wonderful politician, too, of course, and I agree with most of his political stands, but it's his dedication to his wife and children that's his real appeal."

Personally, Riley thought the man was a schmoozer, but then he wasn't about to get into a political debate with Regina. "I'll take your word for it."

Still disgruntled, she said, "He politely posed for my pictures, even did one with him and the intern standing on either side of the fountain. He walked me to my car *and* opened my car door for me."

Maybe he'd been coming on to her after all and Regina was just too naive to realize it. "So what happened at the park that made you feel threatened?"

"Oh, it was as I was leaving the park. I was almost to the main road when some jerk sideswiped me."

Riley straightened. "What do you mean, he sideswiped you?"

"I drive a little silver Escort, and this fancy SUV tried to pass me, but he didn't clear my hood before cutting back into my lane. His rear end hit my front bumper and my car went into a spin, then off the road. I plowed into a tree. The guy didn't even stop, just kept going."

"And you think that's related somehow to—"

"If you'll just let me finish," she said in exasperation.

"Sorry." Riley held up both hands. "By all means." He only hoped she got to the point before midnight.

"It wasn't easy, but I got the car out of the ditch and made it pretty close to the main road. I probably did even more harm to the car, but I didn't like the idea of sitting there alone in the park, especially since it was starting to get dark."

"Smart."

"I thought so. My cell phone had gone dead, so I thought I'd have a long walk ahead of me, but then the senator came by and he drove me to a phone. He even offered to wait with me, but I told him to go on. Wasn't that awfully nice of him?"

"He's supposed to serve the people, honey."

"Not as a taxi. Anyway, I called my boss from a diner. He called for a tow truck then came to pick me up and drive me back to my car. You won't believe what I found."

Numerous possibilities ran through his mind, but he said only, "What?"

"Someone had broken into it."

"You didn't lock it up?"

"Of course I did. But the driver's side window was smashed. I thought for sure my stereo, speakers and CDs would be gone."

"I gather they weren't?"

"No. The car had been ransacked, my glove box emptied, all my papers strewn around, but nothing was missing as far as I could tell."

Riley frowned. He had to admit that sounded odd. Had someone been looking for something specific? "What did the police say about it?"

"That I must have returned in time to scare the robbers off."

Possibly. But he wasn't one to always accept the most obvious explanation. "You have another theory?"

"Yes. Looking back, I think that SUV ran me off the road on purpose. I think he came back later to look for something in my car."

"If that's so, if he was really that determined, why not just follow you home?" Even saying it made Riley's protective instincts twitch. If someone *had* followed her, what might have happened? He didn't even want to contemplate such a scenario. From now on, he intended to keep a closer watch on her.

"I'm not a criminal so I can't know how a criminal's mind works. But maybe he knew I lived in a busy complex, so going through my car wouldn't have been easy. The thing is, I can't imagine what I'd have that anyone would want, but I am really grateful that Senator Welling was there to drive me into town. If he hadn't…"

"You might have been sitting in your car, all alone, when the burglar showed up." Riley reached out and took her hand. "Could be your presence would have deterred him."

"But maybe not. He did run me off the road without much concern, so maybe he'd have just hit me over the head or something. Maybe he'd have even—"

Riley's teeth hurt from clenching his jaw. "Don't." No way in hell did he want her to cavalierly discuss deadly possibilities. They'd already occurred to him, of course, so he didn't need embellishment of his own grisly thoughts.

"Well, after everything else that's happened…"

"Such as?"

"I left work one night after finishing up some research. Phone calls mostly. It was about eight, dark outside already. Just as I started to step off the curb, a black Porsche nearly ran me down. I had to jump back fast to keep from being hit. I landed on the ground, tore my panty hose, broke two fingernails and twisted my ankle."

Anger swelled inside him. "Jesus. You could have been killed."

"I think that was the point. But the police wrote it off as a sloppy driver, not a deliberate intent to hit me. They thought it was unrelated to the other incident and they said there was nothing they could do about it since I didn't get the license plate number."

Rationally, Riley knew they were right. Without a direct witness or a way to track down the car, the police were helpless. But at the very least, they could have taken the threat to her seriously.

Only, he didn't know if he would have either. Not with so little to go on. The first violation appeared to be a bungled burglary. The second *could* have been a drunk driver or a speeding kid....

"A week after that, some bully tried to grab my purse. I held on to it—"

Riley had gotten more and more rigid as the enormity of her dilemma sank in, and now his control nearly snapped. *"You held on?"*

The dog lunged at him for raising his voice. Riley pulled Butch up to his chest with one hand cradled under his body. He bounced him as he'd often done with his nieces and nephews when they were fussy babies. Butch had no idea what to make of it. He looked confused, but he quieted. His eyes were wide, his ear perked up. He peered at Regina, then back at Riley.

"It was *my* purse, Riley. No way was I going to just give it up."

"He could have hurt you, damn it."

"He *did* hurt me."

Through stiff lips, Riley growled, "Tell me."

His tone was so gruff, she gave him an uncertain look. "He...well, he belted me. Gave me a black eye."

"Son of a bitch."

"Riley!"

The dog howled and Riley released Regina's hand to stroke the dog's back, scratch his ears. "What did the police have to say about that?"

In a strange shift of mood, Regina scooted closer to him and stroked his shoulder. "It was weeks ago, Riley. There's no reason to get so upset now."

She attempted to soothe him much as Riley soothed the fractious dog. "I'm furious, not upset," Riley muttered, then added, "Women get upset."

"Your shoulders are all bunched and one eye is narrowed more than the other and you've got this strange tic in your jaw."

"Fury."

"All right, then don't get so furious. That won't help."

Knowing she was right, he drew a deep breath that didn't abate his anger one bit but gave him the illusion of calm. "Tell me what the cops said."

"Well, they were a little more concerned this time because after the guy hit me, my purse was dumped, only he didn't steal anything. My wallet was right there with two credit cards and about forty dollars, but he just rifled through the stuff on the ground, cursed me, and when we heard people coming, he ran off without a single thing."

Butch flopped onto his back in Riley's arms and went back to sleep. Apparently, he liked the rough rocking.

"What did the man look like?"

"I'm not sure. It was raining that day so he had on a slicker that closed up to his throat. He wore a hat and sunglasses, though there wasn't a speck of sunshine to be found. I noticed he was dark because he had five o'clock shadow and dark side-burns. His hands were tanned."

"Did the police try to follow him?"

"By the time they got there, he was long gone. They didn't know what to think until I explained about the other things that had happened. Then they wanted me to tell them about all my recent assignments." She shrugged. "But there hasn't been anything that would upset anyone. I don't write derogatory, cutting-edge pieces." She looked disgruntled with that admission. "I cover parks and new cookbooks and special-interest groups."

"So what had you written?" Riley continued rocking the dog. Butch twisted awkwardly, tucking the back of his head into Riley's neck and nuzzling closer in doggy bliss. Damn it, he was starting to like the dog.

"Let's see. I'd done the park feature...."

"No, before that. Everything started the day of the park, right? So it had to be something you'd done prior to that."

"That makes sense." She scrunched up her nose in thought. "Well, I did do an article on a professional football player arrested for a DUI, but my angle was on the time he donated to underprivileged children, something he'd been doing even before being assigned community service. And I did an interview with the author of a popular cookbook. The book was a hit, but it turned out the author had stolen some of the recipes from her mother-in-law's great-great-grandmother. But she in turn donated half her royalties to her mother-in-law's favorite charity, and they worked everything out amicably."

Riley frowned in thought. "Not exactly life-altering news, huh?"

Sounding defensive, Regina said, "I have done a few more critical pieces."

"Like?"

"About a month earlier I'd covered a dog shelter that wasn't treating the animals right. They were crowded, dirty, underfed, and naturally I was outraged."

The mistreatment of animals would have outraged him as well, but Regina was so softhearted, so genuine, he could imagine how emotional she'd gotten over the whole thing.

"The article I did was small, but it ended up getting a lot of attention. The shelter got shut down and heavily fined. With the help of the paper, I spearheaded a campaign to find homes for all the dogs. We eventually succeeded. I would have loved to have kept a few of them myself, but I had no hopes of getting my own home then, and a small apartment is no place for a dog."

Riley looked down at Butch. The dog peeked at him, turned his head to lick Riley's hand and stretched. Riley grinned. "Unless the dog is really small."

Regina smiled, too. "Look at him. He's already fond of you."

Hearing that special soft tone in her voice gave Riley an idea. He could get closer to her by getting closer to her dog. "He knows I respect him. But I imagine if I touched you right now, he'd go right back to bristling." Riley gave her a long, intimate look. "He's going to have to learn to share. But I'll be patient— with him and you."

Regina's lips parted. She caught her breath, then looked at his mouth.

Oh, she was begging to be kissed. Unable to resist, Riley slowly leaned toward her.

He ended up kissing the dog when Butch leaped up between them. He nipped at Riley's mouth and nose, making an awful racket.

"You ungrateful mutt." Mindful of his intentions, Riley kept his tone friendly instead of irritated. Seeing that no kissing would occur, the dog resettled himself against Riley and gave him a big-eyed innocent look.

Regina smothered a laugh. "How could anyone ever hurt an animal? I can't understand it. I don't regret what happened with the shelter, but afterward the owners showed a lot of animosity toward me. Of course, that's understandable because I started the ball rolling that eventually lost them their business. The thing is, unless they just wanted to harass me, they wouldn't make likely suspects because I don't have anything they'd want to steal."

Riley tried to let the pieces come together naturally in his mind, but he knew Regina was right. He was too personally involved. All he could think of was how she might have been hurt worse. "Is there anyone else you can think of who'd dislike you?"

"Why would anyone dislike me?"

That made him grin. "Why indeed? Any problems with the people you work with? Why did you move here?"

The careful way she masked her expression told him he'd hit a nerve. "I got along with almost everyone at work."

"*Almost* everyone?"

She folded her hands in her lap. "There was one guy who was pretty persistent in trying to get me to go out with him. The more I refused, the more hostile he got."

"You left because of him?"

"Partially. He started showing up at my place at odd hours, watching me all the time. But he wasn't a threat, just a pest. Mostly I left because I thought I might be safer here. I hate to admit to being a coward, but I got spooked. I'm not used to being hit—"

"Hell, I would hope not."

"—and when that man slugged me, that was more than enough for me. I had to wear sunglasses for a week before the bruise faded enough that I could hide it with makeup. So I quit my job, relocated here in Chester and got hired on with the local paper."

Wishing he could get his hands on not only the man who'd dared to strike her, but the weasel who'd hassled her at work, too, Riley shook his head. "And you still found yourself in trouble."

"Right. Unless, as the local police say, it's just a coincidence. Maybe the fire was an accident."

Any time Riley thought of the damn fire, his guts cramped. "I don't think so, Red."

"You don't? Why?" And then she asked with suspicion, "Riley Moore, do you know something I don't know?"

Careful not to disturb the dog, he touched her cheek and gave her a tender smile. "I probably know lots of things you don't know, especially about dangerous situations. But specifically about the fire, no."

"Then why?"

"I dunno. It's just that the day of the fire, you were so jumpy, so nervous. Call it women's intuition, gut instinct, or just caution, you seemed to instinctively know something was about to happen."

"I did feel especially edgy. It felt like people were watching me."

"Maybe they were." After she'd left Riley that day, he couldn't shake off the picture of her nervousness. And her nervousness had become his, until he knew he wouldn't be able to relax for worrying about her. "That sort of thing can be felt," he murmured, more to himself than her.

"That's why you were trailing me?"

"Yeah." He'd known she was meeting Ethan to complete her interview, so he'd gone along, hanging back so that no one would notice him, but close enough to keep an eye out for her. When she'd met up with Rosie first and the two of them had gone to the firework's dealership, his edginess had increased. With good reason.

"I'm glad you followed me," she said. "If you hadn't, who knows what might have happened."

The alarms had brought Ethan to the scene, only he'd thought Rosie was still inside the building. He would have gone in after her if Riley hadn't held him back. Regina and Rosie would have been safe, but Ethan would have died.

Riley shook off the awful memories, then touched the corner of Regina's mouth. It looked tender and ripe and he wanted to kiss her, but first they had to talk. "I was feeling territorial even then." He watched her eyes darken and smiled to himself. "I wish like hell I'd gotten my hands on the bastard who carried you out. He's probably the one who stole your camera."

"Likely, since I'd taken some good photos of the fire hazards. If only I'd realized how serious those hazards were, I could have saved poor Ethan a terrible scare."

"And me as well."

"You?"

"Damn right." The picture of her sitting on the curb, blood on her forehead, her eyes dazed, would stay with him for a lifetime. "I felt like I'd taken a kick to the stomach."

"You didn't look scared. Not like Ethan."

"I'd already found you, and though you were hurt, I knew you were going to be okay. Ethan thought Rosie was in the fire." And he'd been a madman, fighting to go inside after her even though it would have meant his own death. Once Rosie had shown up, having left the building on her own by an upstairs window in the back, Ethan had just collapsed. To this day, Ethan trembled when anyone mentioned the fire. Oh, he was still a fireman, still did his duty with fearless determination, but you didn't mention the fire that almost took Rosie from him.

Riley didn't ever want to be so afraid that he lost all reason and discipline. Which was why he was taking matters into his own hands. He didn't love Regina the way Ethan loved Rosie, but he liked her, he wanted her and for as long as he held a claim, he'd damn well keep her safe.

He dropped his hand. "Maybe I'm just buying into your fears, but it's possible you have good reason to be afraid. I'm not willing to put it to chance."

She pressed back against the couch cushions. "You say that like it has some hidden meaning or something."

"It does." He stared at her hard, keeping her pinned in his gaze. "Regina, I don't want you by yourself until we figure out what's going on."

It took her a second to catch his meaning, then her eyes slanted his way in speculation. "You think you should stay with me?"

"If you move from the apartment, yes."

"No."

He went on as if she hadn't voiced the denial. "Here you're surrounded by people. Help is only a few feet away and anyone could hear you through the thin walls. In a house, you'd be all alone."

Her shoulders straightened. "I'm a big girl, Riley. I'll be extra careful. But I won't—"

"You can't be careful enough. Do you intend to be home before dark every day? And what does it even matter when by your own admission, you've been attacked during the day? You can't imagine how many ways an intruder can get into your house without you even knowing."

Her slim brows pulled down.

"What if someone doesn't want to steal from you at all? What if someone just wants revenge?"

She pushed to her feet to pace away. Riley noticed her hands had curled into fists at her sides, evidence that she'd had the same worry. "Stop it. You're trying to scare me."

Riley set the dog beside him and stepped up behind her. "Bullshit. I *am* scaring you. And you know why, Red? Because you're smart enough to know I'm right." He clasped her upper arms and pulled her back against his chest. Her hair smelled sweet. *She* smelled sweet. And soft and female and delicate. She demolished his control and intentions without even trying.

Riley pressed his jaw against her temple, and in a roughened voice, said, "Will you check every room, every closet, under every bed and in every corner each night when you first go in? What will you do if you find someone, crouching in the dark, waiting for you?"

Jerking around to face him, she said again, *"Stop it."*

His hands closed over her shoulders and he brought her to her tiptoes. "The hell I will. You say the threat is real. I believe you. So don't be dumb, Regina."

"What am I supposed to do?" She was so shaken, she practically wailed, then thumped him solidly on the chest. "Hide? Stop living? I have work and friends and errands…."

He caressed her tense shoulders. "Let me help."

"By moving in?" She shook her head. "No, I won't do that. It wouldn't be—"

"Proper? Screw proper. Who's going to know besides our friends?" She started to walk away from him and Riley crushed her close. Her eyes flared. "Improper beats the hell out of dead any day."

The dog started barking, anxiously looking for a way off the couch. But he was too small to try jumping down.

"You're upsetting my dog."

"Misery loves company." He kissed her, hard at first, but when she went immobile, then soft and sweet against him, he gentled. Her hands curled against his chest, telling him she liked the kiss almost as much as he did. He caught her face, held her still while he sank his tongue in. Her heartbeat pounded against his chest, her soft moan vibrated between them.

Riley carefully pulled back. Her eyes stayed closed, her lips parted. "Listen to me, Red. I'll do everything I can to figure this out before you're due to move. I swear it. But I don't want you living alone."

Her eyelashes fluttered, lifted. Slowly, comprehension dawned and she looked beyond him, then stepped away to scoop up the dog. With her back to Riley, she went about soothing Butch. "If you're that close, you know what will happen."

"We'll sleep together." He crossed his arms over his chest, anxious for it to happen, wondering if she'd admit it.

"Every time you touch me, I forget who I am."

"Meaning?"

"Meaning I'm not the type to get carried away with the moment, but when you're kissing me, it doesn't seem to matter."

She would be ready, more than ready, by the time he got her in bed. He'd see to it. "It's going to happen no matter what, Red. You know that."

She swallowed, then nodded. "I know." She looked none too pleased with that admission, making Riley frown.

A real gentleman would have told her not to worry about it, that he'd control himself, protect her. He wasn't that much of a gentleman, and he wanted her too much to start playing one now. "We'll go slow." As slow as he could manage, considering he'd held himself at bay for weeks already.

She walked over to the balcony doors and looked out. "I'm sorry. I don't mean to be...coy. It's just that I can't be cavalier about sex."

Her honesty was refreshing, something he hadn't expected. "You don't need to apologize to me for speaking your mind. But we're both adults, both uninvolved." When she didn't look at him, he said, "I don't mean to push you..."

Her laugh sounded strained. "That's all you do is push."

His smile caught him by surprise. "For your safety, yeah. But I'm not cavalier about sex either. No one in their right mind is these days."

"Then I know a lot of men not in their right mind."

He wouldn't think about her with other men. It'd make him nuts. But he could be honest in return. "I can't promise not to touch you, Red, because I will."

Her shoulders lifted on a deep breath. She waited, anxious and still.

Seeing her response, Riley took two steps closer. "Is it worth your safety? Is avoiding me worth risking your life?" And because he knew she already loved her little dog, he pressed her, saying, "Is it worth risking Butch's life?"

He waited, and finally she turned. She looked sad, resigned. "No. I tried ignoring the threat. I tried to believe it was all coincidence like everyone said. I wanted to just go on with my life, keep doing what I always did, keep working." She shook her head and said in a nearly soundless whisper, "I almost got Rosie killed."

Riley knew she still felt guilty for allowing Rosie to be involved, even though everyone knew Rosie did just as she pleased. Ethan couldn't control her, so it was for certain that Regina would never sway Rosie from something she chose to do.

"I know the risks now, but the thing is, Riley, I can't just hide away. I love my job and I won't give it up. Yet, that's when a lot of things seem to happen. Out of control cars, purse snatchers…"

"I have an idea about that, too." A stupid idea, one he was sure to regret, but damn it, he had to be certain she was safe. "You wanted to interview me."

Sudden excitement lit her eyes. Both she and the dog stared at him, she with delighted surprise, Butch with mere curiosity.

After clearing his throat, Riley forged on. "Well, here's your chance. I'm on vacation for the next two weeks. While you finish up any current assignments, I'll accompany you—and no, there's no negotiating on that point, not if you want to interview me next."

"That's blackmail," she pointed out, but she didn't sound too upset about it.

"Take it or leave it."

For three heart-stopping seconds she hesitated. Her slow smile gave him warning. "I'll take it."

Already dreading it, Riley nodded. She sounded enthusias-

RILEY   249

tic enough to make his stomach clench. "During the evening
we'll work on your training. I want you to have at the very least
a basic understanding of self-defense. While you're still in the
apartment, I'll check into the things that've happened to you
to see if I can turn up anything."

"But hasn't it been too long?"

"Maybe. But maybe not. Cops file all their reports, so I'll
check through that and see if anything jumps out at me. Back
when things first happened, they were looking at each incident
with the thought that you were a hysterical woman. I'll look with
the thought that you're in danger. Two very different perspectives."

She licked her lips. "It happened in Cincinnati, not Chester."

"Don't worry. I'll find what I need to get started."

Still she stood there.

Riley touched her cheek. "Try not to fret, okay? Everything
will work out."

"And if you haven't found out anything when it's time for
me to move?"

He'd have kissed her again, but Butch started a low rumbling,
ears back, body poised to attack. The little dog had enough to
get used to without worrying that Riley was accosting his new
mistress. "Then you'll continue to stay with me."

"With you? But I thought you—"

"Intended to move in with you? No. My place is already
secure. And look at it this way, you can use the time to get your
new home up and running." And in the interim, he'd have
her—in his home, under his protection and in his bed.

The setup worked for him.

chapter 4

BUTCH DIDN'T LIKE SLEEPING ALONE.

Regina found that out after a long night of listening to pitiful howls that finally broke her down. At two in the morning she gave up, retrieved Butch from his pen in the warmest corner of her kitchen, and carried him to bed.

He did a reconnaissance of the perimeter, sniffing every corner of her bed, her pillow, the sheets, before crawling under the covers. She watched the lump move here and there, then finally settle close to her. He dug—*endlessly*. She had no idea what he thought he was doing, but he ignored her pleas to stop and finally curled up behind her knees. She couldn't move without making him grumble.

For a four-pound dog, he was sure bossy about his comfort.

At six, when her alarm went off, Butch scampered out, yawned hugely in her face, then wanted to play. When Regina only blinked at him, he reared back on his haunches, barked and nipped her on the nose. She groaned, which he took for a sign of life and started bouncing around the covers like a tiny rabbit. He could stop and start so fast, darting this way and that, it was comical. Even half-asleep, she grinned as he raced up to her, gripped the edge of her pillowcase in his teeth, and began tugging.

"Okay, okay." It was a sorry truth, but she wasn't a morning person. She'd tried over the years to become one, only because it seemed like the thing to do. Good, honest people went to bed at a decent hour and rose early to begin their day. They didn't lie around for hours, being lazy.

Well, she was decent and honest, but she just couldn't force herself to be alert first thing. It took her at least two hours and a pot of coffee to get her head together. Before that, she didn't want to face the world. And with the way she looked in the morning, she doubted the world wanted to face her.

Moving around in the dark, she made a quick trip to the bathroom, turned on the coffeepot, which she'd prepared the night before, and put Butch out on his lead so he could potty. Because the morning was damp that late July day, he finished in a flash.

With only a dim light on over the sink, she slumped at the table in her cozy cotton jammies, nursing her first steaming mug of caffeine. Butch curled in her lap, content just to be with her—until a knock sounded on her door.

She froze.

Butch did not.

In what she now considered typical Butch frenzy, he leaped from her lap and ran hell-bent for the door. He made so much noise, she knew any thoughts of ignoring her early-morning caller were shot. Through the peephole, she spied Riley standing impatiently in her hallway, and she ducked away as if he might see her, too. Good God. What was he doing at her door so early?

"Open up, Red. I can hear Butch, so I know you're up and about."

No. A thousand times no. Still plastered to the side of the door, her heart racing, she croaked, "What do you want?"

"You," he said with a discernable smile in his voice. "But I'll settle for conversation."

Eyes closing in mortification, she shook her head. "Not at six-thirty, Riley. Go away till eight." She could be ready by eight. It'd be rushing it since she usually didn't leave for work till eight-thirty, but under the circumstances—

"Not happening, Red. Now open the door." And then he tacked on, "I have a gift for Butch."

"You do?" She chanced another peek out the peephole and saw that Riley held up a stuffed Chihuahua toy. It looked almost like Butch, but bigger and not as cute. She covered her face with her hands. The man had brought her dog a present. She groaned, undecided.

Beside her, Butch continued to encourage her with barks and jumps and circles. She pressed her forehead to the door. "If I let you in, will you not look at me till I've had a chance to get down the hall?"

Riley laughed. "Why?" And then in a throaty tone, "What are you wearing, Red?"

Regina looked down at herself. Sloppy, blue-flowered cotton pajamas hung on her body. Her loose, tangled hair fell in her face. Even without a mirror, she knew that her eyes were puffy and still heavy from sleep.

"I'm waiting."

This was ridiculous. Half her neighbors would hear him if she didn't do something quick. She flipped on the entry light, turned the locks and cracked the door open. "Riley?" she said in a harsh whisper.

"Yeah?"

"You can come in, but I mean it, don't you dare even think to look at me. I'm a mess and I don't like it when people see me a mess."

"All right, honey, calm down. I promise."

She could hear the laughter in his tone. "The door is unlocked, so just give me thirty seconds to—"

Behind her, the shattering of glass disturbed the early morning quiet.

Screeching, Regina whirled around to see the devastated ruins of her patio doors. Shards of glass glittered everywhere. "Oh my God." She snatched up Butch, who had tucked in his tail and darted behind her before yapping hysterically.

Riley stormed in, moved her to the side and took in the mess in one sweeping glance.

"Close and lock this door, then call the cops." He tossed the stuffed toy dog on the couch, and sprinted across the floor, through the broken patio doors and, to her amazement, right over the balcony.

"Riley." They were only about eight feet up from the ground, but still… Regina slammed her door shut and started after him, but she was barefoot and there was glass scattered everywhere, all over her floor, some atop her furniture. Her heart hammered so hard, it hurt.

Cautiously, she stepped up onto the couch, Butch clutched in her arms. "Ohmigod, ohmigod, damn you, Riley, ohmigod…" She stepped off the other end of the couch nearest to her kitchen. Being careful to avoid any sharp shards of glass, she went to the phone and dialed 9-1-1.

In less than two minutes that seemed like a lifetime, Riley was back. This time he climbed up and over the balcony railing. Regina didn't have a chance to worry about her appearance because he barely spared her a glance. "I need a flashlight. It's still too dark out there to see and I don't want to mess up any evidence."

Skin prickling with sick dread, Regina pointed to the middle of the floor. "It was a rock."

Riley nodded. "I know, honey. Where's a flashlight?"

Flashlight? She felt shocked, disoriented. She hadn't had near enough coffee.

"Regina?"

One deep breath, and she felt marginally more in control. "In my bedroom, in the nightstand drawer."

"Stay put." His booted feet crunched over the remains of her patio door. An early-morning breeze blew the curtains in. The blackness beyond the doors seemed fathomless, sending a chill down her spine.

Belatedly, Regina remembered what else was in her nightstand drawer. *Oh no.* Her heart dropped into her stomach and she started across the floor in a rush, the glass forgotten.

Riley reappeared. Not by look or deed did he acknowledge anything he might have uncovered beyond the flashlight. He crossed to her and handed her a housecoat and slippers.

"You okay?"

Maybe. "Yes."

He cupped the side of her face, his touch gentle and reassuring. "The cops should be here any second. Tell them I'm out back. I don't want to get shot by some overeager hero."

Shot! "Riley, wait." She closed her hand around his arm above his elbow. His muscles were bunched, thick with tension. To someone who didn't know him better, he might almost appear calm. But Regina noted the unfamiliar, killing rage in his blue eyes. He felt warm and strong and secure and she didn't want him to walk away from her.

As if he understood, he bent down to look her in the eyes and said with deadly calm, "It's okay, Red. I know what I'm doing. I want you and Butch to wait in the kitchen."

"No. Don't go out there."

Riley scrutinized her. "You should put on more coffee. The officers will appreciate it."

Coffee? That sort of made sense. At least, with her mind in a muddle, it did. "Oh. Right."

For one brief moment, his gaze moved over her, touching off a tidal wave of warmth. He paused at her mouth, her breasts, then shook his head in chagrin. "Be right back."

Butch squirmed to be let down, but she didn't dare, not with so much glass on the floor. A sort of strange numbness had set in. She blocked the kitchen off with his small pen, pulled on her robe and fuzzy slippers, and went about making more coffee by rote.

This time the knock on her door didn't startle her.

Holding Butch like a security blanket, his small warm body somehow comforting, she skirted the glass and made her way to the door again. Two officers in uniform greeted her. Young, fresh-faced and eager at the prospect of a crime, they looked the complete opposite of Riley. Regina wanted to groan.

Butch wanted to kill them both.

His rabid beast impersonation was especially realistic this time. Regina tried, but there was no shushing him, so she gave up.

At her invitation, the officers cautiously ventured inside, keeping their eyes on Butch. The first officer removed his hat, then nodded at the dog. "What is that?"

Here we go again, Regina thought. "My dog, Butch."

"What's wrong with him?"

"He doesn't like you." Regina closed the door behind them. "Would you like coffee?"

They looked at each other, then her. "Uh, sure." They had to speak loudly to be heard over Butch's furor. "Maybe after you tell us what happened here?"

"Oh." She looked behind her at the devastation. "A rock. Riley Moore is out back poking around with a flashlight. Don't shoot him."

"Riley?" The darker-haired officer lifted one brow. "Why's he here?"

"He was, uh…" Why had Riley dropped in? Oh yeah, a gift for the dog. "Visiting Butch."

"That right?" The two cops shared another look, this time of masculine comprehension.

Regina pulled herself together enough to fry them both with her censure. "Riley is a friend," she stated, emphasizing the last word. "He had just knocked on the door when the rock came crashing in."

At that moment, Riley opened the door behind them and stepped inside. His brows were down, his eyes glittering. "I thought I told you to lock this."

"I did, but then they arrived." She gestured at the officers and shrugged.

Riley glanced at both men. "Dermot, Lanny. Thanks for coming over."

The men looked like little boys next to Riley. Regina allowed herself a moment to appreciate the differences, then said again, "Coffee?"

Riley nodded. "Thanks, babe." He kissed her full on the mouth, annihilating her previous claims of friendship. "We'll be right there."

He wanted to dismiss her? Oh no. She squared her shoulders, but it wasn't easy with Butch putting on such a show.

Almost without thought, Riley took the dog from her.

"Good dog." He stroked Butch's back, found just the right spot behind his big ears, and Butch magically quieted. He kept a narrowed gaze on the officers, but the awful racket ended.

Regina turned on her heel and stalked away, muttering under her breath about pigheaded males of both the human and animal variety. From her position in the kitchen, she could hear the men talking in muted tones.

Riley waited, giving the officers a chance to look around. The one he'd called Lanny shone a flashlight over the small balcony—the balcony Riley had jumped from—and shook his head before meandering out there. He came back in and looked around the floor at the broken glass.

"Better call someone to fix that window," Dermot said. "Damn vandals."

"The work of kids, no doubt," Lanny added. "No one supervises them anymore. In my day, my mother would have taken a broom to me for a prank like this."

By the time the officers entered the kitchen, Regina had four mugs out, silverware, a crystal sugar bowl and a matching pot of creamer. "Have a seat, please," she told them.

Lanny nodded. "Thanks." Then, apparently disappointed that he couldn't do more, he said, "I'll take a report, but whoever did this is long gone."

Riley leaned back in his seat, noticeably silent. He continued to stroke Butch who kept looking up at him adoringly, turning his head to get a new spot scratched.

Dermot doctored his coffee, took a long drink, then asked, "You didn't get hurt, did you? The rock didn't hit you?"

Regina shook her head. "No. I'm fine."

Dermot shook his head. "I'm sorry, Ms….?"

"Foxworth. Regina Foxworth."

"Right. You did the right thing calling us but unfortunately, there's not much we can do other than have a squad car drive by and keep an eye on things for the rest of the night."

Same old song, Regina thought. "I understand."

"Well, I don't." Riley blew out a sigh of disgust. "Neither of you went outside to look around the complex."

Dermot frowned at him. "For what? It was a rock."

Lanny nodded. "You know how it is, Riley. We get crap like this all the time."

"No, you don't. And even if you did, that's no excuse for not being thorough."

New tension filled the air. Tones and posture abruptly changed. Lanny was the first to speak up. "Look, Riley, I know you have more training, but—"

"But nothing. I went outside. I looked—just as you should have done. Someone was outside her window for about an hour, just watching."

Regina straightened in new alarm.

"Not a group of unruly kids, but one man. He's a patient son-of-a-bitch, too, and I personally think he was waiting for her to be awake to throw that damn rock."

With sudden clarity, Regina said, "It was right after I turned the light on." She stared at Riley. "Before that, I'd been drinking my coffee in the dark."

"He probably thought it'd shake you up more to catch you when you first woke up." Riley glanced at Regina with an expression close to satisfaction. "Didn't rattle you too much though, did it, honey?"

He sounded teasing, which she didn't understand at all. She calmly sipped her coffee and hoped only she noticed how her hands shook. "No."

Riley smiled, a secret, intimate smile. Turning back to the two men, the smile disappeared to be replaced with a scowl.

"If you'd checked, you'd know Ms. Foxworth has a recent history of threatening incidents. In light of that, I don't think anything, especially a rock through her window at dawn, should be taken lightly."

Lanny didn't like the criticism. "Sounds to me like you're personally involved here."

"I am."

Regina nearly choked on her coffee. Why didn't he just take out an ad in the paper? He could tell more people that way.

"But that's irrelevant." Riley wasn't through lecturing. "What pisses me off the most is that neither of you did your job." He encompassed them both in a look.

Regina thought it might be a favorable time to intercede before Riley got too insulting. She pushed back her chair. "Good grief, Riley, have you had breakfast? Surely, a temper like that is wrought from hunger. Would you like some pancakes? Lanny, Dermot? I can put a batch together if you'd like."

Riley stared at her in disbelief. "You're not going to feed them."

"I am if they're hungry." Her chin lifted. "Pancakes would give you something to chew on besides two officers who are only trying to do their duty."

His expression darkened. "They're not doing it very well."

"It's my fault that I didn't mention the other incidents, not theirs."

"Victims get rattled and forget important details. An officer is supposed to know that and ask pertinent questions."

Regina sucked in a breath at the insult. "Are you saying I'm rattled?"

Dermot stood, interrupting the escalating argument. "So how'd you come to all these brilliant conclusions, Riley? That's what I want to know."

Almost in slow motion, his movements rigid and calculated,

Riley came to his feet and handed a sleepy Butch to Regina. With his gaze on Dermot, he said, "I'll take pancakes. They'll be leaving—after I explain."

Seeing no hope for it, Regina stepped out of the line of fire.

Riley took a step closer to Dermot, which had the other man's eyes flaring a bit in alarm. "There's damn near a pack of cigarette butts below her window. Red doesn't smoke—"

"Red?"

Regina raised her hand. "He means me."

"Oh." Dermot cleared his throat, glanced at her hair. "Yeah, I guess that makes sense."

In a voice raised to regain attention, Riley continued. "—so they sure as hell aren't hers, but they were fresh, one still smoldering. You know what that means, Dermot?"

Again, he cleared his throat. "Uh, that someone was out there just a few moments ago?"

"There's also one set of prints in the ground. Big adult-size prints. There are no rocks in the apartment landscaping the size of the one now in her living room, so whoever threw it probably brought it with him, meaning this was premeditated, not just a last-minute bit of mischief."

Both officers looked dumbfounded and a little awed.

"Can you maybe get some prints off the rock?"

Riley shook his head. "To get prints, surfaces need to be smooth. Since the rock isn't, there's no point in checking it."

"So what have we got?"

"Speculation. When I stand outside, about twenty feet from the balcony, I can see right into her living room. I think he watched, and saw her light come on."

"I let the dog out before that."

Riley slewed his gaze her way. "With a light?"

"Um, no."

Riley nodded in satisfaction. "You need a floodlight out there, Red. And you should never open your door in the dark."

Lanny put his hands on his hips and dropped his head forward. "Okay, so you're a big-shot crime scene tech." He looked up, eyes narrowed. "We're not."

"Learn." That one word fell like a ton of bricks, discomfiting both officers.

Silence throbbed in the kitchen, making Regina more edgy than ever. "I think I'll make those pancakes now."

"Make plenty. I'm starving." Riley didn't spare her a glance as he led both officers to the front door, where he gave them the information they needed to file a report. Regina could just make out the low drone of their voices.

Now wide awake, she mixed up pancake batter with a vengeance. She thought of everything she now had on her to-do list: clean up glass, vacuum her furniture, have the glass replaced in her door... She probably needed to call into work because she'd surely be late.

Butch sat at her heels, staring up at her, just waiting for her to sit down again so he could reclaim her lap. Whenever she glanced at him, his eyes widened hopefully and he wagged his skinny tail in encouragement. Regina shook her head. "There won't be much sitting for me today, sweetie."

Riley strode back in just as she'd pulled out a skillet and set it on the stove top. He didn't stop at the table, though, or even slow down. Startled, Regina drew back as he stalked right up to her, his long legs carrying him quickly to her. He pulled her close and without hesitation, without warning, took her mouth with a surprising hunger that completely caught her off guard.

His big hands, hot and callused, held her upper arms, straining her upward. His head was bent so that his mouth fit hers completely. His lips pressed hard, parting hers, and his tongue thrust in, deep and damp and insistent.

Regina hung in his grip, a little stunned, quickly warmed. Her heartbeat thundered in her ears. He changed position, gathering her to him with one arm tight around her waist so that his other hand could tangle in her hair, tipping her head farther back. He rubbed against her, groaned, then lifted his mouth enough for her to catch her breath.

Against her lips, he murmured, "Christ, you look good."

"Hmm?" With almost no effort, he aroused her to the point of incomprehension.

Damp, warm, openmouthed kisses were pressed to her throat, along her shoulder where the robe had opened and the loose neckline where her pajamas drooped....

Her pajamas.

"Riley!"

He held her head in his hands, brushed her cheeks with his thumbs. In a rushed voice, hoarse and low, he said, "You're beautiful."

Beautiful? Regina blinked over such an absurd comment. Her hair was a mess, more so now that he'd tunneled his fingers through it. Her eyes were sleep-heavy and she had not a single speck of makeup on. The pajamas were comfortably baggy, not in the least attractive. "I...I need to go get dressed."

Slowly, he shook his head. "No. I like you just how you are." He kissed her again before she could argue. This kiss was deeper, hotter. She was aware of so many things—the press of his strong fingers on her skull, keeping her immobile, the heat of his breath, the taste of him.

His tongue retreated, moved over her lips, then licked into her mouth again. When his hands released her head, she kept the kiss complete, unable to get enough of him. His tongue retreated, hers followed. His sank in again and she sucked at it.

She knew his hands were roving over her, not stroking her breasts as he had done before, so she didn't understand what he was doing—until her robe fell open and he pushed it aside.

Oh, but it was hard to think with Riley holding her so close, touching her in such remarkable ways. He smelled delicious this morning, like soap and the outdoors and like himself. He was so warm, the cotton of his T-shirt so soft over solid muscle. His callused fingertips slipped beneath the hem of her pajama top to trace the indentation of her waist, then higher, until he teased just beneath her breasts. He circled, glided over and under her nipples, not touching them but bringing her breasts to a tingly, almost acute sensitivity. She held her breath, wanting more, wanting everything.

In the next instant, his thumbs brushed up and over her nipples. The touch was so electric, so anticipated, she jolted against him, gasped, and her fingers bit into his upper arms, closing on rock-solid muscles.

Regina didn't want him ever to stop touching her; if anything, she wanted more and tried to tell him so by pressing closer with a soft moan. Though he hadn't touched her below the waist, her whole body sang with awareness. Her thighs trembled, her belly had filled with butterflies and a curling, un-dulating sensation of ripe pleasure expanded and retreated within her.

Riley removed his hands, then drew her head to his shoulder, rocking her a little, rubbing her back in a soothing, calming way.

She didn't understand. "Riley?"

"I have to stop, Red. When you agree to sleep with me, I want you to be totally clearheaded, so you won't have regrets."

Regina didn't know what he was muttering about. She

pressed her nose into his throat and breathed in his warm male scent, filling herself up. She wanted to taste his skin, but knew that might not be wise.

Against her ear, Riley rumbled, "While you fix the pancakes, I'll clean up the glass and call someone to replace the door." His tongue touched her ear, traced the rim, dipped inside. Little shivers of excitement raced along her arms and nape and she almost melted. "After breakfast you can pack."

The fog thinned. "Pack?"

"Yeah." His hard hand drifted lower, all the way to the base of her spine. He pressed gently—and she felt his erection against her belly, long, hard.

Regina shoved back. "What do you mean, *pack?*"

As if she should have already understood, Riley held her face turned up to his so she couldn't miss his frown. His gaze bore into hers, insistent, unrelenting. "You can't stay here now."

When she still stared at him in confusion, his frown became a black scowl. "Red, someone is getting pretty bold. And if that doesn't alarm you, then look at Butch."

She glanced down at the dog. He had his tiny front paws crossed over Riley's big foot with his head resting on them. His big brown eyes stared up at her trustingly. He was so shaken, he hadn't even protested their intimacy.

"Do you really want to chance letting him outside to do his business again, knowing someone could be lurking there, that they might snatch him away or, worse, use him to upset you?"

She knew what he was saying, and her heart squeezed tight. *"No."* In a protective rush, Regina scooped him up and hugged him to her breasts. He twisted and rubbed against her, luxuriating in the human attention. She needed the comforting contact as much as her dog did.

"Look at him," Riley said, "he's still shaking."

Without removing her cheek from the dog's neck, she said, "He always shakes and you know it." She had a feeling Riley only used the dog as leverage, and still she had to admit he was right. She'd be heartsick if anything happened to him. He trusted her to keep him safe, to take care of him, and she intended to do just that.

"I have plenty of room." Riley watched her with a sort of cautious regard. "You'll be safer with me."

Regina looked past him, through the kitchen doorway. The sun was on the rise, a crimson ball that reflected like fire on every sharp, jagged shard of glass littering her once secure home. She chewed her lip in indecision, but no other option came to her. If she went with him, it wouldn't be just an agreement to share space, and she knew it. It'd be an agreement to start an affair.

Her heart pounding for an entirely different reason now, she glanced at Riley, drew a breath, and said, "All right."

Riley encompassed both her and Butch in a bear hug.

Butch bit his nose.

Now that he'd gotten his way, Riley grinned like a rascal. "You really do look great in your pajamas and with your hair all loose and tangled." He fingered one long curl. "Sexy as hell."

Heat rushed up her neck to warm her face. She turned her back on Riley and set the dog down. "I didn't even realize…"

"You were rattled, just as I said."

Regina wanted to groan. She was *still* rattled. "I can't believe I sat there in front of those men…"

"They thought you looked hot, too. I wonder if they think we've been sleeping together."

She slanted him a sharp look. "You tried hard enough to give them that impression."

"No choice. With them both eyeing you, I had to stake a

claim." Totally unrepentant, he kissed her ear again and squeezed her waist. "I didn't want them getting any ideas about pursuing you."

Feeling like a fool, Regina smoothed her hair and retied the belt of her robe. "I guess I ought to call work since it looks like I'll be late." She picked up the receiver.

"Go ahead." Riley's blue eyes twinkled with teasing. "While you do that, I think I'll just go put the flashlight back in your nightstand—"

Regina whipped around so fast she almost fell. She grabbed Riley by the back of the shirt. "No."

He cocked a brow. "No?"

She dropped her hands, dusting them nervously across her thighs. "That is, I'll do it." She snatched the flashlight away from him. "You should call about the door."

"Right." And then with feigned confusion, he said, "But I thought you were going to call work."

The unholy grin gave him away, and her temper ignited. "You snooped in my drawer, didn't you?"

"Snooped? Now why would I do that, Red? What are you hiding in there?"

Regina swatted at him, embarrassed, irritated. "You had no right." In a snit, she went past him, stepping over the dog's pen and marching toward her bedroom. Glass crunched beneath her slippers, but she barely noticed.

Riley was right on her heels. "The *Kama Sutra,* Red? That's a little dated, isn't it?" His teasing voice grated along her nerves. "But that other book…what was it called? Oh yeah. *Getting the Most Pleasure in Bed.* Now that's current, right?"

Stopping beside her bed, Regina pointed an imperious finger at the door. "Get out."

He didn't budge. "And no less than a dozen rubbers. Woman,

what have you been planning?" He stepped closer, forcing her to back up until her legs hit the side of the mattress. "More important, any chance you were planning it with me?"

With sudden clarity, Regina knew he hadn't seen the photo. No, being typically male, he'd only noted the silly books and condoms. "No."

"No, what? You weren't planning anything with me?"

She shook her head, felt silly for going mute, and managed to say again, "No."

His smile turned smug. "I didn't really think so. After all, those condoms are smalls." And totally deadpan, "They'd never fit."

Regina's heart jumped into her throat. She licked suddenly dry lips. "No?"

He shook his head. "I'm just an average man, Regina."

"There's nothing average about you."

His slow smile nearly melted her heart. "Maybe you should wait until we've made love to make that judgment."

A tidal wave of awareness nearly took out her knees. They were in her bedroom, right next to her unmade bed. Her heart gave a hard thump, then tripped into double time.

Riley stepped closer, a grin playing about his mouth. "Such a pretty blush, Red." He looked at her bed, gave a small shake of his head, and all teasing evaporated. "So tell me, Red. What have you been planning, and with whom?"

No never. Not in a million years. "The books are just... curiosity."

"Curiosity about sex?"

It wasn't easy, but she gave a cavalier shrug. "About... variety." She knew about sex. She even knew about pleasure. But things didn't always go right, no matter how she tried. With an airy wave of her hand, she explained, "I bought the books and condoms months ago, when I was engaged."

"Engaged?"

His thunderous expression surprised her. "Yes."

"You were in love with someone?"

He said that like an accusation, confusing her even more. Because he looked so red in the face, she decided to admit the truth. "No, I didn't love him. I thought I *could* love him, and I loved the idea of being married and starting a family...."

He'd grown so rigid, she rushed on to explain. "The engagement ended almost as soon as it began. I realized what a stupid move it was, and he made it plain he didn't love me and likely never would. I think he just used the engagement as a sham, a way to..."

"Get you into bed?"

It sounded so stupid, and she'd been so gullible, that she only shrugged. "The, um, condoms have never been opened. I just haven't had the nerve to throw them out. I didn't want anyone to see them in my garbage."

Slowly, Riley relaxed. His frown smoothed out, replaced by a tender expression that seemed so incongruous to the hard man he could be. "Wouldn't be proper, huh?"

"It's private, that's all."

He started to say more, but Butch gave an impatient howl from the kitchen.

Riley glanced that way, then back at her. "I'll get him." He touched her chin, lifted her face and pressed his mouth to hers for several heart-stopping moments. "You better get dressed before I forget my dubious code of honor and the fact that we have a lot to get done in the next couple of hours." He turned and went through the door.

The second he disappeared, Regina jerked the drawer open, took out the framed photograph and looked around for a good place to hide it. She'd just lifted her mattress, ready to shove it beneath, when Riley stepped back in with a wriggling Butch in his arms. He drew up short when he saw her, then his brows came down.

His gaze went from her guilty face to her hand, which she quickly stuck behind her back. "All right, Red. What are you up to now?"

chapter 5

RILEY WATCHED AS REGINA JERKED THE FRAMED photo behind her back. Green eyes wide and innocent, she said, "It's nothing."

"Right." He strode forward, watched her quickly back up and move around the bed to the other side, and his suspicions grew. He set the dog on the mattress. Butch ran to Regina, came up on his hind legs and begged to be held.

Without taking her gaze off Riley, she caught the dog up one-handed. "If you'll leave, I'll get dressed."

Riley crossed his arms over his chest, not about to oblige her. "I'm damn curious, Red, what's worth hiding from me when I already saw the dirty books and rubbers."

Her jaw firmed. "They're not *dirty* books, they're educational."

"Uh-huh."

"And it's none of your business."

"Someone is trying to hurt you. Everything is my business."

Her cheeks colored. "This is...personal. Nothing that anyone else would care about."

"You don't trust me."

"Of course I do."

"Then let me see."

"Riley."

She wailed his name, making him smile. Stalking her, he started around the bed. She took one step back, then planted her feet and glared. Butch licked her chin in commiseration. Absently, she patted his back.

She was such an affectionate woman, so soft and gentle. It didn't take much to make her blush—a smile from him, a touch and her cheeks turned pink. The more he was with her the more he wanted her, and the more he wanted to know all her secrets. She'd kept parts of herself away from him, her engagement, her insecurities...but no more.

He stopped right in front of her and held out his hand.

She shook her head in exasperation. "This is stupid."

Riley waited.

Finally, with no graciousness, she slapped the picture frame into his hand. His curiosity keen, Riley turned it over, and was met with the charismatic smile on Senator Welling's face. Riley decided it must be the photo she took in the park, given the fountain beside him and the large trees behind him. Regina had written at the bottom of the photo, *Senator Xavier Welling,* along with the date of the photo.

The senator was easily in his mid-fifties. He was tall, gray-haired and aristocratic. In order to always make a good public appearance, he'd kept in shape. He had no paunch and his shoulders were still wide from his college football days.

Riley saw red. Through stiff lips, he said, "You keep a picture of the senator beside your bed?" And then with jealousy pricking his temper, he added, "Next to the goddamned *Kama Sutra?*"

Regina drew herself up. "Don't raise your voice to me."

It wasn't easy, but Riley reined in his temper. He tossed the picture onto the bed. "What the hell does it mean?"

"What does what mean?"

"Don't look so confused, Red. You've got his picture in your nightstand drawer, next to your bed, with books on sex and a load of rubbers." Hell, just saying it made him madder. "You got the hots for him?"

She gasped so hard, Butch started to howl again. She absently stroked him. "Of course not. He's a wonderful, respectable man with a wife he loves and a family he cherishes."

"Don't make me puke. He's a politician, first and foremost."

Regina went on tiptoes to poke him in the chest. "Yes, he's a politician. A wonderful senator. He's fought hard for the health and safety of children. He supports local law enforcement. He's won numerous awards and honors for leadership and—"

Riley turned his back on her. "Jesus, you're besotted."

Using her free hand, she caught the back of his shirt. "I am not," she all but shouted. "Senator Welling is an inspiration. I admire him, just as I admire his family and his aspirations and his beliefs." And then, in a smaller voice filled with vulnerability, she said, "I admire everything he stands for."

Riley turned to stare at her, something in her tone touching deep inside him. "Just what does he stand for, Regina?"

Still disgruntled, Regina chewed her lip, not looking at him. "Family. Community. Everything that's good. When you see him campaigning with his wife and kids, you just know that's how it *should* be, all of them smiling, happy, secure." She lifted her gaze to meet Riley's. "I see them together and I know it can happen, because it's right there, live, real."

Riley didn't know how real a politician's public persona

might be, but he could tell Regina believed in it. When she'd talked of her family, she'd done so with very little emotion. He'd found that strange, but hadn't pondered it long, not when most of his thoughts centered on carnal activities.

Feeling like a complete bastard, Riley pulled her into his arms. Butch wiggled until he was up between their faces, making sure no kissing would occur. But Riley felt content just to hold her. At least for now.

"I'm sorry."

Against his chest, she murmured, "For what?"

"For prying. And for not understanding." Keeping one hand on Butch so he wouldn't fall, Riley stroked Regina's back. He wished he could touch her bare silky skin again, but he didn't dare. It had been a close thing in the kitchen, his control severely tested. Only the fact that he knew damn good and well she wasn't thinking straight had kept him from laying her across the kitchen table. She'd been ready, damn it, whether she wanted to admit it or not.

"I guess it's okay," she said while rubbing her cheek against him, setting him on fire again. "It's not a secret that I admire the senator and what he stands for."

"Looks can be deceiving, you know."

She shook her head. "Being a politician does not automatically make him a fraud, Riley."

"No. But the world is filled with cheats and liars, people you'd bet on in a pinch, who turn out to be more unscrupulous than you ever could have imagined."

Leaning back, she looked at him thoughtfully. "Have you known people like that?"

He skirted that question by stating the obvious. "I'm a cop, Red. I see the worst of mankind all the time."

Her hand smoothed over his chest. She couldn't know how

the innocent touch inflamed him. If she did, she wouldn't now be looking at him with so much understanding. "You deal with that element of life. But Senator Welling is just the opposite. He's part of the good team, Riley."

Riley wanted to shake her for her naïveté. He knew first-hand how difficult it was to read the people you cared about. Blind trust was never a good thing, but since he wanted it from Regina, he didn't say so.

Riley tucked a long curl behind her ear. "Can I ask you something, honey?"

She laughed.

"What?" He held her away so he could better see her face.

"You're so funny, Riley. Demanding one minute, requesting the next."

"I'm glad you're amused." He smiled, too. "So is it all right?"

"Sure. At this rate, I won't have any secrets left at all."

That'd suit him just fine. He intended to make her his, but never again would he be made the fool. Knowing everything about her would be a safeguard against unhappy surprises.

He released her and she sat on the bed. Butch circled her lap, then nudged his way beneath her housecoat so he could curl up against her stomach. She tucked him in before looking at Riley in inquiry.

Riley settled himself beside her. "Who footed the bill when your parents died?" If she'd been the only one responsible, it'd help explain her need for doing things right, to always be prepared and proper.

She appeared confused by the question. "I did what I could, but I didn't have enough money to make a huge difference in their care. What I had to give wasn't enough, so instead I spent days researching ways to get them the help they needed. It wasn't easy. That's one of the things about Senator Welling.

His health benefit programs would have done my parents a world of good."

Riley did not want to talk about the damned senator. "What about your brother? Did he help out?"

"I told you, he's just like them. I had to loan him money to buy a suit so he'd have something decent to wear to the funerals."

Damn, that meant she alone had had the burden of her parents' care. "Loan—or give?"

She shrugged, which was all the answer Riley needed. "What about your fiancé? What happened there?"

Hedging that question, she asked, "Just who is the reporter here, Riley? Me or you?"

With a straight face, Riley said, "I just wondered if he could possibly be the one bothering you now." He spoke the truth, but it wasn't the only reason he asked. Possessiveness had a lot to do with his interest, too.

"Oh. No, he didn't help with my parents. Our engagement was after their deaths. And, no, it's not him."

"How do you know for sure?"

She untangled a grouchy Butch from her lap and pushed to her feet. "Trust me. He has no reason to hold a grudge."

Riley took the dog from her. He immediately rooted underneath Riley's shirt, circled into a small ball, and sighed himself back to sleep. Riley looked down at the lump where his flat abdomen used to be, shook his head, and put one hand over the dog. "Men see things differently than women. Maybe your take on the breakup isn't the same as his."

Regina rubbed her head. "It's not. But that has nothing to do with anything."

Her reluctance to talk about the other man couldn't have been more plain. It nettled Riley. "So who did the breaking up, you or him?"

"I did, but he didn't mind."

"How could he not mind? That doesn't make any sense. If he'd asked you to marry him—"

"He didn't want me, all right?" She threw up her hands. "There. Happy? He called me a prude and said I was unappealing. He wanted me to change myself and I can't do that, and he said that no man would want me, especially in bed, and so I *left*. End of story."

Stunned speechless, Riley watched her storm out of the room.

For long minutes after, he remained on the bed, soothing Butch who had gone a little frantic at Regina's raised voice. He'd crawled up Riley's chest, grumbling and growling, then poked his head out the neck of the shirt, just beneath Riley's chin. "Her fiancé sounds like a complete ass, doesn't he, Butch?"

Butch whined.

"I wonder, is that why she bought the books? Had she already realized that things weren't going well between them? Not that I'm sorry to hear it, because if she hadn't, she might have married him."

Butch whined a little louder.

"I agree." Riley had to take off his shirt to get Butch free. "Does she still love the guy, do you think?"

Butch had no answer.

When Riley entered the kitchen, Regina was on the phone with her editor, explaining about the glass. She didn't look at Riley, and after she hung up, she went past him to the living room.

"I won't be going in today at all. Most of the work I need to do for the rest of my assignment can be handled on the phone and typed up on my computer." She paused. "Is it okay if I bring my computer?"

Riley followed behind her, cautious of her new mood. "You can bring anything you want."

"Thank you." She pulled out a phone book from the closet and carried it back to the kitchen.

"What are you doing?"

"Looking up numbers for glass replacement. I want this fixed before the evening."

Riley followed her. "I'll take care of that."

"You said that half an hour ago."

"This time I mean it." He wrested the book out of her hands and plunked Butch into her arms. The poor dog had been passed around a lot that morning. "Go shower and pack whatever clothes you need right away. I'll call for the door replacement, take you to my place, then come back here and get your computer and any other stuff you need. All right?"

"I am not helpless."

"Far from it." He tried a smile that she didn't return. "C'mon, Red. You look stressed and tired and I want to take care of you just a little, okay?"

She stared up at him for long moments. "I'll finish up my work on this current piece today."

The swift change of topic threw him. "Great."

"That means tomorrow, or even later tonight, I can start my interview on you."

His smile slipped a little, but he managed to hang on to it. "Okay."

"I have so many questions, it might take a few...days."

His smile felt like a grimace. "I did agree."

"Yes, you did." She handed Butch back to him. "Can you keep an eye on him while I shower and dress? Thank you."

Both Riley and Butch watched her leave yet again, her walk a little more sassy this time. Oh, she wanted payback with the interrogation, he could tell. Riley wondered how many answers he could give without telling things he never wanted to reveal? It'd be tricky, but he could handle it.

If all else failed, he'd distract her with a kiss—and more. After all, he'd given her fair warning of what to expect. And still she'd agreed.

That thought brought back his smile in full force. In the end, he'd get what he wanted most: Regina. That made the rest worthwhile.

"WELL, THIS ANSWERS one question, doesn't it?" Regina stated.

Riley had parked his truck behind her Escort in his allotted garage space, then joined her. She stood between the car and the opened door, staring at his apartment.

Unlike most women Riley knew, Regina hadn't lingered in the shower. Butch, unwilling to wait in the kitchen while Riley cleaned up the glass, had howled endlessly until Regina stuck her head out the bathroom door and asked Riley to hand him to her. Butch had curled up on a towel and slept while she quickly showered and dressed in white slacks and a sleeveless cotton sweater and sandals. With her long red hair restrained in a French braid, minimal makeup and small earrings, she looked classy and sexy combined.

A large satchel with files and notes from her current project was slung over her arm. Riley hadn't realized that she gathered so much info just for one story. And since she'd told him her current article was about the silly talent show held by a local television station in the mall, he was doubly surprised.

They'd both driven so Regina would have her car handy. Not that he wanted her out driving around alone until he figured out what was going on. But neither did he want her to feel trapped or overly dependent on him. He knew she would rebel over that and he'd lose her before he could get her used to being with him.

Butch was on a thin leash, so Riley lifted him out of the car, then took Regina's elbow to move her forward. He closed her car door. "You disappointed?"

"That you don't have your own house?" She glanced at him over her shoulder and smiled. "No, of course not." Then she asked, "But why don't you?"

Riley shook his head. Before meeting Regina, he'd thought he had enough of hearth and home to last him a lifetime. He said only, "This is easier. Less maintenance." He led her and Butch up the walkway. "I'll show you around, then unload your stuff."

All she'd brought this trip were a few changes of clothes, her bedding—because she claimed she needed her own pillow to sleep—Butch's belongings and the material for her current assignment. She'd packed up more stuff at the house and disconnected her computer, but Riley told her he'd get all of that when he returned to meet the glass repairmen. Everything else they could retrieve as needed.

Since his place was on the ground floor, it'd be more convenient for Butch. He only hoped Butch liked the big golden retriever next door, since they'd be sharing yard space. He unlocked the door and pushed it open for Regina to enter.

"Oh, Riley, this is very nice."

He watched her look around. Luckily, he was a tidy man, otherwise he couldn't imagine her reaction. She touched her hand to the arm of a brown leather sofa, glided her fingers over a marble tabletop. "Did you decorate yourself?"

"Yeah." At the time, he'd taken enjoyment in only pleasing himself, with no one else to consider. He hadn't expected ever again to want the approval of a woman. And Regina wasn't just any woman, but an immaculate one at that.

Only it looked as though Regina liked his choices. "There's only one bath, but we'll work that out." Maybe they could share the shower? He grinned, then covered that reaction by discussing the dog. "I'll hook a lead up for Butch so he can run a little more outside. Oh, and if you need me to pick up any groceries for you, just let me know. I tend to do a lot of fast food."

He tugged Butch inside and closed the door.

Butch's ears perked up with his first glimpse of the place, giving Riley warning. He leaned down to unleash the little rat. In a stern voice, his finger shaking in the dog's face, Riley said, "Now listen up, bud. No piddling on the furniture, okay?"

Rather than feeling intimidated, Butch snapped at his finger, making Riley grin. "I almost forgot, with all the excitement." He pulled the stuffed Chihuahua from his pocket and tossed it toward the middle of the room. Butch jerked about to watch the stuffed animal land, then he reared back on his haunches, did a bunny hop to where the floppy toy lay—and attacked.

Regina started laughing at his antics.

Riley had to admit it was pretty cute the way he shook the toy, threw it this way and that. For such a small dog, he made feral sounds. Then as if expecting it to follow, Butch went into flight. It was so funny to watch him run. Somehow he managed to streamline himself, laying his ears back, tucking in his tail and dashing around furniture and corners so fast he was practically a blur.

His tiny feet made a distinct patter on the wooden floor. He slid around the corner, took a second to get some traction, and was off again.

Regina watched in wonder. "He doesn't know your place yet. How can he be sure he won't run into anything?"

Riley slung his arm around her shoulders, already enjoying having her in his home. "Men have great reflexes."

She cocked a brow at him. "And women don't?"

"Some women do." He pinched her chin, tipped up her face and kissed her mouth. "We'll be working on yours, remember?"

A knock sounded on his door. Regina pulled back in surprise, but Riley just shook his head. He opened the door and there stood Ethan, Rosie, Harris and Buck.

As usual, Rosie was pinned up against Ethan's side, and she appeared most comfortable there.

Harris, a firefighter at the same station as Ethan, looked fatigued, a good indicator that he'd recently come off his shift. Though Riley knew he'd have showered, the scent of smoke still clung to him. He pushed his black hair back with a hand and lounged against the door frame, his blue eyes tired and a little red.

Riley gave him the critical once-over. "Hell, Harris, you look like you should be in bed."

Harris yawned hugely. "Just left bed, actually." His satisfied grin said he'd just left a woman, also.

Riley grunted. "Maybe you should have tried sleeping."

"Did that—*after*. But last night was a bitch so I'm still sluggish."

Ethan nodded. "Had a pileup on the expressway. Three cars caught fire. No one died, thank God, but we worked our asses off."

Buck threw a thick, muscular arm around Harris, nearly knocking him off balance. Being the owner of a lumberyard and used to daily physical labor kept Buck in prime shape and made him the bulkier one in the group. Like Harris, Buck was single and enjoyed playing the field.

Still holding Harris, Buck pulled off a ball cap and scratched his head, further messing his brown hair. Green eyes alight with laughter, he said, "Harris never minds toiling through the night, 'cuz the ladies like to fawn all over him the next day."

"Jealous?" Harris asked.

"Naw." Then with a huge grin and a feigned yawn, he said, "I just got out of bed myself."

Riley laughed and held the door wide open. They all piled in, and Rosie was about to say "hi" when Butch flew around the corner, skidded to a halt, and went into a rampage of spitting Chihuahua fury.

Ethan tucked Rosie close. "What the hell?"

Rosie said, "Oh, it's so cute!"

Harris shrank behind Buck, pretending to cower. "Cute? What is it?"

"Whatever it is," Buck added, "it's demonic."

Riley caught Regina's scowl and laughed. "You might as well get used to hearing that, Red. It seems to be the typical response to your dog."

Buck and Harris said in unison, "Dog? You're kidding, right?"

Riley lifted Butch, who seemed to take extreme dislike to Ethan holding his wife. Most of his ire was directed at him.

"What did I do?" he asked

Rosie laughed, saying, "What haven't you done?"

"Hey." Riley held the dog eye level. "They're friends. You can relax now."

But Butch wasn't having it. Rosie dared to try to pet him and Butch practically went over Riley's shoulder in his effort to escape her. As long as he thought he had everyone cornered, he was as brave as a German shepherd, but let someone reach for him and he tucked his tail quick enough.

Regina took her dog. "He's still getting used to me and Riley. He's...shy."

Buck forced Harris to turn him loose. "Yeah? Is that what you call it?"

"I'd call it rabid," Ethan said.

Now that he was close to Regina, Butch quieted and started to lick her chin. Harris curled his lip. "That's disgusting."

"I think he's adorable."

Harris nudged Buck. "Yeah, Rosie, but you think Ethan is adorable, too, so you obviously have lousy taste."

Riley attempted to get things back on track. "Now that you're here I can explain."

Regina froze. "Explain what?"

"What's going on, of course." He knew she wouldn't like it, but he thought the extra backup wouldn't hurt. "They're friends, Red. And I want Harris and Buck to help me move some of your stuff."

Ethan sent his wife a look, then stared at Riley. "She's moving in with you?"

"Temporarily," Regina rushed to clarify.

At the same time, Riley said, "She is."

Rosie just grinned. "This is great. But what about your house?"

"As soon as it's mine, I'll—"

"As soon as it's *safe,* she'll move in there." Riley didn't want to think about her being on her own like that until he knew for certain that no one would hurt her. "Rosie, why don't you help Red make up the guest bed?" Riley suggested, and saw Harris and Buck start elbowing each other again, "and I'll get these goons to lend a hand unloading."

Rosie frowned. "Why can't Harris help her make the bed? I'd rather hear the scoop."

Harris stepped forward eagerly, eyebrows bobbing. "Oh yeah, I'll help her—"

Riley hauled him back with a hand in his collar. "I need to talk to you." Then to Rosie, "Regina can tell you what's going on."

"Yeah, well, somehow I think I'd hear a different version from you. Guys always have a different version."

Regina looked pained. "Really, I can make the bed myself and there's not that much to carry in."

Ethan grabbed his wife and kissed her. It wasn't a quick kiss or a timid one. Against her mouth, he teased, "Riley's suffering here, sweetheart. Be agreeable for once, will you?"

Dreamy eyed, Rosie said, "I'm agreeable every night."

Ethan touched her cheek and grinned. "Yes, you are."

Harris rolled his eyes. "God, will the honeymoon never end?"

In a quick mood switch, Rosie reached around her husband and shoved Harris, who fell into Buck. In a huff, she turned and grabbed Regina's arm. "Come on. Let them do the grunt work. You'll probably tell it right where Riley will only beat his chest and play Neanderthal."

That observation had Regina laughing. Butch gave the men a bark of farewell as the women disappeared around the corner.

"Okay," Ethan said, now that they were alone. "What's going on?"

"Outside. I don't want Regina to hear me."

Harris said, "Why is it the second a guy starts really caring about a woman, he complicates things?"

Buck nodded. "It becomes one big soap opera, doesn't it?"

Ethan and Riley hauled them out the door. At Regina's car, Riley said, "Someone is trying to hurt her, or scare her. I'm not sure which, and I don't know why."

Harris leaned on her fender. "No shit?"

"She okay?" Buck asked.

"Yeah. She's hanging in there. Regina is tougher than she looks."

Harris snorted, and when Riley glared at him, he held up his hands in surrender. "Hey, I wasn't casting aspersions on the lady. It's just hard to imagine anything tough about her."

Buck grinned, adding fuel to the fire. "She is a rather soft-looking woman, huh?"

Ethan rolled his eyes. "Quit baiting him, you two. He's got enough on his mind as it is."

All humor vanished when Riley said, "Someone threw a rock through her patio doors this morning." Seeing that he now had their undivided attention, he added, "And that's not all." As quickly as possible, Riley explained what had been happening.

"Could be coincidence," Ethan pointed out. "But I gather by your expression, you don't think so."

"No."

"Any ideas?" Harris asked.

"I'm going to check into her old fiancé. Things ended only a few months ago."

"Regina was engaged?" Ethan looked startled by that disclosure.

"Yeah, and there's some idiot who made a pest of himself at her old job. I'll get names from her tonight." Riley also intended to talk to Senator Welling. That might be a little more difficult to accomplish, but if Welling had seen anything the day her car was run off the road, or if he'd noticed anything suspicious at the park, Riley wanted to know about it. The senator had an appearance scheduled at a ceremony for the historical society. Should be easy enough to grab a few words with him then.

"And in the meantime?" Ethan asked.

"I don't want her alone." Which was the main reason he'd gathered his friends together. He couldn't be with her 24/7, so he'd count on them to help out. "For right now, I figured Rosie could stay here with her while we go get some of her things. Plus, I don't want repairmen in her apartment without supervision. They're due in about an hour."

"If it's not safe, then I don't want Rosie involved."

Riley sent his best friend a long look. "Would I put Rosie in any danger?"

"I wouldn't think so."

"Then relax. They're safe enough here, especially since no one knows Red is staying with me."

Ethan scrutinized Riley. "She says it's temporary."

Riley drew a breath. "For now." And then as he walked back to the apartment carrying Butch's pen and bed, he added, "But I'm working on it."

chapter 6

THE SECOND RILEY OPENED HER APARTMENT door, he felt the tension. With a raised hand, he shushed the men behind him and stepped silently inside. There was no noise, but the silence was thick, somehow alive. Automatically, Riley's gaze searched out every nook and corner, fast but thorough. He noted the unfamiliar shadow in the bedroom doorway. As he stared, it shifted the tiniest bit and all his senses went on alert.

He flattened his hand on Ethan's chest. In a nearly sound-less voice, he ordered, "Stay here."

Ethan took exception to that with a muttered, "Like hell."

Unwilling to waste any time, Riley started into the living area. A floorboard squeaked beneath his foot, and in the next instant motion exploded around him. A crash sounded and a tall, dark man dressed all in black bolted out of the bedroom. In one fluid motion, he went through the patio doors and over the railing, much as Riley had earlier.

Without a second thought, Riley went after him.

Behind him, he heard Ethan yell, "Call the police," and then

Riley was at the railing, cursing as he hit the ground. He landed in a crouch on the balls of his feet, took only a single moment to get his balance, and gave pursuit.

The man was several feet in front of him, but Riley was fast and more than a little determined. This could be the man who'd been terrorizing Regina but, either way, he'd been in her apartment where he didn't belong. Riley could easily take him apart with his bare hands—but he was a cop, and so he'd go by the law. Even if the restraint killed him.

When he'd almost reached the intruder, Riley didn't grab him with his hands. Instead, he kicked out, sweeping the man's legs out from under him.

The big man went down with a loud grunt of pain. Riley hit hard, too, jarring his bones but unmindful of any pain. He rolled and was atop the other man before the goon could regain his feet. Riley immobilized him by catching his legs with his own, then twisting the man's thick right arm up and back at a very unnatural angle. The man howled in pain. It wouldn't take much pressure to snap a bone or pull the arm from the shoulder socket, and with the way Riley felt, he was more than willing.

Another loud groan issued from his captive.

"Be still," Riley commanded, then he glanced up to see Buck and Harris standing at his side.

Buck curled his lip. "I'm not a cop, Riley. Want me to break something on him?"

The offer was so ludicrous coming from Buck—a man known for laughter, but never aggression—that Riley almost grinned. "If he moves, kick him in the teeth."

"Right." Buck planted his muscular legs apart in what appeared to be anticipation. His size twelve-and-a-half feet were encased in sturdy steel-toed boots.

Wearing a grimace, the intruder twisted to see Riley. "You're a cop?" he gritted out.

"That's right. But I'm off duty. Some uniforms will be here shortly to haul your ass downtown."

"Christ, man, you're breaking my arm."

Harris nodded. "He's right, Riley." He turned his head, contemplating the strange hold Riley had on him. "Looks like you might be breaking a leg, too."

"Don't tempt me." He nudged the guy. "What's your name?" When the man hesitated, Riley growled, "Say it, damn it. Don't make up a lie."

"Earl! My name's Earl."

"Earl what?"

Rather than answer, he groaned in agony.

"Just Earl, huh?" Approaching sirens split the air. Riley said, "Well, Earl, you want to tell me what you were doing in the apartment?"

Sweat beaded on the man's forehead. "Saw it was open. Just wanted to have a look around."

"Right. Let's try again. What were you looking for?"

"Nothing." His head dropped forward to the ground and he panted. "It's the truth, damn it."

"So you're just a regular, run-of-the-mill burglar? You weren't here earlier, tossing rocks?"

"Rocks? No."

Maintaining his hold on Earl's arm, Riley came to his feet and hauled the other man upright. Earl tried to jerk away, but only managed to cause himself more pain. "Buck, check his pockets."

Earl kicked and fought, prompting Riley to add a little more pressure. The man's back bowed with a rank curse.

Ethan showed up then. He looked far more disgruntled and angry than Riley. "What the hell are you doing, Riley?"

Buck dug in the man's pockets and produced a pack of cigarettes, loose change, and a knife. "Sorry, Riley, no wallet, no I.D."

"Shake out a cigarette."

Buck sent him a look. "It's a hell of a time to start smoking." He smacked the pack until one cigarette emerged, saying to Earl, "Nasty habit, bud. Smoking can kill you."

Earl tried to kick out at Buck and with little effort, Riley forced him to his knees.

Ethan crossed his arms over his chest. "The cops are here. Should you be abusing him that way?"

"Since he keeps fighting me, he's lucky I don't tear him to pieces."

As luck would have it, Dermot and Lanny rounded the corner. They stiffened when they caught the occupants of the scene. "Christ almighty, Riley. What the hell is going on?"

Riley forced the big man flat again, put a knee between his shoulder blades and said to Dermot, "Give me some cuffs."

Dermot rolled his eyes, but did as told. After the restraints were in place, Riley did a quick search of his captive, but found no other weapons. He released Earl into Lanny's legal hands. "Read him his rights."

"I know my job, Riley. You want to tell me what the hell we're arresting him for?"

"Sure thing. He was in Red's apartment when I showed up." Riley handed Lanny the cigarettes. "And he smokes the same brand I found on the ground below her balcony."

"Well, I'll be damned. What'd he do inside? Did he steal anything?"

Indicating the contents of his pockets, which Buck still held, Riley said, "That's all he had on him, and I don't think the blade is Red's, so it must be his own. You can add concealed weapon to illegal entry. I think we interrupted things, but I've yet to have a look around inside. You can go on. I'll be down to the station in a little while." Then Riley thought to add, "Hang on to him, okay?"

Dermot grinned. "Judge Ryder is on a fishing trip, not due back till Monday. I'd say it's a safe bet we'll have him till then."

Lanny and Dermot each took an arm while Lanny started the familiar litany on rights. They led Earl to the cruiser. Riley watched, still tensed, until the big man was folded into the back seat and the door securely closed.

Then he became aware of the silence around him. He looked at Harris, who had his brows raised, Buck who grinned and Ethan who stared at Riley so long, Riley finally said, "What?"

"You're a regular savage, Riley, you know that?"

Riley shoved his way past his friend. "Screw you, Ethan."

Ethan laughed. Buck stepped up and drew Riley to a halt so he could squeeze his biceps. "Pure steel," he crowed to his friends. "Like a real-life action hero, he is."

Harris tucked his hands beneath his chin and said in a falsetto voice, "My hero."

Grumbling under his breath, Riley jerked free and went to the balcony. Damned idiots. When he jumped up and grabbed the railing, all three of his foolish friends started joking again. Riley did his best to ignore them as he swung a leg up and pulled himself over the railing. He noticed Ethan, Harris and Buck followed suit, climbing the balcony rather than taking the long walk around the complex to the front door.

Several neighbors were out, watching the proceedings with great curiosity. Once he'd regained his feet, Riley waved down to them. "A minor break-in folks."

They looked skeptical.

Of course, Buck was still scaling the balcony and Harris had only one leg caught awkwardly over the top rail. Riley shook his head and went inside. When Ethan started to follow, Riley warned him off. "Stay put a minute, okay? I want to have a look around. There's less chance of anything being disturbed if it's just me."

"If you need anything, give a yell."

Riley went to the bedroom first. He knew better than to tamper with evidence or disrupt a crime scene, but this wouldn't be the first time he'd ignored his conscience to do what he thought was best.

In this case, they weren't dealing with a death. More important, Red's feelings were at stake.

If anything would embarrass her, he wanted to know about it and, if possible, spare her. His intentions were altruistic— as unselfish as they'd been the first time he'd broken his own code of honor.

He saw right off that her dresser drawers had been dumped. Lacy panties and bras littered the floor in haphazard disarray, looking like a flock of fallen butterflies. Her pajamas and T-shirts had also been dumped.

Everything from her dresser top had been shoved to the floor, including hair combs, jewelry and perfume. Items from her closet had been sloppily rearranged and her bedding pulled apart.

What really caught Riley's eye, though, were the damn rubbers tossed everywhere. Dragging a hand over his face, Riley considered the situation, but he gave in before he had time to really think it through. Rushing, he gathered up the condoms and stuffed them into his pockets. He had more than one reason for doing so.

If his friends saw them, they might think they were his and

the teasing would be endless, considering the size of the damn things. In fact, he intended to dispose of them posthaste so he didn't get caught with them in his pockets. It would give him a reputation he'd never live down.

But the biggest reason was that Red would be appalled if anyone knew she had them. Obviously, they had nothing to do with whatever Earl—if that was even his real name, which Riley doubted—was looking for.

Her nightstand drawers were now empty. Riley looked around the carnage, but didn't see the photo of Welling or the damn books anywhere. Earl hadn't had them on him, and what would he want with them anyway? That had to mean that Red had taken them with her.

He didn't mind the books—hell, he'd be happy to read them with her. But the last thing he wanted in his home was Xavier Welling's smiling face. Especially since he knew Red saw the man as some sort of paragon of goodness, a damned representation of what men should be. If she expected him to measure up to a precisely staged public persona, she was sure to be let down.

Ethan said, "Everything okay, Riley?"

With the condoms out of sight, Riley called back, "Yeah. You can come in."

Ethan entered the room, followed by Harris and Buck. "Damn, someone is definitely looking for something."

Harris stared toward her underwear. Using only his pinkie, he lifted a teeny tiny thong of shimmery pale pink. "I thought redheads weren't supposed to wear pink."

Riley grabbed the garment from him and stuffed it in his pocket—with the condoms. Hell, it was hard enough for him picturing Red in the sexy bottoms. He'd be damned if he wanted Harris doing the same.

Buck propped his hands on his hips. "Do we clean this up or leave it?"

Riley shook his head. "I have a camera in my truck. I'll take some photos then we'll tidy up before Regina sees it. It'd only upset her."

Ethan crossed his arms over his chest. "All things considered, I want to give Rosie a call. We're going to be a while and I want to make sure she's okay."

"Tell her to get a list of groceries from Regina. I'll stop at the store on my way home."

Harris grinned. "Why, don't you just sound so domesticated?" He started to reach for a satin demibra, and Buck grabbed his arm, but he was laughing, too.

"Leave the unmentionables to Riley before he twists your arm behind your neck."

Riley glared at them both before heading out to his truck, but his thoughts soon left his goofy friends. He had a man in custody. He had Red in his apartment.

Things were moving right along.

REGINA HEARD the front door opening and her heart shot into her throat. Jumping to her feet, she ran to greet Riley.

With his tongue hanging out, Butch kept pace, pretending they were in a race. She knew it was idiotic, knew that Ethan said Riley was fine, but she wanted to see him for herself, to be sure.

He'd just stepped inside the door, awkwardly holding his keys in one hand while juggling grocery bags with his other. Regina halted in front of him.

Riley glanced at her in surprise. "Hey, what's wrong?"

A little embarrassed but still anxious, Regina blurted, "I was worried."

His gaze lingered on her face, his mouth curled. "About me?"

"Yes. And don't be insulted. I know you can take care of yourself."

"And you still worried?"

She nodded, which made his expression warm all the more.

Without looking away from her, Riley kicked the door shut and shifted both bags into one arm. Reaching out, he snagged her close and his mouth brushed hers. "Thanks, Red. But you don't need to fret, okay?"

She sighed. He sounded like the idea was unheard of. "You aren't invincible, Riley. And Ethan called and told Rosie what happened and—"

"And I'm fine." He gave her a squeeze. His hand started down her back toward her bottom, then he looked beyond her. His hand stopped at the base of her spine and he nodded. "Hey, Rosie. Ethan's right behind me."

"I figured as much." She sauntered forward, grinning. "So, hero, how you doing?"

Riley rolled his eyes and allowed Regina to take one of the bags. Suddenly Butch let out a demanding, yodeling howl, and when Riley looked down at him, he came up on his hind legs, dancing in excitement.

"Well, what a greeting." Riley lifted the little dog to eye level. "Met at the door by a beautiful woman and a faithful Chihuahua. What more could a man ask for?"

Regina wanted to smack him. "Riley, please tell me you didn't tackle some maniac who broke into my apartment."

He winked and, still holding Butch close, walked around her to the kitchen. She looked at Rosie, who shrugged, then she stalked after him. *"Riley."*

"Yes, dear." He was in the kitchen, Butch over his shoulder while he unloaded groceries one-handed. "Since you cooked last night, I'll do the deed tonight. Steaks on the grill or spaghetti? They're my two specialties, my only specialties really, so I bought both. Or we can go simple and just have sandwiches. What's your pleasure?"

Regina held on to her temper by a thin thread. She was in his house, and he wanted to help her. She drew a breath. "Do you or do you not have a man in custody?"

"Yeah, we do. Thing is, the bastard isn't talking. We don't even have his name yet. But, luckily, Judge Ryder is out fishing."

Regina shook her head in confusion. "So?"

"So this is a small town, not the big city. Things are done differently here. Ryder's been around forever because no one cares to run against him. Because of that, he feels comfortable taking off for days at a time when the weather looks right to catch a big bass." He winked at her. "The weather looks right."

"What does some judge fishing have to do with the guy who broke in?"

"He can't be arraigned until the judge comes back. That gives us more time to check him out. I have a gut feeling that once we turn him loose on bail, he'll disappear."

Nervousness made her voice tremble. She clasped her hands together tightly, trying to calm herself. "What are you holding him for?"

"Illegal entry and concealed weapon for starters. He ransacked your bedroom, honey, but he didn't steal anything and nothing was really damaged."

The ramifications hit her. "So he was looking for something."

"I'd say so. Whatever it is, he hadn't found it before we interrupted." Riley gave Butch an absent pat as he moved from the cabinet to the refrigerator. "The guys helped me clean up the mess."

The guys. Aware of Rosie lounging in the doorway, Regina eased closer. Her heart slammed in her chest and her palms were damp. "He, uh, trashed my bedroom?"

Riley turned toward her. After a long look, he leaned down and whispered near her ear, "Hey, it's all right, babe. I confiscated the rubbers before anyone could see."

Her relief was overwhelming. "Thank you."

His grin gave her fair warning. "Harris gathered up your panties. Sexy stuff." His gaze dipped down her body. "Makes me wonder what you're wearing right now."

Rosie cleared her throat. "It's rude to whisper in front of guests."

Riley straightened with a sigh. "Since when are *you* a guest?" He glanced at his watch in a show of impatience. "Shouldn't Ethan be here by now?"

"Trying to get rid of me?" Rosie laughed. "And here I was ready to vote for steaks."

Riley looked pained, which mirrored how Regina felt. She wanted to be alone with him, to ask him details on what had happened.

Ethan sauntered in. "Soon as I get everything out of the truck, I'm taking you home, woman."

Rosie turned to drape her arms around his neck. "Really? What for?"

It was Ethan's turn to whisper, Rosie's turn to blush. In a rush, she said, "I'll help you unload."

It was another half hour before Regina was finally able to corner Riley and get some answers.

Not once had Butch left his side. He'd followed Riley to the truck time and again, then around the apartment, watching while Riley helped to put her things away in various places. He hooked up her computer in the room he'd given her to use as an office. It was a guest bedroom, but Regina knew Riley didn't want her using the bed.

With everything now in place, they sat on the back patio so Butch could run the length of the lead Riley had stretched between two trees. Regina stared at Riley, on the edge of her seat.

"What if he'd had a gun, Riley? What if he'd pulled that knife on you?"

Sprawled out on a chaise, his ankles crossed, Riley laid a forearm over his eyes to shield them from the late-afternoon sun. "If the dumb son of a bitch had dared to pull a knife on me, I'd have..." Belatedly, he lifted his arm to take in Regina's expression of horror. His frown smoothed out. "I'd have disarmed him, honey. Okay?"

She couldn't bear the thought of him being in danger because of her. "Are you really that good?"

He sat up and swung his legs around to face her. Treating her to a somber, very direct stare, he took her hands and said, "Yeah."

He'd answered without boasting, just matter-of-factly stating what he saw as a truth. Regina shook her head at such confidence.

"Later," he told her while giving her hands a squeeze, "I'm going to show you how good I am."

Oh, the way he said that. His low tone and sensual smile left her uncertain to his meaning. Cautiously, she asked, "You are?"

"Might as well get started on your training, don't you think?"

Well heck, so *that's* how he meant it. Disappointment warred with common sense. Still, private self-defense lessons wouldn't be at all the same as what they'd done in his gym. There, he'd been all business, politely distant, and a true gentleman given the other onlookers. Here, they'd be wrapped in privacy. The thought of being alone with Riley, feeling his body over hers, touching in all the most sexual places, made her breathless. "I suppose."

"So much enthusiasm." He pulled her off her seat and into

his lap—something he never would have done in his gym. She thought he might kiss her, and truthfully, she wanted him to. In the short time he'd been at her apartment and then at the station, she'd missed him. She'd worried about him, too.

Instead he said, "Tell me the name of the guy who harassed you at work, and that ass you were engaged to."

"Why?" She tried to twist around to see him, but he hugged her closer so she could barely move. The fact that she was thinking about intimacy, and he apparently wasn't, left her flustered.

"I'm going to talk to them both. And no, don't argue, Red. I won't embarrass you. You have my promise on that."

It wasn't Riley she worried about. He'd already proven to have her best interests in mind. But her ex-fiancé… "I don't know what you think they can add to the equation."

Riley shrugged. "Maybe nothing. But it can't hurt to ask them a few pertinent questions, now can it?"

Actually, it could probably hurt her pride a lot. She bit her lip, but finally nodded. Riley was a professional who knew his business inside and out. It would be ridiculous to contradict him. "The man I worked with is Carl Edmond. He's a nice enough guy, just different. Sort of intense."

"Intense how?"

"Not in a bad way. Just overzealous about everything, his work, his life—"

"And you?"

She couldn't deny that. "For a while, maybe. He fixated on me. He told me he loved me, but I knew that wasn't true. His courtship became a bother before he wised up, but he was never threatening."

Riley didn't seem convinced. "And the other guy?"

Regina hated to talk about him. She couldn't mention his

name without memories swamping her, leaving her hollowed out with humiliation.

But this time, seated on Riley's lap, held in his arms, it was easier. "His name is Luther Finley." She closed her eyes and prayed Luther wouldn't reveal anything of their private past to Riley. Not that Luther considered anything private. She'd found that out too late. "I assume Carl still works at the paper. He loves his job a lot. And Luther should be in the insurance building across the street. He's a salesman." She drew a breath. "Want me to write the names down for you?"

"Carl Edmond and Luther Finley. I won't forget." Riley rubbed his big hand up her arm, then down again. He was silent, introspective, and yet he kept touching her as if he couldn't help himself.

When his thoughts finally turned from the men, Regina felt the shift in his mood and she wanted to rejoice. She tipped up her face—and Riley accommodated her by capturing her mouth for a long, deep kiss. She felt the drumming of his heart, tasted the damp warmth of his mouth, and didn't want him ever to stop.

With his mouth still touching hers, he murmured, "Damn, you taste good."

He tasted better than good. Delicious. Regina pressed closer to slip her tongue into his mouth, deepening the kiss again and making Riley groan in response.

The warm sun beat down on them, cooled only by the gentle breeze. Riley's strength wrapped around her, giving the illusion that nothing bad could ever happen. From his wide chest and thick shoulders to his flat abdomen and strong thighs, he was all male. Being with him, alone each night, would make it nearly impossible to keep any emotional distance.

Had it been only a day ago that she thought she needed to know him better before becoming involved?

She knew the truth now. Already she was way too involved, and knowing him better only made it worse. Riley believed in her when no one else did. He put himself in danger for her. By his own admission and by the evidence of his actions, he was more than capable of handling any threatening situation. On every level, he fascinated her.

She was already half in love with him.

Riley's hand moved up alongside her face. His big thumb stroked her cheekbone as he lifted his mouth. "I want to ask you something, Red."

Regina felt herself floating. She smiled. "Hmm?"

"Why did you bring the books and photo here?"

Her sensual haze lifted. She opened her eyes to see Riley watching her, his expression probing, filled with command. Because their noses practically touched, it was a rather intimidating stare.

"C'mon, Red, tell me." She started to straighten, but he shook his head. "No, I like you like this. I enjoy holding you."

"Oh." She shifted a little to get more comfortable, felt his erection, heard his low groan and immediately stilled. No one had ever touched her as much as Riley did. Not even her fiancé had wanted to hold her this way. "I brought the books because I thought, well, we are going to be staying here together. I'm not an idiot. I realize what we'll likely do before too long."

The heat in his blue eyes darkened. "Today." His kiss was soft, gentle. "It's going to happen today."

Such a sensual promise shattered all other thought. She could only stare at him.

"But, honey, you don't need a book."

Brought back to the reality of the moment, she winced and gave an awful admission. "I think…maybe I do."

Without seeming to move, he gathered her closer to his body. He glanced out into the yard at Butch, saw he was sprawled out in the sweet grass in a spot of bright sunshine. Then he looked to make certain they were well hidden between the sections of privacy fence that lined his small patio.

His gaze came back to her, resting first on her eyes, then her mouth. "How can you need a book when everything you do makes me hot? You dress up all classy and it makes me think about stripping you naked. I catch you in worn pajamas and I want to feel how soft and warm you are under them. You cook dinner and I obsess about the way your bottom sways while you stir the food."

She'd been listening with fascinated wonder until the last, then a startled laugh broke free. "You do not."

"I do." And in a growl he added, "Your backside has played prominently in all my most recent fantasies." He punctuated that statement by grasping her firmly in both hands, giving her behind an affectionate, caressing squeeze. "Damn. I can't wait to get you naked so I can explore it in more detail."

Her face flamed. "Riley."

"Regina." His smile touched her heart. "I especially like the charming way you blush. Hell, everything about you makes me hot. Believe me, honey, getting you into bed is the objective. Once we're there, it doesn't matter what you do. I won't be complaining."

Hearing him say it made her almost believe. Had she allowed Luther's spiteful comments to influence her too much? It had been such a difficult time, such a humiliation.

But Riley wouldn't lie to her, she knew. He was better than

that. "All right, I'll forget about the books if you promise to tell me what you like."

He drew her marginally closer. "I like you."

"You know what I mean."

He pressed his face into her neck and gave a gruff laugh. "The way you keep talking about this, like it's going to happen any second now, has me close to exploding."

Regina thought it *was* going to happen at any moment. She frowned at him, but before she could tell him that she wanted him now, he said, "There're a few things I want to clear up before we get sidetracked."

Sidetracked? Is that what he called making love with her? Feeling put out by his blasted patience, she said, "Like what?"

He leaned away. Some of the teasing laughter in his eyes darkened to a more serious emotion. "The photo. And why the hell you brought it along."

chapter 7

BLESS BUTCH'S LITTLE HEART. HE CHOSE THAT
moment to interrupt with a loud spate of barking. Regina sat
up to see that a rather hefty golden retriever had come over to
check him out. Regina started to jump up in alarm, but Riley
stayed her with a hand on her arm.

"That's Blaze. She's a sweet dog, honey. She won't hurt him."

Regina doubted that after she saw Butch try to sprinkle the
gorgeous creature's nose. Yet rather than snap at him, Blaze
lunged back playfully, shook her head, and ran the length of
his lead so that Butch could chase her.

He went so fast trying to keep up, he tripped over his own nose
and managed a complete somersault without stopping. When he
ran out of rope, he yelped, and Blaze trotted back to him.

Regina laughed. "I think Butch is in love."

Riley sat up behind her, his arms looped around her waist.
"Poor bastard. I wonder if she'll keep pictures of other dogs
around just to make him nuts."

Regina turned sharply to stare at him. Was he jealous over

the picture? But no, that would be too absurd. Senator Welling represented strong values, not sexual allure. Surely, Riley understood that.

Riley lifted her away and came to his feet. The dogs were still playing, making a terrible racket that didn't bother Regina at all. She couldn't keep her eyes off Riley as he stretched, then looked up at the blazing sun.

In the next instant he reached for the hem of his shirt and pulled it off over his head.

Regina didn't so much as blink. His upper body was gorgeous. Dark hair liberally covered his well-defined chest. Sleek, prominent muscles in his shoulders bunched and moved as he haphazardly folded the shirt and laid it over the back of her chair. In unselfconscious masculine display, he dragged one hand through his chest hair, scratching a little, then flexed his shoulder and rotated his head.

Regina's mouth went dry. In something of a rasp, she asked, "What are you doing?"

"It's warm out here." He glanced down at her. "And I'm a little stiff from jumping off your damn balcony so many times." So saying, he turned to head inside and Regina caught sight of a bruise on his ribs.

"Riley." She was out of her chair in a flash, catching his arm and holding him still. "What happened?"

He looked down at the darkening flesh she indicated. "Nothing. That must be where I hit the ground when I tripped him. I had no idea there were so many little stones everywhere."

Wishing she could soothe him, even heal him, her fingertips grazed over his warm skin. "I'm sorry."

His gaze stayed on her face, piercing and bright. "No problem, Red." He unsnapped his slacks.

Regina stepped back in a rush.

"I'm going to go change before we have our little chat about that picture. Be back in a second."

Change? As in, change into *what?* Less clothes? It was bad enough when he was at the gym wearing shorts, T-shirt, socks and athletic shoes. But at the gym, there was always a crowd around, plenty of people to keep the situation less intimate.

Here, there was no one. And she just knew if Riley started flaunting himself, she'd end up the aggressor.

He was only gone a minute, but it was long enough for Regina to give herself a hot flash, thinking of the night to come.

"You getting hungry, Red?"

She jerked around, then took an automatic step toward him. Good Lord, the man oozed sex appeal. He wore gray low-slung drawstring shorts, and nothing else. She realized she'd never seen his feet before. They were big, sprinkled with golden brown hair, narrow, and as sexy as the rest of him. Right now, braced apart as they were, he seemed to have planted himself firmly against opposition. Hers?

Not likely. Not when everything about him appealed to her.

Slowly, Regina allowed her attention to climb upward, taking in every inch of his body. Muscular, very hairy calves, nice knees. *Incredible* thighs.

Her heart raced. She already knew firsthand how strong his thighs were. She'd watched Riley grappling with some very big bruisers at his gym and he always dominated. Swallowing, she looked higher still and saw the hem of his shorts, hanging to midthigh.

A little higher and she saw… Oh my. Regina blew out a breath that sounded part whistle, part exclamation, and not in the least ladylike. Under normal circumstances, she would have been appalled at herself. But the soft cotton molded to his sex. He was right, small condoms would never fit him.

Breathing became more difficult. As an intelligent, educated and modern woman, and as one who had recently read some informed books on the subject, she knew size didn't matter. That hadn't been her problem with Luther at all.

So why did it feel like a volcano of heat had exploded inside her?

As she stared at him, unable to draw her gaze away, something twitched. Her brows lifted. Fascinated, she watched as Riley became semierect. She put a hand to her throat.

Riley, blast him, never moved.

Deciding it might be safer to continue on with her visual journey rather than keep staring at him *there,* Regina looked at his hard abdomen. That didn't help one iota. The hair around his navel and the silky trail below it appeared soft, tempting her to touch it. She wanted to so badly, but would that be crossing the line?

At the moment, did she care? How could any woman remain rational when faced with such provocation?

Almost from the start, she'd wanted Riley. Every day the feeling grew stronger. Other than her acute sense of caution and propriety, there were no real reasons for waiting.

She moved toward him.

Riley made a gruff sound of expectation.

Savoring the moment, she put her hands on his sides, luxuriating in the feel of hot smooth skin drawn taut over firm muscle. Experimentally, Regina caressed him, her thumbs inward to trace over the sleek muscles slanting toward his groin.

She looked at his face. He was rigid, flushed, waiting. "I want to touch you, Riley."

"Do."

One simple word that somehow sounded so provocative. When she looked again, she saw that he now had a full erection.

Very full. Just from her touching his waist? Intrigued, she asked, "You like this?"

"Yeah." He drawled out the word, husky and deep.

Emboldened, she slid her hands around his back near the very bottom of his spine, close to his sexy muscled tush. The position brought her closer to his chest and she inhaled deeply. "You smell so good, Riley."

He leaned forward, pressed his mouth to her temple, and whispered, "Is that really where you want to touch me, Red?"

Her nose brushed his soft chest hair when she shook her head. She liked that, so she did it again. "No."

"I didn't think so."

Deciding to try pure honesty, she said, "We're outside...."

"No one can see us."

"But still..."

"I'm a man, not a schoolboy. I can control myself. Nothing happens unless you say so. Feel free to touch all you want and to stop when you want."

Her heart expanded. Such an incredibly generous offer.

Such an incredibly generous man.

She tipped her face up. "Will you kiss me while I do it?"

His expression hardened and his voice went low and rough. "My pleasure, baby."

This kiss felt different. Regina hadn't realized he'd been holding back, that there were so many nuances to kissing until that moment when she felt all his carnal intent in the way he devoured her mouth. It was an eating kiss, hot and hard and overwhelming. He would make love to her now—she understood that and reveled in the reality.

Again and again, his tongue sank past her parted lips and into her mouth, stroking seductively. She felt consumed. That was enough of a distraction that Riley had to nudge himself forward into her belly to remind her of what she wanted, of what *he* wanted.

Bringing her hands around, she first toyed with his navel. His abdomen had grown rigid, the muscles clearly defined, growing more so as she touched him until he felt like granite with no give to his flesh at all. The hair there was just as silky as she'd imagined.

Breathing hard, her awareness suspended, she encountered the waistband of his shorts, the ultrasoft cotton material and finally the long, solid length of his penis.

They both groaned.

Riley's fingers tightened and he lifted his mouth away to gulp for air. Keeping his forehead against hers, he encouraged her by saying, "That's it. Damn, Red..." And he groaned again, harsh and broken.

Regina could have spent an hour just exploring him. On so many levels, he fascinated her, the freedom he allowed, his open response. Her fingertips trailed up his length, measuring him, then back down again—and she felt the shuddering response of his body.

Driven by curiosity, she cupped beneath his shaft, cradling his heavy testicles in her palm and heard him hiss in a breath.

"Easy." His long fingers gripped her upper arms.

"Like this?"

"Yeah." His grip loosened, caressed, encouraged.

They spoke in muted whispers, hers awed, his raw with arousal.

Suddenly he kissed her again, so ravenously that she forgot what she was doing and her hands left him to grasp his neck, holding tight. Strong arms enclosed her, stealing her breath. Her lips were swollen, her head spinning, when Riley again cupped her face to place sweet little pecks on her chin, her cheeks, her forehead.

"You know what I think, Red?"

Overwhelmed, she whispered, "What?"

"That turnabout is fair play."

Her stomach jumped and her heart began a wild race. When she got her eyes open, Riley was smiling at her.

"You'll love having me touch you, Red. I promise. But for right now, we should take this indoors before things get out of hand and neither one of us makes a clearheaded decision."

Her head would never be clear again.

Riley nodded in the direction of the yard. "Butch fell asleep with his new lady friend."

A safer topic if ever there was one. Regina turned and saw that Blaze had stretched out on her side in the thick grass. Her golden fur looked beautiful with the sun glinting off it. Butch was curled up on her neck, his whole head practically in her ear. They made such an adorable picture, Regina's heart nearly melted and stupidly, tears filled her eyes.

"Tonight," Riley whispered to her, "I want to sleep with you curled that close." He didn't give her a chance to reply to that, not that she had a reply anyway. He picked her up and started into the house.

"Butch…"

"Will enjoy his freedom in the yard. I'll leave the window open. Don't fret, honey. We'll hear him if he needs us." Riley walked right past the room he'd given to her and into his own bedroom.

When he reached the bed, he went down with her in his arms. She'd known of his strength, but still he amazed her. He treated her weight as negligible, arranging her as easily as he would a pillow. Straightening away, balanced on one arm, he said, "You're wearing entirely too many clothes, Red. What d'you say we take them all off?" And before she could find her voice, he already had her sleeveless sweater up and over her head.

RILEY KNEW if he gave her too much time to consider things, she'd decide it wasn't proper to be having sex with him in the middle of the afternoon with the window open. He was done giving her time. She now felt comfortable touching him sexually, and he knew, even if she didn't, that they had a future together.

The rest would fall into place.

The second her sweater cleared her head, he reached for the clasp to her bra. He heard her gasping breaths, felt the urgent bite of her nails in his upper arms.

The bra, bless her feminine little heart, was white lace and so damn sexy he could have spent an hour just appreciating the way it decorated her small breasts. Instead, he flicked the front clasp open, pulled the thin cups apart, and visually sated himself.

"Beautiful."

Regina made a sound of startled embarrassment and covered herself with her hands.

Riley forced his gaze from her white breasts to her face. "Harris was wrong. Pink and red go real nice together."

Her embarrassment faded behind confusion. "What are you talking about?"

A long curl of titian hair had come loose, and Riley used it like a feather to tease the side of her breast. "Red hair and pink nipples. It's a sexy combination."

"Oh." More color exploded in her cheeks. "But what does Harris have to do with—"

No way would Riley tell her about Harris picking up her pink panties. "And this pretty blush." He put his mouth to her cheek and felt the heat of her flush. "You're beautiful, Regina, and I don't want you to be embarrassed with me."

He gently caught her wrists, aware of the fragile bones, how small she felt in his big hands. Drawing her arms up, he pressed her hands firmly to the mattress at either side of her head. He released her and her breasts shivered with her nervous, jerky breaths.

"But I—"

Her protest died on a gasp when Riley leaned down and took one soft, plump nipple into his mouth. Regina's back arched and her fingers threaded through his hair.

Holding her shoulders down on the bed, he sucked gently, keeping the pressure light, using his tongue to tease her nipple into a stiff little point. When he lifted his head, Regina had her eyes squeezed shut, her bottom lip caught in her teeth and her body held tight.

"You like that, honey?"

Without opening her eyes, she bobbed her head.

Riley smiled, then looked at her body. Her upper torso was so slim, her rib cage narrow and her breasts pert. He skimmed his palm down her side, then inward to the clasp of her slacks. "I want you naked. I want to see all of you."

Her eyes flew open.

"Once you're naked, I can get naked and think how good that's going to feel."

Her lips parted. "Yes."

Gently, he pried her fingers from his hair and again raised her arms over her head. "I love seeing you like this, Red, stretched out on my bed." He studied her from top to toes, then kissed her belly. "Now don't move."

She agreed by curling her fingers into the bedding, holding on tight.

Her sandals slipped off easily enough, but Riley took the time to kiss each arch, then each ankle. There was one spot just behind the ankle bone that when pinched, could cause agonizing pain, maybe even paralyze the limb. In the same regard, a featherlight touch sent thousands of acute nerve endings on alert. Riley tickled with his tongue, soothed with soft kisses.

She had sexy legs, long and sleek. Her casual white slacks unbuttoned with ease, and building the anticipation, he slowly drew down the zipper. Her belly hollowed out with her sharply indrawn breath.

Riley spread his fingers wide over her hips and dragged the pants down to her knees. Her panties were the same lace as her bra, showing the springy auburn curls over her mound. He wanted her so badly he hurt, but he didn't want to rush her, he didn't want her to start searching for her damn books.

Using one fingertip, Riley traced the triangle of pubic hair. He couldn't wait to taste her, to have her completely naked and open....

"Riley?"

"Yeah?"

A long heavy silence filled the air before she said, "I don't think I can take all this waiting. My patience isn't as strong as yours."

Riley looked up at her face. Her hands were fisted, her pupils dilated, lips parted.

"Just a little longer."

Her pants tangled around her ankles with her trying to kick them off and Riley had to finish that chore for her. Her panties came off next, and then she was beautifully bare.

Her aroused scent filled his head. He kissed her belly, each hipbone, an inner thigh. Alternately, he made the kisses gentle, then rough, sometimes laving with his tongue, sometimes nipping with his teeth. Regina squirmed and gasped, on edge, unsure what the next touch would bring. He could feel the urgency pounding through her.

Parting her legs, he licked the joint of her thigh and groin, where her skin was ultrasmooth and delicate.

"Riley, please…"

Regardless of what she said, she couldn't be ready yet. His mouth open and his kisses deliberately damp, Riley made his way back up her body. She grabbed him, kissing him hard, while his hands covered both her breasts. Her nipples were tight now, her breasts swollen. He caught her nipples and rolled, squeezed, tugged.

She pulled her mouth away. "Riley."

"Shh." He kissed her again, silencing her protests while continuing to torment her nipples. The more aroused she got, the more she'd enjoy his caresses. Her legs shifted restlessly, moving alongside his until he stilled them with one of his own. Caught under him, Regina could barely move, and that suited Riley just fine.

Keeping her legs trapped, he leaned up to look at her face. "I want you as ready as I am, Red."

"I am," she all but wailed.

"No." Smiling, he dragged his callused fingertips over her ribs, her belly and finally between her thighs. The crisp curls were damp, her lips puffy, sleek with moisture. His breath caught. "Well now, maybe you are." He pressed his middle finger inside, just past her swollen flesh, no deeper. She was most sensitive here, at her opening, so he used that knowledge to circle, dip, circle again. He relished her broken moan, the way her body tried to move with him.

"I should… I should be doing something."

"What is it you want to do?"

"Touch you."

His control nearly slipped. "No, not yet. I'm on the ragged edge as it is."

Her eyes opened and her head lifted off the pillow to shout into his face, "Then quit playing around!"

Riley almost laughed. Regina amused him so much, even at a time when laughter should have been eons away. "All right. Tell me how you like this."

Her head dropped back with a groan as he began moving his finger deeply in and out, making her wetter still. As he did so, he kissed his way down her body. The closer he got to her sex, the more she stiffened.

"Riley?"

"Hush." He nudged her thighs farther apart, took a moment to enjoy her scent, breathing deep, then with a groan, he covered her with his mouth.

She gave a small cry, arching hard.

At the first flick of his tongue, her body clamped down on his finger. He licked, stroked, and finally, catching her small clitoris carefully with his teeth, he suckled.

Her body strained away from him, but Riley held her hips, keeping her still. He loved the feel of her voluptuous bottom in his hands, the taste of her on his tongue, the hot, wild sounds she made. As her excitement peaked, he worked in another finger, stretching her, filling her. She lifted up to meet his mouth, grinding against him, so close.

When he knew she was ready to come, he sat up and snagged a condom from the nightstand. Regina cried out in protest at the delay, and the second he got the protection taken care of, she opened her arms to him.

Riley settled between her wide-open thighs. Wanting every possible connection, he held her face to kiss her and nudged his way inside. She was tight, but so wet he knew he wouldn't hurt her. With one hard thrust, he entered her completely and Regina lifted her legs to wrap around his waist. He found a rhythm that quickly had them both straining toward a climax.

Her mouth devoured his, biting his bottom lip, sucking on his tongue. He loved it.

He loved *her*. If only he could make her understand that.

Sweating, his heart thundering in his chest, he slid one hand under her behind to tilt her hips up so he could enter her more deeply. That was all it took. She started coming with broken groans and mewling cries and that pushed Riley right over the edge. He could feel the throbbing clench and release of her body on his cock, the frantic bite of her nails on his shoulders, the way she shuddered and writhed under him.

He pressed his face into her neck and growled out her name. Regina wasn't quite so restrained. She screamed.

Two seconds after Riley's body went utterly limp and he gave Regina his weight, Butch began barking hysterically.

He felt Regina stiffen, but he patted her hip and made the manly offering. "I'll go get him."

Her hands slid off his back to land limply on the bed. "Thanks."

Riley forced himself to his elbows to see her face. Her eyes were closed, her French braid ruined, her makeup smudged. She was sweaty, just as he'd predicted.

And, thank God, she was finally his.

RILEY ATTEMPTED to wake her with a kiss to her forehead. Regina moaned, rolled to the side and slept on.

They'd spent the night making love and apparently, Regina wasn't used to such excesses. Truthfully, neither was he.

It had surprised him how often he'd wanted her. Watching her eat a simple dinner in her robe, seeing her coddle the silly little dog, catching her secret smiles and sudden blushes, had all provoked him. He hadn't been able to keep his hands off her.

And she hadn't minded in the least.

It'd been tricky, getting Butch to leave the room without

kicking up a fuss. Riley figured he'd need to stock up on toys and tasty chews to distract the dog.

After her fourth release, she'd conked out and hadn't really come to since. Once he'd realized she was done for, he'd worked her pajamas back onto her then let Butch in the room. She hadn't protested when the dog burrowed under the covers, or when Riley had pulled her close and held her all night long.

She hadn't even awakened.

It drove home to Riley just how exhausted she'd been, and the toll her worries must have taken on her.

He hoped his presence would ease those worries, because, from now on, she'd damn well be with him. Beyond that, he didn't know if his lauded control extended to sleeping chastely each night, even if they'd made love prior to going to bed.

He hated to disturb her now, but he didn't want to leave for the day without saying goodbye. Butch seemed just as determined to keep him from doing so.

He and the dog had been up for an hour and more than once Butch had whined at her door, apparently wanting Regina to join them. Now that he was back in the bed with her, he dashed from Regina's feet to her head and back again, trying to protect all of her—from Riley.

Riley lifted the minuscule dog. "I may have gone overboard last night, bud, but I don't accost women in their sleep."

Regina's eyes fluttered open. "Riley?"

At the sound of her soft, sleepy voice, some insidious warmth expanded in his chest. "After last night, were you really expecting another man to wake you up?"

He saw confusion flit over her face, then realization. She snatched the sheet over her head. "What in the world are you doing in here?"

He sat on the bed beside her, causing a dip in the mattress. Her rump rolled into his hip. "I slept here. It's my bed, remember?"

She groaned.

"And because Butch wanted under the covers, I put your pajamas back on you, so you don't need to hide."

"It's not that," she mumbled from under the covers.

Ah, Riley thought, appearances again. Silly woman. "Do you have any idea how sexy you look all rumpled and warm?"

She went very still. "I do?"

"Yeah. Makes me want to strip naked and get back into bed with you." He gave a grievous sigh. "But unfortunately I have some stuff to do, so I only wanted to wake you so I could say goodbye."

One slender hand emerged from the blankets, shooing him away. "I'll be out in a second."

Smiling, Riley patted her hip and stood. As an enticement, he said, "I have coffee ready and waiting."

She made a rumbling sound of appreciation. "I'll be right there."

Ten minutes later she emerged with her hair brushed and pulled back in a ponytail, wearing a casual green sundress. Her eyes were still puffy and there was a crease in her cheek probably formed from a pillowcase.

Riley wanted to consume her. Again. Last night hadn't even taken the edge off his hunger. He didn't think a hundred years could do that.

As he watched, she made her way unsteadily toward the table. "Riley? I suppose I should admit that I'm not at my best in the morning." She ended that with an enormous and inelegant yawn, giving proof to her statement.

"Coffee will help. You sit and I'll pour it for you."

She plopped down in the chair. "Thank you."

The dog made a beeline for Regina. She roused herself enough to lift him into her lap and treat him to several kisses to his round head.

Riley could have used a few of those kisses. Not that he was jealous of the attention she gave Butch, and not that he didn't understand how sluggish she felt. But this was the proverbial morning after and she'd barely looked at him.

Then he decided *what the hell*.

He handed her a mug of coffee, but forestalled her from tasting it by leaning down and taking her mouth in a warm morning kiss. "Now that," Riley said as he straightened, "is the *proper* way to say hello after a night of satisfying debauchery."

Regina gave him a bemused look, snatched up her cup and swilled her coffee. There was no other word for it. In two long gulps, her mug was empty. Enjoying this side of her, Riley fixed her another cup then seated himself across from her.

"You do remember last night, don't you?"

Her eyes darted away from his. "Of course I do. No woman in her right mind would forget a night with you. Especially not a night like that."

"Thanks. I wanted verification, given the way you passed out on me."

She groaned and covered her face with one hand. "I'm sorry."

Riley reached across the table and took her slender wrist. Her skin was warm, smooth. "I'm not. You needed the sleep."

"That's no excuse for rudeness."

Riley nearly choked on his laugh. "You were not rude, I was excessive. And believe me, I have no complaints."

"But…"

"*None,* Red. Okay?"

Her expression softened. "I don't have any complaints either. In fact, I think I owe you a few compliments."

Riley grinned with her. "You can give them to me tonight."

"Why tonight?" She looked more awake now and somewhat interested. "I thought maybe we could…"

He groaned. "Don't tempt me, Red. Nothing would please me more than hauling your sexy butt back to bed. But I'll be gone till this afternoon."

Her disappointment was plain to see, filling Riley with satisfaction. "I thought you were on vacation."

"I am, but I want to talk to your two swains, Carl and Luther, then stop by the station and see how things are going with our intruder."

Her brows pulled down. "I'm not at all sure I like this idea."

"Why?"

"Don't look so suspicious, Riley. I'm not hiding anything important."

That clarification *important* rang like a bell in his head. "So you're hiding unimportant stuff?"

"No! And don't twist my words. It's just that I'm sure neither Carl nor Luther has anything to do with my trouble."

"With this type of continued harassment, it's almost always someone you know, and more often than that, it's someone you've been romantically involved with." She quit her protests to groan instead. Riley laced his fingers in hers. "Now, don't take this the wrong way, but I'd like you to promise me you won't take off anywhere while I'm gone."

She rubbed her eyes tiredly. "I have nowhere to go. In fact," she said, giving him a direct look, "I thought I'd finish up my article on the talent show. Once that's done, I can start on your interview."

He didn't want to talk about the damn interview right now. While he intended to discover everything he could about Regina, he detested the thought of her prying into his past.

He came to his feet and stepped around the table to reach her. Caging her in with one hand on the seat and the other on the back of her chair, Riley said, "We've got a lot to do today, sweetheart."

She stared at his mouth. "We do?"

He nodded. "We're going to start on your private lessons today, remember?"

"Oh."

Seeing her disappointment almost had him laughing out loud. Aware of Butch's low growls, he touched her nose. "I'll make sure you enjoy them, okay?"

Her eyes darkened. "Okay."

"Tonight is the ceremony at the Historical Society. They're honoring Senator Welling." He watched her face and added, "I thought maybe we could go."

Excitement brightened her eyes and added a smile. "You mean it?"

Now he was jealous. Welling represented her ideal man, and for most, his stature was as unattainable as the moon. "It won't be a social call, honey. I want a chance to talk to your senator, and this seems like it might be the best opportunity."

Her excitement remained plain to see. "He's not just my senator, and Riley, you'll like him a lot, I know it."

Riley would have liked the guy more if Regina weren't so infatuated with him. "If he cooperates with me, I'll have no complaints."

"I really don't think he'll have anything to share, but it'll be good to see him again."

Because he didn't want to hear her talk about Welling, Riley kissed her quick and hard. He felt Butch nipping at his chin, his ear, doing all he could to scare Riley off. Riley drew back to stare at the little dog. "Where's your toy?"

Butch's ears shot up. He maneuvered down Regina's leg to the floor and took off at a dead run for the hallway. He returned with the stuffed Chihuahua in his mouth and dropped it at Riley's feet.

Riley laughed. "Smart dog. All right, I can play for just a few minutes, but that's all." And to Regina he added, "Finish up your coffee. There's cereal in the cabinet, fruit in the fridge. Help yourself, okay?"

Her expression was tender when she nodded. "Thanks."

Ten minutes later, Riley was on the floor, the stuffed toy caught in his teeth while he and Butch indulged in a feigned tug of war. Butch gave it his all, jerking and growling in his attempt to tear the toy away from Riley. Riley growled back, a stuffed tail and leg caught in his mouth.

Regina laughed. "You're both nuts."

Riley straightened. "Now he knows how to grapple. Did you see his triceps? Or would they be triceps, considering dogs don't have arms?" Riley shook his head. "Either way, he's buff and built like a lean bulldog."

Butch took off in a flash, dragging the toy, but when Riley didn't pursue him he returned only to smack Riley's ankle with it. "No," he told Butch. "I gotta go. Get Regina to play."

Butch dutifully dragged the toy to Regina. She laughed. "Gee, thanks."

Riley tipped up her chin to give her a long, thorough kiss. "If you need anything while I'm gone, just call me on my cell phone."

He knew he had to leave before he decided not to go at all. Today he was going to get some answers. The sooner the better. Then he'd come home to Regina.

Soon he'd have everything worked out.

chapter 8

THE SECOND RILEY WAS OUT THE DOOR, REGINA made plans. She called Rosie at work first to find out Ethan's and Harris's schedule. She didn't want to call either of their homes if there was a chance she'd wake them. As firefighters, their hours varied. Rosie told her they were both on second shift that week, and that Ethan, at least, should be up and about.

She called him and made an appointment for him to visit her at Riley's house. Next, she called Buck and left him a message since he didn't pick up.

Finally she chanced a call to Harris. A woman answered, temporarily throwing Regina off. "Um, is Harris around?"

"Who is this?" the woman asked with heavy suspicion.

Regina was about to reply when she heard some grumbling in the background, then Harris's voice on the phone. "Hello?"

"It's Regina. I'm so sorry I'm interrupting."

"No, you're not." That statement caused another ruckus in the background. Harris covered the phone, did some grousing, then came back to ask, "What's up? Everything okay?"

"Oh, yes. I just… I'm going to be doing an interview on Riley and since he's gone for most of the afternoon and he doesn't want me to leave his apartment, I figured I could start by talking to his closest friends. Ethan's coming over in a few minutes, and I hoped, if you weren't too busy, maybe you could come by after him."

She heard the amusement in Harris's voice when he asked, "Does Riley know you're inviting us over?"

"No, why?"

Now he laughed outright. "No reason. None at all. And yes, I'd love to come over. Hell, I wouldn't miss this for the world. Want me to pick up Buck and drag him along? You can kill two birds with one stone."

"I already called him. He's working."

"He's the boss. If he can't take off for a few hours, who can?"

Regina laughed. "No, that's okay. I'd rather talk to each of you one on one."

Harris snickered. "Really? All right then." He laughed again. "This is going to be fun." He hung up before Regina could ask him what he meant.

RILEY MADE IT to Cincinnati in a little less than an hour. It was easy enough to find the newspaper building. He thought about going in to talk to Carl first, but changed his mind and parked in the lot for the insurance company. At the lobby desk, he asked about seeing Luther, and was told to go to the fourth floor.

On the elevator ride up, Riley thought about what he'd say. He realized he wanted Regina's ex-beau to be guilty, just for the satisfaction of cleaning the guy out of her past. If she did have any residual feelings for him, finding out he was the one harassing her, with nothing but hurt feelings to motivate him, ought to take care of it.

There was no one at the receptionist's desk. Riley glanced at his wristwatch, saw it was lunchtime and waited only a moment before mentally saying, *To hell with it*. He strode to Luther's door, raised his hand to knock—and got a whiff of sickeningly sweet smoke. Pot.

What the hell?

He tried the door, but it was locked. After knocking sharply, he called out, "Luther Finley?"

There was a lot of shuffling movement behind the door before it finally opened. A man close to Riley's height, with straight black hair and shrewd blue eyes, stood there. His suit was immaculate, expensive and in good taste.

He made a great appearance. Shit. First the senator, and now this clown. If Regina was drawn to GQ men, Riley didn't stand a chance.

"Yeah? Who are you? What do you want?"

So this was the man Regina had bought sex books for? This was the man she'd hoped to please in bed?

Riley wanted to punch him in the nose. The urge to do so made it difficult to breathe. Ruthlessly, Riley brought himself under control. He would not behave like a Yeti. He would not prove himself to be a jealous fool.

Looking beyond Luther, Riley saw an open window, a desk drawer slightly ajar. Perfect. If he couldn't hit him, he could at least have the upper hand. There must be a fairy godmother sitting on his shoulder, to be given this advantage.

"Can I help you?" Luther said with strained impatience.

"You Luther Finley?" At the other man's nod, Riley flashed a badge. "I'm Riley Moore, with the Chester Police department. I need a moment of your time."

Luther's eyes opened wide and he reeled back two steps. "The police? What the hell did I do?"

"I want to ask you about an acquaintance of yours. Understand, Mr. Finley, this is an informal visit and you're not in any trouble. Yet. I'd just like some information."

Riley saw the moment the man relaxed, wrongfully assuming he'd ignore the pot. "Yeah? About who?"

"Regina Foxworth. She seems to have gotten herself into a bit of trouble."

The look of curiosity faded beneath a smarmy smile. "Regina is in trouble?" He actually laughed. "Yeah, sure. Come on in and pull up a chair. I'm glad to help."

And Riley thought to himself, *I just bet you are.*

REGINA HANDED Ethan a tall, icy glass of cola. "Now, tell me what you know about Riley."

Ethan looked more wary by the second. He glanced around the obviously empty apartment and said yet again, "I'm not sure this is a good idea, Regina."

"No, it's okay. Riley gave me permission to interview him. And he didn't want me to leave the apartment, so this is a good compromise. He won't mind."

"Uh-huh." Ethan sipped his drink, still undecided. "What exactly do you want to know?"

Regina studied Ethan while she considered what to ask him first. He was a very attractive man with his dark blond hair and deep, intelligent brown eyes. As a firefighter he was, by necessity, built almost as handsomely as Riley. But she'd never had any interest in Ethan. No, she'd seen Riley and been lost. She'd fought her reaction to him, but fighting did her no good. Last night had proven that.

She sighed. "Has Riley had any recent romantic involvement?"

Ethan choked, stared at her, and choked some more. She got up to thwack him on the back, but Butch didn't like that and started to howl. For some unknown reason, he'd taken a real dislike to Ethan.

Gasping and wheezing, Ethan waved her away. Regina resettled herself, allowing Butch to skulk back into her lap with a surly look thrown toward Ethan.

"Well?"

"What does that have to do with your interview?"

In the primmest tone she could muster, Regina lied, "His social habits will be of interest to everyone reading the article. They'll want to know about *him,* not just his work."

Ethan didn't look convinced. He drew a deep breath, cast her another suspicious look, and finally murmured, "He dates. Not seriously, not often."

"Really?" Now that was interesting, considering the amount of energy Buck and Harris apparently put into tomcatting around. And from all accounts, Ethan had been worse before Rosie brought him to his senses. "So he's selective?"

Ethan frowned over that. "I have no idea. It's just that Riley is…different. He's not like most guys I know. He thinks differently and he sees the world differently."

"He's dangerous."

Slowly, Ethan nodded. "I suppose you could say that, but only to someone on the wrong side of the law. To most people he's an advocate, a defender. Riley uses all his skill to help protect people." Ethan settled back in his seat, a little more at ease. "If you could have seen how he took that guy down— the one he found in your apartment—it was something else. Riley didn't look winded, didn't look like he'd used much effort, and he didn't look like he had a speck of emotion in him. Cold, swift and effective. One second the guy was running and the next he was completely immobilized by Riley. It was both awesome and a little unsettling." Then, more to himself than to Regina, Ethan murmured, "It still amazes me that he left the SWAT team to come here."

"Why did he? Do you have any idea?"

"Not a clue. Riley only lets people in so far. I'd trust him with my life and I know he's one of the best men around. But his past is off-limits. Not once in the five years I've known him has he given so much as a single clue."

Disappointed, Regina let out a long breath. Trying not to be too obvious, she asked, "Who has he been seeing most recently?"

Ethan rolled his eyes. "You."

"No, I mean before I moved in here."

"You."

"But we didn't…"

"Date? Doesn't matter." Ethan gave her a warm smile. "I remember we were all at Rosie's for dinner the day after we first met you. Riley talked about you—"

"Saying what?"

Ethan shrugged. "It wasn't what he said so much as how he said it. We all knew right then that he was interested. And the day of the fire…"

Ethan grew silent, stiff. He couldn't talk about that awful day without looking a little green. He closed his eyes, took two shallow breaths, and swallowed. "As distracted as I was that day with Rosie, I noticed how Riley staked a claim."

Regina pulled back. "He did *what?*"

Grinning, Ethan nodded. "He laid claim to you."

Flushing a little with umbrage—and with pleasure—Regina said, "But that's ridiculous."

"What did you think it meant when he picked you up and didn't put you down?"

"My head was bleeding. I was dazed."

"And unable to walk?" Ethan snorted. "He held you because

he wanted to and because he decided you were his. Any guy within seeing distance knew it, and because Riley is who he is, they paid heed."

"But he hasn't asked me out or in any way acted interested." Ethan raised a brow and she quickly amended, "Until recently, I mean."

"Baloney. He's tried to teach you how to defend yourself and he's been following you around, keeping an eye on you, making your welfare his business. And he stares at you, Regina. Cracks Harris and Buck up, just to watch the way he watches you." Ethan smiled at that. So did Regina. "Riley's not one to spill his guts, but if I had to guess, I'd say you are a major distraction."

And then what? "You really think so?" She hated sounding so hopeful, but if Riley cared a little for her, if what he felt was more than just sexual...well, that would change everything.

"I know so." Ethan glanced at his watch, then stood. "Sorry to rush off, but Rosie has a few hours free." His grin told Regina all she needed to know. They loved each other so much. She wanted what they had, the closeness, the caring.

If she could have that with Riley, it'd be more than she'd ever dared to hope for.

RILEY PACED around the desk to the open window. "So you and Regina were engaged?"

Luther snorted. "Is that what she told you?"

Stiffening, Riley kept his back to the other man and asked softly, "Are you saying she lied?"

He snickered. "No. She *thought* we were engaged. But you know how it is. Regina's one of those women who has to have everything right and proper. She'd never have let me in her bed without a ring on her finger."

The clawing need to break the bastard's nose nearly choked Riley. "I see. So *you* lied?"

"I told her what she needed to hear. If you've met her, then you'll understand. She's so ladylike on the outside, I thought maybe she'd be a wildcat in bed. That made the deception worthwhile, or so I thought. But she was still stiff as a broom. No satisfaction at all. It was like sleeping with a damn board." He gave a hoarse laugh. "What the hell does this have to do with the trouble she's in?"

Riley turned to Luther with a cold smile. "Someone is bothering her. Damaging her property, scaring her. I'm trying to figure out who."

Luther shot to his feet. "You're accusing *me?*"

"Just gathering the facts—though it certainly sounds like you have a store of animosity for her."

"No. Hell no. You can stop gathering right now. When we split, I said good riddance to the little prude."

"No regrets, huh?"

Luther grunted. "Hardly." He took two incautious steps toward Riley. "You know what that twit had the nerve to do?"

Riley cocked a brow, but Luther didn't wait for him to reply. "She bought some goddamned books on sex, and she actually wanted to talk to me about them. She acted like I held part of the responsibility for her lack of enjoyment in the sack. I told her it was damned tough to satisfy a cold fish. She got pissed, and whenever she got that way, she got all stiff and righteous with her haughty little nose in the air."

Riley's smile hurt. "Yes, I know what you mean."

"You've seen it, haven't you?" Again, Luther didn't wait for a reply. He nodded, then chuckled. "Well, I was sick and tired of her acting superior so I told her it'd help if she'd try a little harder to get my interest. She's so damn skinny, I suggested a boob job." Here he laughed outright, even slapping his knee.

Riley churned with anger, but not by so much as the flicker of an eyelash did he let Luther know. "She's slight, but I haven't noticed her lacking at all."

"Then you haven't seen her naked. She's got a nice ass, but the upstairs leaves a lot to be desired."

Riley went mute with rage. It was bad enough that Regina's childhood had instilled in her a need to make a good impression, but then to have this jerk tear her down and make her think her best wasn't good enough....

Luther's grin lingered. "Man, she hit the roof. She got all red-faced and told me she wouldn't marry a man who didn't want her as she is."

Satisfaction swelled inside Riley. *Bravo, sweetheart,* he silently congratulated her. Then through his teeth, he asked, "That ended the engagement?"

"Blew it to smithereens, which was more than fine by me. She tossed my ring back at me, walked away and I haven't seen her since. I haven't *wanted* to see her since." He leaned back on his desk and crossed his arms. "You know what? I bet she rubbed some other poor bastard the wrong way and he's retaliating. It'd serve the little witch right to get hassled a bit. Maybe it'll get her to loosen up and live a little."

Riley figured Regina would loosen up when the right man loved her, namely him. With trust would come complete comfort. But until then, he couldn't let Luther get away with insulting her.

He rubbed his chin thoughtfully, then moved forward half a step. Very calmly, giving Luther no warning, he said, "Let me explain something to you." Without haste, he reached for Luther's upper arm, clasped him in his right hand, easily found a pressure point, and applied the right grip to make the man's knees buckle and to force a short screech of pain from him.

Eyes wide with fear and teeth gritted in pain, Luther literally hung in Riley's one-handed grip.

Without compassion, Riley watched him writhe in agony. In a voice more deadly because of its softness, he said, "Regina Foxworth is mine. Eventually I'll marry her. Anyone who insults her insults me."

Luther let out a long broken groan. "You didn't tell me that. Hey, I'm sorry!"

Riley shook his head. "No, not good enough. You see, how do I know that you won't go spreading these nasty rumors about her to other people? I think I should impress on you exactly what I'll do if I ever hear of you even mentioning her name again."

Luther gasped. "Please…"

Riley released him.

Slowly, holding his numb arm, Luther straightened. His face was pale with lingering agony.

Legs braced apart, hands on his hips, Riley said, "You have a lot more pressure points, Luther, places that when manipulated just right, can cause pain you can't even imagine. How many do I need to demonstrate before you fully understand?"

"One's enough. I swear."

Riley said, "I don't know…"

Luther rushed behind his desk, which gave him a false sense of safety. His arm hanging limp and useless, he managed to stand more or less upright. "You better get out of here," he groused in a shaky voice. "You're a policeman. You can't do this to me. I'll report you—"

Riley pulled open his desk drawer. "Yeah? Well, I can haul you in for smoking dope on the job." He lifted out a joint, along with a small bag of marijuana. "What do you think your super-visors will say to that?"

Luther's eyes went wide.

"I'll only say this once, Luther, so pay attention. Stay away from Regina, keep your foul mouth shut, and what you do on the job is your business. I really couldn't care less."

Luther slumped, but then another voice intruded from the doorway. "I care."

Riley looked up to see a slender woman in her mid-thirties, dressed much as Regina often did in business-casual wear, staring at Luther with hatred.

"You're the receptionist?" Riley asked.

Her chin went up another notch. "And I was his fiancée." She pulled off a minuscule diamond ring and pinged it off Luther's forehead. "Not anymore."

Luther groaned.

Riley went around the desk to the woman. "You overheard?"

"Yes. All of it. I came back to my desk a few minutes ago and I eavesdropped."

Riley felt a little uncomfortable. "I should apologize…"

"No. He's a pig and I'm sorry if he hurt your girlfriend at all."

"He hasn't. Regina is too smart to be hurt by him." At least, Riley hoped that was true. He'd find out for sure tonight—*after* he got her naked and let her know in no uncertain terms that he thought her utterly beautiful. Anything she didn't have, she didn't need.

The receptionist's shoulders went back. "What you did to him…the way you barely touched him yet he started whining in pain. How did that work?"

"Why?"

"I think it might be a useful thing to know."

Grinning, Riley fished a business card out of his wallet and handed it to her. "If you ever get over to Chester, stop into my gym and I'll teach you."

"Thank you."

As he left the insurance building, Riley admitted to himself that it probably wasn't Luther bothering Regina now. He'd watched the man's every expression and had seen only weakness, conceit and lewd innuendo. No real deception. Riley would keep an eye on him, but he doubted anything would turn up.

Once outside, he stopped on the sidewalk to stare at the newspaper building across the street.

One down, two to go.

REGINA GRINNED at the determined way Buck tried to make friends with Butch. Buck looked like a felled titan in his black T-shirt and worn jeans, stretched out on the floor on his stomach, his chin on his crossed hands, meeting the dog at eye level.

Butch didn't cooperate.

No matter how softly Buck spoke to him or how he cajoled, the dog continued to give a low, vibrating growl of warning.

Buck glanced up at Regina, his green eyes alight with mischief. "You sure this damn dog isn't part badger?"

"I don't understand it. He's always so sweet to me."

Buck came to his feet, ruffled Regina's hair fondly and said, "Well now, honey, you're very easy to be sweet to."

Half-embarrassed by that odd praise, Regina gave an uncertain smile. "Um, thank you. If you'd like to take a seat, I can get you something to drink."

"No thanks. Let's get right to it. You want the scoop on Riley, right?"

"Well, yes." But she rushed to explain, "I'm doing an interview on him."

"Uh-huh." Buck stretched out his massive arms along the back of the sofa and grinned. "He's hung up on you big-time. Never thought to see the mighty Riley with a weakness, but damn if he isn't acting smitten. It's downright fun to watch."

Regina blinked, then blinked some more. "Oh, but I didn't mean to—"

"What? Find out how he feels about you? Course you did." Buck continued to grin. "I don't mind. Riley's tough, no way around that. But any man who guards his past that closely has a few serious wounds. I'd like to see him happy and I happen to think you can accomplish that. So whatever I can do to nudge things along, count me in."

Such an awesome outpouring, from *Buck* no less, left Regina momentarily distracted and without a single coherent thought in her head. "Uh…"

"I think some woman did him wrong, don't you?"

Regina stared. "Well, I…"

"That'd make sense, huh? If it was a guy, Riley would have just kicked his ass, not quit his job and moved away. And now here you are, putting him into a possessive lather, helping him to focus on better things. I'm glad you moved in with him. Ought to keep him occupied." He winked.

Regina went hot to the roots of her red hair.

"So." Buck slapped enormous hands on his thick thighs. "Is that all you wanted?"

She cleared her throat twice and attempted to get control of the situation. "I, uh, had hoped to learn more about Riley's job, what he does, his training…."

Shaking his head, Buck came to his feet. "Sorry. I don't know anything about that. He used to be SWAT, but left the city to come here. Since Chester has no need of a SWAT team, Riley fell back on his old training of CSI. That's the beginning and end of what I know." Then he frowned. "Well, one other thing."

"Yes?"

He pushed up his T-shirt sleeve over a massive, bulging shoulder and flexed his arm to show off a seriously impressive biceps muscle. "See that?"

"Yes." Regina knew she wouldn't be able to circle that muscle even if she used both hands. "It'd be rather hard to miss."

Buck nodded. "I'm strong. I do a lot of physical work, day in and day out at the lumberyard. Men walk a wide path around me if I'm annoyed. But I don't have a single doubt in my mind that Riley, scrawny as he is, would make mincemeat out of me if he ever had a notion to."

He smiled as he made that claim, especially the ridiculous part about Riley being scrawny. Compared to Buck, he was certainly leaner, but scrawny? Nope, not by anyone's standards.

Buck tugged his sleeve back down and nodded. "That's some serious training that goes beyond what you're taught for a job, even if that job is SWAT. It's a lifestyle, a personality, an inherent part of the man. Riley's like a warrior born in the wrong century. He'd die to protect those people he cares about, and he'd expect loyalty in return."

Was this Buck's idea of a warning for his friend? Regina didn't know for sure, but she touched the arm he'd just bared and offered a smile. "I would never do anything to hurt him."

Buck patted her hand. "I know. That's why I think you're perfect for him."

He started for the door, and both Regina and Butch followed. "You know, Buck, I'm a little surprised. You're usually so quiet."

"Naw. It's just that with Harris around, who can get a word in edgewise?" He laughed, opened the door, and there stood Harris with his hand raised to knock. "Well, speak of the devil."

RILEY EYED the tall, thin fellow with the wire-rimmed glasses and neatly combed blond hair. He wore a suit, complete with a tie and jacket. Everyone else in the room had removed their coats and rolled up their shirtsleeves, loosened their ties. Not Carl Edmond.

The outward attention to detail had probably appealed to Regina, even if the man hadn't.

Bent close to the keyboard, a slight frown on his brow, Carl typed industriously at the computer. Riley snagged a chair and pulled it up close. Carl was so absorbed in his task, he didn't notice Riley until he sat down.

Shifting around, first startled, then polite, Carl asked, "May I help you?"

"Carl Edmond, right?"

"That's correct."

He didn't look alarmed, only curious. He didn't look like a predator either, but Riley had learned long ago that even the most innocent expression could hide deceit. It was a lesson he'd never forgotten. After discreetly flashing his badge, Riley said, "I'm here informally, just to ask a few questions if you're willing."

Looking around the crowded room with a slight blush, Carl said, "Perhaps we should go someplace more private?"

"Sure."

Riley allowed himself to be led into an employee lounge. There was no one else present. Carl glanced at him. "Would you like some coffee?"

"Please." He was so courteous, Riley wondered that Regina hadn't been taken with him. He reminded Riley of a masculine version of Regina. Carl set a steaming cup of coffee in front of Riley, along with a small square napkin.

With those courtesies taken care of, Riley said, "You know Regina Foxworth."

Carl had just started to sip his coffee, but he stopped, face alight with pleasure. "Yes, yes I do." And then with sudden concern, he added, "She's all right, isn't she?"

"She's fine. But someone has made her a target." Riley explained the things that had happened, all the while watching Carl Edmond for the slightest flicker of guilt.

There was none.

"But this is terrible. Regina is… Well, she's a gentle, beautiful person. I don't mean her looks…well, her looks, too. But she's one of the kindest women I know. I owe her a lot. If there's any way I can help you to find this evil person…"

Riley leaned back in exasperation. Carl had a touch of melodrama. "Why do you say you owe her?"

The man actually blushed. "Well, it's a long story, and I really hate to admit it, but I fancied myself in love with her. I'm afraid I made a real nuisance of myself, too, following her around like a lovesick pup." Here he shook his head and chuckled. "But Regina remained kind. She sat me down, explained that she only cared about me as a friend, and then she suggested that I wise up and pay more notice to the bagel girl."

"The bagel girl?"

"She delivers fresh bagels to this room twice a day. I didn't understand at first, but I did as Regina suggested." He held up a hand, showing off the gold wedding band. "Thanks to her, I'm now married to Carolyn. It was love at first sight, at least for me."

Riley ran a hand through his hair. "Great. Congratulations." And another dead end. If the new wedding hadn't been enough, Carl's obvious happiness would have swayed Riley. He pulled out a card and pushed it across the table toward Carl.

"If you think of anyone who might want to hassle Regina, would you give me a call?"

"I'd be glad to." When Riley stood, Carl reached out and caught his arm. "Mr. Moore? Please. Take good care of her, okay? She's a very, very special person."

Riley nodded. "You have my word."

chapter 9

HE HEARD THE RAUCOUS NOISE EVEN BEFORE HE finished unlocking the door. Music, laughter, playful barking.

Brows drawn, Riley turned the knob and silently pushed the door open. No one noticed him.

Regina sat cross-legged on the floor, her back to the sofa where Harris lounged on his side, his head propped up on a fist. Butch ran up Red's body, over her shoulder, along Harris's length, then back down over Regina.

Her shoulders were touching his stomach.

Harris's nose was practically in her ear.

Riley closed the door with a resounding click that seemed more effective than a hard slam. Butch jerked up. His small furry face went blank with surprise, then lit up with blinding pleasure. Yapping with berserk glee, he tumbled off Harris, rolled over Regina and came charging toward Riley. Ears bouncing and little paws moving with lightning speed, he reached Riley and slid to a halt.

"Well, hello to you, too, squirt." Riley lifted him up and got his face thoroughly bathed with a warm doggy tongue. All the while he stared at Harris.

Slowly, his mouth twisted as if to hide a grin, Harris straightened. "Hey, Riley."

Riley continued to stare.

Regina scurried to the stereo and turned it off. Hands behind her back, she smiled shyly at Riley. *Shyly?* Now what was she up to?

She hesitated a second, then with only a bit less enthusiasm than Butch had shown, she came to him, went on tiptoe and kissed him. Not a polite welcome peck. Nope. She cupped his face and moved her soft sweet lips over his until Riley forgot that Harris was behind her. He snagged an arm around her waist, hauled her up against him, and pressed his tongue past her parted lips. When she went limp against him, Riley reluctantly ended the kiss.

"You're home," she said in a breathless whisper.

"Earlier than you expected?"

Harris chuckled. "Gee, Riley, is that a gun in your pocket or are you glad to see...Regina?"

Regina gasped, her thoughts plain on her face, but Riley relieved her mind by saying, "It's a chew toy for the dog."

Regina looked down at his lap and blinked at the ludicrously large bulge there. "Oh."

Harris cleared his throat. "I think I'll take this as my cue to get lost."

He had the nerve to stop at Regina's side, kiss her cheek, and then wink at Riley. When Riley narrowed his eyes, Harris laughed and held up both hands. "Don't hurt me, Riley, okay?"

Riley rolled his eyes. "What are you doing here?"

"Ah, well, I'm just one in a long line of guys who've trooped through your door today."

Regina elbowed him hard. Riley took her arm and pulled her to his side so she wouldn't hurt herself poking at Harris. Regina was red in the face, Butch was squirming to be petted and Harris was trying to sidle out the door.

Riley opened it for him. "Later, Harris."

"Right." With a fast salute, Harris took off.

Riley closed and locked the door, then, ignoring Regina for the moment, headed to the couch with Butch. "So, my man, you missed me?" He seated himself and Butch immediately climbed up on his chest to sniff his face. He barked, bit Riley's chin and then tried to dig underneath his shirt.

Laughing, Riley set him aside. "Anxious for your gift, huh?"

Regina inched over to the couch. She smiled. "You're spoiling him, Riley."

"I thought it might keep him occupied while I carried you off to bed."

He heard her gasp, but didn't comment on it. He was so wired, so damned...*needy* after talking to the other men, he knew if he didn't have her soon, he'd explode. He pulled a large rawhide bone out of his pocket. Butch's eyes widened and his ears came forward in an alert pose.

Setting the bone on the floor, Riley asked, "Think you can handle that?"

The dog ran down Riley's leg and circled the bone, examining it from every angle, making both Regina and Riley laugh.

"It's bigger than he is."

Butch got one corner in his mouth and started backing up with the bone until he was completely hidden beneath a side table.

"That ought to keep him busy." Riley stood and turned toward Regina. "Now for you."

Regina chewed her lower lip. "Yes?"

"I missed you."

Her smile quivered the tiniest bit. "I missed you, too."

Riley slipped his arms around her waist. Staring down at her, he said, "I was going to go really slow, Red. I was going to start by teaching you a few self-defense moves, because that's important. Then I was going to carry you to bed."

"You've been teaching me self-defense moves for a while now," she reminded him.

"Not alone. Not in private where I can mix the lessons with kissing and touching."

"You've changed your mind about teaching me?"

"No, I just don't think I can wait. We'll work on your lessons afterward."

Her smile was sweet, sensual and teasing. "I'm glad. I've been thinking about you all day, too. I don't want to wait."

She caught her breath when Riley lifted her into his arms. He strode into his bedroom, pushed the door quietly shut with his foot, and sat on the edge of the mattress with her in his lap. "How could you have been thinking about me when you had Harris here entertaining you?"

She pushed his jacket off his shoulders. Riley helped, moving his arms until the coat fell to the bed. Next she began undoing his buttons. "We talked about you."

"You did?" He didn't like the sound of that, but with her small cool hands now on his chest, he found it hard to concentrate.

"Yes." She bent and kissed his throat. "I wanted to start your interview by talking to your friends."

Riley stiffened, but she caught his neck and quickly kissed him, scattering his thoughts.

"They respect you a lot, Riley."

"They?"

"Ethan, Buck and Harris."

His groan was due partly to dismay, partly to the way she

removed his shirt and rained tiny kisses across his chest. "Hell, Red, you had all three of them here?"

"Mmm. They don't know any more about you than I do." She pushed him flat to the mattress, straddled his thighs and started on his belt buckle.

Riley settled his hands on her waist, charmed with her seduction, and so turned on he wanted her under him right this instant. "You know everything about me that you need to know."

She glanced up to give him a chastising smile. "No, I don't. But I can be patient. I've decided not to do the interview until you're comfortable talking to me about your past."

"Red…"

"Raise your hips." She had his slacks undone, so Riley did as ordered. She quickly skimmed them, along with his boxers, down his legs. She paused to tug off his shoes and socks, and then he was naked.

Regina let out a breath. "You are such a gorgeous man, Riley Moore."

"I'm glad you think so. Now come here."

"Just a second." She stood beside the bed and stared down at him. "You spoke with Luther?"

"Yeah. I spoke to him." *And I made him very sorry he ever hurt you.*

Regina nodded. She bent to pull off her sandals. "He, ah, told you about our breakup, didn't he?"

Rolling to his side so he could see her better, Riley propped himself up on one elbow. "He explained that he was an obnoxious blind ass who doesn't deserve you."

Her lips curled in a disbelieving smile. "Never in a million years would Luther say something like that."

"No, but that's the gist of it." Riley watched her fidget with the straps of her sundress. Would she be daring enough to lose the dress? He hoped so. "Whether he realized it or not, whether you realize it or not, you're an incredibly sexy woman, Red." With a grin, he added, "I sure as hell realized it the second I saw you."

He heard her inhale deeply. "Thank you." She reached for the hem and tugged her dress up and over her head. After tossing it aside, she pushed her panties down and stepped out of them. She straightened and waited.

It was the oddest feeling, Riley thought, shaking with lust while choking with tenderness. He'd never experienced it before, but then, as he'd just told her, he'd known from the beginning that she'd be different.

He reached for her and toppled her across his chest. He rolled, putting her beneath him, and cupped one satiny breast. "You're perfect."

"I'm—"

"*Perfect*." He looked up into her eyes. "I understand about hurt, Regina. People say and do things that, if we let them, can hurt us deep inside and linger for too damn many days and nights."

Her expression froze. "Someone hurt you?"

Riley decided then and there that he'd tell her. He wanted her trust, so perhaps he had to give it first. He wasn't a polished man and he didn't have the persona of the senator, but he could be honest. "My wife."

She went rigid beneath him. "You were married?"

"Yeah." Her naked body distracted him and he said in a growl, "Luther is an idiot. I wouldn't change a single thing about you." He bent and took a nipple into his mouth.

"Riley wait..." she said on a groan.

"Can't." He gently sucked while pressing his hand between her thighs. She was warm and soft, her springy curls already damp.

Regina waylaid him by catching his wrist. "Riley? There's something I always wanted to try."

Breathing hard, Riley forced himself to stop. It wasn't easy when he ached with the need for release. "What?"

"This." He let her push him to his back. Her breasts were against his chest, one of her legs between his. Her hair hung loose, silky soft and tousled. "Don't move."

He considered that a tall order considering the gorgeous view of her backside that she presented while twisting around to rummage in his nightstand for a condom.

Riley said, "In a hurry?"

"Yes. Tell me if I put this on you wrong." She opened the small packet and bent close to his groin, intent on her task. He could feel her breath and it made him moan. She blinked at him in surprise. "I haven't even touched you yet."

"I know." It was a miracle he could string those two words together. Her hair tickled across his abdomen, his thighs.

She looked down at his cock and smiled. In the next instant, she had him in her small, soft hand, gently squeezing. "Is this what you want?"

His groan mixed with a laugh. "I want you any way I can have you."

"Would you like me to kiss you?"

His vision narrowed; every muscle in his body clenched. He said, "Yes," although he doubted she meant what he wanted her to mean. His body arched in delicious pleasure. "Oh God."

Her mouth was warm, damp, her tongue curious. Riley caught her head in his big hands and guided her, urging her to swallow more of him, raising his hips to help her with that.

Her small sound of wonder vibrated along his shaft, and his fingers clenched. He'd dreamed about this, about the prim Regina Foxworth giving him head—and enjoying it. The reality beat the fantasy all to hell and back.

For several minutes she drove him crazy, tasting, teasing,

humming again. Finally, she lifted away and Riley's heart swelled at the evidence of her excitement. Her green eyes glowed with heat, her cheeks were flushed. "You taste good, Riley," she said in wonder.

Riley curled a hand around her thigh. He needed to come. He needed to be inside her. "So do you."

They stared at each other for a long moment before Regina bent to press one last innocent kiss to the head of his erection. Riley watched her straddle his thighs, saw her frown as she carefully rolled the condom on.

He checked it with her fascinated gaze never wavering, then pulled her over him. "Now what, babe?"

"Now I want to do it like this, with me on top."

"Yeah?" He gave her a crooked smile that almost hurt, he was so turned on. "I like that idea. That means I can see and touch all of you."

Her eyes darkened. "Yes." She lifted up, guided his cock to her opening, and slowly began sinking onto him. Riley held her thighs. She braced her hands on his chest.

It was incredible…seeing her face, watching her expressive eyes and the telling way her lips parted and her breasts rose with each deepened breath. "A little more," he urged, and her eyes closed as she wiggled, seating herself fully upon him.

Neither of them moved. Riley gasped for air, Regina's body clenched and relaxed around him.

"I can feel you throbbing."

He groaned and couldn't stop the lifting of his hips. Through his teeth, he growled, "I'm a nanosecond away from coming."

"Really?" She smiled down at him, then lifted.

"Really." She dropped and he said, "Regina…"

"I like this. Do you?"

Groaning again, he cupped her breasts, brushed her nipples

with his thumbs, then caught them both in his fingers, lightly pinching, tugging. Her back arched, driving him even deeper.

He knew he wouldn't last so he moved one hand between her legs, gliding his middle finger along her swollen lips, taut around him, then up to her turgid clitoris. "Move, honey. Ride me."

Her fingers splayed over his chest and she began to rise and fall, faster and faster. He loved the small sounds she made, the way her face contorted with her concentration, her pleasure. Riley kept his fingers just where she needed them, treating her to a constant friction that worked with her own movements. Soon she was in the same shape as him, shaking, on the verge of exploding.

He brought his knees up to support her back and returned her thrusts, lifting her knees from the bed as he drove into her. With a startled cry, she collapsed against him. Her mouth opened on his shoulder, her teeth coming down in a tantalizing love bite.

The small pain pushed him over the edge. Riley lost control. He gripped her ass and pounded into her, groaning harshly with his own unending climax, the crushing waves of pleasure going on and on....

He wasn't sure how much time passed when he became aware of Butch jumping beside the bed, demanding attention. Regina was a soft sweaty weight over his heart.

"Hey?" He moved fistfuls of her hair aside, kissed her ear. "You okay?"

"Mmmrrmf."

Riley managed a grin. "What's that?"

"I'm fine," she said against his neck, wiggling lazily. "Better than fine. I feel extraordinary."

He stroked her behind. "Yes, you do."

Her giggle was one of the sweetest sounds he'd ever heard.

She was totally relaxed with him. Soon, she'd love him—as much as he loved her.

"We have three problems. We're both sweaty and sticking together. The condom's going to become useless in about two seconds if we don't separate. And Butch is none too pleased to be ignored."

Regina pressed her face into his chest. "You smell good sweaty." Lifting up to see him, she asked, "Do I?"

Damn, but she wrenched at his heart. "Good enough to eat."

She smiled and blushed, then turned her attention to Butch. "You have to wait, sweetie. Give me a second to regain feeling in my legs, and I'll get up and play."

"That dog is worse than an infant."

"How would you know? Ever had an infant?" It was just an offhand remark, not really serious.

"No." Riley rolled her to his side, filling his hand with her hair so he could see her face. "I wanted a baby though."

That bald admission, especially after lovemaking, got her attention. "You did?"

"Yeah." He kissed her, then sat up in the bed. "Stay put. I'll be right back." He headed to the bathroom to dispose of the condom. It also gave him a moment to gather his thoughts and figure out how to say what he wanted her to know, to understand.

When he returned, she was sitting up against the headboard, wearing his shirt and holding Butch. The dog took one look at Riley and tried to keep him out of the bed with his pseudo-attacks.

"You mangy little mutt, I'm the one who brought you the bone, remember?"

At the mention of the enormous chew, Butch's ears perked up and he went to the edge of the bed, whining to be let down.

With a sigh, Regina lowered him to the floor. He ran out the bedroom door in a flash.

Riley found his boxers, pulled them on, and sat on the bed at her side. "You look good in my shirt."

She laughed, making a halfhearted effort to smooth her wild hair. "You know what I think? I think you just like giving compliments."

"Only to people who deserve them." He fingered the collar of the shirt, then undid the button between her breasts. He didn't know if he'd ever get enough of her—

Something solid and damp landed on his foot. Butch had dragged the colossal chew bone over to him, and was now jumping at the side of the bed again.

"Oh no. I don't want that thing in my bed."

A barked argument ensued. When Riley held firm, Butch got hold of the very edge of the bone and tried to stand up against the bed. He couldn't. He looked ridiculous with his mouth full and he made an odd snorting noise during his struggle. Riley couldn't help but laugh. "All right, you pathetic little beggar. You win. But keep it down at the foot of the bed."

He lifted both dog and bone, then laughed again when Butch did his best to hide the gigantic thing under the covers. Riley helped by lifting the blankets for him, then caught Regina's sweet indulgent expression. "What?"

She reached out and touched his jaw. "When I first met you, I knew you were very capable and strong. That's as noticeable as your blue eyes, and I told myself that I needed to get closer to you to learn some self-defense."

"Which you've yet to do."

She ignored that. "Then after a while I decided you were a terrific friend, too. You're so at ease with the guys and with Rosie. I wanted so badly to be a part of that."

"And you are."

"Yes." She touched his mouth, tracing his lower lip with her fingertips. "After I brought Butch home, I got to see how gentle you are. That was such a turn-on, Riley." Her smile trembled. "Now, seeing your patience and generosity, it occurs to me that you'd also make a wonderful father." She laughed. "Although you'd probably spoil your kids rotten."

Riley turned his head and kissed her palm. She was getting into some pretty deep stuff here. So far, she'd admitted to liking and admiring him. He wanted more. He wanted her love.

"I think we can spend a few minutes talking before we need to get dressed for the ceremony."

"I'd like to talk about…things."

"Yeah?" He moved into bed beside her, put his arm around her and tugged her into his side. "I haven't wanted to really talk to a woman in a long time."

"You prefer to just rush her into bed?"

He shrugged. "I haven't been a saint, but I haven't been sexually attracted to that many women either. Now here you are, and I want to talk to you and be inside you at the same time. It's damn strange."

"Gee, thanks."

Riley hugged her. "You go first then."

He felt her nod before she said, "I always knew it wasn't me."

Riley just held her, waiting.

"I've never been ashamed of my build or thought I was lacking. I'm just me and I try really hard to be the best that I can. But even though I realized Luther is a creep, I was still… worried."

"Without reason. You're incredible, a beautiful person inside and out."

"Thank you."

Riley smiled at her continued good manners. "Any problems in the sack were his, Red. It was never about you."

"Yes, I know." She stroked his abdomen and sighed. "Especially now. After today, after being with you, I won't worry anymore." Then she turned into his side, wrapped her arms tight around him as if to protect him, and whispered, "But you didn't know, did you? The woman who hurt you—you blame yourself."

Riley tensed. "It's not the same thing, honey."

"Will you tell me what happened? Not for an interview and not for nosiness, but because I care about you, Riley. And I know from experience that it helps to talk."

A good start, Riley thought, then wondered if she'd feel the same when he finished his tale. "I've never told anyone before." He wanted her to know that, to understand the level of his trust. He shuddered at the small kiss she pressed to his chest, right over his heart. "She died, Red."

A strange stillness settled over her. "Your wife?"

"Yes." He was glad Regina kept her face tucked against him, rather than looking at him. He wasn't a coward, but he couldn't remember those awful days of lies and deceit—his and hers— without feeling raw. "She was having an affair with Phil, one of my friends from the SWAT team." With disgust he added, "A man I respected."

The silence felt heavy, almost suffocating Riley before she asked, "How do you know?"

Riley shook his head, once again wishing he could somehow change things. "I caught them in bed together. I came home from work early and found them in my bedroom, in my bed."

"I'm so sorry."

"I always have control, Regina. Always. But when I saw them, I didn't bother using it. I can't claim temporary insanity or a blinding jealous rage. That would be a lie. I was pissed off, completely furious, and I wanted to beat the hell out of Phil, so I did. I coldly, methodically, hurt him. Not permanently, but I did a lot of superficial damage."

"But listen to what you're saying. You could have killed him, Riley. You're more than capable. But you didn't. Instead you just hurt him, as he deserved."

Riley shook his head. "No one got what they deserved that awful day." He had to draw three breaths before he could continue. "My wife flew around me, screaming and crying. Phil… He was good, but he didn't stand a chance against me."

Regina fisted a hand on his chest. "He was in bed with your wife, Riley. Most men would react the way you did."

"Most men aren't me."

"Meaning you fight better than they could?"

He laughed. "There was no fight to it."

"And don't you see? Another man without your control might have killed him, even if he hadn't meant to."

He couldn't deny that. As a cop, he'd seen more than a few crimes of passion. "You know, it was strange, but a good part of my anger was for Phil's wife. She was seven months pregnant at the time."

Regina curled closer, both arms around him, one leg over his. Absently, Riley stroked her shoulder.

"God, Regina, when Phil finally left my house, my wife went with him and…" He hesitated, but she had a right to know. "They both died in a car wreck."

"They made their own decisions, Riley."

"They were both upset. Physically, Phil was in no condition to drive. I should have stopped them. I should have at least stopped her from going along. But I didn't." His throat hurt, but he said it all. "I wanted her out of my sight. I wanted her gone."

"But you didn't want her dead."

She sounded so sure of that. Many times, Riley had remembered that awful day and wondered. He'd been so detached through it all, as if his heart had been anesthetized. "No, I didn't want her dead." Saying it out loud made him finally believe it. He'd reacted, but without the intent of such dire consequences. "Hell, I didn't even want *him* dead. But when I got the call, I dunno, most of my concern was for Phil's wife. I kept seeing her in my mind, how happy she'd been, all the plans she'd been making for them as a family." He glanced down at Regina. "She was cute as hell pregnant and whenever we got together she'd show us the new baby clothes she'd bought or a bassinet or a toy."

"Oh God, how did she take the news about Phil and your wife…."

He shook his head. "I never told her, Red. Not about the cheating. I've never told anyone." He glanced down at her. "Except you."

Regina's eyes were big and soft, filled with understanding. "How did you explain them being in the car together?"

He laughed, but the sound wasn't humorous. "I was CSI—I knew how to cover my tracks. I made sure no one would know I'd been home when he and my wife left together, then I said my wife must have been helping him with a gift for the baby. I told everyone that they'd discussed it, made plans to buy something wonderful because Phil wanted to surprise his wife. No one doubted it. No one questioned me. Hell, no one even noticed my bloody knuckles." He swallowed down his own disgust. "They didn't see the bruises on Phil either. The wreck was pretty bad and the car caught on fire." His voice went so quiet, it was barely audible. "Neither of them was all that recognizable."

Riley could feel Regina shivering. "Was anyone else hurt in the wreck?"

"No, thank God. They went off the side of the road, down

into a gully. The car flipped and hit a tree. There were no other cars involved."

His stomach started churning; absently he rubbed it, trying to fight off the familiar sickness. Butch appeared, his little furry face so expressive, so concerned. He whined as if he'd sensed Riley's upset, then crawled up onto his chest and curled up under Riley's chin.

Stupidly enough, it helped.

Emotion clogged Riley's throat, but he hugged Regina with one arm, patted Butch with his other hand, and wished the damn story didn't still hurt so much.

Regina was frozen and silent for a long time before asking, "What ever became of Phil's wife?"

"I stuck around until after the birth, trying to help her out. She had a baby boy she named Phil, after his daddy. Phil had a life insurance policy so she's not too bad off financially. After that, I left. I quit my job and moved here. I heard she got remarried about a year ago. Her kid would be... I dunno, almost five now." He stroked his fingers through Regina's hair, taking comfort in her warmth and softness. "I hope she and the kid are happy."

Suddenly Regina sobbed.

Startled, Riley tried to see her face but she pressed herself so close, it felt like she wanted to crawl inside him. Butch panicked, whining at Riley, poking his nose into Regina's cheek.

"Hey. Honey, what's the matter?"

She hiccuped and in a strangled voice said, "I want to give you something, Riley, okay?"

As she spoke, she turned her face up to his and Riley grimaced. She didn't cry well. Already her eyes were watery and red, matching her nose. Her cheeks were blotchy. He smiled. "Yeah, sure. But please, don't cry, baby. I can't stand it."

That made her start sobbing again. She crawled out of the bed, still sniffling, and headed out of the room.

"Regina?"

"I'll be right back," she wailed.

Riley watched her go, enjoying the way his shirttails barely covered her tush. He looked at Butch. "Women." Then he added, "But damn, she looks good in my shirt, doesn't she?" And he murmured, "Even better out of it, though."

She came back into the bedroom, the framed photo in her hand. She plopped into bed, burrowed into Riley's side, and dropped the photo on his lap. "Here, you can have it."

Lip curled in distaste, Riley lifted the smug, smiling face of Senator Welling away from his body and dropped it on the nightstand. "Gee, thanks. Just what I always wanted."

Regina gave a choked laugh, lightly punched him, and then hugged him in a stranglehold. "You asked me earlier why I brought the stupid thing along."

Stupid thing? "Uh, yeah."

"I see the photo and I remember his commitment to his family and how he stands for all the things I value. It gives me hope that someday I'll have those things, too."

Riley rolled his eyes. "Regina…"

"It gave me hope that some day I'd meet a man like him. But I don't need him for inspiration anymore." She smiled up at Riley and even with the blotchy cheeks, she looked beautiful. "You're the finest man I know, Riley. No one else could ever measure up to you."

Oh hell. It was bad enough when he thought she used Welling as a masculine measuring tape. But if he became the damn tape, she was bound for disappointment. "No, Regina, I'm just a man."

"A good man. A real man. And that's better than a public persona any day."

Riley's heart about stopped. Was it possible she loved him, too? Had he finally gotten through to her? He started to tell her so when his phone rang. Riley reached for the nightstand and snatched up the receiver. "Hello?" And then with foreboding, "Yeah, Dermot. What's up?"

Just as he suspected, Earl had been released. The judge returned not more than a few hours ago, but Earl had made his call and somehow gotten things expedited.

"Thanks for the heads-up. I guess all we can do now is hope he doesn't jump bail." He hung up and rubbed his face. "Looks like we're back to square one unless Senator Welling can remember something vital."

Regina gasped as if someone had pinched her. "Oh no. Senator Welling and the ceremony. We're going to be late."

Riley glanced at the clock and cursed. "We'll make it if we hurry." He threw the covers aside and stood.

Regina remained in bed, her bottom lip caught between her teeth. "Riley? Are you sure we can't just skip it? Somehow, I'm not as excited about seeing him as I had been."

He smiled, caught her under the arms and lifted her from the bed. "No, we can't skip it. I don't want to miss this chance. If we get there early, we can talk to the senator before the ceremony begins and get it out of the way."

"Then come back here and make love some more?"

Riley feigned a scandalized gasp. "Why, Ms. Foxworth, you surprise me."

She grinned. "When we get home, I'll surprise you even more."

Home. He liked the sound of that. "It's a deal."

chapter 10

BUTCH PUT ON AN AWFUL, MELODRAMATIC FIT about being left alone. He was a smart little dog who understood *everything* whenever the mood suited him, and right now he understood that two dressed humans heading for the door meant he'd be alone.

He didn't like it, and he didn't hold back in letting them know his deepest feelings. Not only did he howl pitifully, but he lay flat on his belly and did an army crawl, as if his little legs wouldn't work.

They tried stepping out and waiting to see if he'd calm down. He didn't. He made such a racket that he sounded like a pack of wolves. Riley feared complaints from his neighbors if they left Butch carrying on so enthusiastically.

In the end, since the ceremony would mostly be outdoors, Regina gave in and tucked him away in her satchel. She hooked his leash to his collar as a precaution in case he attempted to escape. She kept the leash wrapped around her hand and the strap of the big bag over her shoulder with Butch close to her side.

He seemed to like that just fine. He curled up and went to sleep like a baby in a knapsack.

"And you said *I'd* spoil him?"

Regina scowled at that accusation. "He's still getting used to us. There's been no stability in his life yet, what with me bringing him home, then bringing him here...."

Riley drew her close without mussing her hair, and pressed a warm kiss to her forehead. "I do understand. Even cantankerous little dogs need reassuring." Then he grinned. "Just remember that us old dogs need it, too."

Regina intended to reassure him in a big way as soon as they returned. She was going to tell him how she felt. Love was love and it should never be denied. To get it, you had to give it. That was the argument she'd used when choosing Butch, and now she'd apply it to Riley. She'd give him her heart and hope he gave his in return.

It had worked with Butch.

Riley drove his truck to the ceremony. Regina felt the difference now in just being with him. There was a new comfort, a new ease that existed between them. She thought of everything he'd told her, everything he'd gone through. No wonder he hadn't wanted to get involved again. He had not only the emotional turmoil of an unfaithful spouse, but he also had a battle with his professional conscience for being untruthful.

Regina considered his thoughtfulness for Phil's wife one of the most commendable things she'd ever heard. Riley had put his own hurt aside to protect someone else—and that, more than anything, defined the type of man he was.

Milling crowds filled the lawn in front of the museum center where the Historical Society had planned the ceremony. Keeping Regina tucked close to his side with a precautionary, proprietary air, Riley repeatedly flashed his badge to dispatch a path to the quiet chambers inside the museum where Senator Welling passed the time until his introduction. In the end though, it was Regina who got them beyond the final barrier of guards.

She gave her name and politely asked them to inform Senator Welling that she would greatly appreciate a moment of his time. One unconvinced guard did as she asked, then returned with a smile, saying Senator Welling would love to see her again.

The guards wouldn't let Riley in, though, and Riley wouldn't let Regina in without him. He was most firm on that issue, so Regina stuck her head in the heavy carved wooden door of the museum's inner sanctum and requested that her escort be given entrance as well.

Senator Welling, smiling and as jovial as the last time she'd seen him, rose from behind a large desk and bid them both inside. "Ms. Foxworth—Regina—how wonderful to see you again."

It was enough of a surprise that he remembered her, but he also sounded sincerely happy to see her. Regina smiled with true pleasure. By rights, the Senator should have looked exhausted from his recent travels. The commendation from the Historical Society came at the tail end of a two-week tour. Instead, he looked vital and energetic. "Senator Welling. I hope we're not imposing."

"Of course not. And please, no formality here. Call me Xavier. After all, we're old friends now."

"Why, thank you. I'd be honored."

Another guard came forward to frisk both her and Riley.

"I'm sorry," Xavier said with a wry, philosophical shrug. "They're quite insistent on doing their jobs."

"Oh, I understand. You're a very important man. Of course they have to protect you." Regina held her arms out to her sides and submitted to being patted down. Butch didn't take it well, snapping at the guard and startling him when he peeked inside the bag. The Senator, a lover of animals, was merely amused when Butch peeked out at him and growled.

Unlike the others who'd called her dog a rat and worse, Xavier said, "Such distinctive coloring. A pure-bred Chihuahua?"

"Yes, thank you. I think he's beautiful, too." Regina beamed at Xavier for his exquisite taste in animals.

Riley didn't take the invasion of privacy much better than Butch had, but at least he didn't try to bite anyone. He introduced himself, showed his badge, and still got roughly checked for hidden weapons. Regina watched him warily, unsure what he might do.

When the security check had been completed, he merely nodded. "Senator Welling—"

"Xavier, please," he reminded Riley.

Riley conceded with a nod. "Xavier. Thank you for seeing us."

"It's my pleasure." After sharing a hearty handshake with Riley, he took Regina's hand and winked at her. "We have plenty of time to spare before the ceremony and I've only been sitting here hoping I won't trip over my words."

His charming, self-deprecating grin could win over the worst skeptics, Regina decided. "I'm sure you'll keep them all enthralled."

Laughing, still holding her hand, Xavier turned to Riley. "My biggest fan, or so she tells me."

Riley's mouth flattened. "Yeah, she tells me that, too."

Regina frowned at Riley's tone—and noticed he was staring at Xavier's hand clasping hers. Could he be jealous? He'd made that comment about old dogs needing reassurance, too. Trying to be inconspicuous, she pulled away from Xavier. "Senator, how is your intern? That lovely young lady I met at the park with you."

His gray brows rose in confusion. "My intern?"

Regina forged on. "I recall she was very quiet, but you told me she worked hard and was very dedicated to you."

Xavier cleared his throat. "Yes, a hard worker. I'm sorry, but you know, I can't keep up with all the interns. They come and go, and…" Suddenly he stopped. He turned to his guards and said, "Wait outside."

The guards shared a look, hesitant to obey.

Xavier frowned and rounded his desk to shoo them away. "Really, I'm quite safe here with the young lady and her friend. Go. I'd like some privacy."

Regina was stunned at the sudden turn of events. Both men were forced out a door at the back of the office, behind where Xavier had been sitting. In a heartbeat, Riley was there, standing mostly in front of her, blocking her with his body. She tried to nudge him aside, but he wouldn't move.

"Riley, really," she whispered.

Glancing over his shoulder, he gave her one brief, hard look that stopped all other protests in her throat.

When Xavier turned back to them, his expression had become strained. "There. Much better, don't you think?" His smile didn't reach his eyes. "Please, take a seat and tell me what you've been up to." Xavier returned to his chair.

Regina started to take the nearest chair opposite the desk, but Riley stopped her by backing further into her.

"With your permission, Senator, I'd like to ask you a few questions about that day in the park."

Xavier's complexion paled. He looked down at his desk a moment, then faced Riley squarely. "Is there a problem?"

Regina could feel the tension in Riley, but she didn't understand it. He seemed braced for an attack, ready to charge. But why?

"Since that day, Regina has been repeatedly threatened by someone. I believe it started with the car that ran her off the road."

Xavier swallowed, and in a murmur said, "Thank God she wasn't injured that day. Terrible, terrible thing to happen to a young woman. She could have been killed."

Riley's arms hung loose at his sides. It was a negligent pose, but Regina had taken enough lessons from him to know he was readying himself, keeping limber, poised.

"Yes, she could have. And that wasn't the only incident. She's been accosted several times. The worst, however, was the fire."

Xavier's head shot up. "A fire?"

"Yes. A deliberate fire, in my opinion. It burned a building to the ground and almost took Regina and her friend with it."

Xavier squeezed his eyes shut and shook his head. "This is dreadful. Just dreadful."

By small degrees, Riley started backing up, forcing Regina toward the door where they'd entered.

The sense of foreboding was so thick in the air, Regina thought she might choke on it. "Senator?"

He shook his head. "I'm only a man, flawed, damn it."

"What the hell does that mean?" Riley demanded.

The senator looked up, then beyond Riley. His face went ashen.

Someone had stepped into the room behind them.

Startled, more than a little frightened, Regina jerked around— and let out a relieved breath. Mrs. Welling stood there, elegantly dressed in a turquoise suit with pearl jewelry.

Riley started to move Regina to his side, but Mrs. Welling reached out and took her hand. "Hello. I heard Xavier had guests."

Flustered, Regina all but gushed. "Mrs. Welling! It's so wonderful to finally meet you. I didn't know you were here, too, but then you always accompany Xavier, don't you?"

"'Xavier'?" She slanted a sardonic look at her husband. "I see you're a close friend, to call him by his first name."

"Oh." Regina felt the heat pulsing in her face. "No, not at all. He just—"

"It's all right. My husband has mentioned you, Ms. Foxworth." Mrs. Welling was tall, softened with age, but still striking in appearance. Her brown hair was stylishly laced with gray, her eyes a stunning, clear blue. She held Regina's hand overlong.

Regina was aware of Xavier slowly standing behind his desk, of Riley stepping aside so that he stood between husband and wife. Regina prayed Riley wouldn't lose his temper and do something outlandish.

She was trying to send him a warning look to behave when the door behind Xavier opened. Regina's view was blocked by Riley, but she heard him curse. With Mrs. Welling still clasping her hand, she stepped to the side to better see.

A tall man, probably a guard, stood there. He wasn't smiling, and he kept his narrowed, alert gaze on Riley. Slowly he lifted his right arm and pointed a gun.

Regina gasped. Instinctively, she tried to move toward Riley, but Mrs. Welling kept her immobile. "Meet Earl Rochelle, Ms. Foxworth. I believe he's made himself something of a nuisance to you."

Confusion warred with fear. "You...you're the one who broke into my apartment?" Regina had a hard time taking it in. Mrs. Welling seemed so cold, Xavier was rocking back and forth on his heels, muttering to himself and shaking his head. Riley just stood there, as sturdy and unshakable as a stone wall.

Earl nodded at Riley. "Your lover boy roughed me up. But now it's time for payback."

Riley shifted the tiniest bit. "You son of a bitch." His voice was calm, without inflection. "So you're working for the senator?"

Xavier violently shook his head. "No. No, I'd never hurt anyone...."

Mrs. Welling laughed. "Xavier, be truthful. You hurt me all the time." Her lovely face contorted—with pain, with anger. "Every single time you crawl into bed with another woman. But no more, you bloated pompous ass. I've stuck with you this long, and I'll be damned if I let you ruin our family now."

Regina turned to face her, her brain blank with shock, with disbelief. "Mrs. Welling... I'm sorry. I didn't know."

"Of course you didn't. Along with a good portion of the constituents, you think Xavier is an honorable man, a *family* man. In truth, my dear, he's a lying cheating pig."

Xavier shook his head, his face now bright pink, his eyes pleading. "No, dear. It was only those few times...."

"I'm not a fool, Xavier. I've known of every single affair. Your intern—who by the way, Ms. Foxworth, is no more than a well-paid prostitute—was only one in a long line of young women. You preach family values, all the while you're paying for sex with a common whore."

Her voice had risen with her ire, and Earl moved closer. "Mrs. Welling, please. Discretion is necessary."

She released Regina to wave away his concerns. "I dismissed the guards for now. I told them to return when it's time for Xavier's introduction. We've at least fifteen more minutes."

Regina suddenly understood. "The photograph." She stared at Mrs. Welling. "It has the intern... I mean, the prostitute, in the picture with the senator. They were..." Aghast, she turned to stare at Xavier. "They were having an affair *in the park?*"

"You begin to understand. The stupid park wasn't due to be open. Xavier knew I was watching him, and he thought he could lose my spies in the woods. But Earl kept a tail on him." She glanced at her husband with loathing. "Earl saw everything, including the damn picture you took. Xavier, the idiot, didn't think it was anything to worry about. He didn't think anyone would put two and two together. I know better. If that picture got out, the whole family would be ruined. I had Earl run you off the road, but you kept the camera around your neck and Xavier came to your aid."

Sadly, his shoulders slumped, Xavier said, "I couldn't let you hurt her."

"The way you hurt me?" Mrs. Welling turned away from him. "At the fire we finally got the camera, but it was filled with new film. Since then, we've been unable to find either the undeveloped film or the photograph."

Riley laughed. "She has it framed and keeps it in her bedside drawer."

Regina gaped at him even as she felt herself enveloped in mortified heat. *"Riley."*

Riley ignored her, moving closer to the desk, casually leaning a hip on the edge. Earl stiffened, but kept quiet.

The senator stared at her in astonishment.

Mrs. Welling's face contorted. "So you've slept with him, too?" she wrongly concluded. Outraged, she shook her head and addressed Riley. "Thank you for letting us know." Her lip curled, destroying her image of a respected and elegant politician's wife. "Retrieving the vile thing will be so much easier now, especially with you two out of the picture."

"And how exactly do you plan to accomplish that?"

At Riley's question, she pulled another gun out of her purse, but this one was odd-shaped, unlike any gun Regina had ever seen. "Why don't you let me worry about that, Mr. Moore?"

Riley shifted again. Regina felt sure he planned to do something, but what, she couldn't guess. She only wished he'd hurry up. She was starting to sweat nervously. Things did not look good. She realized that she should have been worried about him, but she somehow knew he'd handle things.

Then Mrs. Welling made the bad decision to grab Regina by the hair. She had the odd gun raised when suddenly Butch exploded from the bag with such a feral, wild snarl it sounded like a pack of demon dogs had been unleashed.

He bit Mrs. Welling's hand, her arm, and ran right up to her face where he sank his small sharp teeth into her nose. The woman screamed in reaction and swatted at the dog.

Regina saw red. She hadn't realized she'd learned anything substantial from Riley, but without any real thought she caught her small dog in one arm, grabbed the arm holding the gun in the other and deftly tripped Mrs. Welling to her back. The woman hit her head on the hardwood floor and stayed there, dazed.

Regina jerked the gun from her hand.

Almost at the same time, Riley moved with blinding speed. His leg came up and over the desk, landing his foot squarely in the senator's face. He went down with a grunt. Earl moved, but Riley already had the advantage. He grabbed Earl's gun arm, pulled him forward and delivered his elbow into his throat.

Gagging and gasping, Earl collapsed to his knees. The gun fell from his hand and Riley kicked it aside. Hesitating only a moment to make certain Earl was sufficiently incapacitated, Riley turned and reached for the fallen gun. Both doors exploded open as guards filed in. Riley groaned, his hands lifted in a non-threatening pose. He started to explain, and finally saw that Dermot and Lanny headed up the cavalry. He actually laughed.

Dermot grinned. "We followed him. You seemed so sure he was up to something more than a break-in."

Lanny nodded. "And you being sure made us sure, so when the judge returned and we had to release him, we decided it might be smart to keep a close watch."

"Good job," Riley told them and they both puffed up like proud peacocks.

"Explaining to these guys wasn't easy though." Dermot nodded to the hired guards with a scowl.

They ignored him.

One stepped forward and picked up the strange gun by Mrs. Welling. "A tranquilizer gun?"

Regina's knees felt suddenly weak. She trembled from her head to her toes. "She was going to use it on us." Her voice was little more than a breathy squeak. "Then he—" she pointed to Earl "—was going to kill us."

The guards looked at her like she was nuts. Earl shouted denials. Senator Welling stirred just in time for a small bespectacled woman in a black suit to duck her head into the room and say, "Senator, it's time for…your…introduction." Her eyes rounded, looking huge behind her glasses.

One of the guards caught her arm and pulled her completely into the room, then shut and locked the door.

The senator moaned. Mrs. Welling, now sitting on the floor holding her head, said, "Forget it. There'll be no more honors for him."

Regina looked around at the chaos and wanted to cry. It was more than just the scandal that was sure to ensue, the political ramifications, the threat to her and Riley. Something she'd cherished, something she'd believed was real, had just been defiled in the worst possible way.

Her stomach actually cramped. She'd been such an utter fool.

Then Riley was there, his hand closing gently on her upper arm. "Babe, you're crushing Butch. Loosen up."

Regina glanced at Butch, at his bulgy little eyes, and saw it was true. She relinquished her hold on him.

"That's it. Here, let me hold him." Riley balanced the dog in one arm, up close to his chest because Butch seemed more than a little rattled by all that had happened. He was curled in on himself, his eyes still wild, and low growls continually emitted from deep in his throat as he watched everyone and everything. Once Riley held him, he looked less threatened.

With his other arm, Riley gathered Regina protectively into his side. Regina knew everyone was looking at her with varying degrees of expression—virulence from Mrs. Welling, disgrace from Xavier, concern from Lanny and Dermot.

She felt like a spectacle, something she detested, a feeling left over from her childhood. Ashamed, she turned into Riley to hide. "You told them where I kept the picture."

At her agonized whisper, he tightened his hold and his voice became hard. "Only to distract them, to keep them talking until I could best situate myself to react."

"Oh." She supposed that made sense. She'd put them into a situation and he'd had to rescue them because of it.

"Damn it, Red, I would never deliberately do anything to hurt you."

He sounded so outraged, Regina tried to soothe him. "Okay, Riley." The last thing she wanted was another spectacle.

To her surprise, Riley murmured near her ear, "Red, you've made me so proud."

"Proud?" She wasn't expecting that and her laugh was bitter and hurt. "I was a gullible idiot."

"No. You handled yourself well, disarming Mrs. Welling, protecting Butch, helping me."

Had she done all that? She had struck out at the crazy woman, but… "I got us in this situation in the first place by being an idiot."

"No." He turned her to face him, his expression volatile. "You're you, sweet and trusting and sincere, and I happen to love you an awful lot."

She jerked back. The suffocating crowd and her own embarrassment seemed to fade away. Her entire focus was on Riley and those awesome words he'd just uttered. "You what?"

With exasperation, he took her arm and towed her into the farthest corner of the room. It wasn't really far enough, merely a few feet away. The guards were watching them while another phoned a supervisor on his cell phone. The situation was sticky and could explode into an ugly scandal if it wasn't handled quickly and efficiently.

Riley cupped the back of her neck and put his forehead to hers. "Listen to me, Regina. I know the human garbage that exists in our world. Hell, I've dealt with them more times than I care to remember. Rapists, murderers, sadists... They're out there and we all have to be careful. But there are a lot of good people in the world, too, the kind of people you believe in."

"Like you."

"Like *you*." He looked pained. "I'm not perfect, Red. I'm as flawed as your senator. But I would never cheat on you or deliberately hurt you and I'll always try to make you happy. You have my word on that."

She stared at him.

"I love you for who you are. I don't want you to change, to be jaded by this. I *like* the things you believe in. Hell, I believe in them, too." He bent to see her face. "You still do, don't you? You won't let one creep distort things for you?"

Her smile came slowly, along with sudden insight. The senator wasn't the man she'd believed him to be—but Riley was. True, he wasn't perfect, so he'd likely make mistakes in his life, just as she would. But he was steadfast, solid, a man you could rely on.

A man she could trust with her love.

"No, I won't let him disillusion me." She touched Riley's chest. She knew Riley, so she knew how incredible a person could be. No one could ever change that. "I love you, too, Riley. I fought it, but I knew last night that I'd lost the battle."

He didn't smile, but new warmth darkened his blue eyes. "I've known how I feel for a long while now."

"Buck and Harris and Ethan knew how you felt, too."

"They *what?*"

Nodding, Regina said, "They told me, but I didn't really believe them." Then in a barely there whisper, she confessed, "I thought you only wanted sex."

He rolled his eyes. "Of course I want sex," he answered in the same low whisper, and then added with gentle awe, "Look at you."

At his very private words, she glanced around the room. She knew no one could hear him, but when Lanny winked at her, she blushed. They really should have found some privacy for this chat.

"I was giving you time, Red, and trying to get this mess sorted out so we wouldn't be distracted." He looked up at the sound of the door opening and two more men—very official in appearance—stepped in. "I think the mess just got messier, but at least you're out of it now. I can concentrate on you."

"On us?" she specified.

He pressed a firm kiss to her mouth. "Yes."

"I do love you, Riley, but now that this is over, I have no reason to stay with you. I'm not the type of woman who shacks up."

He went stiff as a board, and Regina said, "Will you marry me?"

He slumped against her, half in relief, half in amusement. Butch complained until he could squirrel up between their bodies and poke his face out.

"Riley?" Regina prayed he'd said yes.

"Yeah, I'll marry you." He grinned. "It's nice having a very proper woman around. Takes the guesswork out of things."

With that settled, Regina turned back to face the room. "What do you think will happen now?"

"I dunno. I don't really care as long as none of them can ever again threaten you."

A sort of wistful melancholy crept up on her. "It's strange, but I still think he's a good senator—he's just not a good husband."

"Maybe. I promise I'll be a good husband." When she smiled in agreement, Riley hugged her tight. "One thing, Red."

"What?"

"You remember what I said about babies?"

Regina softened all the way to her toes. Her knees felt like butter, her heart full and ripe. "Yes."

"I'm a homebody at heart. I want a house—"

"I have the house," she rushed to remind him, just in case he was getting cold feet.

"—and a dog."

"Got the dog, too. A perfect dog. A dog others will envy." She rubbed Butch's oversized ears.

Laughing, Riley hefted Butch up closer to his face and the dog playfully nipped his chin, appearing very pleased with the situation. "I'd really like a few kids *without* tails if you think we can manage that sometime in the misty future."

Tears filled her eyes. All around them was chaos, but the government could work itself out. This was important. "Since we love each other and we're getting married, and we intend to stay married forever, I'd say it would only be right and proper."

RILEY STEPPED through the door, took one look at Regina, and backed out. With the music she had playing on the stereo, she hadn't heard him. He turned to his friends and said, "Wait out here a second."

Buck crossed his arms over his massive chest. "If you're

going to leave me hanging in the street just so you can grab a nooner, forget it."

Harris laughed. "Men in love are so predictable."

Rosie shoved him for that inelegant remark. "You'll get yours someday, Harris. Just wait and see."

His horrified expression had both Riley and Ethan chuckling.

Shaking his head, Riley said, "No, it's not that. She's just not ready for you. Two minutes, I swear. That's all I need."

"Two minutes? Talk about a quickie," Harris muttered, then ducked behind Buck before Rosie could reach him.

Riley slipped through the door and locked it behind him. He loved the house that Regina had chosen. It wasn't all that large but it had a real family feel to it, a coziness that she enhanced by her mere presence.

Since she'd already taken care of a sizeable down payment, he'd splurged on most of the furnishings. Between their combined efforts, things were really coming together.

The music continued to play, and Regina still had her delectable rump in the air as she rummaged beneath the couch for Butch's bone. The dog sat beside her, his expression anxious and watchful.

"Can I help?"

She screeched, whipped around to sit on her butt, and stared at him. "You're home early!"

"It ended quicker than I thought." He'd had to testify in court on a burglary, then had stopped by to see his friends. They'd invited themselves over, but obviously Regina wasn't ready for company.

Before he could explain that he had them all with him, she was on her feet and racing Butch to the door to greet him. Both woman and dog appeared thrilled with his arrival.

Dressed in one of his shirts—something she knew he loved

seeing—and with her rich hair wound into enormous curlers around her head, Regina launched herself into his arms. Since that day at the Historical Society, she'd grown completely at ease with him. Around others, she remained immeasurably polite and proper, but with Riley she shared every facet of herself, including her less polished moments. Like now.

When the delicious kiss ended, Butch demanded his attention with a yodeling bark. He stretched up to stand on his hind legs, dancing around in what Riley called his circus dog impersonation.

Riley picked him up and treated him to a full body rub before saying to Regina, "Sorry to break it to you, but everyone is with me."

Her hands went to her cheeks and her green eyes widened. "Everyone?"

He nodded toward the door. "Harris and Buck, Rosie and Ethan. They invited themselves over. They're waiting on the porch."

The words no sooner left his mouth than she whipped around and dashed down the hallway to their bedroom. Riley enjoyed the back view of her, watching her long legs and the way his shirttails bounced over her bottom. "I'll keep them entertained while you finish getting ready."

The slamming of the door was her only reply.

Fifteen minutes later Regina emerged dressed in pressed slacks, a beige cotton sweater and a huge smile. "Sorry I kept you all waiting. Usually I'm dressed and ready by this time of the day, but I got behind this morning after Barbara Walter's people called."

Rosie's mouth fell open. Ethan jerked around to face her. Buck, who'd been on the floor playing with Butch, froze. Harris snorted in disbelief.

Riley, the only one with his wits still about him, raised a brow. "Barbara Walters?" He wasn't all that surprised. It seemed everyone in the media wanted the scoop on Senator Welling's sudden withdrawal. With his influence, the senator had put a gag order on the entire event. The guards present that day would never speak a word. Lanny and Dermot had been warned that they could lose their jobs if they released any information to the press.

Riley had assured the senator's people up front that they couldn't use his job to threaten him. All he cared about was that Regina be kept safe. Beyond that stipulation, they could handle the situation as quietly and secretively as they wished. But they *would* have to handle it because he wouldn't tolerate any more threats to Regina. So far, they had things in hand.

Regina was the only one left that could talk—and she wasn't about to.

"What did she want?" Buck asked.

"The same thing the others wanted."

Agog with fascination, Rosie asked, "To hear firsthand what happened with the senator?"

"Right." Regina sat down on Riley's lap, which was the only seat available in the small living room. She leaned back against his chest and smiled. "I told them that they'd just have to find out the nitty-gritty details like everyone else, after the federal investigation ended."

Rosie flopped back against her husband's arm. "Wow. Barbara Walters and you turned her down."

Buck rolled to his back and propped up on his elbows. "I can't believe you don't want revenge after the hell Welling's wife put you through."

Regina shrugged. "What good would revenge do? The senator has lost a lot of credibility with his constituents. They apparently don't like secrets, but with his wife under indictment and his own blame in the whole thing, what else can he do but keep quiet?"

"He could have not cheated in the first place," Harris grouched with feeling, then looked blank when everyone stared at him. "What? I have morals, too, ya know."

Regina sighed. "They have two children, and I think the kids have been through enough. Even with his wife blaming everything on Earl, her involvement is bound to make headlines eventually. The whole family is going to suffer. I won't take part in that."

Harris nodded, giving her a look full of admiration. "You're something else, Regina, you know that?"

Riley scowled at his tender tone, but Harris blew it by saying, "And here I thought you were a nosy reporter."

"I am." Regina gave them all an evil grin. "But I still like the more personal and upbeat human-interest stories." She hesitated just long enough to add impact, then announced, "That's why I told Walter's retinue that if they wanted a real scoop they should bring their TV crew to Chester and check out the local heroes."

Riley choked on his own breath.

Ethan groaned as if in mortal pain.

"You'd never get them here for something like that," Rosie said. "They like stories of worldwide appeal."

"Oh, I dunno. What could be more appealing to the world than the local heroes who keep us safe?" She slanted Rosie a look. "I specifically mentioned Harris and Buck."

Buck bolted upright. "I'm no hero! Hell, I just own a lumberyard."

"You were right there by Riley the day he caught Earl. You may not have a hero's occupation, but you have the soul of a hero."

"I don't!"

"Yes, you do," she insisted. "Think of the interview as free advertising for your business."

Harris said, *"Oh gawd,"* with great disgust. "That's weak, Regina. Very weak."

She didn't seem the least upset by the criticism. "When I told them two of the men were still single, they sounded pretty interested. They told me they're doing this whole segment on singles in America, and heroes would naturally be prime fodder for the piece. They want me to call them back with more information."

Buck and Harris stared at each other, their Adam's apples bopping in panic.

"You wouldn't."

"You didn't."

Riley started to laugh. "I can tell you unequivocally that she would. For some insane reason, she thinks the two of you epitomize all that is good in mankind."

"They're your and Ethan's friends," Regina said with prim regard. "And you two are definitely heroic."

"Hear, hear," Rosie agreed.

"So of course they're good men. And since they won't let me interview them..." She left the sentence dangling with loaded suggestion.

"Hey, I put up with it," Ethan pointed out.

"Me, too," Riley added. His own interview had been carefully edited by Regina. Anything that might have been too personal or hurtful had been omitted.

It was still embarrassing, especially because the love she felt for him had shone through and Harris and Buck had harassed him for days afterward, pretending to swoon, blowing him kisses and asking for his autograph. But the public had gobbled it up, his chief was thrilled with the positive PR for the department and Regina had thanked him oh so sweetly, so he was glad he'd given in.

Buck finally said, "Regina, be reasonable. You have to call off Walters."

Her nose lifted. "I could do that—*if* you agree to give me a story." Her gaze slanted to Harris. "Both of you."

With hardy groans and a lot of grumbling, they surrendered to the inevitable. "Deal."

Regina relaxed. "I'll return their call after dinner. But I need the interviews before our wedding next week."

"Why the rush?" Harris asked, looking somewhat stricken by the whole idea of being in the limelight.

"After the wedding, I plan to be busy for a while—with my own personal hero."

Riley hugged her close. He knew the truth: Regina was the heroic one. With her big heart and unwavering faith in human nature, she had filled his soul. He intended to keep her safe for the rest of their lives. If that made him a hero, too, at least in her eyes, then he'd gladly live with the label.